It Happened
ONE BITE

LYDIA DARE

sourcebooks
casablanca

Published by Sourcebooks Casablanca, an imprint of Sourcebooks, Inc.
P.O. Box 4410, Naperville, Illinois 60567-4410
(630) 961-3900
FAX: (630) 961-2168
www.sourcebooks.com

Printed and bound in Canada.
WC 10 9 8 7 6 5 4 3 2 1

To Mom, Dad, Jill, Ryan, and Nick.
Thanks for always believing in me,
even when you didn't understand me.

For my mom, Rebecca Switzer.
For all the little things you do that you probably think I
don't even notice, I thank you. If we were all allowed to
pick our own mom, I'd pick you a thousand times over. So
would most of the kids you've mentored, encouraged, loved,
and laughed with. They have good taste.

Prologue

Black Dragon Inn, south of Edinburgh
March 1797

ALPINA LINDSAY BREATHED A SIGH OF RELIEF. IT HADN'T been easy locating a vampyre none of them had ever met, but finally, after nights of searching for the man, there he was! He certainly matched the description of the man Fiona Macleod had seen in her vision.

Leaning against the stone façade of the old inn, Lord Kettering drew deeply on his cheroot as he gazed up at the crescent moon, seemingly without a care in the world.

Alpina narrowed her eyes at the gentleman who was, indeed, handsome, dashing, and more powerful than anything or anyone she had ever faced. The bairn in her womb kicked and Alpina protectively smoothed a hand over her belly while Fiona Macleod's warning echoed once again in her mind.

"Are ye certain ye want ta do this?" Bonnie Ferguson whispered in her left ear.

Alpina caught Rosewyth Campbell's eye and nodded,

as there really was no choice in the matter. The man before them had to be dealt with. Otherwise, her daughter's life and future would be in danger. That couldn't be allowed.

From her right, Moira Sinclair's dainty hand slid inside Alpina's, reminding her she wasn't alone. Together they could thwart the evil that Fiona had seen in her vision. Together they would ensure her daughter's future.

A twig snapped beneath one of the witches' feet, and Kettering stood at attention. "Hello?" His crisp English accent sliced through the night air.

It was now or never, and Alpina couldn't take the risk that Kettering would escape. She stepped from the mist that had until now shrouded the coven from his view, pulling Moira alongside her. "Good evenin', my lord." Somehow she managed to keep the fear from her voice.

A charming smile settled on the man's face, and his white teeth sparkled in the moonlight. "It is now." He tossed what was left of his cheroot to the ground and stepped toward the pair. A seducer if ever there was one. "What a delightful treat. Not one beautiful lass, but two."

"Actually, there are five of us," Fiona's waspish voice came from somewhere within the mist.

"Five?" Kettering echoed.

And in the blink of an eye, Moira's misty shield evaporated and Kettering found himself in the middle of their circle. The five witches clasped hands together, trapping him inside the ring.

The Englishman looked from one to the other, confusion lighting his too-handsome face. "Why?" he asked.

"Because of what ye are," Alpina answered. "We canna allow ye ta harm anyone."

He shook his head. "I've never harmed anyone," he professed.

Fiona Macleod snorted at that. "I've seen what ye are and what ye will be with my own eyes, my lord. Pray doona deny it."

"And what are *you*?" he asked.

"Justice," Fiona sneered. "For all yer victims—past, present, and future."

"*Cadail, uilebheist. Caidil gu bràth!*" Alpina's voice rang loud and clear.

"*Cadail gu bràth, cadail gu bràth,*" the others chanted.

Power surged through Alpina's hands where she held onto Moira and Bonnie within the circle. She'd never felt such intense energy. Sparks erupted from their clasped hands, arcing across the circle and creating a perfect, five-pointed star. Thunder cracked above them, and Kettering let out a pained cry. He crumpled to the ground and everything was silent.

The five witches slowly released their hold on one another, stepping closer to the man at their feet. If Alpina hadn't known better, she would have thought he was dead.

"His maker will search for him," Fiona predicted. "The knight will go through Edinburgh, Glasgow, and Aberdeen."

"But no' the Highlands?" Alpina asked, the answer mattering more than her next breath.

Fiona smiled. "Nay. No one will find him at Briarcraig, but we must hurry."

Alpina nodded. Then she knelt beside Kettering,

wishing they could have done more than place him in a dormant sleep; but it would have to do.

"As he is imprisoned, so shall remain his soul," Fiona said as she lifted his hand to stare at the ring that adorned it. She tugged it from his finger and tossed it to Alpina, who caught it in mid-air. The ring glowed, warm and vibrant in the palm of her hand.

"But vampyres have no soul," Alpina said with a shake of her head. "No life."

"As a descendent of Blodswell, *he* could." Fiona pointed her finger at the lifeless man at their feet.

Everyone knew the story of Blodswell. The tale was passed from witch to witch, from cradle to grave. It was a story of true heroism. It was the reason why the rings had been gifted to the knight, as a harbinger of hope, a promise for the future. But the prophecy could only be fulfilled if the wearer of the ring remained pure. For only love could heal the blighted soul.

"The ring contains what he holds most dear," Fiona continued. "It's the essence of him. And his link ta his maker. Take it and go. If ye doona leave with it, he'll seek its power and wake soon."

For the first time today, Alpina doubted this deed. But Fiona had foreseen it. If they didn't take immediate action, the vampyre would wreak havoc upon their lives and upon her daughter in particular.

Alpina stood back and watched as her four coven sisters made quick work of depositing the vampyre's body in the awaiting Macleod coach. They exchanged quick hugs before the four women crowded inside as well.

It didn't feel right to leave her sisters exposed to

such danger. "If he wakes, ye might have need of me," Alpina called out, as the coach lurched forward.

Fiona answered from inside the conveyance, "Ye hold his heart in yer hand. Without it, he is but a shell of a man."

A shell of a man. Somehow Alpina doubted that. However, the further the coach moved down the meandering lane, the more the ring lost its shimmer and warmth. With a shrug of her shoulders, Alpina threaded the ring onto a cord she wore around her neck. No one could ever take the relic from her, and her daughter's future would be preserved.

One

Twenty years later…
Lindsay House, Edinburgh
January 1817

BLAIRE LINDSAY HAD THE OVERWHELMING DESIRE TO throw a fireball at her older brother's thick head and engulf him in flames. Unfortunately, Aiden had excellent reflexes and a lifetime of experience at dodging her blows. Besides, she'd be the one cleaning up the mess. Still, her fingers itched to send him flying into the next room. How could one be so dense? "Have ye lost yer mind?" she said instead.

"I'm no' a fool, Blaire," he replied patiently, as though *she* was the one who had insisted the family pick up in the dead of winter, leave Edinburgh, and travel through the Highlands to some place she'd never heard of. He settled on the threadbare divan across from her, his silver eyes hopeful, and raked a hand through his dark hair. "I just want ta see it. Can ye no' understand?"

She could understand his desire to see the supposed

inheritance for himself. Ever since Aiden had returned from the battlefields of Belgium, he'd seemed different. The young man who'd once been quick to smile was now sullen and dispassionate. Yet, the idea of Briarcraig Castle brought back the sparkle that once had shone in his eyes. Still, she had duties in Edinburgh, and leaving was not in her plans.

Blaire sighed and toyed with her mother's old ring, which hung on a cord around her neck. "It's no' a good time, Aiden. Elspeth and Caitrin are both in England. Someone has ta keep an eye on things here in town."

He rolled his eyes and kicked his long legs out in front of him. "How much trouble do ye think Sorcha can get herself inta? I'm certain Rhiannon can keep her eye on the little witch while we're away."

"It's no' Sorcha I'm worried about. It's no' a good idea ta leave the coven so exposed. It's bad enough we're already down ta three."

"*Mo chreach!*" he moaned. "Ye act as though we're leavin' forever. It's just a wee trip ta Loch Calavie. We'll be back before anyone even notices ye've left."

A wee trip to Loch Calavie? She'd never even heard of the place. And it didn't make one bit of sense that Aiden had inherited the supposed castle. "It's probably just a pile of rocks, ye ken. I'm sure it'll look better in the spring or even the summer," she said hopefully.

His response to that was a scathing glare. "I've got nothin', Blaire. I sold my commission and returned home with only the clothes on my back."

He'd come home to find that everything he believed was his had been sold to pay their late father's creditors. That's what he meant. Though Aiden never said so, Blaire knew he blamed her. But Colin Lindsay had been a drunkard long before she was born, and, if their mother hadn't reformed him in all their years together, there wasn't a thing Blaire could have done to do so during Aiden's absence.

"But *now* I've got land, lass. A castle. I doona want ta wait for the spring ta lay eyes on it. Are ye no' even the least bit curious ta see it for yerself?"

Not in the least. Blaire was happy in Edinburgh. She had her coven and a purpose. But...Aiden had neither.

Just a wee trip to Loch Calavie. It really wasn't so much to ask, was it? The dead of winter. Traveling through the Highlands. She'd obviously lost her mind to have allowed him to talk her into this madness.

Blaire's shoulders sagged forward. "All right, Aiden, if it's that important ta ye."

His face lit up. Before he could properly thank her, a knock came from the front door. The next instant, it sounded as though a herd of elephants was racing down the steps. Brannock must have been keeping an eye on the street.

"*Havers!* What's he in a rush about?" Aiden complained.

Blaire shrugged, then rose to her feet. "I doona ken, but I intend ta find out." She crossed the small parlor, and as she reached for the door, it swung open of its own accord.

Brannock, Blaire's junior by a decade, raced into the room, his face slightly red. "Rhi and Sorcha are here."

In his wake, her two younger coven sisters entered the room. Aiden rose at their entrance and bowed his head. "Ladies."

Blaire embraced both Rhiannon Sinclair and Sorcha Ferguson, surprised to see them in her home as they'd planned to converge at Arthur's Seat, the coven's normal meeting place, later that evening. "What are ye doin' here?"

A smile lit Sorcha's innocent face. "Papa said ye had excitin' news, but he wouldna say what it was. So we came ta find out."

The indulgent smirk Rhiannon wore made it obvious that Sorcha was behind this impromptu visit. Still…exciting news? Blaire shook her head. "I doona ken what ye're goin' on about."

Both girls sat in matching chintz chairs near Blaire, while Aiden resumed his spot with Brannock settling in beside him. Her exuberant younger brother's light eyes danced. "I think they mean Aiden's news," he said, swinging his legs back and forth as though sitting still was too much of a trial.

The blasted castle. How had Mr. Ferguson gotten wind of it so quickly? Aiden sat a little taller, and Blaire could sense the pride that must be flowing through his veins. The Lindsays' bad fortune had come to an end; at least that's what she read in his expression.

"Aye," she said more brightly than she felt. "Aiden is the proud master of Briarcraig Castle. We'll be leavin' tomorrow ta see it."

Sorcha sighed wistfully. "Briarcraig Castle? It sounds so romantic."

Rhiannon and Blaire exchanged a look. The youngest witch in their ranks tended to be quite naïve, though in the sweetest of ways. It was hard not to adore the little sprite, and Blaire sometimes wished that she had just a touch of Sorcha's charming innocence. Could one feign innocence when fireballs rested beneath one's fingertips though? Probably not very well.

"I thought ye said," Brannock began with a frown, "wild dragons couldna carry ye ta Loch Calavie."

Blaire turned her gaze to the lad. "Little brothers who listen at keyholes will have ta be dealt with."

His childlike laugh echoed around the room. Brannock knew the threat was empty. Blaire might have the blood of warrior witches flowing through her veins, but she'd raised the lad without any help from their father and she treasured Brannock beyond anything else. "Are we really goin' ta see Aiden's castle?" he asked hopefully.

Blaire couldn't help but smile at her younger brother, who wanted an adventure more than anything. "Aye, Brannock. We really are goin' ta see Aiden's castle."

The lad jumped to his feet with a shout. "When do we leave?"

"Did ye no' hear me, lad? We'll leave at first light tomorrow." Blaire sighed. "Otherwise, Aiden will be a pain in the arse until we do so," she mumbled low enough for only Sorcha and Rhiannon to hear.

"We should have had the coach resprung before we left Edinburgh," Aiden complained again.

Having the coach repaired before they departed was a luxury they could ill afford. In fact, it was a wonder they still had a coach, bedraggled as it was. If Sorcha hadn't insisted on loaning them one of the Fergusons' drivers, she and Aiden would have had to trade turns sitting in the coachman's box and freezing their arses off instead of just bruising them.

Blaire pointed a finger into her chest and said, "*I* am no' the one who was in such a hurry." She turned the finger on him as she shifted to adjust her own aching bottom. "Ye were the one in such a hurry." She mocked his masculine voice. "I have ta see my castle, or it will get up and walk away before I get ta Loch Calavie."

"How did ye get ta be so cruel, Blaire?" he asked, an unrepentant grin tugging at one corner of his mouth. "Mother was a kind soul, a good woman."

"Aye, and she dinna pass a single trait down ta me," Blaire said smugly. Then she turned her palm up and allowed sparks to shoot from her fingertips, just enough to make a bright show of lights within the carriage. "Aside from this one." She smiled again at her brothers.

"Ye need ta be careful who ye do that around at Briarcraig Castle, Blaire," Aiden scolded. "Ye doona have yer coven ta protect ye where we're goin'."

Did the dolt really think she needed to be told such things? Although the modern age seemed to be here to stay, people still were a bit squeamish about witches, and Blaire had no intention of being burned alive by a group of uneducated Highlanders. She rolled her eyes heavenward.

"Oh, ye think we'll stumble inta a workin' castle full of servants and beautiful things, Aiden?" She snorted. "It's more likely that we'll drive up ta a big pile of rocks that collapsed years ago. Then we'll have ta make the poor coachman up there turn around and head back home."

"And try ta act like a lass, will ye?" he continued as though he hadn't heard one word she'd spoken. "Ye doona have ta best every man ye see."

Blaire leaned over and covered his hand with hers. "I hate ta inform ye, but I'm no' made ta wear petticoats and pretty jewels. I am a warrior, Aiden, and my body is designed for fightin'."

"Fightin' what?" Brannock interjected.

"I doona ken," she shrugged. "Whatever danger exists in the world. Dragons or trolls or arrogant Englishmen."

Brannock dissolved into a peal of laughter while Aiden heaved a dramatic sigh. "The only danger ye have seen so far was when Wallace Ferguson tried ta kiss ye in the stables. I still canna believe ye blackened the big oaf's eye. He weighs three times what ye do."

"Well, he should have kept his lips on his face, instead of tryin' ta put them on mine," Blaire mumbled.

"Please, *try* ta be a lady, will ye?" Aiden pleaded, his face finally serious.

Blaire frowned. She would like to think that her brother could accept her as she was after all this time. But he was forever trying to change her into a laces-and-fripperies kind of lass, when hunting and shooting ran through her blood. It was a shame those sorts of accomplishments weren't highly regarded as particularly feminine. Perhaps someday she would find a man who could accept that she would always best him at manly arts and not be afraid of her strength and power. And perhaps all the stars in the sky would turn to diamonds and rain bracelets and earbobs across her path, too.

No, she was doomed to live a solitary existence.

She refused to endure the sort of life her mother had had, settling for a bitter drunkard who could never accept her gifts, hiding her true self, and dying a little more each day. They'd all suffered from that situation, and Blaire would never willingly live that way again. Being alone couldn't possibly be worse.

The coach hit a bump so hard that Blaire bounced from her seat to knock her head on the roof of the carriage. She groaned and pressed a hand to the offending lump that quickly grew at her hairline.

"Are ye all right?" Aiden asked as though he was suddenly concerned for her well-being.

"Aye, I'm well. But I will be quite happy when we arrive so I can stretch my legs." She lifted the curtain and looked out the small window. "Look at that, Aiden." She nudged his leg.

"What is it?" he asked as he sat forward.

The golden sun was setting behind a large stone structure, and it looked like a beacon of light that was guiding them home.

"That's Briarcraig Castle," Aiden breathed in awe.

"Let me see!" Brannock cried as he edged himself in between them. "*That* is yer castle?" He sat back with a disappointed huff.

"Well, it's no' a pile of rocks," Aiden said brightly. "At least it's still standin'."

"Barely," Brannock sniffed.

Blaire shot him a look, and the boy immediately sat up and removed the scowl from his face.

The stone structure was surrounded by a low rock wall that opened to a courtyard, and what might have been gardens at one time were now covered in thick weeds and vines, even in the dead of winter. If she returned in the spring, Blaire would need to bring Sorcha with her. The youngest witch could enchant the plants, encouraging them to bend effortlessly to her will and making at least the outdoors hospitable.

The castle itself was a huge monstrosity, probably born of some wealthy laird's imagination. But even Blaire had to admit it looked quite pretty with the setting sun and shimmering loch in the background. Almost enchanting in its own right.

Their coach rumbled to a stop on the bumpy drive, the stillness of it a bit ominous after such a long journey. Aiden stepped out quickly, followed by Brannock. Neither of them waited to hand Blaire out, and she didn't expect them to. She was perfectly capable of vaulting out under her own strength.

She stretched tall, extending her arms over her head to lengthen her long body. That she was a half inch taller than Aiden had always been a source of contention for her older brother. And Aiden was taller than the average man. She'd grown accustomed to looking down at most of the men she knew.

The low stone wall that surrounded the property had a rusty iron gate in the middle. Aiden gave the gate a quick push, and it promptly fell from its hinges. Even still, the look of boyish wonder never left his face.

"It's beautiful, is it no', Blaire?" he asked over his shoulder.

"Aye, it has a bit of charm," was all she could manage.

Two

AIDEN SLID A POLISHED KEY INTO THE BOLT, BUT THE LOCK refused to click. He rattled the key until Blaire felt certain it would break. She cleared her throat, and when her brother looked over his shoulder at her, she raised her brow expectantly. "Would ye like me ta give it a try?"

He scowled but handed her the key anyway.

Blaire looked at the key, which seemed much too small for the lock. It clearly wasn't for the front door. "Where did ye get this thing? It doesna fit."

"Mr. MacDonald."

Blaire pocketed the key and then brushed past Aiden. She bent down to peer into the keyhole, which was rusted from non-use. "*Fosgail*," she whispered. Then she tapped the door handle and turned it.

"Cheater," Aiden muttered under his breath.

Blaire winked at Brannock, and the two of them giggled as their older brother pressed his way through the door. They quickly followed. As soon as Blaire's foot landed inside the castle, she reared backward. One moment she was fine, and the next, she felt as though the breath had been sucked from her lungs.

The ring she wore around her neck seemed to suddenly weigh ten times more, and it grew warm against her skin.

"Perhaps we shouldna go any further," she warned. "This place feels…" She let her voice trail off. Voicing her own fears would serve no one.

Aiden scoffed. "Doona tell me the great warrior witch is frightened."

Blasted brother. She shouldn't let him goad her into doing anything she didn't want to, but after two decades together, he knew exactly what to say to spur her forward. Blaire took a deep breath and pressed into the darkness, her senses on high alert. Something was far from right.

Whatever charm the castle had seemed to possess from the outside was long forgotten. Cobwebs stretched from one end of the long corridor to the other, filling every bit of open space. Brannock sneezed, and a plethora of dust motes scattered about.

"*Havers!*" Blaire turned her palm heavenward and a fireball sparked to life, lighting the way. Medieval wall sconces lined the corridor, and she threw her spark at each one, bringing a warm glow to the dismal atmosphere.

She first looked inside what must have once been the great hall. Old sheets covered settees, tables, and chairs. And layers of dust and grime covered the sheets.

"It looks haunted," Brannock mumbled behind her, grasping her skirts with one hand.

Haunted. The very idea sent a chill straight to Blaire's soul. Then she shook her head at the thought of such foolishness. "There are no such things as ghosts, Bran."

"A lot of people doona believe there are such things as witches either," her little brother countered.

She supposed he had a point, not that she was about to admit that to the lad. Blaire tugged Brannock to her side and entered the great hall. "It's just a bunch of old sheets." She pulled the cloth from an old chair, scattering years' worth of dust around the room and causing both of them to clutch their stomachs as coughs wracked their bodies.

Aiden entered the great hall, frowning. "Are ye all right?"

Blaire caught her breath and shook her head, wiping the tears from her eyes. "This place is awful."

He waved his arm negligently in her direction. "Well, say a few magic words and clean it up."

She scowled at him. "It doesna work that way, and ye ken it." Though the truth was, being magical, she could make lighter work of the cleaning than her brothers would be able to do, not that she was about to admit it when Aiden was so haughty. "I'm ta use my powers for the purpose for which they were given ta me. So if ye have a dragon or a demon hidden away in this godforsaken place, I'll be happy ta fight it for ye."

The wind whipped through the hall and slammed the door shut loudly behind them. Brannock nearly knocked her over in his quest to hide in her skirts. "Bran," she groaned, throwing her head back in defeat. "It's just a little wind."

He stuttered as he began. "I—I've never felt the wind move like that."

She hadn't either, but she'd be loathe to admit that.

Aiden looked nearly as fearful as Brannock, and she didn't want to make the situation worse.

Aiden crossed to the door and gave a hard tug. It refused to budge. He yanked once more and ended up falling to the floor, but he had managed to open the door. Aiden stood up and dusted himself off. He pulled a taper from the wall and held it out to Blaire. "Would ye mind?"

"I never did mind very well."

"I hope ye have a daughter just like yerself some day, Blaire," he grunted as she lit his taper and he started down the corridor.

"Where is Aiden goin'?" Brannock cried. Blaire soothed him with her hand on his back. But his teeth still chattered loudly enough that she could hear them.

"Explorin', I would imagine," she said absently, and she turned her attention to take in the uncovered furniture. Even after years of misuse, the settees and chairs looked to be in much better condition than what they were accustomed to in Edinburgh. How strange this place was.

"What if a monster eats him?" Brannock pressed.

Blaire swiped her finger across the mantel over the imposing stone fireplace and grimaced. Filth. "Then it would have a horrible stomach ache later. I imagine he's no' very tasty."

"That is no' humorous," the youngest Lindsay grunted.

"Ye ken how much I love ta entertain." Blaire winked at him, hoping to tease him into better spirits.

"B-Blaire," Brannock stuttered as he stepped back from her, his finger pointing at her as all the blood drained from his face.

"What is it, Bran?" she asked.

"Ye're g-g-glowin'," he croaked.

Blaire looked down at herself, and sure enough, the signet ring she normally wore around her neck had a definite shine to it. "It's just the light from the wall sconces," she said with a dismissive wave of her hand. "It reflects off the stone."

But it was more than that. And Blaire knew quite well that the glow wasn't benign. She picked the ring up and gazed at the ruby-red stone. It almost seemed to mock her. She dropped the heirloom inside her dress where it rested heavily against her skin. She fingered it absently through the material. It seemed warmer to the touch than it should have in such a cold room.

What was this place they'd stumbled into? And why had she never heard of it before? "Help me fold up the cloths, will ye?" Until she had a firm understanding of the goings-on at Briarcraig, she didn't want to worry Brannock for no reason. Keeping him busy would keep his mind occupied. At least she hoped so.

For a time, they folded the sheets and tried to keep from inhaling the dust that drifted up with every step they took. A scratching sound from the chimney caught Blaire's attention, and she stepped toward it. A moment later, a bat flew from the opening and she cursed softly as she ducked to avoid the creature.

"I heard that," Aiden admonished as he entered the massive room, heavily burdened by one of their trunks. "Ladies do no' curse."

"Then it's a good thing I'm no' one," she said smartly, a smile on her face as she turned toward him. "What did ye find down the corridor?"

Aiden chuckled. "An exit. And lots and lots of rooms. But at least it appears to be safe, even if it is dirty." He stomped his foot. "The structure is sound, so at least I have somethin' ta build upon."

Blaire yawned behind her hand. "Did ye find any beds? I am exhausted."

"Aye. Several bedchambers upstairs are full of furniture draped with cloths. Pick one ye fancy, change the bedclothes, and then ye can go ta sleep." He nodded toward the trunk, which she knew contained fresh linens and several counterpanes.

Falling asleep would be heavenly. "Tomorrow, I'll have to clean," she moaned.

"Tomorrow, there's a lot ta be done. Are ye ready ta eat?"

She shook her head. "I'm too tired. I'm goin' ta go ta bed." She started for the corridor.

"Oh, Blaire," Aiden called.

She turned back to him.

"A neighbor stopped by as Ferguson's coachman headed toward the village—"

Even the bloody coachmen knew better than to stay inside the castle. "We should have gone with him."

Aiden frowned at her. "Frightened?"

"Hardly," she insisted, folding her arms across her chest.

"Well, anyway, the neighbor—"

"Are ye sure ye're no' delusional?" Blaire shook her head. "I havena seen any evidence of anyone livin' near Briarcraig." Who would be mad enough to stay in these parts?

"Well, people *do*," Aiden insisted. "Mr. Fyfe is the

local magistrate, and he tends sheep in the valley. He and his daughters saw the coach as we were comin' in. Ye might like the lasses. They're about yer age."

Blaire leveled him with a haughty stare. If he was trying to talk her into staying, he was out of his thick skull.

Aiden cleared his throat. "Anyway, I invited them ta visit tomorrow, once we're settled in. It might do ye some good ta be surrounded by some *normal* lasses for a change."

"Settled in? Have ye taken a good look at yer castle, Aiden? It would take a team of servants ta clean this place by tomorrow." She let the comment about normal lasses go without a response. It was a fairly common sentiment after all. At least from Aiden.

He shrugged, the picture of an unconcerned male. "We'll get the great hall and a parlor or two done by then."

"I dinna traipse up here ta entertain Highlanders, Aiden Lindsay. Surely, ye doona think I'll be stayin' in this drafty old castle any longer than a sennight."

"A sennight or a fortnight, no' much of a difference really. Fyfe says the villagers think the castle is haunted."

"Oh, what rubbish," Blaire scoffed, hoping Brannock wouldn't get worked up again after hearing such a thing.

"I agree!" the lad said at the same time.

Perfect. Nothing to do now but minimize the damage. She patted Aiden's shoulder as she walked by him. "If ye hear any wailin' or rattlin' of chains, Aiden, ye can come and crawl under my covers. I'll protect ye from whatever goes bump in the night." Then she laughed at her brother's horrified expression.

"Canna ye be serious for a minute?" he scolded.

Blaire shrugged. "What do ye want me ta say? I am no' afraid of some ghost that doesna exist."

Aiden mumbled something under his breath, and though Blaire couldn't quite make it out, she was fairly certain it was far from complimentary.

"Tomorrow, we need ta look around and try ta find out what that stench is," she said, hoping the talk of ghouls had ended for the evening. "It smells as though somethin' died in here and no one has taken the time ta bury it."

Aiden nodded absently, though his mind seemed miles away.

Blaire started for the doorway but stopped to retrieve an armful of bedclothes, and then she slid from the parlor and down the musty corridor with Brannock quick on her heels. She shivered. Now that she was here, she couldn't believe she'd let Aiden talk her into this. Lindsay House was far from a castle, but it was clean, comfortable, and near people they knew.

Briarcraig was the most isolated place she'd ever been, different in every way from Edinburgh. She couldn't imagine actually *living* here. She shuddered at the thought. Aiden was daft if he thought she'd even consider it. The smell alone was enough to drive one mad.

She turned the corner to where she thought the staircase was, but instead she found another dank corridor. Blaire's eyes took in the dismal scene, and she cringed. This was not the sort of place where one would want to be lost. So she turned around and went back in the direction from which she had come.

After several attempts to locate the staircase, she finally found the right corridor and breathed a sigh of relief.

"I wonder who haunts the castle?" Brannock commented as he followed her into one of the bedrooms. She noted that he hadn't let more than two steps separate them as they'd twisted and turned down the maze of corridors.

"The only ghost who'll haunt these halls will be yers," she said, pointing a finger at him, "if ye doona get ta work and help me get the beds ready."

"I wonder if he was murdered."

Blaire rolled her eyes as she handed him half of the linens. "Probably no', but ye might be the next victim if ye keep on talkin' about it," she complained.

"Do ye think he's a good ghost or a bad ghost?" he asked over his shoulder.

"Bran!" she groaned.

He went on as though she hadn't said a thing. "Maybe the ghost will show itself ta me and tell me where it buried a long lost treasure."

Blaire couldn't help but laugh at the image his words brought to mind. The lad was positively starved for an adventure of his own, even if he was scared to death. "If ye see the ghost, Bran, ask it ta clean up a bit, will ye?"

He snorted, and though Blaire couldn't see his face, she was fairly certain he'd rolled his eyes.

Three

JAMES MAITLAND, BARON KETTERING, GROANED. It felt as though someone had coshed him over the head with an anchor and left him for dead. His temple pulsed angrily. How odd. He couldn't remember the last time he'd been in pain. Centuries ago perhaps, but nothing in recent memory.

He tried to blink his eyes open, but his lids were too heavy. How very strange. Then he noticed his arms wouldn't move, not even his pinkie finger. Nor would his legs. What the devil had happened to him? James focused all his energy on his eyes, willing them to open; to no avail.

He was lying flat on something cold, something damp, but that was all he could tell for certain. If he could just remember how he had gotten here…

That blasted coven. A memory flashed through his mind. Five witches had accosted him in the coaching yard. They must have cast some spell on him that rendered his limbs useless. What had they said? Something about monsters and acquiring justice for his victims. Had James been able to scoff, he would have.

Victims! What utter nonsense. Any woman who shared her life's blood with him enjoyed the experience as much as he did. Not once in more than two hundred years had he taken something that wasn't freely offered. Blodswell had belabored the point, and it was a code they lived by. It was expected. And he would never disappoint his maker.

Blodswell!

Relief washed over James. Blodswell, his old friend, was sure to find him wherever he was. He'd set things to rights, and then those five witches wouldn't know what hit them. They thought he was a monster, did they? He'd show them what a monster truly looked like. Damnation, being paralyzed was a bloody inconvenience.

I'm outside Edinburgh. The Black Dragon Inn. I need your help. Please find me. That blasted coven of yours has attacked me.

Then a sound hit his ears. The pitter-patter of footsteps and then a childlike laugh.

"Brannock Lindsay!" a woman cried, "I doona have time for such nonsense. Climb inta bed. We've got a long day ahead of us tomorrow."

"But, Blaire," the child complained, "I just want ta catch the kitty first."

"Aye. Ye always have somethin' ye have ta do first. But tonight I doona have the patience for it." Her voice dropped as she grumbled, but he heard her nonetheless. "Only ye, Brannock, could befriend a mangy, mottled bag of fur as soon as we arrived. Ye're lucky it dinna scratch yer eyes out."

"It's no' a bad cat, Blaire."

"There's no such thing as a good cat," the feminine voice continued her grumble. Against his will, James felt the corners of his mouth begin to turn up.

"But what if it's lost and scared?" the child continued. "Or what if the ghosts or ghoulies snatch it up?"

"I'm sure the cat kens the best places ta hide in this old pile of rocks. Now, I'll no' tell ye again: off ta bed with ye."

The sounds drifted further away, and James was more confused than ever. Pile of rocks? Ghosts? What a bizarre conversation. Now that he thought about it, he didn't hear the sounds of a working inn. There were no groomsmen in the courtyard repeating ribald stories. There were no sounds of cooks or maids scurrying about the kitchens. No smells of freshly baked food wafting upward. No uproarious bellows of drunkards in the taproom. There was nothing but strange bits of conversations between some lad and his sister or nursemaid. Where the devil was he?

Pile of rocks. What had the lass meant by that? Anger swamped James, and he struggled once again to open his eyes, to open his mouth, to move one inch. But nothing happened, and he'd never experienced such torture in his previous life, or in the current one. Once again, righteous anger at that blasted coven coursed through his veins. When he got free from this trap, there wouldn't be a place in the entire world where those five witches would be safe from him.

❧

Just as Blaire closed her eyes, a knock sounded on her door. She sighed. Would this day never end? "Aye?"

The door creaked open. "Blaire?" Brannock's small voice preceded him into the room.

"Bran!" she groaned. "What are ye doin' out of bed?" It had taken the better part of an hour to get him calmed down and tucked under his counterpane. She didn't think she had the strength to start the process over.

"I'm worried about the kitty."

The dratted cat again. Blaire cursed the thing for ever crossing her brother's path that evening. "The cat lives here. There's no reason ta be worried about it. We'll try ta find it in the mornin'."

The lad sighed, and Blaire finally sat up in bed to look at him. He clutched the red Lindsay plaid tightly around his shoulders and shivered. "Blaire, can I…" his voice trailed off.

"Can ye what?"

"I doona want ta stay in my room. I think it's haunted."

He looked so pathetic, quivering in the doorway, that she took pity on him. "All right. Ye can stay with me tonight." Before she even finished her sentence, he'd launched himself onto her bed. She couldn't help but smile at the lad, and she ruffled his hair. "But tomorrow ye need ta stay in yer own chambers."

Brannock quickly nodded his head in agreement.

Within a moment, he settled in beside her and rested his head on her shoulder. "What do ye think about Briarcraig?" he asked.

"I think we have our work cut out for us."

"Do ye think Mama ever lived here?"

Blaire shook her head. "Mama only ever lived in Edinburgh."

He sighed wistfully. "I saw a portrait that looked like the miniature Papa had of her."

"A portrait?"

"Hmm." He toyed with the cord around her neck. "I thought maybe it was—Ouch!" He yanked his hand from her and stuck his fingers in his mouth.

Blaire bolted upright. "What happened?"

"Burned," he managed around his fingers.

"Burned?" Blaire glanced down at the ring hanging around her neck. It wasn't her imagination. The stone was most assuredly glowing. She gingerly touched a finger to it, and though the ring was much warmer than normal, it didn't burn her.

Brannock pulled his fingers from his mouth. "What's wrong with it?"

Blaire shook her head. "Honestly, I doona have any idea." Had her mother not told her on her deathbed to never remove it from her neck, Blaire would have thrown the ring across the room. But it would keep her safe, her mother had promised. It could very well save her life one day. And it was behaving so oddly, she was more afraid not to have it on her person.

She moved the cord away from her brother and then inspected his hand. There was a faint red mark on his index finger, and she pressed her lips to the area. "There, all better."

From the glow of the ring, she saw Brannock roll his eyes. "I'm no' a bairn, Blaire."

Of course not. He was a strong, brave lad who'd jumped under her blankets rather than face the night alone. She winked at him and smiled. "Just try ta get some sleep, will ye?"

The lad settled deeper under the covers and was asleep within moments. However, Blaire wasn't quite so fortunate. Just as her eyes drifted closed, she heard a loud crash from belowstairs.

"Damnable cat," she muttered as she rolled over and punched her pillow in frustration. Between the snores that were already erupting from Brannock's mouth and the crashing objects that fell when the cat ran through the dining hall, Blaire would be incredibly fortunate to get even an hour of sleep.

Just as the castle quieted and the cat finally lay down to rest, a loud bellow came from the bowels of the castle. Blaire glanced quickly over at Brannock, who still slept soundly. Her imagination must be playing tricks on her. Out of nowhere, her brother kicked her shin with all his might. Damn it, she'd never get to sleep at this rate. She slid from beneath the counterpane, shrugged into her wrapper, and then slipped out the chamber door.

The ring around her neck caught her attention momentarily, as the glow seemed to fade and brighten like the cadence of a beating heart. She tucked the ring back beneath her night rail and started down the stairs.

She'd brew a cup of relaxing tea to help her sleep. That was all she needed; an enchanted sleeping draught ought to do the trick.

৵৹

A tingling began first in James' toes and fingertips. He cried out in pain because the tingle was more like being jabbed by the sharpened points of hundreds of needles as his limbs came to life. He hadn't felt pain in decades. Actually, in over two centuries, not since he'd been human. But he was feeling it now. And it was none too pleasant. He'd like to think that he had blood rushing to his extremities, but that was highly unlikely. Damn if he wasn't unusually parched. A thirst tugged at him like none other had before. He needed to feed. And he needed it soon.

He glanced around himself, unsure of where he was. The dark room that held him was so black within that he couldn't even see his hand when he was finally able to raise it in front of his face. He tested his limbs gingerly as they slowly came to life. He blinked his eyes open and closed. Of course, the darkness was all he could see. But it felt good to open them, which was more than he could do earlier. A definite improvement.

He wished he knew how he'd come to be in this bizarre place. He rolled to a seated position and groaned loudly as he unbent his long body. He leaned against the frigid stone wall behind him and laid his head on his knees.

After a time, his eyes began to adjust to the surrounding darkness, and James smiled when he was able to make out a door. Freedom. Thank God.

James rose to his feet but nearly stumbled under his own weight. He clutched the wall to steady himself. Had he been drugged? Just one more sin to add to the mounting list of injustices the coven had placed upon him.

On weak legs, James slowly made his way across the cold floor and grasped the door handle. He tugged, only to find it locked. That shouldn't have been a surprise, but it was disheartening just the same. Not that a locked door could keep him trapped. All he had to do was pull it from its hinges.

He yanked on the handle, but it didn't move an inch. He slammed his shoulder against the wood, but he didn't even hear a satisfying crack. For God's sake, how weak was he? Then the most glorious sound he'd ever heard reached his ears. Footsteps came from the floor above him. He looked up. "Hello?" he called. The footsteps stopped. "Hello?" he said again, resting his head against the door. If he was loud enough, perhaps the person could hear him. "Please!" he yelled one final time. "I'm trapped. Please let me out."

The faint voice of the female he'd heard earlier trickled like rain down to him in the darkness. A bump and a muffled curse word reached his ears, which brought a smile to his face. The lass did have an interesting vocabulary. He'd teach her a few more colorful words if she'd just open the door.

Then once the lass freed him, James would be on his way. He felt his ring finger and growled. Damn witches. Hopefully it was dark outside as traveling by daylight would be impossible since one of the magical she-devils had apparently absconded with his ring.

"Come on," he cried from his prison. "Come and find me. Please."

When her footsteps slowed, James thought he'd wither away and die. He closed his eyes, willing her to continue. He couldn't lose the lass. Not when she was so close to finding him. "Hello…" he called, allowing his voice to linger at the end of the word, drawing it out like a song. "Can you hear me?" His throat burned with the force of his words. He reached one hand into the darkness, as though he could grab onto whoever was moving about above him. "Help me!" he called.

The footsteps stopped completely.

"Please!" he begged. "I know you can hear me!"

Her steps moved across the floor again, faster this time. Had James still possessed a heart, it would have leapt at the sound. "That's it," he whispered to himself. "Come this way."

Finally, footsteps, slow and measured, clipped against stone steps, the noise ringing in his ears.

"Hello!" he cried.

She stopped again.

"No! Keep coming. I'm in here, but I'm trapped."

Another step. She didn't back away. Thank God. She was still coming toward him. A flash of light crept beneath the door. It was nearly painful to his eyes. He gasped and covered them quickly. Then he cracked one eye open and took in the room, which he could now see much better from the warm glow that slid beneath the door.

He jerked at the door handle once more, but it still refused to budge. He could almost taste his freedom. Until he smelled the scent of blood that pumped within her veins. She smelled of sweet lavender, earth, and strength. He wanted to taste her more than anything. James dropped to his stomach beside the door and spoke beneath it. "Please, free me," he crooned.

"Are ye real?" The soft Scottish lilt of her words moved through him like thunder breaks a storm-laden night. He shuddered. Scottish lasses would be the death of him.

"I'm real."

"I doona believe ye." She sounded odd to his ears all of a sudden, as though she was in a trance of some sort. The tiny thread of hope he had held began to unravel in his hands.

Still he was so close to freedom that giving up seemed foolhardy. "I'm very real, lass," he promised, pressing his whole body against the door. If he could slide himself beneath it, he would. "Set me free and I'll show you." James felt the door move a bit when she tugged on the other side.

"It's locked," she said wistfully, dreamlike.

"Of course, it's locked. I told you I was trapped."

"Oh."

"Can you look for a key?" What was wrong with the lass? She didn't seem to grasp much of what he said, nor the urgency with which he said it. Had the coven trapped and drugged her, too? Was she a victim of their treachery as well? "Blasted witches," he ground out beneath his breath.

A startled gasp rang out from the other side of the door. "Blasted ghost!" she countered.

Ghost? Clearly the chit wasn't in her right mind. "Lass, if you'll just find the key."

"Find it yerself," she snapped.

What the devil was wrong with her all of a sudden? James heaved a sigh. "Please," he begged. But then her footsteps moved away from the door and James' hope plummeted once again "Don't go!" he cried.

"No such thing as ghosts," she barely whispered, but he heard the words clearly.

Her footsteps clipped back up the stone steps.

James cursed beneath his breath and begged her to come back, but she didn't answer him. He heard her move across the floor above him. Then silence. She'd vanished as quickly as she'd arrived.

Why had she run off? What had she said? He tried to remember her exact words. Did she think he was a ghost? Was that what she meant? He scoffed to himself. He was the furthest thing from a harmless specter. But, he'd be whatever she desired, right up to the moment she freed him.

Four

Blaire ripped off a piece of crusted bread and popped it into her mouth. She glanced around Briarcraig's dismal dining hall, which was not much improved in the light of day. Her eyes were tired and aching, and there was an insistent pounding in her head. Sleeping draughts always had that effect on her. Not that she'd had much of a choice the night before.

It was her own fault for allowing Brannock to remain with her during the night. How could she have forgotten that the lad kicked in his sleep? She must be covered in bruises all along her left side. Making matters worse, he also snored like an old man, making the bed rumble all night long. No, she hadn't had a choice about the sleeping draught. But she did wish it didn't make her mind feel quite so foggy.

Her dreams had been fitful. Trapped ghosts and glowing rings. Though the ring wasn't a dream, was it? She tugged the cord from beneath her serviceable dress and held the ring up for inspection. Under the daylight, it didn't seem to possess the otherworldly glow from the night before. If it still weighed more, she'd grown accustomed to the difference and didn't notice it now. She ran her fingertip along the griffin etched on the side. The symbol of the valiant soldier. Passed from one warrior witch to the next for generations. Never had she seen it behave so strangely.

It was a shame Caitrin wasn't here. As the seer of their coven, Cait would understand the situation with a close of her eyes and a few magical words. Thinking of her sister witch brought Blaire's attention back to her own hasty departure from Edinburgh. Perhaps she'd send her all-seeing friend a note explaining her absence. Truly, she should have done so before she left Lindsay House.

Blaire tore off another hunk of bread and started to compose the letter in her mind. Before she finished her thoughts, Aiden strode into the dining hall as if he owned the place. Blast him for looking so well rested and bright-eyed this morning.

"Why are ye scowlin'?" he asked, sliding into a place at the table beside her.

"Difficult night," she grumbled.

"Indeed?" Aiden's eyes widened in surprise. "I slept like the dead. Was the bed uncomfortable?" He broke off a hunk of cheese and bit into it.

She shrugged. "Brannock knocked on my door last night, scared half ta death of ghosts and other such nonsense. I let him stay with me."

"Ah, rotten luck there." Aiden winced. "The lad kicks."

"I'm well aware." She somehow managed to keep the growl from her voice. "And his paranoia is infectious. I had the strangest dream last night of a ghost."

His silver eyes lit up. "I dinna think ye believed in ghosts."

She shook her head. "In the light of day, I doona believe in such nonsense. But the dream felt so real in a strange way, Aiden. I canna describe it properly."

"Ye should go back ta bed for a while. Ye doona look quite right."

Blaire laughed. "A lady of leisure I'm no'. Besides we have quite a lot ta do today."

"There's no rush."

Of course, he wasn't rushed. He'd gladly spend the rest of his days in the crumbling castle, which was not appealing in the least to Blaire. "I'm goin' ta jot off a quick note ta Cait and then start ta work on the first-floor parlors."

Aiden sighed. "If ye insist."

"Well, I wouldna insist, but ye did promise ta entertain some sheep farmer this afternoon."

Blaire climbed to her feet and wiped her sweaty brow with the back of her hand. "I canna believe Aiden talked me inta comin' ta this filthy place," she mumbled under her breath as she carried a bucket of dirty mop water and rags to the door. "Brannock!" she bellowed.

She tilted her head to listen for the sound of footsteps. She knew Aiden was busy with chores, but the littlest Lindsay had to be constantly guided back to the task at hand, which was cleaning years' worth of dust from the interior of the main rooms. The boy was underfoot when she *didn't* want him to be but was nowhere to be found when there was work to be done.

Blaire took the stairs two at a time and then called for Brannock as she walked the corridors.

"In here, Blaire," his quiet voice finally said. She followed the sound, which led her to a long corridor adorned with one large portrait after another. There at the far end sat Brannock on the floor, looking up at the last painting in the gallery.

"Takin' a break from yer work?" she asked, striding toward him. But as she got closer, the air from her lungs was nearly sucked away. Her mother stood proud and confident in the final portrait, holding a broadsword in her hands.

"I ken ye said Mama never lived here, but it does look so like Papa's miniature."

Alpina Lindsay had been gone for ten years, but Blaire would never forget her mother's regal face. It was most assuredly staring back at her from the portrait. "I do believe ye're right, Bran. That is indeed Mama."

He looked up in surprise, and a tinkling of metal hit the floor. "How did it get here?"

Blaire wished she knew. "Perhaps she visited when she was younger?" Not that it made any sense. She'd have to ask Aiden again what the solicitor had said about the place. Perhaps she should have listened better the first time he'd told the tale. She looked back down at her young brother and noticed a small pile of pewter figures. "What have ye found there?" She pointed at the floor.

"Bruce was in a wardrobe with these," Brannock said absently as his eyes drifted down to the playthings.

"Bruce?" Blaire echoed.

"My cat," he replied, now arranging the little pewter pieces in lines and circles.

Blaire couldn't help the giggle that escaped her. "Ye named yer cat *Bruce*?"

Brannock shrugged. "He was Scotland's greatest warrior."

She sunk down to her knees beside her brother and ruffled his hair. "He was indeed." Though he'd most likely turn over in his grave if he knew he was the namesake of that scrawny cat. She turned her eyes back to the portrait and stared into the past. "Have ye been comin' here ta look at the paintin' while Aiden and I have been workin' our fingers ta the bones?"

"Doona be mad, Blaire," he begged. "I…I just wish I kent her. Ye canna tell much from the miniature. She looks so strong and brave."

Blaire kissed the top of his head. "I wish ye'd kent her, too. I wish she was still here with us." She heaved a sigh. She had at least known their mother, but Brannock had never gotten that chance. "Ye can come and see the portrait all ye want, but we do need yer help as well."

Brannock nodded. "All right. Can I put my toys away first?"

Blaire winked at him. "Aye. I'll help ye."

He held out one pewter piece to her. "I think this one looks like ye."

Blaire took the shiny object from him and clasped the cold metal in her hand. Indeed, the figure was a woman, the dress she wore making that fact unmistakable. But in her hand she held a bow and arrow. Blaire's heart clenched. She'd seen a piece like this before in Sorcha's collection. What would something like this be doing here of all places? "Let me see the others," she said as uneasiness settled over her.

He scooped up the remaining figures and dropped them into her hand. It was odd indeed to see the set. One lass held her hand over her eyes. One held a bolt of lightning in her hand as though she'd snatched it from the sky. Another held a flower outstretched as a gift, and the last lass held a mortar and pestle. "Humph," she grunted. It was an exact duplicate of Sorcha's figures. "Where did ye say ye found these again?"

"In a wardrobe in one of the rooms. Bruce was usin' it as his house."

"Can ye show me?" She dropped the figures into her pocket,

Brannock nodded. "There's nothin' else there, no' that I could see."

Still, she needed to see it. Brannock led her to one of the many bedchambers and opened up an ancient wardrobe. The interior was vast and dark, almost big enough to be a small room of its own. She kicked a tattered pillow from her path, most assuredly the cat's bed. A fireball sparked to life in Blaire's hand so she could better see inside. At the back of the large wardrobe, her flame glittered against the brass casings of a dark chest.

"*Havers!*" Blaire muttered.

"It's like a pirate's treasure chest." Brannock tugged at her skirts. "Can we open it?"

Blaire laughed at her adventure-starved brother. Though, truly her excitement mirrored his, if she was completely honest with herself. "Of course."

The two of them stepped toward the back of the

wardrobe, and Blaire lowered her flame to inspect the chest more thoroughly. The brass lock sparkled shiny, as though it had recently been constructed. In fact, it had the same luster as the key Aiden had received from the solicitor. The one that didn't fit the front door. "Bran, run back ta my chambers. The key from Mr. MacDonald is on my dressin' table."

Her brother pouted. "Why doona ye just open it with some magic words?"

She could do that, of course, but doing so wouldn't answer her question. "Because I want ta ken if it fits the trunk. Now do as I ask."

Brannock grumbled, though he started for the entrance of the wardrobe. "Doona open it without me."

"Cross my heart."

Blaire ran her fingers over the brass casings. How strange that the chest retained its luster when everything else at Briarcraig seemed dusty and dull. The wardrobe must have kept it safe from the elements, but one would still think a little dust would have settled on the chest, especially if that damn cat had been in and out of the space.

In less than a moment, Brannock was back inside the wardrobe, huffing and puffing as though he'd run a footrace. She never ceased to be surprised at how quick he could be when he wanted something. "Here." He held out the key for Blaire's inspection, still trying to catch his breath.

Blaire bounced the key in her upturned palm, as though testing its weight. "Hmm." It did indeed appear to be the same brass. She slid it into the lock and smiled when she heard a very satisfying click.

Five

BLAIRE GASPED.

"What's inside?" Brannock complained, bouncing up and down on his feet as he tried to look over her shoulder. "Let me see."

Blaire moved to the side, allowing the warm light from her flame to illuminate the contents of the trunk. She couldn't even speak. Never in her life had she seen so much money. Not shillings nor farthings but real golden guineas filled the trunk to the brim. More than she could ever count, she was sure.

"It *is* a treasure chest!" Brannock gushed, awe lacing his voice.

"Aye," Blaire barely managed.

"We're rich! We're rich!"

The lad bolted from the wardrobe and out of the room before Blaire could even call for him to stop.

"We're rich! We're rich!" he bellowed through the corridor and down the stairs, his exuberance bubbling over.

"Brannock!" she called after him. "Wait."

"Aiden!" the boy wailed. "We're rich!"

Blaire chased after her younger brother, nearly stumbling on the last stone step in her pursuit. She righted herself just in time to see Brannock dart into the great hall. That lad was going to be the death of her one way or the other.

"For the love of God, Bran!" Blaire stopped in the threshold of the vast room to find Brannock barreling toward Aiden who was reclined like a king on the settee. Unfortunately, her oldest brother was not alone. Across from him, two golden-haired lasses in cheerful homespun sat in matching high-backed chairs, and an older man of stoic disposition stood near the blazing hearth.

"We're rich!" Brannock blurted out.

"Brannock!" Blaire hissed.

The two lasses exchanged mercenary glances with each other and then turned their attention to Aiden. "Captain Lindsay," the first one began, "have we come at a bad time?"

Aiden shook his head and gestured to Blaire, still standing in the corridor. "No' at all. Allow me ta introduce my sister. Blaire, this is Miss Heather Fyfe, Miss Crissa Fyfe, and their father, Mr. Fyfe. I told ye they'd be payin' a visit."

Both Miss Fyfes raked their gazes across Blaire and she suddenly had the urge to bolt. "Pleasure," she lied.

"Well, come in, come in," Aiden ordered, patting the spot beside him on the settee. Then he gestured to the older lass. "I was tellin' Miss Fyfe how ye love ta sew."

In other words, he'd been lying through his teeth. "Ye shouldna have said so. Truly." Blaire forced one foot over the threshold and then managed a tight smile as she took the place beside her prevaricating brother.

"Aiden!" Brannock stamped his foot. "Will ye listen ta me?"

Her older brother sent a scathing glance at the lad. "My apologies, ladies. The lad's governess has been derelict in her duties."

Governess? Blaire almost choked. What Banbury tales had Aiden been spinning? And why did he care about impressing the golden-haired Fyfe sisters anyway? "Aye. Ye really should have a word with Miss…Gulverness. She has been so lax of late."

"Gulverness?" the younger Miss Fyfe, Blaire wasn't certain which was which, piped up. "Yer governess is called Miss Gulverness?"

Blaire sat up straight, daring the woman to call her on her lie. "Aye. Gulverness. I think that is why she went inta this line of work, Miss…uh."

"Crissa," the lass added, her light blue eyes narrowed with suspicion.

"Aye, Miss Crissa. I think Miss Gulverness became a governess because the name suited her. Much like a blacksmith named Smith. No one thinks that odd, now do they?"

Crissa Fyfe's blond brow furrowed. "I suppose no'."

"Of course no'," Blaire agreed.

"Why doona ye go find *Miss Gulverness*, Brannock, and I'll meet with the two of ye later?" Aiden ground out.

Brannock thrust out his lower lip, glowered at their older brother, and then stalked from the room. The poor lad. He had such delightful news and was being disciplined by having to seek out the nonexistent Miss Gulverness for his punishment. If Blaire wasn't so annoyed with Aiden, she would have laughed.

"Now, then." Aiden shifted in his seat. "Blaire, ye'll be happy ta ken that Miss Fyfe loves her needle and thread."

So the lasses were bragging about their accomplishments to the handsome new owner of the local castle, were they? Not that Blaire thought Aiden was handsome, but she'd heard others in Edinburgh lament the fact nearly all her life. And now the enterprising Fyfe sisters had just heard Brannock announce they were "rich." How the devil would they ever get rid of the pair now that Aiden was a handsome, wealthy Army captain in possession of a castle? "Ye doona say?" she asked in a sickly sweet voice. "That is positively fascinatin', Miss Fyfe. Needle *and* thread, ye say?"

Heather Fyfe narrowed her green eyes at Blaire in a most calculating manner. "I say, Miss Lindsay, ye have," she gestured to Blaire's head, "somethin' in yer hair." Then she shuddered for dramatic effect.

Blaire's hand flew to her hair where she discovered a rather stubborn cobweb interlaced with her locks. *Havers!* That was a bit embarrassing under the circumstances.

"My sister is so excited about seein' every inch of Briarcraig that she must have been investigatin' a place the servants have yet ta clean."

The servants meaning Blaire and Brannock. "Oh, aye," she agreed quickly. "So many corridors and alcoves ta see."

"Are ye no' afraid of the ghost?" Crissa Fyfe asked, sliding forward in her seat.

"I doona believe in ghosts," Blaire informed her.

"Blaire is a brave lass," Aiden added.

"Well, Captain," Mr. Fyfe pushed away from the hearth, speaking for the first time since Blaire had entered the room. "My girls and I had best be off. I hope ye will enjoy yer time here in Strathcarron."

Both girls shot quelling looks at their father as Aiden rose to his feet. "It was such a pleasure meetin' ye both. I do hope ye will visit Blaire again while we're in residence."

Neither Heather nor Crissa Fyfe spared Blaire a glance, as they were too busy batting their eyelashes at Aiden. "We'd love ta," Heather Fyfe gushed.

"Well, why doona ye all join us for dinner tomorrow?" Aiden asked, offering his arm to Heather. "Then ye can become better acquainted."

Blaire resisted the urge to grind her teeth together. "I'm no' sure if the servants will be quite ready, Aiden. We've been workin' the poor dears ta their bones."

Her brother waved her off, as though they truly did have a castle full of servants. "Such a tenderhearted lass," he confided to Heather Fyfe.

He was a tenderheaded dolt.

"Thank ye, Captain." Mr. Fyfe and his younger daughter followed Aiden from the great hall. "We'll look forward ta it."

Blaire settled back against the settee, waiting for the imbecile that was her older brother to return from seeing the Fyfes out. What the devil was wrong with Aiden? She sighed.

She didn't have to wait long. A moment later, her brother entered the great hall, a grin spread across his face. "They were delightful."

"Our ideas of delightful differ wildly."

He rolled his eyes. "So do our ideas of what constitutes a decent name. Gulverness? That was the best ye could do?"

It wasn't the best name, but she wasn't about to admit to it. "Apparently my talent for prevarication isna as well developed as yers."

He had the audacity to chuckle.

Blaire rose from her spot. "We have ta talk, Aiden."

"I ken ye dinna care for the Fyfe lasses. Just give them a chance. That's all I ask."

She couldn't care less about the Fyfe sisters. "Aiden, I have somethin' ta tell ye. Brannock and I—"

"What the devil was wrong with the lad? Where is he?" Aiden started for the door. "Brannock!" he called.

Havers! Getting the man's attention was next to impossible. "Aiden Lindsay!" Blaire barked. "Will ye shut yer trap for a minute and listen?"

Her brother's brow furrowed. "There's no reason ta talk ta me that way."

Oh, there were plenty of good reasons to talk to him that way. Dragging them all into the Highlands. Inviting the Fyfe twits for dinner the next evening. The stream of lies that had flown from his mouth to impress the magistrate and his daughters. But that was neither here nor there at the moment. "Brannock and I found a chest, Aiden. It's filled with guineas."

"Guineas?" Aiden finally looked interested.

"More than I've ever seen," she confessed. "The key from the solicitor. It opened the trunk."

"Indeed?"

"And there's more. Brannock found some little pewter figures." She tugged the pieces from her pocket and dropped them in her brother's hand. "Just look at them," Blaire ordered.

He did take a good long look, and the color from his face drained away. "The *Còig*."

"Exactly." She heaved a sigh. "And there's a portrait gallery, Aiden. A paintin' of Mama is among the collection."

Aiden collapsed back onto the settee, but he said nothing. He just stared blankly at the pewter figures in his hands.

"Tell me again what the solicitor said. How did ye inherit the castle?"

Slowly, his gaze rose to meet hers. "It was Mama's," he finally said. "Her dowry, her birthright. The home of the battle-born witches. An entire trunk of guineas, ye say?"

But that didn't make any sense. Again uneasiness settled over Blaire. "Mama would have told me about it, Aiden."

He winced. That didn't bode well. Exactly how talented was Aiden at prevarications?

"What is it ye're no' tellin' me?" She sank into a chair across from him.

He raked a hand through his dark hair. "Honestly, Blaire, I doona ken." Aiden sighed. "I remember Briarcraig from when I was a child. That's why I was so excited ta see it again."

"Ye remember it?" Why the devil hadn't he said so?

Her brother shrugged. "No' a trunk full of guineas." He sighed. "But we spent a lot of time here, Mama and me. It was a sanctuary of sorts from Father. He never came with us." Aiden shrugged. "Then we just stopped comin'. I asked Mama about it, and she said I was never ta mention it again."

"How old were ye? Did I come here, too?"

He shook his head. "Nay, it was before ye came along. Mama was expectin' ye though, the last time we visited."

Blaire looked around at the tattered walls and tried to pull the essence of her mother from the place. "The home of the battle-born witches? Why dinna she tell me?"

"I was just a lad, Blaire. I doona ken. For the longest while, I thought this castle was a figment of my imagination, in fact, until I met with Mr. MacDonald last week."

The solicitor who had finished going through the last of their father's papers, Mr. MacDonald had seemed glad to be done with the Lindsays. "Why dinna ye tell me this in Edinburgh?"

He hung his head. "I suppose they were my memories, the best of my childhood, and I dinna want ta share them. I forgot about the portrait. She had it commissioned when she knew she was expectin' ye. I played out by the loch while the artist painted her, day after day. Ye should see the place in the summer, Blaire. Loch Calavie sparkles like glittering diamonds under the sun."

Blaire barely heard his words. She was sitting in the

ancestral home of the battle-born witches. Her mother and grandmother and every generation of warrior witches before that. For some reason her mother never told her about the place. Why? Did she think Blaire was undeserving of her birthright? Had she disappointed her mother in some way?

Her mind spun with memories, trying to sort out the reason. Why would her mother have kept the castle from her? It didn't make sense. Was that why her ring had reacted so strangely upon their entrance? As though it was being returned home to its rightful place? It had certainly returned to normal since. No more glowing, no more radiating heat.

"Are ye all right, Blaire?" She looked up to see Aiden hovering over her. When had he left his seat?

"Fine," she mumbled.

"Ye doona look it." Her brother frowned, worry etched across his brow. He touched his hand to her head. "Ye dinna sleep well. Perhaps ye should lie down for a bit."

She must truly look bad if Aiden was concerned about her well-being. "I just canna understand why she wouldna tell me. Why she would stop visitin'." Blaire stared into her brother's eyes looking for any sign of deception. "She said ye were never ta mention Briarcraig?"

Aiden sighed. "It was so long ago, Blaire. I was so young that I thought I'd imagined the place. When I saw the name on a piece of foolscap on Mr. MacDonald's desk, I couldna believe my eyes. I had ta see it again, see if it was what I remembered."

"And it is?"

"Some of it. Will ye take me ta the trunk ye found with Bran?"

She nodded. "It's in a large wardrobe." Blaire started for the corridor.

Aiden was quick on her heels. "Do ye suppose there are other trunks or chests hidden away?"

Blaire shrugged. "I have no idea what ta think or believe about this place."

"True," he conceded as they began to climb the stairs. "I'd like ta be sure, though. I'd like to search the castle over if ye and Bran doona mind stayin' here a while longer."

Wild dragons couldn't drag Blaire away from the castle now. It was her birthright, and she intended to discover all of Briarcraig's secrets. All the things her mother had neglected to tell her. "I imagine with the money we found ye could staff a hundred castles ten times over. If we're ta stay here a while and entertain the featherbrained Fyfe sisters, we probably should go about hirin' a real staff."

Aiden sighed wistfully. "A real staff. I do like the sound of that."

Six

JAMES LEANED AGAINST THE COLD STONE WALL AND counted his blessings. It was one of the covenants he lived by. Never take from another in anger. Always remember that life is a gift. Never forget the world from which he came, nor its societal rules. Love as though you still have a heart.

He scoffed at that last one. Though he'd been infatuated many times during the past two hundred years, he'd not once found a lady he could love. It probably centered around the fact that women held a purpose for him, aside from being a partner in life. They were a food source. Albeit one always taken willingly, always taken with care.

His maker had always stressed that even though James was a predator, living on the lifeblood of others, he was still a human being somewhere deep inside. He didn't doubt it, but he would have to find a woman who would offer herself to him, trusting him implicitly, before he could love. That lady would be the one he spilled all his secrets to, the one who completed him.

James jumped when he heard quick footsteps growing louder and louder. They could only mean that someone was coming in his direction. Hope soared within him when a golden light shone through the crack beneath the door.

She'd come back. Thank God.

James walked closer to the door so he could speak to her through the crack. "Set me free, lass."

"Who are ye?"

Probably your worst nightmare. "Who do you think I am?"

"An annoyin' Sassenach," she said quietly, but he heard her all the same.

A smile teased at his lips. Her scent, clean lavender and the earth, drifted through the crack in the door. He cleared his throat. "I have been called worse."

"I will warn ye once." He could almost see her in his mind's eye with her hands on her hips, her face full of righteous indignation. "If ye hurt my family, I will have no choice but ta kill ye."

Good luck with that. "I promise not to hurt you or your family." And he meant it. If she'd just set him free, he'd be on his way. He had a few things to set straight after all.

Heavy footsteps sounded on the steps, and then a masculine voice called, "What are ye doin' down here, Blaire? Did ye find somethin' else?"

A man? Perhaps it was her husband. James wasn't sure why he was perturbed by that idea. Although dealing with husbands was always a bit of a chore.

The warm light was quickly doused. Damnation, he had been so close to freedom! If he ever made it out of his cell, he'd kill the Scotsman simply for delaying his release with his very presence.

"Bloody hell, Aiden," the lass complained. "Ye made me drop my fire. What did I tell ye about sneakin' up on me?"

"What are ye doin'?" the man asked again, ignoring the indignation in her voice. "I havena had time ta search around down here yet. Find any more chests?"

"Perhaps," she murmured. Then she said with a voice strong and clear, "*Fosgladh, còmhla, fosgladh.*"

The soft snick of the lock bounced off the walls of James' prison. Freedom. He didn't move. He didn't even breathe, afraid that any sound from him would cause her to close him back up in the cell where he'd awakened. Had she found the elusive key? Or had her words freed him? It most certainly seemed like the latter. Until James knew what powers she possessed, it was best to be cautious.

A loud creak sounded as she pushed the door open. James stepped back and tried to assume an unthreatening air. It wasn't a simple task when what he wanted more than anything in the world was to draw the lass to him, take her in his arms, and enchant her so deeply that she'd lean her head to the side and offer herself up for his pleasure…and her own. He'd make sure she enjoyed it.

Dear God, he needed to feed. Soon.

The lass was beautiful. Hair as dark as a moonless night hung down to her shoulders, making her look as innocent as a newborn babe. Silver eyes sparkled with intelligence. Beautiful, full lips the color of ripe berries were pursed tightly together. If he was standing close to her, he could kiss her forehead with a mere dip of his head, she was so tall.

She wasn't part of the coven who'd imprisoned him. He knew that much. He'd never forget those five witches. Though this lass had many of the same features as the raven-haired one. Perhaps a sister?

"Who the devil is that?" the Scotsman with the same chilling silver gaze breathed.

She ignored him completely and spoke to James instead. "Doona move," she said as she tossed a ball of fire lightly in her palm.

A ball of *fire* in her palm? He nearly laughed. She was definitely magical. That question had been answered.

Her silver eyes narrowed at him. "I dinna think ye were real."

"Flesh and blood," he said quietly. Well, not yet. But soon. He could almost taste her.

The Scotsman nearly fell over. "Ye were aware there was a man livin' in the cellar and ye dinna tell me, Blaire? Have ye lost all yer wits?"

"Being sequestered in a smelly old castle has been known ta drive the sane straight ta Bedlam. Were ye no' aware, Aiden?" She paused briefly as her gaze danced down James' body. "And I believe we found the source of the odor."

The Scotsman inhaled deeply. "I believe ye're correct," he said as his face scrunched up with displeasure.

James scratched at the stubble that lined his jaw before he glanced down at himself. In the light from her ball of fire, which hovered at the ready for her use, he could plainly see he was filthy. Dust covered him in layers and flew from his clothes in waves that caught on the flickering firelight as he bent to dust himself off.

"Pray forgive my appearance. I'm typically more presentable than I find myself at present." He held out a hand to the man, hoping he'd take it in friendship. The man she referred to as Aiden glanced at her as though asking for permission. Strange. Why would he need permission to be sociable from the witch?

"Captain Aiden Lindsey," he began. Then he shook his head with wonder as he clasped James' hand. "How did ye end up in my cellar?" the man asked.

"To be quite honest, I don't recollect how I came to be here. Where *is* here, by the way?"

"Briarcraig Castle," the Scotsman said quietly. "Ye doona ken how ye came ta be locked away in the bowels of my castle?"

"No earthly idea," James muttered. Though unearthly seemed to be the dominant trait in his present situation. "The last thing I remember was five w—," he glanced at the lass. "Women," he finished. "Five women who didn't appear to like me very much."

Blaire stood at the ready, though she felt like an interloper when the men began to talk as though they were meeting at an assembly hall instead of a musty cellar of an old Highland castle.

She found it difficult to look away from the stranger's dark gaze. His eyes appeared to be black in the flickering light from her fire, but it was hard to tell. However, it was impossible to miss his strong body with broad shoulders and well-defined muscles. Even beneath the odd, filthy clothing he wore, Blaire could see that he was more than the average man. But what he was, aside from being most unfashionable, eluded her completely.

One thing was for certain, however. The Englishman was dangerous. His presence in the castle didn't make sense. He'd been trapped by magic. There was no denying its force upon the lock she'd just opened. The question was why.

She stepped into the room and lifted her fireball high in the air. Nothing but dingy walls, damp stone, and darkness were visible. How long had he been there?

"Where did ye come from?" Aiden interjected.

Instead of answering, the stranger stared at her fire. "That's a nice bit of magic you have there," he said. But she saw no curiosity in his gaze. No surprise. Any sane man would be worried over a strange lass who could hold a fireball above her naked palm. Perhaps he wasn't sane at all. Not even close. His wardrobe certainly argued that point.

"Aye, it comes in handy at times," Blaire replied. She took a deep breath. A warrior never hesitated to jump into the fray. "Why did they lock ye up?"

"They?" He arched a dark eyebrow.

"The witches. Ye almost said 'witches' earlier. Ye're no' surprised by my ability ta hold fire in my hand, which means ye ken what I am. And those who trapped ye here were witches, too. What I want ta ken is why ye were left ta rot in the bowels of this castle. What type of bein' are ye? And how long have ye been here?"

He whistled softly. "You know of a lot of other beings, lass?"

"A few," she clipped out. She'd heard all sorts of legends when she was younger, though she'd never quite believed those tales. Until recently when Elspeth met Benjamin Westfield, she'd thought witches were the only anomaly that truly existed. However, now she was quite the expert on Lycans. What else was out there, she wasn't exactly sure.

"How interesting," he said, his voice husky and slow. "I'd like to discuss them with you."

Discuss them they would. The unfashionable Englishman wouldn't step foot outside Briarcraig until he answered her questions and she decided what to do with him. "Aye. Right after ye wash some of the stench off yerself, I'll be happy ta entertain ye."

"Blaire!" her brother scolded.

She frowned in response. Aiden would be less than helpful during her interrogation. "Doona pretend like ye canna smell him. Do everyone a favor, and prepare a bath for our guest," she said, sending Aiden the most pointed glare she could muster. Without her brother's prying eyes, she might be able to force the Englishman to tell her some truths, instead of the evasive comments he'd made thus far. She shooed Aiden away with her hands. "Off with ye. Go on."

Aiden grumbled all the way up the stairs. She couldn't quite make out all the words, but knew they were far from complimentary. With her brother disposed of for the time being, she turned back to their uninvited visitor.

He closed his eyes and inhaled deeply. Blaire was nearly afraid he'd expire on the spot, just from taking in that much of his own stench. But a small smile curved the corners of his lips. "You smell like heaven, lass."

"I wish I could say the same for ye. And doona change the subject. What are ye?"

"I am a man," he said, holding his hands out in front of him with his palms pointed up, as though she could find the answer within his reach.

"I hardly believe that's the extent of it. I'm waitin' for the truth," she encouraged as she began to tap her foot.

The Englishman tipped his head backwards and laughed. "And what would you like for me to say? You're looking at me with your own eyes. What do *you* think I am?"

That was the question, wasn't it? "Someone who doesna own a mirror?" she quipped.

He scowled at her response. "I'll set myself to rights in no time. Thank you for ordering the bath."

"Do ye own clothes from this century? Or do ye travel around the countryside lookin' for masquerades ta attend?"

The Englishman's eyebrows drew together in confusion. He glanced down at his grimy knee breeches and high-heeled boots that had gone out of style many years before. "Good God," he muttered to himself.

What had she said to elicit such a reaction? "I beg yer pardon?"

But he said nothing and merely shook his head.

Blaire pursed her lips. What was he hiding? Why the look of confusion on his face? "Who are ye?"

Finally, his black eyes sparkled. He dipped his head.

"Kettering," he answered proudly. "*Baron* Kettering of Derbyshire."

Whatever else he was, Lord Kettering of Derbyshire was full of English pride. She would be surprised if his ego fit through the door. Blaire winced. Heaven help her when Aiden learned their *guest* was a peer of the realm. "Well, my lord, why doona ye tell me exactly what ye did that made the other witches so angry with ye."

A roguish smile lit his lips, and, despite his state of dishabille, Blaire almost gasped at how handsome he was when he smiled. Almost. A warrior never allowed an enemy to see a weakness. Her discomfiture when he smiled was most certainly a weakness.

"You have me at a disadvantage, lass," he replied, his voice dripping with seduction.

"Disadvantage?" she echoed. Blast! Did her voice crack on that word?

Kettering stepped closer to her. His eyes darkened, though she didn't know how that was possible. "You know my name, but I've yet to learn yours."

Blaire wanted to step away from him. In truth, she wanted to run and never look back. Yet she merely straightened her stance and planted her feet. Something about Kettering was most definitely not right, up to and including the fact that he appeared to have stepped out of the pages of a book written two or three decades earlier. However, she would *not* retreat. She would not let him know he had any effect on her whatsoever. "Blaire Lindsay." She forced her voice to sound smooth and unconcerned.

The baron's gaze flashed to the stone stairwell.

Then his eyes narrowed and twinkled, almost as though he held a secret. "Not Captain Lindsay's wife. Most definitely not."

She couldn't have kept the snort from escaping her if she'd tried. "I pity the woman who ends up with him."

Kettering smiled again, and Blaire felt her knees weaken. What was the matter with her? Weakening knees. No wonder her mother didn't tell her about Briarcraig. She was the most undeserving warrior witch who had ever lived. She'd known the man for five minutes and was nearly ready to surrender at his feet in exchange for his smile.

"A brother, then?" he asked.

Blaire nodded, unable to speak coherently when he stared at her so…hungrily? Was that the look he had? His attention swung from her lips to the base of her throat and back. Chills raced up her spine.

"Blaire?" Brannock bellowed from the top of the steps.

She'd never been so glad to hear Brannock yell at the top of his lungs. Normally, she would have chastised his behavior, but not this time. This time she thought she might kiss the lad. "Aye, Bran?"

"Aiden says ta bring yer Sassenach up ta the family wing."

Kettering offered her his arm. "Shall we, Miss Lindsay?"

Seven

JAMES FOLLOWED MISS LINDSAY AND HER IMPISH LITTLE brother up the darkened stairwell and then down one corridor after another. Briarcraig Castle was one big tangle of corridors and stairs, yet he tried to pay attention to his surroundings so he could find his way out, if the need arose. It was difficult with the lovely Miss Lindsay walking beside him. Her heart beat like a soldier's drum within her chest, and he could very nearly hear the wash of blood as it moved through her veins, as though it called to him.

The boy chattered like a magpie and tugged on his sister's arm. Though James tried to keep up with the conversation, the heavy brogue back and forth didn't make it easy. The real problem, however, was trying to sort out where and, perhaps more importantly, *when* he was.

Blaire Lindsay's words still echoed in his mind. His clothes were sadly out of fashion. He should have noticed the differences between what he was accustomed to and Captain Lindsay's attire, but he'd missed it, focusing on the lovely witch before him instead.

However, there was no missing her cutting remarks about his clothing. How long had he been asleep? How long had he lain in that cellar?

He'd have to sort it out somehow. He certainly couldn't ask Miss Lindsay; she was already suspicious by her very nature and would seize any opportunity he offered her to reveal a weakness. The lad, Brannock, never seemed to stop talking, however. Perhaps he could wheedle the necessary information from—

A searing pain broke James from his plotting. "Agh!" he cried as he rushed into a shadowed corner of the corridor, away from the sun that threatened his very existence. He bent forward in an attempt to block out the pain, which thankfully was fading. The blasted sun! He'd never had to avoid it. Until now, he'd always been in possession of his ring. He rolled the pad of his thumb against the inside of his ring finger, missing not only the weight of the relic but also its protective properties. Never had he felt less human.

James winced one last time and looked up to find both Blaire and Brannock Lindsay before him, concern and confusion evident on their faces. He shook his head, hoping to find the power to speak. "The sun," he muttered, as he straightened his bent frame. After all, what else could he tell them? He couldn't walk through the sunlight, and he couldn't stand in the corridor all day waiting for night to settle in. "I must have become adjusted to the darkness of the cellar, because the sun hurts my eyes as it never has before." That much was true.

"Shut the drapes, Bran," Miss Lindsay ordered.

As her brother ran off to do her bidding, she turned back to James. Her silver eyes raked him from top to bottom. He was certain she'd piece the puzzle together. Especially if she was connected to Blodswell's blasted coven in some way. And then what would she do with him? He was already weaker than he'd ever been. Well, at least weaker than he'd ever been in *this* life.

"How long have ye been in the cellar?" she asked, her head tilted at an angle as she regarded him quietly. And closely.

James shook his head. If only he knew the answer to that question himself. "Time is relative, is it not?"

Thankfully, the corridor grew dark at that moment and James pressed forward, following the youngest Lindsay toward a circular set of stone steps.

"No, time is no' relative," the witch called from behind him, quick on his heels. "It's the same every day. Sixty seconds in a minute. Sixty minutes in an hour. Twenty-four hours in a day."

James didn't respond. What could he say? She was, of course, correct. "How much farther?" he asked the lad.

"Almost there." Brannock bolted up the steps and turned down yet one more corridor.

Less than a minute later, James found himself standing on the threshold of a good-sized chamber. The lad rushed to the drapes and pulled them closed, and then turned around with a wide grin. He was endearing in a strange way. James liked the boy despite himself.

Captain Lindsay was dumping a bucket full of water

into a tub in the middle of the room. "I'll get ye some more hot water."

James nodded. "I do appreciate your generosity, Captain."

The Scotsman inclined his head. "We'll find ye some clean clothes, and once ye're all squared away, I'd like ta hear how ye ended up in my cellar."

James smiled. He'd have the length of his bath to come up with a plausible story. Miss Lindsay wouldn't believe a word out of his mouth, but he'd do what he could to convince her brothers for the time being. At dusk he'd be off. Before then, however, he needed to discover *when* and *where* he was—and how the devil he could find Blodswell.

"I'll find somethin' for him ta wear," the pretty witch muttered, and then she escaped the chamber. A moment later, Captain Lindsay followed her departure.

James turned his attention to the youngest Lindsay and winked at the lad. How fortuitous to be left alone with the weakest member of the family. "You appear to be a smart boy."

Brannock Lindsay puffed out his chest proudly. "Thank ye, sir."

"Show me how smart you are, lad." He sat in an old high-backed chair and began to tug the high-heeled boot from his foot. "Do you know who the monarch of England is?"

The boy frowned a bit at the question, and James tried not to let on how important the answer was. Was he being too obvious with this tactic?

"Are ye tryin' ta trick me?"

Damn. He *was* being too obvious. James shook his

head, hoping to give off an air of nonchalance. "Of course not. Just a simple question. One must always be up on such things."

"Well," Brannock sat at James' feet and twisted his face up, "King George III is king…"

James sighed with relief. He couldn't have been imprisoned too long if George III still sat on the throne of England.

"…But," the lad continued, "since the Prince Regent is the actin' ruler, I think ye *are* tryin' ta trick me."

Acting ruler? What the devil did the boy mean by that? His expression must have given something away, because Brannock leaned closer to him, worry on his face.

"Are ye all right, my lord?"

James forced a smile to his lips. "You are indeed a clever boy. You are impossible to trick." Acting ruler. Good God. "But can you tell me *why* the Prince Regent is the acting ruler?" he asked as though he already knew the answer to the question.

The lad appeared as sober as a vicar on Sunday morning. "On account of the King's madness."

Madness. George III was mad? James shouldn't have been surprised by the fact. There'd been rumors to that effect for many years. Still it was a bit shocking to hear aloud. "And how long has the Prince Regent been sitting in for his father?" he continued conversationally. Meanwhile, his mind spun. The Regent must be the Prince of Wales. George III's inept, debauched oldest son. How the devil was England faring under that oaf's rule?

Brannock shrugged. "As long as I can remember."

That wasn't helpful at all. Perhaps the boy couldn't remember as far back as last week. "How old are you, Master Brannock?" James tugged at his other boot.

"Ten," the boy answered. "I just turned ten."

"Which means you were born…?"

"November 20th."

The *year*, damn your eyes. "What year?" He hoped he kept the frustration out of his voice. He'd not get any useful information from the lad if he lost his temper.

The boy laughed. "Are ye testin' my mathematics now, sir?"

"Indeed I am."

"I was born in the year of our lord 1806."

And ten years later meant James found himself sitting somewhere in late 1816. He'd slept nearly twenty years. Twenty bloody years! A red rage clouded the corners of his vision. Never in his life would he forget the faces of the five witches who'd trapped him; but if he saw even one of them now—twenty years later—would he recognize her?

Miss Lindsay was his only solid lead. She was a witch, and she knew the five that imprisoned him were witches as well. If anyone could lead him to the bloody coven, it was Blaire Lindsay. How would he ever get her assistance? Of course, he already knew the answer to that question. It was the same way he got what he needed from any woman. Seduction. He smiled to himself. With Miss Lindsay, he would enjoy the journey as much as the destination.

Captain Lindsay barreled through the door with

another bucket of water. "I think just a few more will do it, sir."

⁂

Blaire listened to the splashing of water as Aiden filled the tub for the stranger. She shook her head in dismay. There could be nothing good about this situation. Nothing at all. In fact, it could be very, very bad.

Kettering had been imprisoned by the *Còig*, by her own coven. Even if a different generation of witches had done the deed, the reason for his imprisonment was still of concern. The group of five would never make such a choice lightly. She couldn't even imagine a scenario that would inspire her friends to take such an action. He must be the worst sort of villain imaginable, and Blaire's imagination was fairly vivid.

She searched Aiden's trunks for clean toweling, soap, and tooth powder. From the smell of the baron, he needed all of that and more. She couldn't help but wonder if the stench would ever come off him. She'd have to spark a small fire in the grate and burn the clothes he was found in.

Blaire heard the splash of more buckets being brought upstairs as she rifled through Aiden's wardrobe, choosing clothing for the gentleman. A man of his stature was probably used to better quality clothing, although anything would be a marked improvement over his own. She passed the items to Brannock and sent him to the baron.

Blaire paced back and forth in the room, trying to come up with a solution to her dilemma. She had to find out why he was imprisoned and then continue from there. She had a healthy concern for their safety. Not just her family. Not just the coven. But for all of humanity.

She walked back toward the guest chamber and listened intently at the door. More water pouring into the tub. Heavens, one would think they'd be through with that chore by now, but apparently not. Well, there was no point in wasting any time. Perhaps she could get a few answers out of Kettering while he waited for his bath to be ready.

Blaire rapped quickly on the closed door and stepped inside the dimly lit room.

When she did, she immediately stilled, unable to do anything but sputter as she gazed upon the very strong, very naked body of Baron Kettering. The man stood in the middle of the small tub, a bucket of water in his hands as he poured it slowly over his head. His eyes were closed, his face lifted to the gentle downpour, a smile of pure pleasure tilting the corners of his mouth. Suds slithered down his body, rolling slowly across his sculpted chest and lower. Blaire gasped out loud but, for some baffling reason, could not tear her gaze away from his naked body.

"You're letting in a draft," he said slowly, his voice suddenly husky and deep. Blaire jerked her eyes up to his face as heat crept up her own. He made no move to cover himself. In truth, it would be a shame to cover such a beautiful body. The water made his skin glisten, the glow from a candle the only illumination in the room. The single candle created shadows that played across his skin. His shoulders were broad, his chest strong. His hips were narrow, and Blaire's mouth fell open when she saw the rest.

The baron stepped from the tub, reached over and plucked a towel from atop the bed, and wrapped it snugly around his lean hips. "If you keep looking at me like that, I won't be responsible for my actions," he warned. There was no smile upon his face. The gentle teasing that had been present in his earlier manner was completely gone.

What had possessed her to walk into the man's room? Blaire spun to face the wall quickly. So quickly that the edge of the door hit the side of her head. "Ouch!" she cried as she reached up to rub it. "I'm sorry!" she blurted out. "I thought ye were still fillin' the tub. I dinna ken ye would be n-n-n…" She bit her tongue rather than continue.

"Naked?" he supplied as he stepped toward her. "It's all right." His voice made her heart skip a beat. "I'm sure you didn't plan to walk in and find me in the bath." He paused, his voice deepening if that was possible. "Naked." He just had to add that last word. He just had to.

"Of course, I dinna plan it!" she hissed, raising a hand to fan her overheated face.

"Relax, lass. I believe you." His voice was smoky and deep, and it rumbled across her skin like a caress as his hand rose over her shoulder and he very slowly pushed the door closed. Somewhere in the back of her mind, she registered this bit of information, but she overlooked the immediate danger. His nearness made the hair on her neck stand up. His breath across the shell of her ear made her shiver.

Before she could blink, he had spun her around and into his arms, pulling her close against his body. She didn't even protest. She didn't even make a sound, aside from the choked little gasp that escaped her throat.

"Ye promised ye wouldna hurt me," she said, relieved her voice didn't quaver.

"*Am* I hurting you?" he asked as his hand spread out on her back, his fingers splayed like fans. The clean scent of the tooth powder he'd already used teased her nose.

"Nay," she whispered in response.

A mischievous twinkle lit his eyes. "I promised not to hurt you. I never promised not to *kiss* you."

Before she could protest, he claimed her mouth. He tasted of power, sinful and sweet. He softly teased her into opening her mouth so he could sweep inside. Blaire wanted to weep with the sheer pleasure of it. Where her lips were hesitant, his were fearless. He toyed with her like a cat with a mouse, leading her into temptation. His lips left hers to travel across her cheek and then down below her ear. She reached for his shoulders to steady herself when he gently nibbled on her neck.

"A small taste, Miss Lindsay?" he asked, his voice a mere whisper by her ear.

"What?" she asked, the beating of her heart pounding in her own ears so loudly that she couldn't hear her own thoughts, much less his words. She desperately needed to get control of herself or she'd be completely lost.

"A small sip of pleasure? Pray allow me to take—" His voice suddenly came to a halt. His hands extricated themselves from around her waist.

With a heavy sigh, he held his hands out by his sides.

"A simple *no* would have sufficed," he muttered. His eyes were dark as night, betraying the surfeit of emotions that crossed his face. "You can remove the dagger from my person, Miss Lindsay," he continued. His voice was much calmer than she'd imagined it would be when she'd pulled the small knife from its hiding place upon her body and pressed it to the side of his manhood, which swelled quite impressively against her belly.

"Do no' think ta distract me, Kettering," she said, happy to hear that her voice was strong and composed. It was not what she felt inside at all.

"Not a mistake I'll make again, Miss Lindsay," he grunted.

"I certainly hope no'," she said as she turned back toward the door. She reached for the handle and jerked the door so hard in her haste that it hit her in the head again. Then she tripped over her own two feet as she tried to walk from the room. When she slammed the door behind her, she was mortified to find that the skirt of her dress was caught between the door and the doorjamb. She gave it a healthy tug, pulling it free.

"Damn it all ta hell," she snapped.

A chuckle sounded from the other side of the door, dark and silky, touching her as no other sound ever had.

Eight

JAMES CHUCKLED AS HE HEARD MISS LINDSAY STOMP down the corridor. He still couldn't quite believe the enchanting witch had actually pulled a dagger on him, and threatened to unman him with a flick of her wrist. Taming her would be rewarding in so many ways. He strode across the floor and retrieved the set of clothes the lad had left him. Brown doeskin breeches and a white shirt that felt soft against his skin.

He pulled the shirt over his head, but he couldn't get it over his shoulders. Good God. If the shirt was this tight, he wouldn't have a prayer with the trousers. But he had to wear *something*, if just long enough to find something else a bit more suitable. Abandoning the shirt, he pulled the breeches up over his hips. He had no hope of fastening the buttons, and the legs almost reached his knees. James tugged the shirt back over his head and held it in front of his nether regions. After all, he couldn't go traipsing through the castle on display. Miss Lindsay might decide to use him for target practice.

James opened the door to find Brannock Lindsay waiting for him in the corridor. "Did ye want ta ask me anymore questions ta test how clever I am?" Then the boy took in James' appearance. His eyes widened in surprise, and then he doubled over with laughter, nearly tumbling to the floor.

James frowned at the boy. "I hardly find it amusing."

Brannock's merriment brought his sister from her own chamber, and she covered her mouth with her hand to hide her giggle. James glared at her.

"*Havers!*" she muttered with a mock seriousness James would normally have found charming. "Doona move," she ordered. Then she flicked her fingers in his direction at the same time she said, "*Mòr!*"

In the next instant, his trousers expanded. The legs stretched down to his ankles, and, if she hadn't been present, he'd have had the room to button the top. Even the shirt in his hands seemed to have grown larger.

"There, that should work," she said dusting her hands against her skirts, apparently quite pleased with herself.

Never one to give up an opportunity to garner a woman's favor, James winked at her. Flattery always worked. "You are so very talented, Miss Lindsay."

Her silver eyes twinkled. At this rate, she'd be his in a matter of days. He could almost taste her.

Brannock seemed to have control over himself now, and he nodded in agreement. "It saves money when I outgrow my clothes, too. But now we're rich."

"Brannock!" his sister chastised. Then she turned her gaze back to James. "Sorry about the size." Her husky voice reached his ears. "Ye are bigger than Aiden. It was all we had on hand."

"And *my* clothes?" he asked, walking toward the enchanting lass. "What have you done with my clothes?"

"Burned," she nearly sang. "The odor made them beyond repair. I do hope ye doona have a masquerade ta attend anytime soon."

The only masquerade he'd be attending was the one where he pretended to be a lost baron in search of answers. Answers be damned. He was in search of vengeance. After he seduced Miss Lindsay into giving up that blasted coven, he'd find Blodswell and things would get back to normal. After he'd made certain those five maddening witches never took aim at another of his kind again. After he returned to his *life*. "And my pocket fob?"

She shrugged. "Pocket fob?"

Was he to be robbed by every witch in Scotland? First his ring and now his blasted watch, which had been a gift from Queen Elizabeth herself. "Yes." He narrowed his eyes on the lass, who was too beguiling for her own good. "My pocket fob was in my waistcoat."

She shook her head as though he was speaking Greek. "I have no idea what ye're talkin' about, Kettering."

The little liar. James could see it in her eyes. But what the devil did she want with his watch? "See that it's returned to me, Miss Lindsay, or I'll—"

"*Frith*," she said, flicking her fingers toward him.

James gasped as his clothes shrunk back to their normal size, squeezing him like a tourniquet.

"Doona threaten me, Kettering." She let her gaze travel the length of him. "I doona think ye'd like ta see my other talents."

"Blaire!" The boy sucked in a breath.

She never removed her eyes from James. "Brannock, go see if dinner is ready."

"But, Blaire—" he protested.

"Do as ye're told," she replied calmly.

Hanging his head in defeat, the boy slumped off down the corridor.

James nodded appreciatively at her daring. Still, he wasn't about to let her run roughshod over him. "I suggest you put my clothes back to rights, Miss Lindsay."

"Or?" she prompted. Her slender brows rose as though she waited for him to threaten her again.

James had never failed a lady's expectations. "Or I can drop the shirt I'm holding."

Miss Lindsay gulped, apparently just now realizing the bit of cloth he held in front of his trousers was the only thing keeping him decent. Of course she'd already seen all of him today. Perhaps she wanted another look. James was happy to oblige her if that was the case.

"Try it and see what happens," she said, her spine stiffening before him.

"Is that a dare? How many daggers *do* you carry, Miss Lindsay?"

"Blaire!" Captain Lindsay called out before she could answer. His quick footsteps sounded on the steps.

He tried to bite back a grin. Could the fates be any more kind? Certainly, she wouldn't want her older brother to find them in this compromising situation. "Well, what's it to be? Shall I drop my shirt?" His fingers inched downward.

Her face shone instantly red. She glanced away from him as she muttered, "*Mòr*," and flicked her wrist in his general direction. At once the clothes he wore and the shirt in his hands righted themselves.

James smiled at her, though she still had her face turned away. "Many thanks, Miss Lindsay. And I'll expect my watch by the end of the night." He buttoned his trousers, pulled the shirt over his head, and tucked the ends into his waistband.

At that moment, Captain Lindsay turned down the corridor toward them. "Blaire," he called again. "Brannock said ye were quarrelin' with Lord Kettering."

James shook his head. "Nothing quite so dramatic, Captain. All is well."

"Wonderful," the captain said as he neared the pair. "Dinner is ready, my lord, and I am dyin' ta learn how ye ended up in my cellar."

"As are we all," Miss Lindsay muttered under her breath.

James inclined his head to his host. "Of course, Captain. My memory is somewhat spotty, but perhaps we can put the pieces together that I do remember. It's a bit disjointed."

"And, Blaire," the captain said as he glanced at his sister's disheveled appearance. "Make yerself presentable." The man disappeared back down the stairs.

"I'd sooner be boiled in a vat of bubblin' oil," the lass muttered as she turned toward her own chambers, presumably to make herself presentable despite her protestations. He liked her quite a bit in her homespun gown, which was still damp from where he'd pulled her against his naked, wet body. He hardened in response. Dinner. He had to find dinner very, very soon.

≪≫

Mutton stew! Blaire nearly groaned aloud. What awful stuff. Still, it was her fault. Mutton stew was common fare when Aiden was in charge of meals. She wondered if she could last until morning without a bite to eat. Tomorrow, they would go into the village of Strathcarron and see about hiring staff. Perhaps there was an inn where she could break her fast in the morning.

Blaire glanced across the table at their *guest*, and what small appetite she did have quickly evaporated. Kettering's dark eyes seemed to bore into her as though he could peer into her soul, and, for a moment, she wondered if he did, in fact, possess just such a power. Was that why he'd been trapped at Briarcraig? Could he see into others' souls? What would one do with a power like that? Something nefarious, no doubt.

She watched as Kettering took a cursory glance at his own bowl before returning his attention to her. The watch she'd taken from his clothes rested heavy in her pocket. She had no intention of stealing the thing, not really. She'd just thought it might give her some clue about his purpose. A little ceremony with the piece under the light of the moon could possibly tell her something of the man before her. Blast him for realizing it was missing so soon.

"So," Aiden began from his spot at the head of the table, "we are all curious, my lord, ta learn how ye arrived at Briarcraig."

A heart-stopping, charming smile appeared on the baron's face. "I don't know precisely how I ended up in your cellar, Captain, but I can give you an educated guess. What, may I ask, is the date?"

Aiden frowned. "January 19th."

Something flashed in Kettering's eyes, but it was gone as soon as it appeared. "I suspected as much." He shook his head. "Are you familiar with Lord Totley?"

Lord Totley? Hardly. Blaire had never heard the name. However, the Lindsays were far from the sort who rubbed elbows with peers.

Aiden shook his head. "I doona believe so."

Kettering sighed. "Well, apparently, I should have become more familiar with the man before I agreed to visit his country home in Roxburghshire. He's a friend of the Regent's and always has a fine hand at cards, but…"

"But, what?" Aiden asked, sliding to the edge of his seat.

Kettering looked back and forth between Blaire and Brannock and cringed. "Some vices are better left unspoken, Captain. Suffice it to say, a number of the guests were a bit more *unsavory* than one might hope to spend time with."

"The five *women*?" Blaire prodded, not believing one word of his Banbury tale. "Ye mentioned them initially."

Kettering glanced briefly at her and then turned his attention back to Aiden. "I believe one or more of them put something in my port one evening. "Those *women* are my last memory before waking up here."

Blaire didn't even try to suppress her snort. "And why would they bring ye here? Had ye done somethin' ta deserve imprisonment?"

The baron's eyes flashed back to her with a look so smoldering that she gasped for breath. "I have my whole life, Miss Lindsay, been a gentleman. No one has ever before thought I deserved to be drugged and stashed away in some castle. I'm not at all sure where I even am, to be honest."

"The Highlands," Brannock piped up.

"So five *women* drugged ye in Roxburghshire and drove ye inta the Highlands in the dead of winter ta dispose of ye in my brother's castle?" Blaire shook her head. What nonsense. "Do ye truly expect me ta believe that?"

Kettering smiled. "Oh, I intend to find the women in question and determine just why they would assault me in such a way. You can be assured, Miss Lindsay, that I will find the truth."

And that sentence was the first sincere thing he'd said, in Blaire's estimation. A chill raced down her spine, though she wasn't at all sure why.

"Tell me, did one of these *women* happen ta look like me?" Blaire crossed her arms beneath her breasts with impatience. Five witches. She only knew of one coven with that number.

"In fact, Miss Lindsay, one of them bore a striking resemblance to you." His eyes narrowed at her. Blaire's heart began to beat double time at the admission. It really was her mother he sought. How was that possible? Alpina Lindsay had been dead ten years. Certainly he hadn't been locked in that cellar for a decade. Yet his clothes were from another time, longer than ten years if she had to guess.

"Would you happen to know where I can find her, this witch who resembles you?" Kettering's voice broke into her thoughts.

Brannock sat forward and opened his mouth. Blaire

snapped her fingers, and her brother sat back with a huff. She couldn't allow the lad to tell Kettering that the witch he sought didn't exist anymore or she'd never discover the true reason why he was locked in the cellar. And until she knew that reason, she couldn't let him leave. He was too much of a threat.

"I'm no' aware of any witches who look like me. I was simply curious. But I will do what I can ta help ye find what ye're seekin'."

"I would be thankful for your assistance," he said as he bowed his head in her direction.

"Is your dinner no' appealin' ta ye?" Ever since he'd sat at the table, he'd simply dipped his spoon into his stew over and over, though he'd yet to take a single bite of the stew. Shouldn't he be starving? Even Aiden's cooking had to be better than nothing.

"I find myself a bit distracted, I admit," he said quietly, and then he immediately turned to Aiden to speak, still without taking a bite. The man had been locked in the cellar for God only knew how long, and he wasn't in search of a meal? That wasn't normal. It wasn't natural. Had the man truly gone ten years or longer without sustenance? She shook her head at the foolish notion. No one could survive that long. She was missing something important. Was there some sort of food source in the cellar? She'd have to take another look at the room.

Safely tucked beneath her dress, the ring around Blaire's neck seemed warm against her skin. Just as she was about to reach for the relic, a clatter arose at the front door. The ornate brass knocker Blaire had seen earlier banged heavily against the oak. "Who the devil could that be?" Aiden mumbled to himself as he wiped his mouth, dropped his napkin in his plate, and rose to his feet.

"I'll get it!" Brannock bolted from his seat and down the corridor.

A smile crossed Lord Kettering's face. It was unlike any she'd seen grace his lips since she'd found him. It held no malice, no temper, no condescension, and no lack of trust. It was simply pleasure. "That will be for me," he explained to Blaire as he came to his feet as well. She followed him down the corridor toward the great hall, with Aiden quick on her heels.

"Someone kent ye were here?" she called to his retreating back. Why hadn't that someone helped him escape the room before now? Kettering was indeed an infuriating mystery.

"Some bonds are difficult to break," he murmured, more to himself than to her. "Thank heavens."

Blaire touched a finger to her hidden ring and toyed with it absently as she trailed behind the baron.

When she reached the great hall, she stopped dead in her tracks. But Kettering didn't. He nearly flew into the man who stood in the entryway beside her brother. The two men clasped hands tightly, and it almost looked as though they both took a long, deep breath together.

"He said he was lookin' for Lord Kettering," Brannock announced proudly.

"And do ye ken just who ye've admitted inta our home?" Blaire eyed her young brother with a raised brow.

"Pardon me, Captain Lindsay," Kettering said after

he coughed lightly into his hand and cleared his throat. Was the man emotional? A better question would be what was the bond between these men? She'd find that out, too. "This is my oldest and dearest friend, Matthew Halkett, the Earl of Blodswell."

Aiden extended his hand. "It's nice ta meet ye," he said warily. Aiden had good instincts, even if he wasn't magical. Of course, he sensed that something was amiss.

Blaire made a noise. A very unladylike noise.

"And the lovely lady?" the earl asked, gesturing toward Blaire. His dark gaze slid across her, disturbing in the same way Kettering's was but different. Only she couldn't discern the difference. It was there, but Blaire couldn't name it.

"This is Miss Blaire Lindsay, the captain's sister." The baron stepped closer to her as he spoke and even closer when the earl bowed in her direction. Blodswell raised an eyebrow a fraction. Only a fraction. But she noticed it.

Then Kettering introduced Brannock, who preened under the attention.

"I never thought I'd find you," Blodswell muttered under his breath to Kettering, but Blaire heard the admission anyway.

"I feared you wouldn't, either, old friend, but I am happy to see you." The camaraderie between the two was real. That much was obvious.

"If it's quite all right with your friends, perhaps we could stroll the grounds for a time. I do have something to discuss with you, James," the earl said. "Although I do hate to interrupt dinner. Something smells delightful here," he said as he inhaled deeply. His dark gaze danced across Blaire, making her shiver.

Kettering stepped closer to her, and his brow furrowed. Strange. Very strange.

"Aiden's mutton stew is nothing ta boast about." Brannock inhaled deeply and then groaned. "It doesna even smell appetizin', sir. But we're gettin' servants tomorrow."

"Ye are welcome ta stay," Aiden said hesitantly. "For dinner."

Blaire punched his arm. "Invite them both ta stay the night," she hissed at him. "Now."

"Why the devil would I—" he began to say, until she stomped on his instep. Hard. "Bloody hell, Blaire. What is wrong with ye?"

The earl stepped to the door and opened it. Kettering scurried out of the sunlight with a wince, moving into the shadows as he'd done earlier. "On second thought," the earl said, shutting the door, "perhaps we could beg some privacy in one of the Lindsays' parlors instead. Just for a short time so we can become reacquainted."

"Aiden!" Blaire hissed again. If Aiden didn't ask soon, she'd overstep the bounds of propriety and invite them herself. Damn it all to hell. She couldn't allow them to leave Briarcraig. Not until she knew why Kettering had been trapped and locked up. She glanced at the handsome earl beside her brother. He was just as dangerous as the baron, if she wasn't mistaken.

"Ask them!" She glared at her brother. Aiden pursed his lips together. Stubborn man. Fine, she'd take matters into her own hands. "We'd love ta have ye both as our guests here at Briarcraig," Blaire blurted. "I'll go and prepare another room for the earl."

Blodswell bowed swiftly. "I'd be honored to be your guest, Miss Lindsay."

He cut a fine figure and was honestly a gentleman. What else he was, she had no idea. But she planned to find out.

Nine

"WHERE IS YOUR RING?" WAS THE FIRST THING OUT OF Blodswell's mouth when they finally found themselves alone. They'd talked about inanities the entire time the witch lurked in the corridor eavesdropping. They'd both known she was there. Finally, her brother had retrieved her with a stern word. Her cursing in response made Matthew smile.

James held up his hand and rubbed his ring finger. "I have no idea. It wasn't there when I woke up."

"It's nearby. That much is obvious."

"Is it?" James swung around quickly to face him. "How do you know that?"

"It connects us. If it's lost to you, we lose the connection. I lost you for twenty years, old friend. I thought you were dead."

"I may as well have been. I slept for two decades, Matt, thanks to your blasted coven."

"*My* coven?" Blodswell placed a hand over his heart and opened his mouth in mock-astonishment. "When did the *Còig* become *my* coven? The last I heard, they were an entity unto themselves."

"They're a force to be reckoned with," James grunted. "They attacked me."

"Why would they do such a thing? It's not like them to take action lightly." His eyes narrowed. "What did you do? Did you attempt to entrance one of them?"

"Of course not," James scoffed. "I was standing outside an inn, minding my own business and enjoying a perfectly lovely cheroot."

"Stalking prey, in other words," Matthew said with a nod. "Since you have no need to inhale."

No, James had no need to inhale, and Matthew had taught him the little trick with smoking. It made them appear more human if they adopted some of man's more basic habits. "I may not need to inhale it, but I can still taste it," James muttered.

Matthew gestured at him impatiently. "That's neither here nor there. I'd like to hear your tale, James."

And James was ready to tell it to someone he trusted. "The night had just fallen."

"And you were thirsty?"

"Yes, I suppose I was. A lovely young woman, one who resembles Miss Lindsay quite closely, by the way, approached me. The night was incredibly foggy, so foggy I could barely see my hand in front of my face, but I could see her. Very clearly. Actually, there were two of them."

"A moment," Matthew said quickly. "You say one of them looked like Miss Lindsay? The captain's sister?" He gestured toward the corridor.

"An amazing resemblance," James confirmed. "The silver eyes. The raven hair."

Matthew frowned. "Go on."

"Well," James snapped his fingers, "just like that the fog lifted, and there were five of them. Then the next thing I remember, I woke up locked in a dank cellar of this castle, which I believe to be somewhere in the Scottish Highlands."

"In the middle of nowhere," Matthew confirmed. His dark gaze raked across James. "You haven't been outside yet?"

James held up his hand and once again pointed out the absence of his ring. "I've never been suicidal."

"No, you have not." A small smile curved Matthew's lips. "Tell me, have you fed? You're looking quite pale."

"Not yet." James tugged at his waistcoat.

"But the lovely Miss Lindsay," Matthew began.

"Is an innocent," James snarled. Even he was surprised by the amount of bite that was present behind his growl. What should he care where his next meal came from? And the woman had been nothing but a thorn in his side since she'd freed him. Yet she *had* freed him, and she did have the loveliest silver eyes.

"It's like that, is it?" A corner of Matthew's mouth lifted as he turned and adjusted a crooked painting on the wall.

"Go to the devil, Matt," James replied, but he wasn't able to keep the smile from his face any better than Matthew had. Blodswell could read him. Hell, he could *feel* him.

"The *Còig* is a benevolent lot, James. They do not act lightly, and they do not tempt the fates. Everything they do is done with purpose. I can't think of any reason why they would imprison you and steal your ring. There is something we don't know."

Though what it was, James had no idea. He clucked his tongue as he rolled the thought over in his mind.

"Does Miss Lindsay have powers?" Matthew suddenly asked. "Have you seen any evidence that she's magical?"

She didn't make an effort to hide the fact. "Fireballs in her own hand. She hides daggers about her person. And wields them with stealth and purpose."

"How the devil do you know that?"

"Because she nearly unmanned me with one when I had the nerve to kiss her."

"And therein lies the crux of the matter." Matthew whistled softly.

"She's a means to an end. Nothing more. I need her so I can find the other witches." He needed to find out why they'd stolen twenty years of his life.

Matthew folded his arms across his chest. "I'm sorry to disappoint, but if Miss Lindsay has verifiable powers, and you say she does?" He waited for a nod from James. "Then the witches you seek cannot be found."

Matthew's statement didn't make one bit of sense. He couldn't possibly know that. "I beg your pardon."

"There's only one *Còig*."

"Thank God," James muttered. They were a menace. He couldn't imagine more than one malicious coven running loose.

"The powers pass from the mother to the eldest daughter, though not fully until the mother's death."

James groaned aloud. "You're saying the witches who imprisoned me are...*dead*?"

"More than likely, all of them," Matthew confirmed. "Unless I am mistaken, I have already met their current seer, a Miss Macleod. Breathtaking lass, like her mother. Her powers were amazingly strong. They'd have to be considering the company she keeps."

None of this made any sense to James, but he listened and nodded his head for his maker to continue.

"It's only that way when the coven is complete," Matthew explained. "Not a mix of one generation with the next, but with the women who are supposed to be linked together. In fact, when the first witch goes, the others are often not far behind."

What horrible news. James scrubbed a hand down his face. "I'll never know why they did it then."

Matthew shrugged. "Not necessarily. Miss Lindsay can fill in the missing details. One generation of witches trains the next."

"But the lass acts as though she doesn't know a thing." Was it an act? She didn't seem the sort. Subterfuge didn't seem to be in her nature; she was much more direct than that.

"Looks can be deceiving, my friend. I'm certain you didn't expect her beautiful mother to be all that she was when you encountered her, either."

"Obviously," James snorted.

"We need to get you fed, or you'll soon wilt like a flower in a glass."

"My options are a bit limited just now." He once again held up his hand and wiggled his fingers at his friend. "So, we'll hunt tonight? When darkness falls?"

"I saw some sheep in the valley."

James made a face. Mutton was bad enough in stew.

He still couldn't shake the awful smell of Captain Lindsay's cooking.

"A spotted calf?"

"Would be better than *sheep*."

"Miss Lindsay had an enticing scent," Matthew muttered.

"She is not on the menu."

"Something tells me you could easily add 'not yet' to the end of that statement and have it still be true."

"I'll be done with Miss Lindsay today. Find out what she knows, and then we can leave for England as soon as we've dined." He turned toward the door to exit the room, but Matthew sighed and grabbed his friend's shoulder.

"I see two problems with your plan, James." That sigh did not bode well for James' ambitions.

"Which are?" Matthew was almost as bad as the witches with his riddles and open-ended statements.

"Your ring is nearby. Without it, you're doomed to a life of darkness. It must be found."

"You haven't any others, have you?" James hoped aloud.

"You know I haven't. I was given three. Thrice blessed and all that."

"One of which you wasted on Sarah." If only he could get his hands on it. But to do so, he'd have to cross her path, and life in darkness was preferable.

"It wasn't wasted, not at the time anyway. And everything was perfectly fine for decades upon decades until *you* finally broke her heart."

James scoffed. "One must have a heart for it to break."

Matthew heaved an unnecessary sigh. "Not this again."

James didn't relish the argument, either. Matthew insisted they still possessed hearts, but James disagreed. The subject had been discussed to death, and neither of them would ever change his mind. "No, not now. I don't have it in me."

Matthew nodded, a look of relief on his face. "But speaking of Sarah, she's your second problem."

She always had been a problem. But that wasn't what Matthew meant, James was certain. "Beg your pardon?"

"If I can sense you, James, so can she."

"She'll come here and wreak havoc upon anyone in the vicinity." James smacked himself with the heel of his hand on his forehead out of frustration. Would he never be free of the vindictive wench?

"Hell hath no fury and all that," Matthew answered his unasked question. "And there's another problem."

"I thought you said there were *two* problems?" James didn't know how much more he could take. Sarah, for God's sake. "One more makes three."

Matthew tugged a piece of lint from his jacket. "Well, actually the last two are connected. Perhaps you've forgotten that Sarah had thrown her lot in with Padrig Trevelyan before your little nap?"

James honestly tried not to think of either of them. Ever.

"They are still in one another's pockets. They'll be traveling together."

James winced. Perhaps it would be best to go back to sleep for another decade or two. "Too late to stop them, I suppose."

"Most assuredly. I've not seen her in years, but I can still feel her well enough. She comes in this direction."

And was bringing with her the most vengeful vampyre of James' acquaintance. He shook his head. If anyone should have been imprisoned, Padrig Trevelyan was the one the five blasted witches should have captured and hidden away for safe keeping. He was a creature who killed not for sustenance or survival but to ruin as many lives as he could touch. He cursed himself anew for having created the monster.

"But since she and Trevelyan are together, she can only travel at night. So we do have a bit of time to find your ring and be gone."

"I don't suppose either of them have decided they hate me less since I vanished?" Wishful thinking, he knew, but he couldn't help but ask.

Matthew shook his head. "Sorry, old friend. More annoyed that someone else had dared to end your existence before they got the chance."

Perfect. His two-decade nap had done nothing to solve his problems. He was exactly where he started when that damned coven had encountered him, except now he didn't have his ring.

Blaire paced her chamber back and forth, listening for any sounds from their guests' quarters. But there'd been none for the last hour. The two gentlemen had actually *gone out*. Who went out at night during the winter in the bloody Highlands? The wind alone was enough to freeze a man. Nothing the two of them did made a bit of sense. She blew the hair out of her eyes in frustration. What she wouldn't give to have her coven sisters with her! Together they could sort out this mystery.

But they weren't there, and they wouldn't be coming to help her. Elspeth was in Hampshire, and Cait was either with her or on her way back to Edinburgh. At the most, she could beg Rhiannon and Sorcha to attend her, but unless the five of them were together, it wouldn't do any good. She had no one's power to depend on but her own.

She was all alone in this, and she'd never felt so powerless. Why would her mother and the others capture Kettering? There had to be a reason. Since the previous *Còig* had apparently done something of this magnitude, why didn't she know of it? Why hadn't her mother passed on the knowledge and information like she had everything else?

Well, she didn't know for a fact that her mother had passed everything on, did she? Blaire hadn't even known Briarcraig existed a fortnight ago. Yet it was the ancestral seat of the battle-born witches. Her birthright. What else had her mother kept secret, and why? How was she to know what to do if she didn't know what she was up against?

Blaire sat down on the edge of her bed and tugged Kettering's gold watch from her pocket. It was a beautiful piece with an ornate griffin engraved on the case. She ran her fingers over the regal beast, the symbol of the valiant soldier. After a moment, she clicked open the spring-hinged cover and stared at the dial adorned in rubies, so red they looked like blood against the white face.

She'd stolen the man's watch. What the devil was she thinking? She couldn't perform a discovery ceremony alone. She'd need the others to be successful. Still, nothing ventured, nothing gained.

Blaire dropped the watch onto her bed and then moved across the room to open her trunk. She tossed a few old chemises and a tattered Lindsay plaid out of the way, and then retrieved a small, black cauldron. On her hands and knees, she scrounged around the bottom looking for the necessary ingredients and began to collect little glass bottles.

Alfalfa. No. She tossed it aside.

Rum. She shook her head, searching for another bottle.

Bayberry leaves. She growled, never having been the most patient member of the coven.

Pomegranate seeds. Perfect. One down, two to go.

After emptying the contents of the trunk, she finally had everything she needed. She poured a spot of water from her pitcher into the cauldron and then added the pomegranate seeds and a healthy amount of dried witch grass and pepper. Blaire lit a beeswax candle and trickled the wax over the rim of the cauldron.

She dusted her hands on her dress and doubted Elspeth could have done it better. So far, so good. She hung the cauldron on a handle above the fire in her hearth and planted herself beside it.

"*Lorg freagair timcheall* Kettering." She chanted as she dipped the baron's gold chain into the cauldron, letting it bond with the concoction. "*Lorg freagair timcheall* Kettering. *Lorg freagair timcheall* Kettering." With her free hand, she dropped a moonstone into the mixture, which bubbled. Her heart soared. She just might get her answers yet.

As a flash of light lit up the room, Blaire tossed

the pocket watch to her bed, wrapped a rag around her hand, and retrieved the cauldron from the fire. She placed it on the hearth and peered inside. But no vision appeared, and no answers leapt to her mind. All she was left with was a mixture that looked disgustingly like a vat of blood.

Damn it to hell. She crossed the room, raised the window, suppressed a shiver from the frigid air, tossed the contents of the cauldron to the ground below, and cursed herself for being a fool. She'd known the ceremony wouldn't work when she was alone, but what other choice did she have? It wasn't as though Kettering was going to tell her all his secrets.

Just then she heard the two Englishmen's voices filter down the corridor as the pair apparently made their way toward their borrowed quarters. Then their footsteps slowed outside her door. "Do you smell that?" Kettering asked. Had she not had her ear pressed to the door, she'd have missed his comments completely.

"Blood? In Miss Lindsay's room?" the earl replied with a question of his own.

"They're not here yet. You'd feel them, wouldn't you?" Another quick murmur from Blodswell that she couldn't make out. "Then what *is* that smell?" Kettering asked.

Certainly, they couldn't smell her concoction. It was simply by chance that the earl thought there was blood in her room. *Who* could smell blood? What did blood smell like, anyway? She'd hunted for years and often found herself dressing the animals. Yet she couldn't remember any *strong* odor that came with the letting of blood. It was highly unlikely that Kettering could pinpoint an odor like that either, especially through her closed door.

Before she could take a step, her door burst wide open. She was forced to dodge it to avoid being knocked over in Kettering's haste to enter her chambers. She landed on her bottom with a grunt.

"What the devil…?" Blaire complained as she came to her feet. She shook her nightrail and wrapper so that her legs were covered and dusted her hands together.

Kettering stopped inches from her and tipped her chin up until she met his eyes. Like a ninnyhammer, she froze. The powers-that-be should take away her supernatural abilities, the ones she received simply by being battle born, because she was completely and totally unworthy. That much was quite obvious. She bit back a curse.

"Are you all right?" Kettering asked, his voice rumbling across her like a caress.

Blaire shook her chin loose from his hold. "Of course, I am. Why would I no' be?" She noticed the earl as he raised one hand and quietly squeezed Kettering's shoulder. The baron relaxed, but not by much.

"I'll be along in a moment," Kettering said quietly to his friend, still not removing his gaze from her person. Had she not known better, she would have again thought he could look directly into her soul. The man's dark eyes were the most intense she'd ever seen, and Blaire fought back a shiver.

She vaguely noted when Blodswell stepped out of

the room, bowed a quick farewell from the doorway, and vanished down the corridor. Her attention was centered on the man who still stood much too close for comfort.

Ten

JAMES LOOKED DOWN INTO THE MOST LIQUID EYES HE'D ever seen and tried to force himself to concentrate. How unfortunate that he failed so miserably.

"Is there a reason why ye're in my room, sir?" the mesmerizing witch asked, with a tilt of her head. But she nearly vibrated there standing in front of him, so she wasn't as calm as she appeared. To a casual observer, she would have succeeded in her desire to portray ambivalence. But Miss Lindsay was very much aware and at the ready.

"I thought there might be a problem," he said as he stepped back and allowed his gaze to slide down her body. "You're not injured?"

She held out both hands. "No' that I'm aware of," she snipped at him.

He took her hand in his and turned it over in his palm, searching for wounds. He'd smelled blood. He was sure of it. He never mistook the coppery scent of the life-giving essence. Yet she appeared to be unharmed. She jerked her hand from his grasp. He reached for the other one, but she put it behind her back and took one step away from him.

"Are you hiding something from me, Miss Lindsay?" he asked. "If you're injured, I may be able to help. It appears as though your brothers are asleep."

"I am no' afraid ta wake my brothers if I need assistance." She tossed her hair over her shoulder, where it hung like a dark curtain down her back. James wanted nothing more than to bury his face in it and inhale her essence. He shook away the errant thoughts. One would think a meal like he'd just enjoyed would have quelled this insatiable thirst for the girl. One would, apparently, be wrong.

"Why are you still awake?" he asked quietly.

"I could ask ye the same question," she said without hesitation.

He couldn't fight the smile that her comment provoked, but he crooked a finger and tugged at his nose, hoping she wouldn't notice the corners of his lips tip up. He appreciated her gumption. But there was no need for her to know that. "I was out with Blodswell," he explained, watching her face as he spoke. He lowered his voice, softened his expression, and set out to entrance the witch. But she was having no part of it. She spun to face the other direction, the edges of her nightrail spinning around her legs. He nearly groaned aloud. "We went for a walk."

She spun back to face him quickly. Every movement showed a good bit of her ankles. When did ankles become so erotic? "Where did ye go?" she asked, her eyebrows drawing together.

"Just out by the loch. Does it matter?" he asked her, just as plainly. If he couldn't entrance her, perhaps his forthrightness could put her off the scent of the chase.

"Just curious," she replied as she flopped into a chair and tucked her legs beneath her. Well, almost. The big toe of her right foot stuck out from beneath her hem. James had an instant and absurd desire to kiss it. Yes, it was official. He'd lost his bloody mind. He scrubbed a hand across his forehead and tried to wipe the errant thoughts away. If Blodswell knew, James would never hear the end of it.

"Did ye at least have a nice time?" she asked quietly, resting her chin on the heel of her overturned hand. She looked absolutely adorable.

"I haven't seen Blodswell in quite some time. So, yes, it was very nice to become reacquainted. Thank you for allowing him to stay for the night."

She waved a hand breezily in the air. "A day, a fortnight… Stay as long as ye like. Both of ye." She paused briefly and then smiled at him. "Please," she offered last.

"You are a conundrum, Miss Lindsay," he murmured to himself.

Her eyebrows lifted as she grinned. "I doona believe women are supposed ta be easy creatures ta figure out. I'm simply upholdin' my end of nature's bargain."

He chuckled. The witch could make him laugh, something he needed just now with his mind focused on his problems. There was something about the woman before him. Something magical, and not the fact that she was a witch. He stared at her for the longest while, just soaking in her stunning silver eyes and delectable figure. When she cleared her throat, he shook his head, regaining his composure. "I'll bid you good night," he said then.

"Is that a question? Or a statement of fact?" the witch asked as she came to her feet.

She was a cheeky little thing. "You're certain you're well?" James asked again. He knew he'd smelled blood. It was unmistakable. And he didn't *want* to go. He wanted to take her place in that chair and pull her down into his lap.

She lifted her arms out to the sides and sighed heavily. "Do ye need ta search my person for wounds so ye can get a good night's rest?"

James immediately hardened at the very thought of running his hands all over Miss Lindsay's body. "I trust that you would tell me if you needed assistance," he said instead.

"Do ye, now?" she asked quietly.

"No, actually I don't," he scoffed. "But it sounded good in my head before it came out of my mouth." He turned away from her to hide the evidence of his desire. Despite her bravado, he'd scare the life out of the little innocent if she had any idea how much he wanted her. When he turned to face her, his gaze immediately landed on the bed—and on his gold pocket fob, which lay atop her counterpane. "That's my watch," he said as he approached the bed and reached for it.

"Aye, I found it doin' the wash," she said quickly.

"Shouldn't you have someone else do the wash for you?" He wasn't quite sure where that came from. She was a brazen little thing, one who clearly made her own decisions; but there was still a prideful air about her. She might not be a typical lady, but she was a lady just the same. One who shouldn't be reduced to menial household chores. "I have it on the highest authority that the Lindsays are quite rich, after all."

His statement had the satisfying effect of making her stammer. "A–aye, well we're hirin' a staff tomorrow. But for now ye're left with me."

"I like being left with you." He'd like his watch back, too. He turned back toward her bed and scooped the fob up in his hands. The chain was coated in *something*, and he nearly dropped his own heirloom. "What the devil's on it?" he growled.

James spun to face her, ready to throttle her if she'd ruined his watch. He'd had it for ages. And ages. More than one lifetime, to be sure.

Miss Lindsay plucked it from his hand and began to wipe it with a soft cloth, rubbing until it shone brighter than any sun he could remember. "I was just cleanin' it up for ye. Ye caught me right in the middle of it." She dried the chain and then passed it to him.

He turned away from her and flipped the catch, opening the watch so he could be certain it was in the same shape as when she'd stolen it. And he knew she'd taken it. Why, he had no idea.

A lock of her hair fell over his forearm as she leaned over his arm, peering at the open watch face. James nearly groaned aloud. Instead, he simply raised his brows at her and tried to appear amused. Aroused was more like it. Highly aroused. "Is there something you wanted to see, Miss Lindsay?"

She had the nerve to blush. Color seeped into her cheeks. Could she be any more charming? "I was just admirin' yer watch," she murmured. "I dinna realize there was an inscription. What does it say?" One of her hands lay flat on his back where she steadied herself to lean around him. He'd feel that touch for days. Years, probably.

"Curiosity killed the cat, you know," he teased, attempting to sound unconcerned.

Her eyes narrowed at him. "Yer watch has a quote from Shakespeare?"

She was as intelligent as she was beautiful. He turned and tweaked her nose, which provoked a scowl from her. "Shakespeare performed it. Ben Jonson wrote it." Thirty years after James was born. What might she think if she knew his age?

"So, that's what's written in yer watch? 'Curiosity killed the cat'?" He had to give her credit for being tenacious.

"No, it's not," he said crisply as he closed the watch and slipped it back into the pocket of his waistcoat. The heavy weight of it felt right. She muttered something that sounded very much like *insufferable man*. He chuckled as he crossed his arms and leaned against her bedpost. "I suppose I should leave. The dawn will arrive before we know it. Have you slept at all, Miss Lindsay?"

"Aye, yer stompin' boots woke me when ye returned home."

"Fibber," he accused.

Her back straightened. "I havena gotten accustomed ta the new accommodations," she said as she gestured to her room.

"I'm certain your new staff will make sure all is to your liking tomorrow."

She snorted and shook her head, her black hair swaying across her back in one glorious mass. "If we're able ta find someone ta take us on."

Oh, they'd find someone, he had no doubt. She did nothing by half, and if she intended to staff Briarcraig, she'd have it done by the noon meal. "I like you, Miss Lindsay," he blurted out. Then he bit back an oath. Where the devil had that come from? He could almost hear Blodswell cackling in his head.

She crossed her arms beneath her breasts. "Do ye, now?"

One step brought him toe to toe with her. "I do." He said it loudly and clearly. And knew it was the truth. He lifted one hand to cup the side of her face. "How many daggers do you wear beneath that nightrail?"

Her voice trembled a bit when she replied, "Why are ye so concerned with what's under my nightrail, Lord Kettering? One might think ye'd like ta inspect my person."

"Oh, I'd like that very much, and you should call me James. May I call you Blaire?"

"That would be highly improper," she reminded him, but she didn't shove him away or attack him with darts or lances. Not even a sharpened hatpin.

"And propriety is something you worry about? Is that before or after you curse like a man?" Her gaze left his, and he immediately wanted to take back his words. She was positively enchanting. He liked her cursing. Wanted to hear more of it, in fact. He would particularly enjoy it interspersed with a gasp or two of pleasure. "How do you do it?" he finally asked.

"Do what?" She folded her arms across her chest,

obviously annoyed with him. Good. It was safer for
her that way.

"Manage to look so beautiful on the outside, and
maintain so much strength and purpose on the inside."

Before she could answer, he bent to quickly touch
his lips to hers. She froze, her lips pressed tightly
against his. He opened his eyes briefly, only to find
her staring at him, her lips puckered against his. He
chuckled against her mouth and drew her to him with
his arms around her waist. She stepped toward him
with no reservation at all and let him draw her close
enough that her breasts pressed against his chest, close
enough that his legs tangled in her nightrail.

"Lord Kettering," she protested mildly when his
hand slid down her back and cupped her bottom,
almost as though it had its own free will. But she
didn't pull away. She should have pulled away.

"James," he whispered as he briefly lifted his mouth
from hers. This time, when he bent his head, he
coaxed her lips apart with gentle nudges, and then he
swept inside. She teetered on her feet, but he used
her wobbliness as an excuse to pull her closer to him.
He would draw her into him if he could. What he
wouldn't give for her to draw him into her.

The beating of her heart began to skip like she'd
run a great distance, the soft breaths that escaped her
nose tickling his cheek as she tilted her head to kiss
him more deeply. The witch wasn't afraid of him, that
much was obvious. Perhaps she should be.

Their brief interlude was long enough to show
his desire for her. But short enough that it wouldn't
scare her. It wasn't nearly enough to quench his thirst

for her, but it would do for now. He pulled back, looked down into the interminable depths of her eyes, and forced himself to release the little innocent. She wobbled slightly on her feet when he let her go, and one of her hands landed on her chest. "Dear me," she whispered.

"Good night, Miss Lindsay," he said as he turned and quit the room.

He strode quickly and quietly to his bedchamber and wasn't a bit surprised to find Blodswell sitting back in a chair by his four-poster and wearing a huge grin.

"Oh, I believe you're in trouble now," the man gloated. He nearly glowed with glee. What was bad was that the damned blackguard was one hundred percent correct.

"Go to the devil," James grumbled.

"You'd hardly be the first to wish me there. The poor devil will be waiting forever." Matthew chuckled. "Now, why don't you tell me all about Miss Lindsay?"

James scrubbed a hand across his face. "I already told you all I know about the lass." Though he'd neglected to tell Matthew how she affected *him*. That was not particularly any of his friend's business.

"Come now," Matthew prodded, "I've known you all your life. Don't think you can hold out on me. I know you too well."

Too well, indeed. Matthew owned the estate neighboring his in Derbyshire. He'd been a friend of James' father centuries ago. He'd even taught James how to sword fight when he was a boy, though at the time James had had no idea that the earl was so proficient with the weapon due to having actually been a knight in the Crusades. But most importantly, Matthew had been there when James most needed him, the night he'd been attacked by highwaymen and left for dead. And he would have died, had Matthew not come to his aid, had he not eased the way for James' life-after-death.

He heaved a sigh. "I don't know what to tell you. Something about her calls to me. That's all."

Matthew's grin faded, only to be replaced by a grim expression. "Calls to you?"

"I just want to be near her." He couldn't explain better than that. He felt like a green lad. He scrubbed his hand against his forehead.

His friend nodded knowingly. "Developing an attachment for humans does happen on occasion."

"Has it happened to you?" James asked, though he knew the answer. Matthew cared for all creatures and was the most loyal of men, but he'd never formed an *attachment* with anyone. Not in over six hundred years.

"There's always the future." Of which they both had an endless supply. Matthew rose from his seat and started for the door. "May I offer a suggestion?"

"Of course."

"An attachment for one of the witches isn't wise. Enchant her, and be done with it."

James winced.

"What's the meaning of that look?"

He might as well tell him that unfortunate bit. Matthew wouldn't let up until he knew the truth, all of it. "I tried."

"I beg your pardon?" His friend stepped closer to him.

"You said to enchant her. I tried. This very evening. It didn't work."

"Well, now *that* I've never heard of." Matthew's brow furrowed with deep concern. "I wonder…"

The way his friend said those two words sent an icy chill down James' spine. "You wonder what?"

Matthew shook his head. "I wonder what sorts of spells the *Còig* might have cast upon you in your dormant state."

"Preventing me from being able to enchant, you mean?" Had James needed to breathe, all the air would have rushed from his lungs. The witches had said something about victims, hadn't they? Were they trying to level the playing field? What else might they have done while he slept?

Then again, if a spell cast could disarm him… "Perhaps Miss Lindsay could be persuaded to restore my abilities."

Matthew shook his head only slightly. "She's not their healer. But even if she were, you're not ill. Your inability to enchant others is the result of magic, not a natural occurrence."

Which again led him back to Blaire Lindsay. "Then magic can reverse the spell."

His friend smiled weakly as though he was a simpleton. "If the *five* of them did this to you, it'll take all five to undo it. Miss Lindsay alone is not enough."

The entire coven. The daughters of the five women who'd wronged him. He felt a bit hollow at the prospect. "Then we'll have her take us to them. I can't go around 'til the end of time unable to enchant humans. I'll starve." Or take up an unseemly diet of spotted calf and sheep. He still couldn't get rid of the awful taste in his mouth. Sustenance was sustenance after all, but he couldn't imagine living on such things forever.

Matthew nodded. "But we'll need your ring first. It's here somewhere. We have to find it."

Eleven

MORNING SUN FILTERED IN THROUGH BLAIRE'S BEVELED windows. She opened one eye to stare accusingly at the light as though it alone was responsible for her lack of sleep. But alas, she had no one to blame but herself. And him. She mustn't forget him.

James. He'd asked her to call him James. She shook her head at her own foolishness. James indeed!

Lord Kettering had actually kissed her! How was she expected to sleep after that kiss? Brief as it was, she'd felt it all the way to her toes, like a burst of warmth that washed over her entire body, leaving her breathless in its wake. And then he'd disappeared before she could regain her composure and properly thrash him for it.

Blaire groaned again. Why had she allowed such liberties? Though she didn't think she could have stopped him. Then there was the niggling little feeling deep inside that whispered she hadn't wanted to stop him. Even worse, she'd relived it in her mind all night. His strong, sculpted lips pressed ever so gently to hers.

She turned on her side and crashed her fist into a stray pillow. What a complete dolt she'd turned out to be. "Dolt" was the correct word on so many levels. Not only had she allowed liberties to a man she barely knew, but what she did know about him wasn't at all reassuring. He was dangerous. He was some sort of villain, or he'd never have been imprisoned here. Her mother had helped trap the man, for heaven's sake. And she'd let him kiss her. No doubt about it, she was a dolt.

The intelligent thing would be to stay as far away from the man as possible, since she didn't seem to have any self-control where he was concerned. But that was impossible. If she stayed far from him, she couldn't learn why he'd been locked away here. And she couldn't let him go gallivanting off about the Highlands until she knew exactly who or *what* she was dealing with. What a conundrum.

That was it then. She simply *had* to gain control of herself. There was no other way to get the answers she needed. The blood of generations of battle-born witches who'd come before her coursed through her veins. They had been strong. She could be strong, too. And no matter what, she couldn't allow him to kiss her again. Ever.

Her mind made up, she rose from bed, tore open her wardrobe, and retrieved the dowdiest dress she owned. Grey wool. Not alluring in the least. Kettering wouldn't want to kiss a woman wearing scratchy grey wool. It would remind him of a washerwoman. The grey dress was perfect.

Blaire quickly dressed and fixed her hair in a simple chignon, which wasn't the least bit complimentary.

That should do well. She looked like an impoverished governess. Splendid.

She was finally ready to start the day with enthusiasm, despite her lack of sleep, but she desperately needed answers to her questions. She threw open her door and then took an immediate step backward and gasped.

Standing before her, waiting for her, it appeared, was Lord Kettering, who was holding Bruce, the feral cat, in his arms. "Good morning," he crooned, his deep voice touching her soul.

Blaire shook the effect off. She was *strong*. At least she was going to be today. "What are ye doin' with that beast?"

"He was hiding out in my wardrobe. I thought he might belong to you."

"No. I meant ta ask what ye're doin' with the beast all cuddled up in yer arms like that. He's wild." Although Bruce didn't look very wild at the moment. In fact, he looked into Kettering's eyes with an adoring gaze.

"Some beings find me to be quite enchanting, in case you didn't know," he said slowly, the corners of his lips turned up in a smile as he leaned his weight against her doorjamb.

"I had no idea," she murmured. Oh, she knew. She knew the man was mesmerizing. Poor Bruce seemed almost as besotted as she was herself. "Some creatures are no' so bright." She rested her index finger on her chin and pretended to think it over. "Are they blind? Deaf?" she tossed in for good measure.

The man had the good grace to chuckle.

"Are ye plannin' ta tell me that ye like me again, Lord Kettering?" If her dowdy garb didn't turn him off, perhaps her flippancy would.

"I thought we were past the 'Lord Kettering' business, Blaire. I asked you to call me James." He stroked across Bruce's head, and the cat leaned in to him. He was missing half of his left ear, but Kettering still crooned to him as though he was the most beautiful of beasts.

"Aye, ye did. I dinna accept." She pushed his shoulder to move him out of her doorway and then closed her door behind her.

"Where are you off to in such a hurry?" Kettering asked from one step behind her. The man moved as fast as she did.

"Breakfast," she muttered.

He hovered like a gnat. Which made her want to swat him. "Then what are your plans?"

She spun quickly to face him. So quickly that he nearly ran into her. He reached out to catch her, dropping Bruce to the ground. The cat sent her a caustic glare. She bumped the feline gently with her foot to shoo him away, and got a hiss and raised claws for her trouble. "Blasted cat," she hissed back.

"Your plans, Blaire?" Kettering asked again.

"I am headed inta the village of Strathcarron ta hire whatever staff can be found. Why are ye so interested in my plans, James?" she asked, then winced aloud as she realized she'd used his first name. It couldn't roll around in her head through the wee hours of the morning and not come out of her mouth at some point, she assumed.

"The sound of my name on your lips is one of the sweetest I've ever heard, darling girl." He reached out to caress the side of her face, but she brushed his hand aside. In truth, she wanted to be just like Bruce and lean into him. And almost caught her eyes closing as she did so. She shook off the thoughts.

"Doona get used ta it," she tossed at him as she shoved his arm away.

"I like your hair like that," he said as he caught her hand in his and squeezed it gently, his eyes searching hers.

Now she was certain. The man *was* daft. Or foxed. She reached up to touch his forehead with the back of her hand, like she might if Brannock was feverish. "Are ye ill, Lord Kettering?" She caught his face between her hands and looked into his black-as-night eyes. They weren't bloodshot. And he looked right as rain. He wasn't foxed. "Or does madness run in yer family?" She put her hands on her hips and glared up at him. Blast him to Hades! Kettering still wore that annoying grin.

"You think I'm daft because I like your hair?" He cupped the side of her neck against his palm, with his thumb moving toward her collarbone. "I like the way it shows your neck." He leaned in and said very quietly by her ear, "So graceful and strong. And your pulse pounds at the base of your throat. I think it's beating like a drum right now. In fact, I can see it." He touched his lips to the side of her throat.

Blaire gulped. "Ye have lost yer bloody mind, Kettering."

He lifted his lips long enough to whisper the word, "James."

Blaire clenched her jaw and fought the flutters in her belly. "Ye're about ta lose yer bloody hand, Kettering, if ye doona remove it from my arse."

❧

How the devil had that happened? One moment, he was trying to enchant the witch. The next, his hand was on her lovely little bottom as he clutched her to him and set about devouring her whole. Yet, he hadn't entranced her at all. At least not in the way he'd attempted.

Oh, James had affected her, but it was on a very primal level. The witch was aroused. He could tell by the way her heart beat at a runaway rhythm. The way her pulse jumped beneath the delicate skin at the base of her neck. But he hadn't entranced her at all.

James froze. His hand that was so gently kneading her ass stopped its movement. Blaire reached behind her and took his wrist within her grasp, pulling his hand away from her derriere. He felt a tremendous sense of loss at that removal. Like that pitiful cat might feel if someone stole a juicy mouse from him.

He was hard against her belly and knew she'd take note of it if he lingered. She was an innocent, for pity's sake. James took a step back, bowed quickly to her, and said, "Miss Lindsay," as he left her standing there in the corridor.

She mumbled something that sounded a lot like *Blasted groping man…should keep his hands to himself before I chop the bloody things off.*

James shook his head, running back through the events that had just taken place as he returned quickly to his bedchamber. He'd made eye contact. Established contact with her hands, a powerful connection when trying to enchant someone. Then he'd caressed her until he was certain he had her attention. Every other time he'd done so, the woman in question would drop at his feet if he'd willed it, ready to bend her neck and ready for…anything else he desired.

But not this time. Not with her. He'd touched his lips to her skin. And that was when *he* was lost. The witch had somehow entranced *him* instead. He cursed beneath his breath as he stalked into his chamber.

"I am almost ashamed to call you my creation," Matthew said quietly from his seat beside the bed.

James stopped and glared at him. "In my quarters again?"

"Well, I *was* in the corridor." Matthew sighed. "But then I stumbled upon you with Miss Lindsay, when you were begging her to call you James."

James folded his arms across his chest. It was bad enough that he'd failed to enchant Blaire, but having Matthew witness the debacle was more than a bit embarrassing.

His friend rose from his seat. "So, I assume it didn't work, or you'd be in a much better mood." He crossed the room and clapped a hand to James' back. "Not to worry. We'll get everything set straight."

"I hope so. I don't feel like myself." Which was an understatement.

A small smirk appeared on Matthew's face. "Did my ears deceive me, or did the lass actually threaten to chop off your appendages?"

James held in a groan. "She's formidable."

Matthew laughed. "You certainly picked an unusual woman with whom to form an attachment. In the future, you might consider a more malleable lady."

But a more malleable lady didn't seem remotely appealing. James loved Blaire's fire and bravado, combined with her innocent blushes and the way she warmed at his touch. But he'd rather not go into all that with his old friend. "Let's just focus on finding my ring, shall we?"

"Whatever you wish," Matthew placated him.

James scowled. "Miss Lindsay is headed into the village to hire staff for the castle. She's already suspicious of me. We should wait until she departs before we start tearing the place apart."

"All right," his maker agreed.

Where did one go about searching for a ring in a castle this size? It must have a million different hiding places, and those were the ones out in the open. A priest hole behind a false chimney or a bookcase would be nearly impossible to find.

❧

"I wish Brannock had come with us," Blaire complained as the carriage jostled her forward. But he'd insisted on chasing after that blasted feline, and they'd had no choice but to leave him to it.

"The lad's fine," Aiden replied dismissively. Then he speared her with a piercing glare. "I doona like those Englishmen stayin' in my castle though. I'm waitin' for ye ta tell me why ye insisted they do so."

If she told Aiden the truth, that their mother had trapped Kettering a decade ago, her brother would think she was out of her mind. No one could survive that long without food or drink. It wasn't possible. But somehow it was, and she needed to find out exactly how Kettering had survived, and, more importantly, why her mother had imprisoned him.

A howling wind rocked the carriage from side to side, which broke Blaire from her reverie, and she pulled her plaid closer around her shoulders. Across from her, Aiden folded his arms across his chest. He clearly wanted his answer, and he wasn't about to be diverted until he got it. Damn his Lindsay persistence.

Blaire pasted on her most accommodating smile, though she wasn't certain she could pull it off. "It's the middle of winter. Ye canna toss them inta the Highland chill."

Aiden snorted. "Blodswell has a fine travelin' carriage. A few bricks for their feet and a lap blanket or two, and they'll be perfectly fine."

And he meant it, too. Blaire couldn't let that happen. "Doona be rash," she protested.

Aiden uncrossed his arms and leaned forward on his bench, peering into her eyes with his soft grey ones. "Tell me the truth, Blaire."

"I want Kettering ta court me," she blurted out, before thinking it through. Then she added in a softer voice, "I think he intends ta." Or at least that was what she would think if a normal *man* had kissed her the way the baron had the night before.

Had a speck of dust landed on Aiden, he'd have collapsed in a pile on the floor of the coach. As it was, his mouth dropped open and his eyes grew wide with surprise. "Beg yer pardon?"

Well, she had to make it work now, didn't she? "I think he'd make a fine match for me."

"Aye." Aiden shook his head. "A fine match indeed. English lords doona marry Scottish lasses with no connections, Blaire."

She sighed and glanced out the window to avoid his ever-knowing eyes. "Well, wealthy Scottish lairds doona marry daughters of shepherds either, but the Fyfe sisters have clearly set their caps for ye."

"I'm no' really wealthy," he began and then stammered, "well, I suppose I am now, but I wasna before yesterday."

"Well, ye certainly put on a performance for the lasses, tryin' ta convince them of the fact. Servants and governesses. If Bran and I hadna discovered that trunk, we'd have had ta work our fingers ta the bones tryin' ta prepare dinner and get the blasted castle presentable for the enterprisin' Misses Fyfe."

Aiden grumbled something under his breath, and Blaire turned her attention back to her older brother.

"Did ye say somethin'?"

"I said," he gritted through his teeth, "they were nice lasses, and I wish ye'd try ta be a bit more like them."

Blaire rolled her eyes. "The day I spend my time with needles and thread will be the day ye can admit me ta Bedlam. I doona ken how many times I have ta tell ye that I'm no' a lace-and-fripperies kind of lass. And I never will be. What's more, I think Kettering likes that about me. I just wish my older brother did."

"Kettering?" Aiden raked a hand through his hair, all the while looking at her as though she'd sprouted a second head. "Ye canna be serious. Ye doona ken the first thing about the man."

"Ye're the one, Aiden, who has been beggin' me ta try and catch a man's eye. That's all I'm tryin' ta do."

"Blaire—"

She so wished that she could cry on command as Sorcha could. She blinked her eyes rapidly, the way she'd seen the youngest witch in their coven do many a time. Apparently it was good enough.

"Are ye gonna *cry*?" Aiden leaned back against the squabs, completely appalled.

Blaire shook her head and huddled further under her plaid, hoping he couldn't see through her ruse. "Aiden, promise me ye willna toss Kettering and Blodswell from Briarcraig. Or I'll never get the chance ta see if somethin' could come of this."

At that moment, the carriage rumbled to a stop. Aiden frowned a bit as he reached for the door. "I willna throw them out. No' yet anyway, if it's so important ta ye."

She didn't trust her voice not to give her deception away, so she nodded instead.

"Just doona cry, all right?"

Blaire nodded again.

Aiden opened the carriage door and stepped out into the bright Highland sunlight. Blaire followed his lead. She shaded her eyes with her hand to take in the sleepy village before them. Strathcarron seemed desolate, not quite as desolate as Briarcraig, but bleak just the same. The clearances must have hit the region hard. Of course, they had hit most of Scotland hard. Living in Edinburgh, the Lindsays hadn't been affected too badly. But they'd seen an influx of Scots looking for work and shelter in the city, and those people had all come from villages such as this one.

Aiden pointed to a tiny pub and inn at the end of the street. "Why doona ya start over there, and I'll head over ta the blacksmiths.'"

It was as good a place as any. Blaire started down the frozen street, clutching her plaid closer about her shoulders. A frigid wind from a loch at the southern tip of the village threatened to freeze her in her steps. She shuddered and increased her gait until she reached the safety of the taproom.

Blaire rushed inside the building. A small group of locals sat around a couple of dingy tables. Their mouths dropped open when their eyes landed on her, and one man dropped his pint into his lap. Apparently it was never too early to start drinking in Strathcarron. Then again, a pint might keep the chill from one's bones.

She smiled tentatively at the assembled men whom she'd taken by surprise. "Mornin'."

A short, ruddy faced man pushed his seat back and rose to his feet. "Hello, lass. Are ya lookin' for someone?"

An old man beside him chuckled. "I could be someone."

Blaire stepped forward, ignoring the last comment. "I *am* lookin' for someone. A great many someones. My brother, Captain Lindsay, has inherited Briarcraig Castle, and we are hopin' ta hire locally."

"Mother o' God," the old man's eyes rounded in horror.

"Briarcraig?" another muttered.

The ruddy faced man shook his head. "No one goes near the castle, lass. Place is haunted."

Silly, superstitious Scots. Blaire smothered a laugh with her fingers. "Come now," she began again. "I've slept in the castle the last two nights and have neither seen nor heard any evidence of ghosts. Surely, ye big strappin' Highlanders are no' squeamish of a couple old tales."

No one said a word. It had to be the most quiet this taproom had ever seen.

"Or do ye think a lowland lass is more brave than the lot of ye?" she goaded the villagers.

"Hirin' locally, ye say?" A young, smooth-faced man stood up from one of the nearby tables. "What positions are ye lookin' ta fill, Miss…Lindsay, is it?"

Blaire nodded to the youngest man of the group. "It is. And we are in need of…well, everythin'. Maids, footmen, a butler, a cook, a housekeeper, a groom or two."

"I'm Malcolm, and my Glenna and I would be happy for the opportunity." And he meant it. Blaire could see a bit of optimism in his eyes.

Her heart soared as though it had wings. With the amount Aiden had come into, they could help others who were in need. The people of these parts could use some good fortune themselves. "Can ye be by this afternoon?"

"Aye." Malcolm nodded. "And my mother can cook."

"Wonderful." Blaire smiled at the taproom at large. No more of Aiden's mutton stew. The smooth-faced Malcolm was fast becoming her favorite Highlander. "Anyone else?"

Behind her, the door opened again, bringing with it the icy Highland air that had nearly chilled her to her bones. Blaire glanced over her shoulder and shouldn't have been surprised to see Aiden standing in the threshold. "The blacksmith isna there."

The ruddy faced man stepped toward her brother. "I'm Hamish. Do ye have need of my services, lad?"

"Ye're the blacksmith?" Aiden's eyes widened. He clearly hadn't expected the smithy to be drinking so early in the day and not at his place of work. But this was not Edinburgh, not in the least.

"Aye. And ye are?"

"Captain Lindsay." Aiden's gaze swept across the room, taking it all in.

"Well, Captain," the old man began, "do ye really have the funds ta staff that castle of yers?"

A hundred times over at least.

Aiden nodded his reply. "As long as there are men and women lookin' for honest pay for honest work. The castle has been vacant for so long that there's a lot to do."

"That," Malcolm said proudly, puffing out his chest, "willna be a problem, Captain."

Twelve

BLAIRE LED A TROOP OF NEW MAIDS OVER THE threshold of the great hall. Gathering the necessary servants had not been as difficult as she'd originally thought. As soon as the villagers realized Aiden and his money were real, fears about haunted castles evaporated like mist from the loch.

After a quick dispersal of duties, Blaire led Mrs. Fraser toward the kitchens, relieved Malcolm's mother had agreed to come on as their cook and even promised she could have dinner prepared for all their guests that very evening. The old woman so exuded confidence in her abilities that Blaire believed every word from her mouth.

As they reached the kitchens, Brannock burst through the door and barreled right into Blaire. She gasped and put him out from her, shocked at his disheveled appearance and scratches that marred his neck and arms. "What the devil happened ta ye?"

The youngest Lindsay shrugged, as though he had no idea what she was going on about. "I was just hopin' ta meet the staff Aiden said ye hired."

"Do ye mean ta tell me Aiden saw ye like this, all covered with slashes, and he dinna do anythin' about it?" The injuries looked swollen and angry, turning redder by the minute.

"Oh, that." Brannock glanced down at his own arms. "I dinna have the scratches then."

"Brannock Lindsay, what exactly did ye do ta yerself?"

"Bruce dinna like the new home I made for him. That's all, Blaire."

That damn cat. "Brannock," she began, but the new cook held up her hand, silencing Blaire's words.

"I have always said, Miss Lindsay," Mrs. Fraser put in, "that lads doona feel bumps and scrapes the same way we do. My sons could've lost legs or arms, and they'd have kept at whatever held their interest."

Blaire shared a commiserating look with the new servant and shook her head. "Does it no' get easier as they get older?"

"Wish I could tell ye it does," the older woman replied with a shrug, "but I'd be lyin'. But if they catch the ague, ye'd think the world was comin' ta an end." She looked Brannock over. "Come along, lad. We'll get an ointment for yer injuries."

Brannock's mouth fell open as the cook began to tow him toward the great hall, and Blaire held in a laugh. She'd never seen the boy handled so swiftly before.

"Blaire, do ye ken why Lord Kettering is crawlin' around on his hands and knees in the cellar?" Brannock called, trying to extricate himself from the cook's hold.

"Crawlin' on his hands and knees?" Blaire echoed, stalking toward the servants' staircase that led to the lower level. What in the world was the baron doing on his hands and knees in the cellar? She'd scoured the room from top to bottom looking for clues about the man. Had she missed something? What was he looking for? She nearly tripped down the steps in her haste to reach Kettering.

She rounded a corner, and before she could stop, Blaire barreled right into Lord Blodswell's backside as he blocked the cellar from her view.

The earl spun around in a flash and kept her from falling. "Are you quite all right, Miss Lindsay?" He set her from him.

She paid him no attention but strained her neck to see around his broad shoulders, hoping for a glimpse of Kettering. What was he searching for? Blodswell, however, was again in her way, continuing to block her view.

A moment later, Baron Kettering was at his friend's side, a look of concern on his ruggedly handsome face. "Blaire?"

"What are ye doin' here?" she choked out, for lack of anything intelligent to say.

A slight smile appeared on Kettering's face. "Is it possible you missed me, Miss Lindsay?"

His twinkling dark eyes completely disarmed her. "I-I…"

"Did you have any luck in Strathcarron?"

Blaire gestured toward the empty cellar. "Did ye have any luck in there, my lord?"

Aiden chose that moment to call from the top of the stairs, "Is there a soiree goin' on in my cellar?"

Blodswell stepped around Blaire and started for the

steps. "Ah, Captain, so good to see you this afternoon. I was hoping to speak with you."

"With me?" Aiden mumbled.

"Yes. I'm quite impressed with your property, what I've seen of it anyway. May I impose on you to show me around? I adore the medieval feel."

Aiden grumbled something unintelligible but finally said, "Very well. Where would ye like ta begin?"

"Oh," Blodswell gushed as he climbed the steps, "I think I should like to see the library, Captain. Always the most fascinating things are found in libraries, don't you agree?"

Blaire couldn't remember the last time her brother had cracked open a book. Not to mention that the library at Briarcraig was in a most horrible state of disrepair. She would have giggled about the situation if she didn't realize that she was unexpectedly, once again, all alone with James. Suddenly, he seemed to take up most of the space in the small confines. As he stepped closer to her, the smell of citric shaving lotion and a freshly smoked cheroot wrapped around her. She had to stop herself from closing her eyes and simply enjoying his scent.

Strong. She was supposed to be strong today. "What are ye doin' down here?" She straightened her shoulders and looked him in the eye.

He watched her for the longest while, and she had the strangest feeling he was gazing at her neck. What an odd place for a man's eyes to linger. But he had mentioned her neck earlier this morning, as well, hadn't he? "I, um, I've lost something, and I thought perhaps I'd left it in here."

Nothing was in the room. She'd searched it over more than once. "What are ye lookin' for? Perhaps I've already come across it."

"Like my watch fob?"

She knew a blush stained her cheeks. No, not like his watch fob. Whatever he'd lost this time, she hadn't absconded with it. "I could help ye look," she offered.

A charming smile graced his face, and Blaire felt warmth wash over her. "Would you truly help me, Blaire, if I asked it of you?"

Look for whatever he'd lost? The opportunity to discover his secrets? She nodded.

"Hmm. I wonder." His eyes took on a far-off gleam.

Blaire wasn't at all certain they were talking about the same thing. "I'll be happy ta help ye find whatever ye've lost, James."

"What if I want *you* more than what I was looking for? What then, Blaire?" he asked as he took a step toward her. "Would you still be as amenable?"

❧

His intent had been to disarm her, to remove some of the guardedness that was her constant companion. But James found himself just as stripped. She gazed up at him with those shimmering grey eyes, open and trusting. And James wanted nothing more than he wanted to take her in his arms.

Yet she spun away from him after a moment. "What is it that ye're looking for?" she asked. He heard the tiny quaver in her voice, the hesitance. Her back stiffened. Obviously, she heard it, too.

Initially, he'd been looking for a way to enchant

her. But once again he was the one suddenly and completely disarmed. "Blaire," he began softly as he stepped up behind her. He hovered within an inch of her body, knowing full well that if he pushed too far, he wouldn't get to inhale her scent, to enjoy her.

"James," she whispered softly, still facing away from him. Then her body backed into his, almost as though a magnet drew her to him. She fit him. Her forehead nestled beside his chin, her back against his chest.

He slid one of his hands around her waist, where he opened his fingers wide and pulled her bottom even tighter into the saddle of his hips. God, she smelled so good. Felt so good. With his free hand, he brushed aside the tiny tendrils of raven-black hair that had escaped the knot at her neck to cascade over her shoulders. And then he placed his lips against her tender skin.

She tasted like all the things he'd forgotten because he'd gone so long without, like freshly baked tarts. Like sugar in one's tea. She smelled like sunshine and the clean air after a quick spring rain. Her gasp sounded like the winter wind, quiet but cutting. She looked as delicate as a flower in spring, yet she felt like firm, hot, *human* flesh in his arms. *Willing* human flesh.

He nearly cursed aloud when his incisors descended. He couldn't help it. His body associated all pleasures of the flesh with a meal, the ultimate sharing of one's self. But if she knew, she wouldn't be so warm or willing.

There was no doubt in James' mind that she was in his arms because she wanted to be there, rather than because he'd enchanted her. She liked him. She wanted him, too. He could nearly taste her desire.

Her hand came up to cover his upon her belly but not to push it away as he momentarily feared. Instead, she threaded her fingers with his and gripped him tightly. Her hand shook slightly as she leaned her head to the side at the insistence of his questing lips. He groaned against her skin, his incisors gently abrading the sensitive skin.

James fought his most basic instinct to take from her. He fought it for as long as he could. He could bring her pleasure. He would cause her no pain. He would seal his mouth over her pulse point, take all of her pleasure inside himself, and give her his own in return. It would be most wonderful. He nipped at her with his teeth. Then sucked gently. A prelude of what was to come.

"James," she cried as she spun in his embrace, her arms rising to wrap around his neck. Her lips sought his. He lifted his head for no more than a moment and took her offering, sipping at her lips gently and then nipping her lightly. The metallic taste of copper flooded his tongue, and he froze. *What had he done?*

James caught her face between his hands and stared down at her. Her eyes were limpid pools of silver, dark as a storm-laden day. With her eyes half-closed in pleasure, she barely saw him. "Doona stop," she whispered, her lips seeking his again.

He'd bitten her. He'd nipped her hard enough to draw blood, and she was coming back for more?

"Did I hurt you?" he breathed against her lips.

She shook her head quickly, affirming the negative.

"I'm sorry," he said. "I didn't intend to do that." At least not there. Not like this.

"Do I look ta ye like someone who might break, James?" she whispered, a grin turning up the corners of her kiss-swollen lips. A tiny drop of blood beaded up on her mouth, and he bent to kiss her, to draw it into himself.

"You look like someone who wants to be loved," James admitted.

That made her draw back.

"This has nothin' ta do with love."

"It doesn't?" He probably looked like the worst sort of fool, but in his experience, women wanted to be loved. That made his seductions easier to conduct.

"It was just a *kiss*," she said as she stepped out of his grasp. James felt the loss immediately. He reached to draw her back to him. But she stepped farther away and then raised her hands to tuck the stray tendrils of hair back into a loose chignon.

Heavy footsteps sounded on the stairs above them. "Blaire!" the youngest Lindsay bellowed from the top of the servants' stairs.

She stepped into the doorway and called back to him, "What do ye want, Brannock?" She sighed.

Was she disappointed? In him? That their brief interlude was over? Never had James felt such warring emotions, not since he was a green lad.

"Ye'll never believe who's here!" the boy called back.

Blaire started up the steps. But James wasn't about to let her go alone. He followed so closely behind her that his view all the way up the stairs was her sweet little bottom. She ignored his presence. When they reached the kitchen, Brannock was standing at the top.

"Who is it, Bran?" she asked with a sigh.

"What happened ta yer neck, Blaire?" the boy asked. "Do ye need some of Mrs. Fraser's ointment?"

"My neck?" she mumbled, covering her neck with her palm. Her frantic eyes met James'.

He turned her toward him and gently uncovered her neck. He'd left a purple love-mark upon her skin. It shone like a bright beacon on a clear night. He was a damned idiot. He quickly tugged the pins from her hair, letting it fall over her shoulders, and then drew some of it forward to cover his marks.

"It looks as though that spider did bite you after all, Miss Lindsay," he said to appease Brannock, who looked on with a worried tilt to his eyebrows. "I'm so glad I was there to kill it for you."

Brannock snorted. "*Blaire* needed a man ta kill a spider for her? I find that hard ta believe."

Blaire cuffed his shoulder. "Mind yer manners, Bran," she hissed. "And ye shouldna go around bellowin' anymore. What will the servants think?"

"Sorry," the boy muttered, though he looked far from it.

"Now what were ye yellin' about? Did ye say someone is here?"

The boy nearly bounced on the edge of his toes. "Ye'll never guess who."

"Oh for pity's sake. Please tell me it's no' those Fyfe twits already." She rolled her eyes, which made James bite back a smile. Amazingly, she had no idea how charming she was.

"No." Her brother shook his head. "Ye'll never guess who it is."

"If ye willna tell me who, then will ye tell me *where* our guest is?"

"He's in the great hall. I told him I'd get ye. And it's no' a secret. I just wanted ye ta guess again."

She folded her arms across her chest. "Ye want me ta guess again? And ye doona think I'll ever figure it out?"

Brannock bounced on his toes.

Blaire sighed, but there was devotion in her eyes. "Well then, is it Wellington come ta bestow an award for Aiden's bravery at Quatre Bras?"

The boy choked on a laugh and shook his head.

"Elspeth and Caitrin and the others?"

Again the lad shook his head.

"For the love of God, who *is* it, Brannock?" James asked, realizing his tone was a little too sharp as soon as the words came out of his mouth.

The lad sobered a bit and looked at his sister. "It's Mr. MacQuarrie."

Blaire looked puzzled. "Alec MacQuarrie is here? Why on earth would he come ta Briarcraig?" She stormed down the corridor with her brother in tow.

Who the devil was Alec MacQuarrie? James followed closely behind the pair. But he came up short, a tiny pain erupting in his chest when he saw Blaire fly into the arms of another man just inside the great hall.

The dark-haired gentleman caught her close to him, a huge smile upon his face. James tried to tamp down his feelings of imminent destruction.

The man was tall, his eyes shining with something

James had lost decades ago—a kindhearted soul. It shone through in every move the man made, from his impromptu hug with Blaire to his ruffle of Brannock's hair.

James didn't like him. Not one little bit. In fact, if he didn't remove his arm from around Blaire's shoulders, James would remove it for him. Right off her shoulders. Off his body, in fact. James took a step toward them.

"MacQuarrie!" the captain bellowed from behind him, where he and Matthew had entered the great hall. The captain rushed forward, his voice full of friendly camaraderie. "What brings ye ta Briarcraig?"

"It's quite a long tale, actually," the man hedged, his gaze sliding across James and Matthew in a most peculiar way. The newcomer apparently had a secret, something he didn't want everyone to know.

James coughed into his hand, which earned him a scowl from Matthew. Did Blodswell think he would just stand by while someone put his hands on Blaire? Without even learning the man's identity? How ridiculous.

"I believe we've met once before." Matthew spoke up from beside him.

They had? What the devil?

"Blodswell?" the man asked, surprise lighting his face. "What a coincidence."

"You were traveling with a woman the last time I saw you," Matthew remarked.

That blasted MacQuarrie nodded and gazed down at Blaire. "I was with Caitrin."

Blaire's eyebrows drew together, but she squelched

the gesture when he blinked hard at her. Oh, that was not good, whatever it was. A red rage clouded the corners of James' vision.

Blaire chimed in, "Lord Kettering, I'd like for ye ta meet Alec MacQuarrie, a dear friend from Edinburgh."

"I'd love to meet him, if he could take his arm from around your shoulders long enough to shake my hand."

A tinkling laugh that wasn't the least bit genuine escaped Blaire's lips. MacQuarrie didn't remove his arm from around Blaire's shoulders, but he reached to take James' hand anyway. James wanted to knock it away, but he clasped it in his own. "Nice to make your acquaintance," he muttered.

"My lord," the Scot replied, eyeing him suspiciously.

Jealousy bubbled within James like steam in a cast-iron kettle.

"Kettering, let's allow them some privacy, shall we? I've something I'd like to show you." Matthew's hand on his shoulder brooked no argument. If James didn't have such respect for his maker, he'd have refused.

He bowed lightly to Blaire and turned on his heel. "What the devil did you want to show me that's so bloody important?" he hissed as they walked down the corridor.

"Not a damn thing," Matthew answered calmly. "I just wanted to keep you from thrashing the poor man. It would not suit your purpose to be removed from Briarcraig, not at the moment anyway. The sun is high in the sky, or have you forgotten?"

Frustrated, James raked a hand through his hair. Who the devil was this MacQuarrie fellow, and why

had he come all the way from Edinburgh? He pulled
Matthew into the closest parlor and shooed a new
maid from the room. As soon as they were alone, he
glared at his maker. "All right, let's have it. Where
did you meet MacQuarrie? And what do you know
about him?"

Matthew cocked his head to one side, a small
frown forming on his face. "You're not behaving like
yourself in the least. Is this all due to Miss Lindsay? Or
is something else wrong with you?"

"MacQuarrie!" James gritted out, his patience
trickling away like sand in an hourglass.

"Very well." Matthew shook his head and then
slid into an old high-backed chair. "I was near the
border, and I bumped into Mr. MacQuarrie's traveling
companion, Miss Macleod, or rather she bumped
into me. You remember I mentioned her, the *Còig*'s
current seer?"

One of the other witches. James rubbed his temple.
Was that important? Then he remembered the rest of
Matthew's tale. "You said the seer keeps dangerous
company?" And he'd just left Blaire with the blackguard. He started back for the door.

"Wait!" Matthew ordered. Then he gestured to an
old threadbare settee. "Sit down before you go mad."

"But you said—"

"I didn't mean MacQuarrie." His friend sighed.
"Miss Macleod's beast was not with her when our
paths crossed. But I saw evidence of him on her neck."

"One of us?" James finally dropped into the seat
across from his friend.

Matthew shook his head. "No. Something different.

The mark was not one of ours. I'm not certain what it was."

"But you have a guess?"

"If I had to guess, I would say it was Lycan."

A werewolf? The coven was consorting with were-wolves! "And MacQuarrie?"

"Harmless," Matthew supplied. "A scholar, would you believe it? Told me the tale of Sir Matthew Halkett, the very first Earl of Blodswell. Quite a knowledgeable fellow, actually."

So all it had taken was MacQuarrie waxing poetic about Matthew's feats of bravery to win the earl to his side. James scowled at his friend. Traitorous vampyre.

"Enough of this. MacQuarrie is not your problem," Matthew continued, leveling his most serious look on James. "Did you have any luck with Miss Lindsay?"

The best sort of luck. James remembered holding her against him, the taste of her on his tongue. Though he wasn't anxious to divulge such things to Matthew. "Miss Lindsay?"

The earl looked at him as though he was the most inept creature. "I hauled Captain Lindsay away so you could try to engage her assistance in finding your ring. Does any of that sound familiar?"

Of course, that's what he meant, but just Blaire's sweet scent had wiped his mind of all purpose. "I didn't get a chance to ask."

Matthew leaned forward in his seat. "I've never seen you lose your head like this before, James. And you're going to need it, if we're to find your ring and depart before Sarah and Trevelyan arrive."

Sarah Reese and Padrig Trevelyan. How could he have forgotten them? Because Blaire made him forget everything except for her.

Blaire…

Panic shot through James. "We can't leave."

Matthew sighed impatiently. "I know you've developed an attachment for the chit, but—"

"What do you think Trevelyan will do if he arrives here to find us departed?"

Realization dawned on Matthew's face. "The Lindsays and everyone else at Briarcraig."

"We can't leave," James repeated. "I won't leave everyone here to face the two of them alone."

Thirteen

WHEN JAMES AND THE EARL QUIT THE GREAT HALL, THE breath rushed from Blaire's lungs. She turned her gaze to Alec MacQuarrie, whom she still couldn't believe stood beside her, his arm draped companionably around her shoulders. Having him there was surreal in so many ways. There were places one expected to find Alec—a cozy study, a well-lit library, or chasing after Caitrin's skirts. However, seeing him at Briarcraig seemed completely out of place.

She slid from his hold. "Did ye say somethin' about Cait?" Had something happened to her friend? Blaire's pulse began to race at the thought.

Alec winced a bit and then looked at both her brothers. "I need to speak with you."

Mo chreach, it was worse than she'd thought. Blaire clutched at her heart. "What is it, MacQuarrie? Just tell me."

He met her eyes but spoke to Aiden. "Lindsay, do you mind giving me a moment with your sister?"

"Whatever it is, MacQuarrie," Aiden began, "we Lindsays doona have any secrets from each other."

Blaire nodded in agreement. "Please just tell us what's wrong."

He frowned. "No secrets?"

"None," she confirmed. Well, she hadn't told Aiden the truth about James, but that was an entirely different matter than whatever *this* was.

"They know what you are?" he whispered.

The better question was how did Alec know what she was? "And just what am I?"

"Caitrin confessed the truth of it."

That didn't make one bit of sense. Coven members didn't discuss their powers or admit to being witches except to their own families. It just wasn't done. It was too dangerous otherwise. But Cait had apparently told all to MacQuarrie. "Did she finally accept yer proposal?" That was the only thing Blaire could come up with to explain his sudden knowledge.

But as soon as the words left her lips, she knew she was wrong. Poor Alec looked as though he'd been hit in the stomach. He managed to shake his head.

"Then I doona ken what ye're referrin' ta."

Alec sighed. "You know exactly what I'm talking about, Blaire Lindsay. The only thing that surprises me is that I didn't realize it earlier. The *Còig* was in front of my own nose for years, and I never put it together. You with your archery and sword fighting. Elspeth and her healing touch. I never did understand Rhiannon, who doesn't have the sense to come in out of the rain. Sorcha and her plants. And Caitrin…"

There was that look again, as though he'd lost his very best friend in the world. "Has somethin' happened ta Cait?" Why was the man being so tight-lipped? She'd never professed to have patience, but MacQuarrie's equivocation was enough to drive her mad.

He straightened his shoulders, but a frown settled on his face. "I'm sure she's happy in her new role. At least she assured me she would be."

"Her new role?"

He inclined his head with a tight nod. "Aye. I left before the nuptials, but I am certain that by now she is the Countess of Brimsworth." He took a steadying breath and focused on Blaire. "But that's not why I'm here, lass. Cait sent me, you see—"

"Who the devil is Brimsworth?" Raking her brain, she couldn't recall ever hearing the name, not even anything similar. Cait had married some stranger? In the few days Blaire was gone? She couldn't quite believe it. In fact, she thought she might faint, something she'd never done in her life. "I always thought she'd marry ye."

"So did I," he said quietly.

"Who is this man?"

Alec heaved a sigh. "Brimsworth is a fellow she met in England, heir to a wealthy marquessate, evidently. But, honestly, Blaire, I'd rather not discuss that particular situation, if you don't mind. That's not why she sent me."

Aiden stepped forward and steadied Blaire with his hand, though his eyes never left MacQuarrie. "Why *are* ye here? And why did Caitrin confide the truth ta ye?" No matter their differences, Lindsays supported each other, and at the moment she was very grateful for her older brother.

"Cait had a vision." Alec focused on Blaire. "You're in danger. She sent me to warn you."

"In danger?" Aiden echoed, clearly concerned.

"What vision?" Blaire pressed forward. "What did she see?"

MacQuarrie shook his head as though he didn't believe it himself. "A monster," he admitted. "She said it was a monster with black eyes, coming for you. A *dead* monster. I don't know any more than that. She said the visions aren't always clear, but she was nearly hysterical with whatever she did see."

It must have terrified her if she had confided the secret of their coven's existence to MacQuarrie. Black eyes? A vision of James flashed in her mind, but she shook the thought away. She wasn't certain what he was, but he wouldn't ever hurt her. At least she didn't think so. He might kiss her into oblivion, but the man was *alive*. She was fairly certain parts of him were, in any event. A blush crept up her cheeks at the thought.

James nearly dragged Matthew from room to room in his search for his missing ring. They moved from parlor to parlor, from kitchen to retiring room, from the library to the dungeon and every bedchamber they stumbled across. His ring was nowhere to be found. They'd upended beds, rifled through wardrobes, and knocked on walls, looking for secret openings. They'd scared one of the new maids to death, or nearly. Fortunately, Matthew still possessed his ability to enchant humans, or she'd have brought the whole household down on their heads.

Just as the sun began to sink in the sky, James

finally pushed to his feet from the floor of the last bedchamber, dusted himself off, and sighed heavily. "It's not here," he complained.

"It has to be," Matthew insisted quietly. "It's here somewhere. If it wasn't, I wouldn't have been able to feel your presence. You wouldn't have awoken." They turned to walk down the long corridor that led to their own chambers.

"When, exactly, did you begin to feel my presence?" James asked.

"I assume it was when you woke," Matthew said with a shrug of his shoulders. Then he turned toward James quickly and stopped. "*Of course*, it was when you woke."

"I don't understand." And he didn't, not any of it. If this mess became any more tangled, James would never find his ring, would never see sunlight again.

"You slept for nearly two decades, correct?"

James could see the story unwinding in Matthew's mind. "I assume so," he said slowly, beginning to catch on. "I woke when the Lindsays arrived." He rolled it around in his mind. What an idiot he'd been! "When my *ring* arrived," he growled.

"I can't think of any other way it could have happened," Matthew agreed. "The rings tie us together. Mine allows me to feel you, and vice versa. The only way I wouldn't feel you would be if there was a great distance between you and your ring."

"Such as the distance between Briarcraig Castle and Edinburgh?" The distance between the witch's residence and his prison. The distance between her comfortable home and the damp walls of the cellar where he'd lost twenty years of his life-after-death.

"Evidently." Matthew looked truly shocked at his own discovery. "It would make sense."

Sense? Nothing made sense. Why he'd been attacked. Why he'd been locked up. Why his ring had been taken. None of it. "Where could it be?" he asked, more of himself than Matthew. They'd searched the castle from top to bottom, including the bedchambers occupied by the Lindsays.

"The stables, perhaps," his friend suggested. "We haven't looked outside."

Well, that was true. They had vast acreage yet to search. But something about that didn't feel right. Why would the Lindsays return to Briarcraig, bringing with them the key to James' escape, and then leave it lying about the property unguarded?

They wouldn't, of course.

It would be protected, and who better to protect it than a battle-born witch?

A sinking feeling hit James squarely in the gut. "You said the mothers trained their daughters, the next generation?"

Matthew confirmed this with a nod.

"Then she *must* have it." She must have known all along. But what game was she playing with him? James intended to find out.

He stormed from the musty bedchamber and stalked down the corridor toward the rounded staircase, ignoring Matthew's warnings that he stop and think. He'd been thinking long enough, all day on his hands and knees searching for something he'd never find because *she* had it all along.

James could hear her tinkling laugh on the main

level, and he followed it down the steps and to a small parlor at the end of one corridor. Furious, he tossed the doors open and burst inside. Everything went quiet. An old fellow with wispy, white hair and two golden-haired lasses sat across from Blaire and the MacQuarrie fellow. All of them stared at James as though he'd sprouted horns and a forked tail.

"Blaire." James didn't even try to hide the growl in his voice. "A word, if you don't mind."

A warm fire blazed in the hearth, lighting the room with warmth, but James could only feel the chill in Blaire Lindsay's stare. Well, damn her. He didn't care what she thought of his manners at the moment.

When she rose from her place on the divan, Mr. MacQuarrie stood as well. "Ah, Kettering," the interloper began smoothly, "we wondered where you had gotten off to."

James didn't even spare the man a glance. He only had eyes for the warrior witch who gestured to the newcomers. "Lord Kettering, allow me ta introduce our neighbors—Mr. Fyfe, the local magistrate, and his daughters, Miss Fyfe and Miss Crissa. And this," she waved her hand toward James, "is Baron Kettering of Derbyshire."

Both girls sucked in breaths at the mention of his title, and one of them actually twittered.

"Pleasure," he growled. "And now, Miss Lindsay, I'll have that word."

"Ah, but dinner awaits," MacQuarrie interjected.

Dinner indeed. James leveled Blaire with his most scathing gaze. If she didn't hand over his ring, he'd just as soon dine on her. Matthew's rules be damned.

"Why don't you escort the nice lasses into the dining room and tell the captain we'll be right along."

MacQuarrie squared his shoulders and stood his ground. "Under the circumstances, my lord, I think it would be best for us all to go in together."

Blaire's brow furrowed as though she was working through a difficult arithmetic problem in her head. Then she met MacQuarrie's eyes. "It's all right, Alec. I'm certain Lord Kettering and I will be right behind ye."

James barely managed not to snort.

"But, Blaire," MacQuarrie continued, "I don't think it's wise—"

"*Havers*, Alec!" She laughed, though it sounded hollow to James' ears. "I can certainly take care of myself, as ye well ken."

That seemed to appease the interfering Scot, and he slightly inclined his head before offering his arm to one of the golden-haired lasses, the one who twittered. Then he directed the Fyfes from the parlor, even if it was a bit reluctantly.

Blaire folded her arms across her chest and scowled at James. *She* was annoyed with *him*? "Just what do ye think ye're doin'? Stompin' around, barkin' orders? Actin' like the lord of the manor? I doona even like those lasses, but the way ye're behavin' is inexcusable."

The last thing James wanted was to hear her chastise his behavior. It was beyond the pale, considering everything her coven had done to him. Before he could stop himself, he stormed across the floor and backed her against the far wall. He ignored the gasp that escaped her and tipped her chin back so that she had to look him in the eyes. "I want my ring, and I will not wait any longer for it."

"Ring?" she sputtered.

Her innocent grey eyes blinked at him. Beneath that beautiful exterior lay a witch. A very devious one at that. "Don't play me for a fool, Blaire. I *know* you have it, and I want it back. Now."

She pushed at his chest with a strength he'd never found in a woman before, and he stumbled back a few steps before finding his feet. He advanced on her, but a fireball burst to life in her palm and she looked prepared to engulf him in flames. He stopped inches from her, just as she pulled her arm back to throw her fire, and he stepped back.

"I doona ken what ye're talkin' about, Kettering, but this evenin' is difficult enough without ye makin' it worse."

The liar. He glared at her as he tried to figure out how to disarm her. "You thought to distract me with your pretty eyes and silky hair, and it almost worked. But I *do* need my ring to go on with my life, and nothing will make me forget that."

❧

Blaire could only gape at him. She had no idea what he was so angry about. He looked positively enraged, and, for a brief instant, Cait's warning echoed in her mind. *A monster with black eyes.* Surely it couldn't be James. It couldn't be. Though, at the moment, he didn't seem remotely like the James she had known these past few days. He barely resembled the man who was so easy to smile and who kissed her until her mind spun. He seemed something else entirely. Something dangerous.

"On my honor, Kettering, I have no idea what ye're about."

"My ring," he gritted out, wiggling the fingers of his right hand. "I know you have it."

"I think ye've taken leave of yer senses, my lord. I found yer *pocket fob*, but I have no' laid eyes on yer ring. I doona even ken what it looks like. I offered ta help ye, but ye've told me nothin'."

"Don't pretend with me." He stalked toward her, and Blaire lifted her ball of fire higher so he wouldn't forget the power she held. "You know your mother and the others attacked me. Deny it."

She could not. Blaire shook her head. "I suspected as much, and I'd very much like to ken why."

"Suspected." He snorted. "I have it on the highest authority that one generation of witches trains the next. Which means *you* know exactly why they attacked me. *You* know why they stashed me away in this godforsaken castle. And *you* have my bloody ring."

Blaire nearly lost her breath at the power of his words. She didn't know any of those things, and the fact that she didn't almost brought her to her knees. Why didn't she have his answers? Why didn't her mother prepare her for this moment? What she *did* know was that she'd been right about him; he'd admitted as much. Her mother had trapped him. He'd said so himself. "What are you?" she asked, making certain her voice remained even. Not a tremor would escape her lips. Not if she could help it.

Kettering chuckled, though no joy could be

detected in the sound. "You know that, too. Don't you, my pretty little witch?"

No one ever called her pretty. Why did the first man to do so have to act as though the admission was painful to his soul? "What I ken is that ye're a suspicious, self-absorbed Sassenach."

A bitter laugh escaped him. "Suspicious? I suppose one becomes such after being locked away for two decades."

Two decades? Nearly double the time she suspected. Kettering had been here at Briarcraig her entire life, and yet her mother never breathed a word of it. Had she ensnared the baron right before her death and forgot to mention it, Blaire could possibly understand—but for *twenty years*. Her mother could have told her the truth of the matter at any time. Yet she had not. The room began to spin a bit, and Blaire struggled to maintain her composure. She edged away from the baron and started for the door.

"Don't even think to run away from me." Kettering advanced toward her again.

But Blaire didn't pay him any attention. She made it to the door first, and she bolted up the stairs and down the corridor to her bedchamber. She shoved a wooden chair under the handle, though she doubted that would keep the baron out if he was of a mind to gain entry to her room. Blaire paced the floor, back and forth. None of this made any sense. So what did she know?

One: Briarcraig was the home of the battle-born witches.

Two: Her mother had stopped visiting the place before Blaire was born and had forbidden Aiden from ever speaking of it when he was a child.

Three: The property had only resurfaced after her father's death when the meticulous solicitor Aiden had hired at Mr. Ferguson's suggestion searched every nook and cranny for a way out of their debt. If the solicitor hadn't stumbled upon Briarcraig, the castle might have lain untouched for decades, perhaps centuries even.

Four: James Maitland, Baron Kettering, whatever he was, had been locked away in that tiny cell for two decades, presumably to be sealed away until the end of time. At least that's how it appeared at the moment.

And five: after twenty years in a tiny cell, Kettering looked no worse for wear. In fact, he seemed healthy, vigorous, and strong. And handsome. She mentally removed that last from her list. Regardless of his physical perfection, he didn't seem remotely like a man who could have *lived* through such an ordeal, let alone look so hale and hearty afterward. Which brought back her original question—what exactly was he?

A knock sounded on her door, eliciting a startled gasp from Blaire.

"Aiden's waitin' on ye for dinner." Brannock's voice filtered into the room. "And the Fyfes too."

Blaire squared her shoulders. Whatever Kettering was, she wouldn't let him chase her away or allow him to endanger the others' lives. "Just one moment, Bran, and I'll be right there."

⁓

James had watched Blaire escape into her room, unnoticed from the shadows of the corridor. He wasn't certain what to think about her performance in the parlor, if it even *was* a performance. At the time, he'd been so furious, but looking back, she did appear unsettled by his insistence that she had his ring.

Still, it didn't seem possible that she *didn't* know, not from what Matthew had said of the covens' practice. She just seemed so sincere in her denials. Even now, he wanted to believe her; he wanted to believe that she wasn't toying with him as her predecessors had done, that the connection between them was as real to her as it was to him. He had no doubt that he was developing feelings for the witch. But he wasn't at all certain what to do with them.

How was he to know the truth?

"One would think that after the many years we've known each other, you'd pay some notice to my advice," Matthew said at his side.

James hadn't even noticed Blodswell's approach. Apparently, he wasn't himself in many different ways. The witch had cast her spell on him, whether she'd meant to or not.

"I never expected to see a battle-born witch retreat," Matthew said. "What did you do?"

"How many battle-born witches have you known?" James flung at his maker. "And what makes you think I've done anything?"

Matthew scratched at his temple. "Oh, perhaps the way the lovely Miss Lindsay ran from you up the stairs like the hounds of hell were nipping at her feet."

Perhaps they were. "She didn't admit to having the ring. And I can't tell the truth between fact and fiction." He'd let himself get too close to the girl. So close he couldn't remain objective.

"I heard," Matthew murmured. "She seemed sincere. And truly bothered by your accusations."

Indeed she had. Which was why this was so confoundedly difficult.

James realized Matthew hadn't even responded to his query. "How many battle-born witches *have* you known in your lifetime? You didn't answer my question."

"Several. But I only knew one of them well. I met her during the Crusades, though I had no idea what she was at the time. She fought beside me like a man until she was wounded and her ruse was exposed. I came between her and a blade that would have taken her life." He inhaled deeply and scrunched up his eyebrows, as though he was digging for a memory or two. "That was how I became thrice blessed." At James' confused expression, he clarified. "Three rings. Thrice blessed."

Matthew cocked his head to the side as though listening for something.

"What is it?" James needed to know.

"They're in this area." Matthew's cheek jumped as he clenched his teeth.

"Who?"

Before he could answer, quick footsteps sounded in the corridor.

"We'll discuss it later," Matthew said, though he'd truly worried James at this point.

Brannock Lindsay skidded into the corridor, his

breaths coming in gasps. "Oh, there ye are. Aiden said ta tell ye that dinner is ready, and everyone is waitin' on ye."

Matthew reached over and ruffled the lad's hair. Then he reached into his pocket, pulled out a coin, and flipped it with his thumb so that it flew through the air, right into Brannock's hand. It was a shame that Matthew never had children of his own. He'd have been a great father.

"Thanks!" the lad cried as he spun on his heel. "I need ta show Aiden!"

Matthew turned to James and spoke to him as though he was still in leading strings. "Why don't you escort Miss Lindsay to dinner. Be a gentleman, for God's sake." Matthew cracked a smile that made James groan.

A gentleman. The last thing he wanted was to be a gentleman when he was around Miss Lindsay. He either wanted to pin her to the wall and kiss her. Or pin her to the floor and force her to tell him all her secrets...by kissing her into submission. He was a complete and utter fool. He scrubbed a hand down his face in frustration, but he trudged up the winding staircase anyway.

He knocked softly on Miss Lindsay's door.

"I said I'll be there in a moment, Bran," Blaire called back.

James leaned close to the crack between the doorjamb and the door and said softly, "It's not Brannock." He steeled himself. "Allow me to escort you to dinner." Wasn't that what Matthew had told him to do? Be a gentleman? He hadn't forgotten how. He just forgot how whenever he was alone with Miss Lindsay.

"I can find my own way downstairs. This is *my* castle, after all. Yer assistance is no' needed, Kettering."

James leaned his forehead against the door. "But I need *your* assistance, Blaire. I need it terribly." He continued to speak softly to her, hoping his tone would ease some of her anger. "I'm not myself, you see."

The door flew open with such force that James stumbled inside. Blaire stepped to the side and allowed him to flounder, moving nothing more than her eyebrows as she watched his clumsy movements. James hadn't been clumsy in years. What was it about this woman that confused him so?

He reached for her hand to place it upon his arm. Matthew had said to be a gentleman. Damn Matthew. She jerked her hand back and crossed her arms beneath her breasts. He scowled at her. Heavily.

"Do ye always look so pleased when ye're playin' the gallant?"

He never *played* the gallant. He just was. Usually.

"I am pleased because I have a beautiful lass who might allow me to escort her to dinner if I remember how to act properly." He cleared his throat. "My apologies, Blaire, for my earlier behavior."

"Ye suddenly are no' quite so intent on findin' yer jewelry?" she asked skeptically. The toe of her slipper began to tap against the floor.

"It's not jewelry." James sighed. "It's a ring. It was stolen from me, if you must know. And I think your mother passed it on to you as the next in the line of battle-born witches." She started to speak, but he held up his hands to stop her. "You say she didn't. But I don't know what to believe. My instincts are usually spot on. Just not right now, apparently."

Blaire glared at him. So much for soothing her with his gentlemanly ways. He nearly chuckled at the absurdity of it.

"What are ye?" she asked, her voice strong and clear.

"Are you certain you wish to know what I am, Blaire?" he asked, watching her face closely. She barely blinked.

"I believe I have a right ta ken what ye are. If I'm ta help ye find yer ring, I'll need all the details ye can give me."

He wanted to tell her. He needed to trust her as badly as he needed blood to survive. James stared at the beautiful witch across from him and hoped he wasn't making the biggest mistake of his life. He stepped close to her, prepared to bare his soul; and she looked up at him warily.

"Very well. Allow me this concession," he said quickly, before he could change his mind. "And I will show you what I am. Do you agree? I promise not to hurt you."

"Do ye plan ta sprout wings and fly away, James? Because, honestly, that is the only thing that would surprise me at this point."

She was adorable when she was sarcastic. *And when she was angry. And when she was overcome with passion.* James allowed his thoughts to linger on the last. If he was a small bit aroused, it would make his incisors descend all the quicker.

"May I?" he asked as he stepped closer to her and

pulled her into his arms. She came to him warily. Yet still she came.

James inhaled the scent of her. Absorbed the warmth of her. Felt the sweet remembrance of her life's blood.

Then he stepped back and smiled at her. Blaire's eyes widened to the point where he felt almost certain the silver orbs would fly from her head. Then she covered her mouth and laughed.

That was her reaction? "It's not a good idea to laugh at a vampyre, Blaire. Truly, it's not."

Fourteen

Vampyre?

Blaire's mouth fell open. She hadn't meant to laugh, not really. She'd just been so surprised that the sound had escaped her. Never in a million years had she expected to see fangs appear in James' mouth. *Fangs* for heaven's sake. And a vampyre? She had heard of them, of course. For whatever it was worth, her mother had at least told her about vampyres, immortal monsters that live off the blood of others to survive. Parasitic creatures that scour the night and entrance their victims before draining them of their life force.

Vampyres were to be feared and avoided at all costs. After all, they were indestructible. However, the *Còig* had held one in great esteem long ago, or so the tale went. He was a noble knight who'd fought alongside a warrior witch, both having followed Richard the Lionheart into battle. She'd always attributed the tale of vampyres to those of legend, like fire-breathing dragons or trolls who lived under bridges.

James folded his arms across his chest. He was not a legend, but a man of flesh and... "I've never seen you at a loss for words."

She never had been before, not that she could remember anyway. "I doona suppose ye were a knight in the Third Crusade?" Even as she asked it, she knew he had not. Had he been that benevolent knight of the legend, her mother and the others would never have captured him.

The baron's eyes narrowed on her. "So you do know."

What was she to know? What a vampyre was? Why he'd been held prisoner for two decades? The location of his all-important ring? Blaire shook her head. "I doona ken what ye're askin' me."

"Don't play me for a fool, Blaire." A frown marred his too-handsome face. "I don't have the patience for it."

"Why must ye talk in riddles? I doona ken what ye are askin' of me. Just speak plainly, will ye?"

James turned his back to her. He walked across the room and leaned against her hearth, staring into the flames. Still he said nothing.

Blaire thought her head might explode. Why did he ask her questions repeatedly, act as though she knew the answers, and then fail to respond to any of her inquiries in return? She stomped across the room after him. Somewhere in the back of her mind, she thought that antagonizing an angry vampyre might not be the best idea. But she had endured all of his evasiveness she intended to. Before she even reached him, he spun on his heel so quickly that she lost her balance watching him.

James hauled her into his arms, which kept her from tumbling to the floor. She stared up into his black-as-night eyes and felt completely lost to him. Even knowing what he was, she wasn't afraid. Not of him, only that he'd release her.

"What do ye want of me?" she asked, her voice breathless to her own ears.

"More than I should." James lowered his head and very softly touched his lips to hers.

But the pressure wasn't nearly enough. Blaire pressed herself even closer to him and wrapped her arms around his neck. He ran his tongue across the seam of her lips, and she gladly opened to him, welcoming him into her mouth. He tasted of cheroot, danger, and all-encompassing sin. She couldn't get enough of him. If he'd only pull her closer.

As though he could hear her thoughts, James groaned and clutched her tighter to him, his fingers so wonderfully spreading across her back. Then his hand went lower, across her bottom, and Blaire's heart skipped a beat. A chill touched her calves, and she realized James was gathering her skirts in his hands. At that moment, she didn't care as long as he kept touching her, kept kissing her.

An impatient knock broke the spell. "Damn it ta hell, Blaire," Aiden bellowed from the corridor. "How long does it take for ye ta come down ta dinner?" He pounded again. "Our guests are waitin'."

James slowly released Blaire's skirts and took a step away from her. He did appear as lost as she felt, but there was no time to discuss it. One more bang and Aiden was likely to knock the door from its hinges.

The last thing she needed was for her irrational brother to find James in her room.

"Just a moment!" she called.

"Sorry," Aiden grumbled from the other side of the door. "I ken we're no' the upper echelons of society, Blaire, but it's beyond even ye ta keep the Fyfes and Alec waitin' on ye."

"I said I'd be down in a moment." Blaire's eyes sought James', but he now was staring at the floor. Why wouldn't he look at her? She prayed he didn't regret what was happening between them. She didn't think she could take that.

"Aye, ye said that *ten* moments ago."

"I havena been feelin' myself, Aiden. A little patience would be most appreciated."

"What do I care?" her brother complained. "Either come ta dinner or do no'. I'm tired of beggin' for yer attendance."

As soon as Aiden stomped down the corridor, James' gaze rose to meet hers. The intensity of his dark stare took Blaire's breath away. "You should go down to dinner," he said quietly.

She reached her hand out toward him. "Come with me?"

A self-deprecating smile settled on his face, and this time Blaire didn't find his elongated incisors surprising at all. On the contrary, everything about him was wildly appealing, and she didn't want to walk away from him. "It would be best if you'd make excuses for Blodswell and myself."

"Blodswell?" Blaire echoed as her heart sank a bit. But of course Blodswell. He was an old friend of James'. He must be a vampyre as well. There was no other explanation for his presence at Briarcraig or his lack of surprise that his friend hadn't aged in two decades. Not one vampyre but two were under their roof, and yet Blaire wasn't concerned in the least.

"Ye have ta come, or Aiden will wonder why ye're no' at dinner and there are guests."

"He will wonder more if two of his guests don't touch a bite of their food. Go on, Blaire. You need to eat. I'll be waiting for you here when you've finished." James' voice rumbled over her like a caress.

She shook her head stubbornly. She wasn't sure if it was because his plan was ridiculous or because she simply didn't want him out of her sight. "Aiden is tryin' so hard ta impress those featherbrained twits that he willna pay the least bit of attention ta yer plate. I promise."

James nodded. His fangs retreated, and he offered her his arm. "Whatever you wish, my dear."

Together they descended the steps and found Blodswell waiting for them outside the dining hall. "Glad you both could make it."

Blaire's cheeks warmed. She had a fairly good idea that the earl knew exactly what had kept them. "So sorry ta be late."

Blodswell grinned good-naturedly. "Save your apologies for the Captain, lass. You don't owe me any explanations."

The three of them entered the dining hall, which caused several sets of eyes to land on them. Blaire cleared her throat. "My apologies. I was detained."

Aiden glared at her, though she chose to ignore his stare. She settled into an empty spot beside Alec.

"Ah, my fault entirely," James offered as he slid into the chair on Blaire's other side.

Blodswell took a seat across from them, next to the icy-eyed Crissa Fyfe, who looked extraordinarily pleased at her good fortune. Footmen poured wine in their glasses, and Blaire noticed that the young fresh-faced Malcolm Fraser, amongst their numbers, gave her a warm smile in the process. She took a deep breath. They could get through this evening. It couldn't last forever, after all.

"Forgive our tardiness," Blodswell said smoothly. "Allow me to introduce myself. I am the Earl of Blodswell, and my dear friend here is Lord Kettering. We are generally more punctual, but circumstances prevented that this evening."

Heather Fyfe twittered from her spot beside Aiden. Blaire could see the glee in the mercenary girl's green eyes. A wealthy captain next to her, two English lords, and a well-to-do Scotsman all in attendance. She was probably pinching herself under the table to make sure she hadn't dreamed the whole evening.

Crissa Fyfe narrowed her blue eyes on Blaire across the table. "Will anyone else be joinin' us? Miss Gulverness perhaps?"

"Gulverness?" James muttered, but Blaire kicked him under the table.

"I am afraid Miss Gulverness is no longer with us. My brother had ta let her go this mornin' right before we went inta Strathcarron."

"Aye," Miss Fyfe glanced around the room at the footmen standing near the doors. "I do recognize many of these faces. I had thought ye'd arrived at Briarcraig with yer staff from Edinburgh."

Alec frowned beside her, and Blaire winced. Prevaricating to the Fyfes was one thing, but Alec knew the true state of their finances, or at least he did before they'd stumbled across Aiden's fortune.

"Well," Aiden's voice carried all the way down the table, "we did come with a skeleton staff, but we sent them back ta attend the house in the city as Miss Gulverness was leavin' anyway. And as we intend ta keep Briarcraig workin' throughout the year, we thought it best ta go ahead and hire locally."

"Good of ye," Mr. Fyfe agreed. "Very admirable. This area's been hit hard. It will be good for everyone ta have Briarcraig Castle returned ta its former glory."

Aiden preened under the praise, and Blaire tried not to roll her eyes. Her dolt of a brother must truly have eyes for Heather Fyfe, or he wouldn't go to such extremes to impress the lass. She slid a sidelong glance at James beside her. *He* wasn't telling *her* Banbury tales, was he? She didn't think so. The man had confessed to being a vampyre and even showed her his fangs. Something about that honesty suddenly made her heart warm.

Alec glanced across the table at the Earl of Blodswell. "When Miss Macleod and I met you in England, I had no idea you were acquainted with the Lindsays."

"Our acquaintance is a new one, Mr. MacQuarrie. Though I am happy for it. Miss Lindsay is a diamond among paste imitations, don't you agree?"

"Blaire is indeed one in a million."

At the end of the table, Aiden's brow rose in

question, which Blaire took as an inquiry about whether she'd still prefer James or the earl after that last exchange. She hadn't truly set out to catch either man, but after the soul-searing kisses from James, she could almost feel herself falling for him. That afternoon she'd told him their connection wasn't about love, but perhaps she was wrong. Or perhaps she was a fool. A vampyre for heaven's sakes. A vampyre her mother had helped trap. She was apparently losing her mind.

Footmen began ladling cock-a-leekie soup into their bowls, for which Blaire was extraordinarily grateful. In the first place, the Fyfe sisters would be occupied with eating, so she wouldn't have to listen to any of their inanities. Secondly, dinner smelled delightful. Mrs. Fraser must be a genius in the kitchen. After a year of Aiden's cooking or her own dismal failures, the soup promised to be heaven.

Beside her and across the table, James and Blodswell lifted empty spoons to their lips. The ruse of dining with the others was so practiced that she would never have realized their subterfuge if she hadn't known to look for it. Some cheeky imp inside Blaire made her glance at the vampyre baron beside her and ask, "Is everythin' ta yer likin', my lord?"

One black brow rose with mirth. "Indeed, lass. I like everything I see. I can hardly wait to taste the fare you have to offer."

Across the table, Blodswell choked.

She probably should have been embarrassed by James' words, but instead she was giddy at the suggestion and the twinkle in his black eyes.

"Well, I hope ye enjoy it."

"I'm certain I will."

Crissa Fyfe batted her eyelashes in Blodswell's direction. "How long do ye intend ta stay in Strathcarron?"

The earl smiled at the lass beside him. "Not long. I shall be spending the season in London, Miss Crissa."

"London?" the girl sighed wistfully. "I've always wanted ta go ta London."

"Indeed?" Heather Fyfe sent an arch stare toward her younger sister. "I've always wanted ta see Edinburgh." Then she tipped her head toward Aiden. "Will ye tell me about yer home, Captain? I find the lowlands so fascinatin'."

Blaire barely managed not to roll her eyes.

The Earl of Blodswell tapped the side of his bowl with a spoon, catching Blaire's and James' attention. Then he slightly nodded his head to the left toward the main doors, though what he was trying to indicate, Blaire had no idea.

Someone cleared his throat, and Blaire looked over her shoulder to find the new butler, whose name escaped her at the moment, standing just inside the dining hall. "Captain Lindsay, there are some people in the great hall…"

Blodswell's chair legs scraped along the floor as he rose from his spot. "I believe the people are here to see Kettering and myself."

Blaire blinked at the earl in surprise. Who would even know to find them here of all places? Before she could ask the question, James leapt to his feet as well. "Do excuse us, Captain."

James looked down at Blaire and shook his head. "Stay here," he silently mouthed.

Like hell. Blaire rose from the table as well. "I'll just see ta the new visitors, Aiden."

Her brother scowled and James growled, but she paid neither of them any attention as she brushed past the new butler and down the corridor with two vampyres quick on her heels.

"Blaire," James hissed. "Go back. This is too dangerous."

Dangerous? She glanced back over her shoulder at the baron. "I am perfectly capable of handlin' danger, James."

"Not like this," he warned as they turned the corner. "Wait just a moment. There's something I should explain."

She spun on her heels to look at the man. Worry lines marred his face, and a sense of foreboding settled in the pit of her stomach. Something *was* terribly wrong.

"Jamie, is that you?" A feminine voice filtered down the corridor.

"Jamie?" Blaire echoed. Who exactly did that voice belong to?

James winced and clutched Blaire's arm in his hand. "Keep your voice down. Don't say anything."

"Doona say anythin'?" she whispered. Was that all he intended to tell her? If so, he was sadly mistaken.

"And don't look them in the eyes," James muttered.

Before she could demand to know what was going on, a striking woman stepped from the great hall.

"Ah, there you are." The stranger's voice floated down the hallway once more.

Pretty brown locks billowed scandalously over the woman's shoulders, nearly shiny from the warm glow of the sconces. The hair on the back of Blaire's neck stood as the stranger's dark eyes raked across her.

James' hand settled low on Blaire's back. "Why doona ye return ta yer guests, lass?" he whispered in her ear.

And fail to learn what exactly what was going on? Leave him to this woman? Blaire shook her head. "Aiden has it well under control. Why doona ye introduce me ta yer friend?"

"Come in, come in," directed a rich, disembodied voice from inside the great hall.

Blaire didn't wait for James to try and dissuade her again. Instead, she steadied her shoulders and started for the threshold. The woman stepped aside to let her pass, though James was directly behind her.

Lounged across the settee, an uncommonly handsome man looked as though he thought he was Caesar upon his throne. There was something so innately dangerous about the man that Blaire's natural instinct was to engulf him in a ball of flames. She clasped her hands before her to prevent a spark from going off awry. The man's brow rose in question. "Do forgive us for calling so late," he drawled. His melodic words flowed over Blaire like heavy syrup, coated with something that could easily bind her wits.

James touched her waist at that moment, dragging her back to reality. Then he spun her around slowly, all the while making it look as though she was a willing participant, until he had gently thrust her behind him. Danger. He *had* warned her, hadn't

he? And she hadn't listened. James managed to place
her between himself and Blodswell, who Blaire didn't
even realize was still there until the earl touched her
arm. The pair nearly vibrated with the challenge the
newcomers presented. What she wouldn't give to
know what was going on.

James slightly inclined his head in greeting. "It has
been an age, Trevelyan."

The woman swept further into the room with
such grace that Blaire almost swore the stranger was
floating. Her eyes trailed over James as she slid behind
Trevelyan, dropping her arm to his shoulder. "Indeed.
It's been too long, Jamie."

A smile that was obviously false broke across James'
face. "Sarah, you look lovely as ever. I can't imagine
what has brought you to the Highlands."

"Can't you?" One slender, condescending brow rose.

Trevelyan leaned forward in his seat, ignoring the
exchange. Confidence nearly rolled from the man in
waves. "For a while, Miss Reese and I thought some
tragedy must have befallen you."

Miss Reese tossed her dark, wavy hair over her
shoulders, making it appear as though she'd just
tumbled out of bed. "I was overcome with worry
about you." Her crisp tone belied the comfortable
camaraderie one might find in her words.

Blaire's mind spun in confusion. Who *were* these
interloping vampyres, and what the devil did they
want? Oh, there wasn't a doubt in her mind that the
two new visitors were creatures of the night. If their
dark eyes weren't enough of a clue, it was obvious
from their words that the four of them had known

each other for many years, even centuries perhaps. A shiver snaked down her spine.

How could she possibly get these dangerous creatures to leave Briarcraig without making Aiden aware of their presence? Without endangering any of the lives of her brother's dinner party or their newly hired servants? At that moment, she wished desperately for the strength of her coven. How could she protect everyone all by herself? It didn't seem possible. There was only *one* of her, after all.

Blodswell slid Blaire even further behind him as he stepped forward. "Miss Reese," he began smoothly, "allow me to take your coat if you plan to stay."

The woman tipped her head back and laughed lightly. "Taking coats? Oh, what a change in circumstance, Blodswell."

"We are all equals here," the earl replied. "No need to stand on ceremony."

At that statement, the woman leveled her eyes on Blaire. "We're not *all* equals. I believe you're beginning to go a bit senile in your old age, Matthew."

The earl laughed. "Charming as ever, Sarah."

Sarah. Blaire hated the name instantly. As Blodswell moved closer to the intruding vampyric pair, James grasped Blaire's hand in his and squeezed with reassurance, which was surprisingly comforting. She wasn't necessarily all alone, was she? James *was* at her side and Blodswell…? Well, the earl seemed devoted to James. That was something. Hopefully he wasn't equally devoted to the other pair as well. If so, he couldn't be counted on. She had so many questions and no answers at all.

Blaire pinched James' arm to get his attention. "What—" she began with the softest voice possible; but he shook his head, his eyes imploring her to stop talking, and he clutched her tighter to his side.

Perfect. The bloody vampyres apparently had superior hearing, and she couldn't ask James anything the others wouldn't overhear. Perhaps if she could just get him alone with her, far enough away for just a moment so the others couldn't overhear her, she could figure out what they were dealing with.

"Would anyone care for tea?" Blaire asked as inspiration struck her mind. She *could* ask James to go to the kitchen with her. It wasn't the best solution, just the best she could come up with at the moment.

Mr. Trevelyan smirked, and Sarah Reese laughed out loud, a sound without any true pleasure and full of scorn. "Heavens!" The woman touched a hand to her chest. "She hasn't been with you long, has she?"

James growled at Blaire's side. "Some creatures are simply more hospitable than others."

The smile on the woman's face fell, and a furious blaze lit her eyes. "Hospitable?" she nearly spat.

"Now, now," Blodswell soothed, taking a step toward the female vampyre. "It has been so long. Can't we have a nice conversation without dredging up the past?"

"Ah," Trevelyan began, rising from his place on the settee, "but the past is all we have, is it not, Blodswell?" His voice had a slight musical quality, and Blaire tried to place his accent. It wasn't quite English; it was…something else. Welsh, perhaps?

The earl shook his head. "I'd have to disagree. We all, each of us, have a *future* as well, Mr. Trevelyan."

"Perhaps not all of us," Sarah Reese countered, settling into the seat her companion had vacated.

"I'm afraid we have been ill-mannered. Miss Lindsay, is it?" Mr. Trevelyan asked, crossing the floor toward Blaire in only two strides.

James slid his arm around Blaire's waist, securing her to him. "That's close enough, Trevelyan."

The man laughed. "For decades you chastised my lack of decorum, Kettering. And now that I'm trying to be *hospitable*, you won't allow me to make the acquaintance of your little plaything?"

"The fact that you see her as a plaything is reason enough to raise my guard. You don't need to make her acquaintance. She's under my protection, and that's all you need to know." Blaire's eyes flashed to back to James. *His protection?* Did he realize what he'd just said?

An evil smirk spread across Trevelyan's face. "And when you're gone, who will protect her then?" The corners of his lips tipped up in a hateful smile. "Hmm. And something tells me you haven't even had her yet."

Had her? James released his hold on Blaire and started toward Trevelyan, a murderous expression lighting his eyes, until Blodswell cleared his throat with a subtle warning.

"Come now," the earl began, "no one will be gone. And Miss Lindsay and her family are also under *my* protection."

If Trevelyan's coal-black eyes hadn't been focused on her, Blaire would have sighed from relief. Blodswell was clearly James' ally, and that did make her feel a bit better about their circumstances. She only wished she knew *what* those circumstances were.

"Gallant knight to the end, eh?" Trevelyan asked.

Gallant knight? Blaire's eyes shot toward Blodswell. Had he been a knight? Had he been *the* knight of the legend? More questions that would go unanswered until she could get James alone.

"The end is not here." Blodswell smiled. "Not yet anyway. And certainly not tonight. Your little disagreement with each other has gone on long enough. Don't you think it's time it was laid to rest?"

"Exactly what I have planned," Trevelyan answered.

"Blaire?" Brannock bellowed from the corridor.

She sucked in a breath at the sound.

"Is that a child?" Sarah Reese rose from her spot. "Oh, how delightful." Her incisors lowered, confirming Blaire's suspicion that the woman was indeed a vampyre.

Before she could react, James thrust Blaire into Blodswell's arms, and, within the blink of an eye, he had Sarah Reese by the throat. He'd moved so fast it was a blur. "You will not touch one hair on his head," James threatened. "Everyone within these walls is mine."

"*Havers!*" Brannock chose that moment to enter the great hall. His silver eyes widened at the sight of James with his hands around a strange woman's neck. Blodswell released Blaire so she could clutch her little brother to herself. Even so, the earl hovered over both of them protectively.

"Bran," Blaire hissed, "what are ye doin' here?"

He gulped. Brannock was as much in the dark as Blaire was. But even he seemed to grasp the severity of the situation. "Aiden sent me ta check on ye," he whispered back.

Trevelyan laughed heartily, which didn't make any sense. There was nothing humorous at all about the situation. She and Brannock were terrified. James still held Trevelyan's companion by her throat. How could he laugh? Was the man mad?

"Blodswell is right. For now," Trevelyan announced as though he was king. "Release Sarah, and we'll be on our way."

James dropped his hand, though he held his ground, staring at the woman before him. "Do not return."

Sarah Reese tossed her head back regally, and her long hair bounced over her shoulders. She stepped around the baron and toward her companion. Then she glanced back at James. "You hold no power over me, over either of us, and I find I'm enjoying the Highlands quite a bit."

Before anyone could respond, another blur of color appeared as Trevelyan and Sarah flashed past them, out the front door of Briarcraig. Brannock held tightly to Blaire's hand. "Did ye see her teeth?" he asked. "They looked like the Fergusons' hound. Long and pointy." He shivered dramatically.

"Aye." Blaire squeezed his shoulder. Then she rose to her full height and met James' eye across the room. "Tell Aiden I'll be there in a minute. First I need ta speak with Lord Kettering."

James shook his head. "Go back to dinner, Blaire. We'll talk once your guests have all departed. Our conversation will be a long one."

Fifteen

BLAIRE FOLLOWED BRANNOCK DOWN THE CORRIDOR toward the dining hall. Her younger brother stopped mid-step and looked up at Blaire, confusion and a little fear still evident on his face.

"Who were those people, Blaire?" Brannock asked.

She didn't have any idea what to say. *Well, I'm no' sure, Bran. But I think they were evil vampyres, no' ta be confused with the good vampyres, or at least I think they're good vampyres, currently in our great hall.* No, that wouldn't do. "Someone Lord Kettering kent a long time ago," she said instead.

"I dinna like them." Brannock shuddered. "That woman. She looked mean."

Mean and vicious, indeed. Blaire couldn't let Brannock re-enter the dining hall with those awful thoughts filling his head. She smoothed a hand across his brow. "I'm certain we willna see the pair ever again." And she prayed that was the truth. "Doona worry. Ye ken I would never let any harm come ta ye."

"Her teeth…" Brannock let his voice trail off.

Her teeth. The same pointy teeth that were so

similar to James'. Blaire frowned at her brother. "We should no' judge people by their appearances, Bran."

"Ah, Miss Lindsay." Malcolm Fraser stepped into the corridor from the dining hall. "I am so glad ta have found ye. The next course needs ta be served. Do ye ken if there are other guests?"

Blaire shook her head. "No, Malcolm. In fact, it will just be Brannock and myself returnin'."

"Very good, Miss." The new footman nodded, and then he opened the door to the dining hall. "I'll see ta the next course right away."

Blaire directed Brannock back to his seat and slid, once more, into her spot beside Alec MacQuarrie.

"Is everythin' all right?" Aiden asked, frowning.

Nothing was all right. Not one blasted thing. Blaire smiled and nodded. "Of course," she lied. "I just thought ta let Kettering and Blodswell reacquaint themselves with their friends." She shot Brannock a look, making it clear that any contradiction would not be appreciated.

"Did ye invite everyone in for dinner? We have plenty."

Hysterical laughter bubbled up inside Blaire, but she tamped it down. Inviting Sarah Reese and Mr. Trevelyan in for dinner was the last thing any sane person would do. She shook her head. "They've already dined." Then she glanced around the table at her brother's guests. "I am truly sorry for all the confusion and interruptions this evenin'."

"Think nothing of it, lass." Alec smiled in her direction, though the look didn't truly reach his eyes. "As long as all is well."

But all was not well for Alec. Blaire's heart clenched for her old friend. To one who didn't know him, Alec would appear as a gentleman who possessed all of life's fortunes. But he wasn't that man, not anymore, if he ever had been. After all, he never had truly possessed Cait, had he? "I received a letter from Elspeth a couple days before we headed for Briarcraig."

Alec nodded. "I saw Benjamin and Elspeth sometime ago in London. She seemed to be getting along well."

Blaire shrugged. "Do ye ken if Benjamin's family was welcomin'? I ken she was anxious ta meet them."

Footmen began placing dishes of salmon in whisky sauce before all the guests, and Blaire took a relieved breath. The food did smell wonderful. The faster everyone finished their meals, the faster they could leave. That wasn't the most hospitable thought, but getting through this meal would be torture when all she really wanted was to get answers from James Maitland.

"Elspeth has nothing to worry about," Alec confided as soon as the table had been served. "The Westfields will adore her. After all," his warm brown eyes twinkled, "she puts up with Benjamin. I'm sure Blackmoor will have the lass put in for sainthood."

Blaire giggled. "He's no' that bad." Not that she ever would have dreamed she'd come to Benjamin Westfield's defense. When she'd first met the Lycan, she'd disliked him instantly. Though, in all honesty, she'd really just disliked the fact that he'd come to steal one of her coven sisters away. But in the months since, she'd learned to accept and had even came to like the boyish werewolf, not that she ever intended to admit as much to him.

"Finally won you over, did he?"

Blaire shrugged. "He grows on ye."

"He does indeed," Alec agreed before sampling the main course.

Mrs. Fraser was a dream come true. Wherever the cook had learned her skills, Blaire was eternally thankful. The salmon literally fell off her fork, and the flavors were like nothing Blaire had ever tasted. Fortunately, dinner had the same effect on their guests, and Blaire had to endure very little in the way of conversation. After finishing off a helping of black buns for dessert, the men were ready for their port.

Blaire rose from her seat and feigned a smile for the Fyfe sisters. "Would ye care ta join me for tea?"

Heather and Crissa rose from their chairs. They mumbled some parting words to the gentlemen and then followed Blaire down one of the corridors toward a cheery, yellow parlor. "We were so glad ye were able ta join us for dinner," Blaire said as soon as she'd handed the sisters each a cup of tea.

Heather sat forward on a golden settee, her green eyes narrowing on Blaire. "I get the feelin' somethin' strange is goin' on around here, Miss Lindsay."

That was an understatement, and not one Blaire was going to confirm. "Indeed? And here I thought ye were so focused on my brother ye dinna have time ta worry about anythin' else."

Crissa Fyfe giggled.

Heather shot her sister a quelling glance. "I hardly think my interest has been so noticeable, Miss Lindsay."

"And yet I *have* noticed, Miss Fyfe. So ye clearly are mistaken."

This time Crissa contained her laugh.

Heather took a deep breath, and then her shoulders sagged forward. "Have I been that obvious?"

And then some. Blaire shrugged instead. "He's a man, Miss Fyfe. Odds are ye'd have ta hit him upside the head for *him* ta notice. They're a thick-headed lot."

Crissa frowned at that and then took a long sip of her tea. "How do ye ken so much about men, Miss Lindsay?"

"I've grown up with Aiden. I ken how he thinks."

That seemed to make sense to the girl, and she nodded in response. "Is that it? Ye have ta ken how they think?"

"What exactly are ye askin' me, Miss Crissa?"

The younger girl bit her bottom lip, but then she continued. "At dinner, ye had every single man's attention. Lord Kettering. Lord Blodswell. Mr. MacQuarrie. Is it because ye ken how they think?"

Blaire took a sip of her own tea to give her time to answer. What was she to say to that? *Alec is just watchful because he thinks a monster is after me. And while James is a monster, I don't believe it's him. Blodswell, is just keeping an eye on me.* No, they'd think she'd lost her mind. And they might be right. "I've kent them a long time is all," she lied. "They're all like brothers, in a way."

"What can ye tell me about Captain Lindsay?" Heather Fyfe's green eyes implored Blaire to give her something useful. "How do I get his attention?"

Blaire was fairly certain the lass already had it, but she decided to offer a bit of assistance anyway. After all, if Aiden was occupied with thoughts of Heather Fyfe, he might not pay too much attention to the vampyres invading their residence. "He has a sweet tooth," she offered. "Do ye bake well, Miss Fyfe?"

Crissa giggled again. "She's terrible." Then she sobered at her sister's quelling glance. "But I'm proficient enough. I'll see what I can whip up for ye." Crissa then speared Blaire with a look of her own. "They're all like yer brothers, ye say?"

Blaire nodded. "Aye."

The lass grinned. "Then what can ye tell me about Lord Kettering?"

That he's mine! Blaire choked on her own tongue. Why had she said something so utterly foolish? *They're all like brothers, in a way.* What a ridiculous thing to have said.

"Does he have a sweet tooth, too?" Crissa asked, hope filling her blue eyes.

Aye, he had two of them. Though the sight would probably send both Fyfe sisters running for cover. Blaire took a steadying breath and very calmly returned her cup to her saucer. Giving insight into Aiden's tiny mind was one thing, but James? She was not about to give up one bit of useful information. Blaire shook her head. "Trust me, ye doona want ta focus any of yer attention on Lord Kettering."

"Why no'?"

"He's a bit of an ogre," Blaire lied. Then inspiration struck. She could actually tell the truth, or part of it anyway. "I ken he looked dashin' at dinner, but he's been kent ta go forever without bathin'. Quite disgustin' ta be honest."

The young blond turned up her nose. "Truly? He seemed so…clean."

"We actually had ta burn a set of his clothes just ta get rid of the odor."

Before she could continue to fill Crissa Fyfe's ear with less than complimentary tales about James, the parlor door opened, and Aiden, Mr. Fyfe, and Alec rejoined them. Hmm. They hadn't been gone terribly long. Perhaps her brother couldn't stand to be separated from Heather Fyfe any longer than was necessary.

As Aiden made his way toward the Fyfe sisters, Blaire found herself in Alec's company. "I think your brother is a bit besotted with Miss Fyfe," he confided softly.

Blaire giggled. "Aye. And she has most definitely set her cap for him."

Alec sighed. "Well, then I wish him the best of luck. Works much better when the lass returns your affections."

Any fool could see the pain Alec suffered from. Poor man. Blaire still couldn't believe Cait had married some stranger. Still, she'd never known Cait to do something without reason. If her friend had married this Brimsworth fellow, she must have seen it, must have known he was her destiny. But even so, seeing Alec suffer tore at her heart. Blaire reached for Alec's hand and squeezed it with her own. "I am sorry. I wish I had somethin' more than my condolences ta offer."

Alec looked down at their clasped hands. "She kept saying she wasn't for me."

Then she wasn't, but Blaire couldn't bring herself to say the words, not when he looked so forlorn. "Cait always could drive one ta the edge of insanity." She laughed, hoping to cheer him a bit. "Poor Sorcha has begged her for the last year ta tell her what the future has in store for her, but Cait willna say a word. Rhiannon gave up hope of even a clue long ago."

Alec's warm brown eyes focused on Blaire. "She won't tell any of you your futures?"

Blaire shook her head. "Doin' so could jeopardize the natural course of events. It's no' fair of us ta ask her, but still it does make ye wonder what she sees in yer future. Is it good? Is it bad? Is it somethin' ye never would have guessed?" Something like a big, strapping vampyre for example.

"Wouldn't it be comforting to know?" Alec whispered.

Blaire shrugged. "Perhaps, but if it's no' what ye're hopin' for, it can be disheartenin' as well."

"And is she always right? Has a seer never been wrong?"

"I'm no' certain." Blaire released Alec's hand and folded her arms across her middle.

"What does that mean?"

Blaire shook her head. Cait's mother *had* been wrong at least once that they knew of, or she had lied about her vision. Neither of which was comforting. "Too much knowledge about yer future is dangerous. Trustin' too much in a vision is dangerous. It's best just ta live yer life the way ye feel it should be lived."

Alec rose to his full height. He clearly couldn't understand all of this. "Then what is the point of even seeing the future?"

"Well, sometimes the natural course of events needs

a little help." Was that what the previous coven had done with James? What had they seen about him that would inspire them to lock him up? The image of Sarah Reese and Mr. Trevelyan flashed again in her mind. What if the reason James had been trapped had something to do with the malevolent pair she'd met earlier that evening? James Maitland had a lot of explaining to do about that situation.

She must have frowned or looked off, because Alec leaned in closer. "Something else on your mind, Blaire?" his asked, his gaze full of concern.

Blaire frowned. "I was just thinkin' about Kettering." She must sound as besotted as Heather Fyfe. In all honesty, she probably was, but at the moment, her overriding concern was wondering what sort of danger she and her brothers were in because of the vampyre.

Alec sighed. "Why don't you go check on him?"

"Because Aiden will slowly murder me if I abandon his guests again."

With a nod of his head, Alec gestured to where Aiden and Heather Fyfe sat side by side on the settee, speaking in hushed tones. "I can't imagine he'll notice your absence, Blaire. And I can entertain Miss Crissa. No one will be left unattended."

She smiled at him again. "Ye really are wonderful, Alec."

He winked at her. "Go on."

"If Aiden asks where I've gone, will ye just tell him I've retired early?" The last thing she wanted was her brother interrupting her interrogation of their vampyre guest.

Alec shook his head. "It's really too bad you aren't

feeling well, Blaire. Perhaps you should retire a little early this evening."

If they weren't in a room full of guests, she would have kissed his cheek.

❧

James paced back and forth across the great hall while he waited for Blaire to return from her social responsibilities. Meanwhile, Matthew lounged in a settee as though he didn't have a care in the world. How could he be so relaxed? Did such ease stem from living six hundred and fifty years?

"Sit down," his maker said. "Wearing a path in the rug won't do you any good."

James scowled at his friend and increased his pace. At the very least, Matthew could help him think of a plan. What in the world were they going to do? After all, they didn't have many options. They were connected to Sarah, and, though they had no desire to be in such close proximity, she and Trevelyan would not retreat any time soon.

Blaire stormed back into the room and slammed the door shut behind her. "All right, ye *will* explain, Kettering!" she snapped. Fury made her all the more lovely. He absently shook the thought away.

James scrubbed a hand down his face and heaved a sigh. "Of course, I will," he said slowly. "Though you may not believe a word I say."

"I'm waitin'." She blew her hair from in front of her eyes with an impatient gust of breath.

Blodswell leaned forward in his seat. "Well, those two people—" he began.

But Blaire raised her index finger at him and said,

"I said 'Kettering.'" Then she swung back around to James. "Now, out with it."

James watched as Matthew bit back a grin and regarded her with newfound respect. It wasn't often a chit stood up to a vampyre who was centuries old. "We're all connected in an odd sort of way, Blaire," James started, not entirely certain where to begin his tale. He shot a look at Blodswell. "It's his fault, but that's neither here nor there." He was mumbling now. He knew, he was, but blast and damn, he didn't know how to explain the situation so it made sense.

"She called ye Jamie. What was she ta ye?" Blaire's silver gaze was so clear it was nearly painful to look into her eyes. But he forced himself to do so. "A mistress?" she pressed.

"Nothing quite that grand," James muttered.

"No' so grand as a mistress? So, she was a whore?"

She was just that. A whore. "Yes?" he tried. What did Blaire know of such things?

"Are ye askin' me? Or tellin' me?" Her foot began to tap impatiently on the floor. "Bloody hell, it's like pullin' teeth ta get the truth from ye vampyres," she groaned.

Well, it wasn't the sort of thing a man liked to admit to a woman he cared about, was it? Still, he had to tell her. She was in danger because of him. James stood tall, ready to get this all over with. "Long ago, Sarah was a whore I *knew* for a short time back when she was alive, during her first life. Do you understand?" He watched her face, trying to gauge her reaction. Blodswell still sat silently across the room, as though this was all a stage and he was the audience.

Blaire waved impatiently at James. "Aye, I

understand. Ye wanted a tumble, and ye met a willin' lass. How did she become tied ta ye?"

She would never cease to amaze him. "She was injured by one of my kind. It was somewhat my fault. So I made the decision to save her. She seemed like such a sweet chit at the time. But I was wrong."

"We all were, my boy," Blodswell said quietly as he rose from his spot and came forward to squeeze James' shoulder. "Having a woman with us helps with the ruse," he explained to Blaire.

"So Matthew gave her a ring," James blurted. He was going about this so poorly.

"My mistake compounded his," the earl said slowly as he held up his hand and pointed to the ring he wore. "Our rings symbolize life. Our hearts. Love. They allow us freedom to move as humans do without detection. They were gifts from your coven centuries ago."

"My coven," Blaire breathed as she sank into a chair and laid a hand on her chest, as though feeling beneath her gown for something. He'd seen her do so before.

"Three rings. Thrice blessed, after I saved the life of a warrior witch in battle. It was my reward."

"Ye're the knight," she whispered.

Matthew nodded. "Yes, in the flesh, so to speak. I gave one of the rings to James. And one to Sarah after she joined us. But her heart was long gone before her life was ever taken. So, she gets little benefit of it, though it does connect her to us."

"My family!" Blaire looked stricken. "We'll have ta leave. Go back ta Edinburgh at first light."

"It's too late for that, Blaire," James said. Though,

even to his own ears, it sounded like a death toll. "They will follow. Simply because I care about you."

"You weren't very good at hiding that little fact." Blodswell snorted.

Blaire dropped her head into her hands and growled in frustration. "I doona understand!"

He stepped close to her and pulled her from her seat. "I care about you." Her mouth dropped open slightly as her eyes danced across his face. "And she's finally speechless," he laughed.

She punched him none too delicately in the side. He was unable to bite back the wince she provoked. His witch was strong; he'd give her that.

"Unfortunately, Trevelyan knows I care about you. So does Sarah. That's why she was so annoyed by your very existence. She still is a small bit jealous."

"Over ye?"

James nodded once.

"And how long since ye were together?" she asked softly, almost as though she didn't want to know.

"Several lifetimes," he whispered as he traced a finger along her jaw.

"I'll just excuse myself," Blodswell mumbled as he started for the door.

"It's about time," James tossed back at him.

"You know there's only one way?" Matthew asked with a raise of his eyebrows.

Yes, he knew. James nodded tightly.

"There's only one way for what?" Blaire yelled to Blodswell's retreating back. Then she refocused on James. "Out with it, Kettering." She punched him again. "Let me hear all of it."

"If you'll stop trying to do me bodily harm, I'll tell you, you little witch," he grunted as he rubbed at the offended area.

"Is that supposed ta be an insult? And I'm no' little." She stood up even taller, reaching his chin.

"You are to me," James laughed. He forced himself to sober when she didn't laugh with him. She had a right to be worried. "Blodswell and I can protect you all. And we will."

"Why do I imagine that the word 'however' is comin'?" she muttered.

"However," he said loudly, "Sarah and Trevelyan know I care about you." Blaire's eyes softened momentarily. "That means you will be their first target. The others will be after."

"I'm no' worried about myself," Blaire insisted. "But Brannock. She wanted him. I could see it."

She had indeed, and the memory made James shiver. He pushed the thought away and tucked a fallen lock of hair behind her earlobe. "He'll be safe, and I'm worried enough for all of us," he said as he bent to kiss her lightly on the tip of her nose. James took a deep breath. "But the only way for me to protect *you* is for me to have you first. Otherwise, they won't stop until they've destroyed you."

"Have me?" she croaked. "Ye mean as in for dinner?"

He laughed. His witch made him laugh more than anyone had in decades. "Well, yes and no."

"Again with the riddles? Aye, ye want ta have me for dinner? Or no, ye doona want ta have me for dinner?"

"I want to have you for *everything*," he said quietly.

"But yes, for dinner, as you so indelicately put it." He tweaked her nose, which made her grimace.

"Ye'll turn me inta a vampyre?" she whispered, showing the first obvious bit of fear she'd ever displayed in front of him. "Is that how ye think ta protect me?"

"No," he laughed. James bent and placed his lips at the side of her neck. "It doesn't work that way. I'll simply mark you as mine and take from you, as you'll take from me. It will help protect you."

"How will I take from ye?" Her eyes darted from place to place in her confusion.

"Pleasure," he said quietly by her ear. "It's a bit of a sensual experience."

"Ye mean in the biblical sense?" Her voice shook a bit.

"Biblical?" he asked, raising his head. "I'm not certain that's the word I'd use. But I think I know where your thoughts are leading."

"Ye'll take my innocence," she clarified quickly. And she didn't look sad about it at all. In fact, she looked excited. Her heart began to beat faster. He could hear it in his head, like the clip of hooves on a runaway horse.

He couldn't help but smile at her eagerness. "Tempting as that is, Blaire, it wouldn't be honorable." Giving her pleasure and taking a bit for himself was one thing, but James could never take her innocence. Men of flesh and blood could offer her more than he ever could, and he would never take her future from her.

She surprised him by wrapping her arms around his neck and touching her lips to his. "And are ye honorable?" she whispered.

He'd always tried to be, though she was making it

much too difficult at the moment. It would be easier if she didn't put such trust in him, if his honor wasn't tested. James pressed a hand to where his heart used to be as a sudden flash of pain hit him unaware. He'd not felt pain like that in a very long time.

"Are ye all right?" She took a slight step away as though to inspect him.

James fought through the ache and took her hands in his, bringing them to his lips one by one and placing a gentle kiss there. "Never better," he lied. Thank God, she believed him. He could see the relief cross her face.

"When?" she asked. "When will ye have me? We'll have ta do it soon."

"We have hours yet. Before the dawn. They won't be back tonight."

"My brothers and the others…" she began.

"Blodswell is nearby, looking over them. I can sense his presence." He kissed her quickly and then stepped back from her. He wanted nothing more than to devour her. "So for now, go to your bedchamber and get some rest."

"Rest?" she echoed. "Wh-where will ye be?"

Counting the minutes until he could join her. "I'd like to check the perimeter, make certain everything is secure and be sure Captain Lindsay is in his own bed and fast asleep before I join you."

"Oh, of course." Blaire blushed, which was a delightful look on her. "Well, then, I suppose I'll just wait for ye." She smiled nervously and then rushed from the room.

Sixteen

BLAIRE DARTED UP THE STEPS THAT LED TO HER bedchamber. She didn't have to run. James wasn't even following her; but she needed to be alone. To drop across her bed and think about the situation she somehow found herself in. Upon entering her chamber, she tossed her spark to a couple of candles by the bedside and took her first calming breath of the night.

Her hand went to the cord around her neck. She tugged the ring from inside her dress and weighed it in her hand. There was no need to inspect it; she'd seen it her entire life. Still, she could not help but do so. It looked identical to the ring the Earl of Blodswell wore on his right hand. Was *this* the ring James sought? It couldn't be. It just couldn't be. It had been her mother's ring and the ring of every battle-born witch before her. Hadn't it?

Blaire closed her hand around the ring. The truth was that she didn't know what to believe anymore. It could be James' ring, or it could simply be a ring *similar* to Blodswell's. The earl himself admitted the rings had come from her coven. Why should her ring look different? The similarity between the two meant nothing, not really.

Her mother had told her never to remove the ring. That it would save her life someday. What to do? Show the ring to James and let him tell her whether or not it was the one he sought? Or tuck it away inside her trunk? Blaire shook her head. That didn't seem the answer. Her mother had begged her never to remove it from her neck.

She sighed, then stepped out of her slippers and fell onto the bed, staring up at the canopy. When had life become so complicated? A fortnight ago she hadn't suffered from any of her current worries. Her biggest problem had been finding the funds to pay the butcher or making certain Brannock was studying his arithmetic. Mystical rings and vampyre vengeances were a far cry from those normal domestic matters.

Then there was the matter of Cait's vision. Alec's warning once again echoed in her ears. Cait had sent him all the way from Edinburgh to protect her. She'd even confided the truth about their coven to the man to keep Blaire safe. Who had Cait seen in her vision? Was it Sarah Reese or Mr. Trevelyan the clairvoyant witch had seen? Or was it James? Kettering *was* dead, or at least the undead. If Cait meant him, she certainly had the right of it. But a monster? Blaire couldn't imagine anyone referring to James in that manner. On the contrary, he was a true gentleman. An honorable one. Yet the previous *Còig* had trapped him for some reason. Blast her mother for not confiding all to her!

James' ruggedly handsome face flashed into her

mind, but Blaire shook away the image. She couldn't afford to lose her heart to James. She needed to keep a clear head, but that seemed near impossible whenever she was in his presence. And would it be even more difficult after he marked her as his? Her face heated at the thought. What *did* he intend to do with her this evening?

A pleasure, he'd said. Heaven help her. Would she live through whatever he had planned for her? She turned on her side and hugged a pillow to her chest. Question after question popped in Blaire's mind. How long would she have to wait for him? Patience had never been her strong suit. Though, at the moment, she was relieved he hadn't yet come to her.

And what sort of warrior witch did that make her? Shouldn't she be a bit braver than that? If only she knew what to expect, it would relieve her anxiety tenfold. Question after question popped into Blaire's mind. What would he expect of her? Should she know what to do? Would it come naturally? And what should she wear? The dress she'd worn to dinner or her nightrail?

She sat up, and the ring thudded against her chest. The ring. Blaire sighed. She wasn't quite certain what to do about that situation at the moment. Show it to James or hide it? Finally, she tossed it over her shoulder so it hung down her back. She'd worry about the ring tomorrow, after she knew what she was dealing with. After all, she wasn't completely certain it even was the ring he sought.

Blaire rose from her spot and began to pace the floor. Time was ticking away. She really should change. She crossed the room to her wardrobe and shrugged out of her dress and into her nightrail. Then she flopped back on the bed to await her fate. She closed her eyes and inhaled deeply, then exhaled just as slowly. If he didn't arrive soon, she'd be a bundle of insatiable nerves by the time he did. She jumped up to pace again. As she made her first pass across the room, the soft snick of her door opening jerked her from her tumultuous thoughts.

James stepped inside and closed the door softly behind him.

"Where have ye been?" she asked quickly.

"You left me mere moments ago, Blaire," he reminded her with a smile. "But once I heard you begin to pace, I knew you'd wear a groove in the floor if I didn't make an appearance soon."

"Are ye certain this is best? Truly certain, James. I'm a battle-born witch. I can come up with somethin' ta protect myself. And my family."

"You might be able to." He nodded indulgently. Then he was across the room in a flash, tilting her chin up. "But I want to take you more than anything I've ever wanted, Blaire. Allow me a moment of selfishness in the guise of keeping you safe."

He wanted her. He truly wanted her?

"Do ye want *me*, James. Or would any pretty lass do?"

He growled lightly, his grip tightening almost imperceptibly. "If I wanted any lass, I could have gone off to find one as soon as you woke me, Blaire. But I've wanted you so badly that I've only taken sustenance from nonhuman sources since I came back to life."

"I doona understand." Her head was spinning more than a bit.

"If I'd wanted *any* lass, I could have charmed one easily and taken from her. Yet no one but you will do." He spun away from her quickly.

She tugged his sleeve sharply. "James!"

He turned to her slowly, his black-as-night eyes revealing more than his words ever could. His fangs had distended and toyed with his lower lip. Blaire stepped back.

"You have two options, love," he teased her as he took a step in her direction.

"And they are?" Her voice shook a bit.

He smiled. Of course, he noticed. "I can tuck you into bed and give you a nice glass of warm milk to help you relax. I could even tell you a story."

She swatted his chest. "Stop teasin' me."

He forced her backward with his steps until the backs of her knees hit the bed and she had no choice but to sit. It was an odd sensation, allowing him to have this power over her.

"Scoot back," he said. She didn't even think twice before she scrambled back on the bed, allowing him room to sit beside her.

"Should I just lie here quietly?"

"Do you know how to be quiet?" He chuckled. The blasted man *chuckled* as he tugged off one of his boots and let it thunk to the floor.

"Ye are no' humorous," she grunted.

His other boot hit the floor as he said, "I don't want you to lie beneath me, solid as a stone, no." His black eyes twinkled. "I like for my prey to still be moving."

"Bloody hell, I've become prey," she groaned.

"Where did you learn to curse like a man?" he asked, a grin pasted across his pretty mouth.

"I was born ta battle. It's no' likely ye will find me practicin' my parlor manners before ye'll find me sharpenin' my blade." She glanced over at him. "I am fully aware that most men find it ta be a detriment. But I never could bring myself ta care. Does it bother ye?"

"I find it charming."

"I could tell ye I'll try ta act like a lady, but I'd be lyin'."

"I prefer you just as you are." He shrugged his shoulders, as comfortable as if they were discussing the weather.

"What will I taste like?" she asked in a very small voice. She'd never been afraid before in her life. But the very thought of James sinking his teeth into her skin made her both fearful and anticipatory at the same time.

"Heaven, I'd wager."

"Ye are no' amusin' in the least, James. I am bein' serious. This is *my* flesh we're talkin' about."

"And such lovely flesh it is," he said as he trailed his fingers down her exposed forearm and then back up to rest beneath the ruffled cuff at her elbow.

"Is that where ye'll bite me?" She flipped her wrist over so he could see the blue veins that rested just beneath the surface.

"Probably not," he said absently as he lifted her wrist to his mouth and inhaled deeply. The wind from his breath tickled her sensitive skin.

"James!" She shoved him, but he just chuckled in response.

"All in due time, Blaire. Have patience, love."

"What *are* we waitin' for? I am here. Ye are here. Let's get on with it."

"Are you always so impatient?"

"Probably."

"If I wasn't here to slow you down, you would suck all the enjoyment right out of the moment."

"I am no' the one who will be doing the suckin', James."

His gaze darkened perceptibly.

❦

If James had to wait for one more moment to taste her, he'd lose what little bit of control he had left. The lavender scent of her combined with the sound of the blood pulsing within her veins was enough to make him embarrass himself completely. After all, it *had* been decades since he'd had a woman.

"Now what do we do?" she asked as she tugged at her sleeve, exposing her wrist for him again. She held it out to him. "Is this what ye want?"

"Why are you in such a hurry?" he asked as he tucked a lock of her sable hair behind her ear.

"Is it supposed ta be done slowly? Ye have ta tell me if I do somethin' wrong. I've never been a meal before."

"You could not possibly do anything wrong." He chuckled. She was absolutely perfect. Her quick wit made him laugh. Her intelligence was like an aphrodisiac. Her scent made his mouth water.

"Ye will no' hurt me, will ye?" she asked quietly as she tilted her head at him.

"I'll do my best not to hurt you. It has been decades since I've had fresh human blood." He paused briefly to search her beautiful face. So trusting. So, perfect. "Not to mention a lovely female beneath me."

James dropped his head and pressed his lips to the side of her neck. He was right. She tasted like heaven.

"Tell me what it will be like, James," she said softly as her hand came up to clutch the back of his neck. The pulse at the base of her throat sped up.

He gently lifted her and righted her in the center of the bed, then climbed slowly on his hands and knees to where he hovered over her. She looked up at him with her soft, anxious grey eyes, her dark lashes sweeping across her cheeks like fans.

James touched his lips to hers, intending to give her a comforting kiss, one meant to show her affection. But she pulled his head down to hers when he would have lifted from on top of her and moved into his kiss.

"If you do that again, I'll lay all the blame at your feet when this goes poorly," he growled.

"Ye said ye wanted yer prey ta still be movin'," she quipped.

He pressed his face into her neck and inhaled. "I'd never expect you to just lie beneath me."

James tugged at the laces of her nightrail, exposing her neck to his gaze. She shifted her body to allow him better access.

"You might have to take this off," he muttered, but watched her expression.

"Why?" Her eyes grew wide.

"I need to find the best place to bite you. And you have places all over to choose from." A poor excuse he knew. He'd probably have fared better if he'd just said 'because I want to see you naked' as she looked at him like he was speaking in tongues.

"James?" she asked hesitantly.

"Yes, love?"

"Ye plan ta only take my blood and no' my innocence?"

"That's my plan." It would be deuced hard, but he'd do it. His number-one objective was keeping her safe. His own needs were secondary.

James studied the side of her neck for another moment and frowned. "If I bite you there, it'll leave a mark."

She covered the area protectively. "So, other people would ken?" she cried, sitting up quickly.

"Aye, but only if I take you there. I can take you down there," he pointed down below her waist, "and no one will ever know. Aside from the two of us." *And I'll think about it day and night. I'm afraid I will never forget the taste of Blaire Lindsay.*

"Where is *down there*?" Her voice quavered.

"I'll show you," he assured her. He tugged at the hem of her nightrail. "Can I take this off?"

"No!" she gasped.

"There's no need to be fretful," he said softly.

"How the devil would ye feel if ye thought ye were goin' ta be a meal and then find out ye have ta be a *naked* meal?"

James bent quickly and kissed her. If he allowed her any more time to think about their situation, the sun would be up and the night would be lost. Blaire would be lost—to him.

She hesitantly kissed him back. "That's it, Blaire," he crooned to her as he kissed down the side of her neck, abrading her gently with his teeth, which were still distended. He tugged at the collar of her nightrail until he'd exposed the swell of her breast. Her nipple lay trapped by the offending fabric where it insistently pressed, as though aching for his touch.

"Blaire," he groaned. "I can't get to you if you're all covered up."

Blaire lifted her bottom from the bed long enough to tug her nightrail from beneath her and draw it over her head. James sat back and devoured her with his gaze. He'd never seen a more perfect woman. His Blaire felt no need to cover her body. Not in the least. In fact, it appeared as though she took great pride in the fact that she had his complete attention.

James reached down and shifted his trousers. She'd have to be blind not to see the length of him pressing insistently against the fabric.

"Take those off," she said. Dangerous suggestion that it was, James couldn't help but follow her command. Within seconds, he sat before her as naked as she was, his length jutting before her. She reached for him, but he grabbed her hands.

"Not tonight."

James pressed her back against the bed, coming to rest on top of her, his hot, hard body in a position where it could completely overwhelm her. In any other situation, she'd probably have fought for the upper hand. Did she trust the man who was about to take from her?

"James," she sighed as he tongued her nipple with

the utmost care. He drew the peak into his mouth as his hand explored the rest of her body. Soon she'd be begging if he didn't do something to ease the ache he was building within her. He could already tell.

"In the interest of full disclosure," he said quickly, "I'm going to bite you down here." His hand slid down her belly and into her curls, where his thumb began the most delicious movement that had her arching against him.

"There?" She sat up on her elbows and looked down at him.

James slid down between her thighs until he hovered over her most secret place, stroking softly.

"More," she cried as her hands slid into his hair, just before he pressed his lips to her center. "Bloody hell," she ground out. "Please, James," she begged.

James licked lightly across that little spot that drove her wild and closed his mouth gently over it to draw deeply on her flesh.

Blaire's heels dug into the bed as she arched against his mouth, completely unashamed of her nakedness. Unashamed of his actions. She cursed fluidly as she got closer and closer to that peak.

He replaced his mouth with his thumb and turned his head into her inner thigh, where he licked slowly across her skin. James licked across her soft flesh as his thumb continued its slow torment. He followed the cues from her body, the arch of her hips, the sounds of pleasure that left her lips, the tug of her hands in his hair, and the bite of her fingernails against his bare shoulders.

When she finally tensed, her pleasure erupting, he

bit into the soft flesh of her thigh, drawing the essence of her life into him quickly, drinking her in, ready to drown in her. He took her pleasure inside himself. And gave her his own in return. "James!" she called as he reached his own peak like a green lad against the linens. Of course, she'd felt it. Just as he'd felt her pleasure within himself, she'd felt his within her.

Blaire cried out so loudly, he feared she'd raise the rest of the family from their beds. He slowed his thumb and decreased the pressure of his mouth against her skin until he broke his hold. Then he licked gently across the wound to close the two small pricks in her skin.

James crawled up her body slowly, looking down at her, hoping his adoration shone in his eyes.

Blaire reached up a shaking hand to gently wipe the corner of his mouth where her blood had spilled over the seams of his lips. "Since that's yer first meal in decades, I'll forgive ye for bein' a little messy," she laughed lightly, her body rumbling with mirth beneath his. James flipped over onto his back beside her and then rolled her over to rest on top of him. She looked down at him, a dreamy look in her eyes. "So, how was I?"

James licked his lips and smiled. "You're a tasty little witch."

In truth, she was more than he could ever have hoped for. More than he'd ever wanted. More than he deserved. She was Blaire. His Blaire.

James sighed, knowing the idea was fanciful. If only she could be his in every way until the end of time. But it wasn't to be. Time was fleeting, he knew quite well. Still, he couldn't help but wish for more. If he could only have her always, living for eternity wouldn't seem quite so lonely. Though *always* for a vampyre and *always* for a human meant two very different things. A quick twinge of pain pulsed within his chest, and James sucked in a surprised breath. What the devil was wrong with him?

"Are ye all right?" Concern clouded Blaire's pretty grey eyes as she peered down at him.

"It's nothing," he lied once more. She had enough to worry about with Sarah and Trevelyan lurking nearby. He wouldn't give her anything else to fret over, especially not when she should still be basking in their shared moment. "Just reacting to my first bit of human blood in ages."

A relieved smile lit her face. "Ye scared me." She pressed a soft kiss to his chest.

Truthfully, he was a little scared himself. He needed to be at his strongest when he faced his enemies and this strange pain did not bode well. Hopefully, Blodswell would know what was to be done about this unfortunate complication.

James urged her to snuggle beside him, and he draped his arm protectively over her middle. "Try to get some sleep, love. We have a long day ahead of us tomorrow."

Amazingly, she heeded his advice, and before long she was fast asleep...

James' eyes flew open. It was still dark. He'd probably just dozed for a few minutes. At least he hoped it was only a few minutes. He unfolded himself from Blaire's arms and tucked the counterpane over her lithe form. No matter how strong she was in the light of day, at night she was as soft as any flower.

From the threshold, James watched the soft rise and fall of Blaire's sleeping form. She was nothing short of perfection. The last thing he wanted to do was leave her. But he needed answers and hoped beyond hope that Matthew had some for him. He quietly stepped from her room and closed the door.

He spun around and took a surprised step backward.

"Just what," Captain Lindsay began, "were ye doin' in my sister's bedchamber in the dead of night?"

Seventeen

IF JAMES HAD STILL HAD A PULSE, IT WOULD HAVE BEEN thundering through his veins. As it was, his mouth did fall open, but only for the briefest of moments. He feigned his most pleasant smile and took a step toward the captain. "Is this Miss Lindsay's room?"

Aiden Lindsay's light eyes narrowed dangerously. Had James been human, he would have feared for his life. "Aye, and ye just stepped from inside. So, I imagine this is no' new information for ye, Lord Kettering."

"So dark in there, I couldn't see my hand in front of my face. I was looking for Lord Blodswell's room and must've gotten lost."

"Gotten lost?" the Scot repeated incredulously. "I find that hard ta believe. Now, I'd like the truth, my lord, or ye can take yer things and yer noble friend and get the hell out of my castle."

And leave the Lindsays exposed for Sarah and Trevelyan? Leave without his ring? Leave without Blaire? James could still taste her on his tongue, and the very last thing he would allow was Aiden Lindsay tossing him from Briarcraig. "The truth, Captain, is I got *lost* looking for the earl. Certainly you're not challenging my honor?"

Lindsay snorted. "Honor, ye say? Would that be the same *honor* ye showed me when ye dined at my table this evenin', arrivin' late and departin' early? Or the same *honor* ye showed when ye met Mr. MacQuarrie and snarled like a beast? Or the same *honor* ye show every time my sister is within yer sight, lookin' as though ye want eat her whole?"

James gritted his teeth.

But the captain showed no sign that he recognized the threat that was certainly rolling off James in waves. "I fought with honor at Quatre Bras. I ken the meanin' of the word, better than some wealthy English peer who's never had ta show his honor in any real way. So doona think ta intimidate me, Kettering. With my years in the army, I'd wager my shot is more sure than yers." Lindsay folded his arms across his chest, and though he was shorter than James by several inches, ire shot from his eyes. "I ken the sort of man ye are."

"Do you indeed?" James clipped out.

"Aye." The captain nodded once. "I served with many men who thought they could take their pleasure with whomever they wanted without consequence. And though Blaire may no' act like it, she is a lady. One ye will no' treat lightly. If ye think ta use her in any way, I will cut yer heart right out of yer chest."

He'd have the devil of a time finding it, not that James could say as much. "There is no need for threats, Captain. I have the utmost respect for Miss Lindsay."

"Do ye now?" The man gestured to Blaire's closed

door at James' back. "Because I just watched ye leave my sister's bedchamber, and I ken full well she's been in there for quite some time. So, if ye have the utmost respect for her, am I ta expect an offer of marriage come tomorrow mornin'?"

Marriage? The desire to have Blaire rose inside James. To have her with him for the rest of her life would be a gift he would cherish for the rest of his. But he couldn't ask for such a sacrifice from her. It wouldn't be fair. A niggling thought in the back of his mind said it might not be a sacrifice if he turned her, but he shook the thought away as soon as it entered his mind. He'd watched his parents and everyone who'd been dear to him pass from this world to the next. He wouldn't wish that on her.

"I thought no'." Aiden Lindsay rose up to his full height, which barely reached James' shoulder. "I want ye gone with the mornin' light."

Blast that damn coven for taking away his power to enchant humans. It would come in bloody handy at the moment. Still, one more attempt couldn't possibly make matters any worse. James leveled his eyes on Aiden Lindsay. He focused intently on the captain's pupils, looking for the man's soul. "You never saw me this evening."

All the expression on Lindsay's face vanished, and James smiled to himself. What a stroke of luck. He could still do it. Thank God. The coven's power must have worn off. "Now go straight to bed, and I'll see you in the morning."

"In the mornin'" the captain muttered as he turned down the darkened corridor.

Relief washed over James, but it was only for a moment. Thrilled as he was to have his power of enchantment returned to him, he still didn't know what caused the pain he'd felt this evening. That worried him more than anything. Matthew had better have some damned answers.

He stormed into his maker's chambers without knocking. The vampyre barely glanced up from the book he was reading but very casually, very quietly said, "I hope things went smoothly with Miss Lindsay."

"You know damned well they did," James snarled.

Matthew finally raised his eyes from the pages of his book and lifted a brow at James. Matthew was his maker. He could feel every strong emotion James had. If he felt anger, Matthew felt it as well. If he experienced sadness, Matthew also had a sense of melancholy. If he experienced extreme pleasure as he had with Blaire, Matthew was well aware of it.

Matthew flipped his book and laid it to rest on his knee. "And yet you're in a foul temper. Why is that?"

James began to pace. Matthew simply crossed his hands in front of him and waited.

"I'm not in a foul temper," James muttered.

"Yes, everyone who attempts to wear a hole in the rug is really hiding a jovial heart." Matthew sighed dramatically, which made James want to roll his eyes since the man didn't even have to breathe to survive. "Why don't you go ahead and tell me what's the matter? Then we can solve the problem."

"I'm afraid my problem cannot be easily solved."

Matthew didn't say a word. He simply regarded him quizzically.

"I fear I want more from Miss Lindsay than I can have," James grumbled quietly.

"Beg your pardon?" Matthew asked as he sat forward.

"I swear, Matthew, it's almost like I have a heart!" James finally blurted. "I haven't felt like this in years. Decades. A very, very long time. Not since I died."

"You're falling in love with Miss Lindsay?" Matthew had the most incredulous look upon his face.

"I don't know!" James shouted.

"Would you be quiet?" Matthew reprimanded. "You'll wake the entire castle."

"Oh, Aiden Lindsay just caught me leaving Blaire's room, by the way," James admitted.

"Oh?" Matthew chimed.

"That's it? *Oh*? That's all I get? Some mentor you are."

"I have never fallen in love," Matthew said quietly. "It's difficult for me to counsel you on something I've not been through. I'm sorry."

"It's not love," James scoffed.

Matthew avoided his gaze. "You forget that I could feel a small portion of what you experienced."

"Which is *not* appropriate. A man should be able to have some secrets."

"I completely agree," Matthew said. The vampyre seemed almost too calm.

"I keep getting this pain within my chest."

"Pain?" Finally, he had Matthew's attention.

"That's what I said," James repeated as he spun to face Matthew. He looked perplexed.

"We don't experience heartache. Longing. Love. It's one of the sacrifices of having eternal life." He met James' gaze. "Allow me to ask you a question?"

"As though I could stop you," James replied.

"Would you give up eternal life for a heart? For the ability to love? For Miss Lindsay?"

James rubbed the heels of his hands into his eyes and groaned. "Without a moment's hesitation," he finally said beneath his breath. "Though there's no need to wish for such a thing, is there?" he added quietly.

"No, I'm afraid there's not."

Blaire stretched an arm over her head and slowly awoke to the sight of moonlight streaming through her window. She'd had the most wonderful dream about James and wasn't quite ready to face the world, preferring to roll it around in her mind instead. She rolled to her side and startled when she felt the cool press of the bed linens against her bare skin. Her bare skin? She'd never slept without a nightrail, not once in her life.

Blaire lifted the edge of the counterpane to confirm that she was, in fact, completely unclothed. *Havers!* Was the dream real? With shaking fingers, she touched the inside of her thigh, which was still a little sore, right where James had pierced her skin.

It wasn't a dream. Breathless, she bolted upright, clutched the counterpane to her chest and searched the room for signs of her vampyre. A shiver raced down her spine at the memory of what they'd done the night before. It was a most delicious shiver that made her toes curl up of their own volition.

On wobbly legs, she crossed the room and tossed on the first dress she touched. The sun was still an hour or two from making its appearance in the sky. She had time to make preparations to protect her family from Miss Reese and Mr. Trevelyan. Hadn't James said she'd be protected once he'd had her? And he'd certainly had her. Her belly flipped at the memory of it. He'd most definitely had her.

Blaire crept quietly from her room, down the stone steps, and out the front door. The wind from the loch rushed around her, cold and damp. She would only take a few moments. A protection spell would protect Briarcraig and its inhabitants. To do so, she needed to mark the five points of the star formation around the property. One mark for each force within the *Còig*. The marks would form a solid barrier against those who would do harm.

The only sound Blaire heard was the gentle lapping of the icy water in the loch. Cool, damp fog rose from the ground as she pressed farther into the dark night. She located a good place to etch the first point in the five-pointed star, in a huge oak that stood at the back of the property. She lifted her finger, and with a slow simmering flame, she etched a star into the century-old tree. One for each of the witches. Four more to go.

A twig snapped behind her. Blaire spun and dropped into a protective crouch, searching the darkness. "Who's there?" she called out.

Sarah Reese stepped out of the fog and into her line of sight. "I had no idea you were so talented," she said as she nodded toward the still-smoldering design.

So she'd seen that little bit of power. Blaire could show her more than that, especially if the vampyre ever looked at Brannock the way she had the night before. A fireball sparked to life above her palm, and she tossed it from hand to hand. "There's probably a lot ye doona ken about me," Blaire replied quietly.

"Apparently," the female vampyre agreed with a nod, stepping closer to her. Blaire could see the woman plotting, sizing her up, and trying to figure out how to disarm her.

Sarah Reese was certainly in for a surprise if she thought to try something so foolhardy. Still, part of Blaire hoped she would try as she ached for the opportunity to destroy James' former lover. How *did* one kill a vampyre? "I am surprised ta see ye still on Briarcraig property."

The woman laughed, though no humor emanated from her. "These days I only listen to my own counsel, Miss Lindsay. Those two can find someone else to order about."

"What do ye want?" Blaire asked. And where was Trevelyan? She doubted they separated often, so she glanced over her shoulder, searching for the intimidating vampyre.

"Where is James?" Sarah countered as she toyed with a twig she picked up from the ground, spinning it within her fingertips.

"I'm no' certain where he is at the moment. Perhaps ye'd like ta come back and call on him in the light of day. Ye can go out in the light, can ye no'? Since ye have a ring?"

The vampyre's eyes narrowed, and Blaire felt an immediate sense of satisfaction.

"James speaks too freely with you," she said crisply.

Blaire pressed on. "And I'd wager that's why ye're alone. Because yer cohort in mischief canna go out in the light of day." She glanced up at the sky. "And the sun will rise any moment."

"Smart girl," Sarah mumbled, but Blaire could almost feel the anger radiating from her.

"If ye think ye can take me easily, ye have a misguided notion of who I am, Miss Reese." Blaire twisted her cupped hand, causing the fireball to spin above her palm like a top set free by a precocious child. It caught Sarah's attention immediately, just as Blaire had planned.

"I have a feeling, Miss Lindsay," she said calmly, "that killing you would be worth being burned." Her dark eyes narrowed as she stared at the fireball.

"What ye fail ta realize is that I've already been taken," Blaire taunted, then watched closely for a reaction. "From what I hear, ye lose much of the drive once a person has been claimed by another vampyre." She allowed a small smile to cross her lips. "He already marked me, ye see."

Fury rose within the other woman. It was a fury unlike any Blaire had ever sensed. She mentally counted the weapons she had on her person. A scabbard in her boot. A knife in her pocket. A dart in her hair. Not enough. Not nearly enough to kill her. Though she could certainly try. Possibly maim her.

"Your blood may not tempt me the way it did earlier this evening, but that doesn't mean I don't have it in me to drain every drop from your body." She spoke with such coldness, such hatred, that a shiver ran down Blaire's spine.

Still, Blaire had never backed down from a fight, and she wasn't about to start by letting this no-hearted, blood-sucking vampyre ruin her record. "Interesting, is it no'?" she asked as she tossed the fireball into the opposite hand and then sent half of it back. Now she held two at the ready. Ready for her to move. "I do love the flames. See how they're infused with hues like purple and gold. So, pretty but so hot. One would think the flames would lose some of their beauty since their only fuel is my hatred for ye."

"Hatred is such a strong word," Sarah replied, her icy smile falling from her face like a crack in a looking glass. It was there one moment and the next was not.

"And yet so accurate," Blaire taunted her. "I doona ken what caused the animosity between Kettering, Blodswell, and yerself, but it doesna concern my family. Briarcraig belongs ta my brother, and though I canna keep ye from visitin' the Highlands, I would ask ye ta keep yerself from Lindsay property."

Sarah's dark eyes narrowed, and Blaire thought perhaps she'd pushed the vampyre too far. She took in the wooded area and knew that if she ran, Sarah would be on her before she could take a step.

The vampyre smiled broadly. Blaire nearly dropped the fireballs she tossed when she saw Sarah's incisors descend. The sight was chilling, not at all the way she'd felt when James had done the same thing.

"Tell me something," Sarah demanded. "Did Jamie lie and tell you that the only way to save you is for him to have you first?"

Lie? Was it a lie? No. It wasn't. It couldn't be.

The vampyre continued, "He probably told you

that the only way to save you from me was for him to claim you as his very own. Then he stripped off all your clothes and put his mouth on your most private places before he pierced the skin of your thigh and drank your life force." She shook her head softly as though she was dealing with an ignorant child. "I've been watching him use that trick for years."

He'd done just that. Blaire's heart clenched. Was it a lie? Truly? Had she been foolish to trust him? Her mother *had* captured the man, after all. Maybe there was a reason she'd imprisoned him in the cellar. Did he pose more of a risk than Blaire had assumed?

Blaire turned to walk deeper into the woods. If she only had herself to depend on, then she alone held Aiden and Brannock's future in her hands, and keeping them safe was her highest priority. And if there was one thing she could do, it was to lead the woman farther from the castle, farther from those she loved. She might not be able to kill her, but she'd do what she could to protect her family. And would die trying.

"What can you do with your flames?" Sarah asked quietly. "Aside from tossing them in the air like billiard balls?"

"Let's see," Blaire started. "I can light the path in front of us."

"And you are doing that quite well."

"I can start a fire if we should get cold."

"That's good to know."

"I can kill ye," she said in the same amiable tone.

"I don't think so." The vampyre shook her head slowly.

"It would be a mistake ta underestimate me."

"No doubt it would." Sarah stopped walking and turned to face her. "But no matter how far you try to lure me from your home, I can return there within seconds and kill them all."

"Thank ye for keepin' me informed," Blaire replied in the same sickly sweet tone she'd used before. "Tell me, have ye ever seen fire from within a whirlwind?"

She shook her head. "Can't say I have."

"That is a shame." Blaire lifted one hand to her mouth, allowed the flame to sink to that of a candle, closed her eyes, and gently blew. Almost instantly, Sarah's grunt met her ears. Then a cry of pain.

Blaire's eyes flickered open to find just what she'd suspected. Sarah stood within a swirling circle of flames that flew around and around her like wind caught trapped within a cave. If she moved one inch to the left or right, she would be burned. Unfortunately, the fire would die down in a couple of hours; but that would give Blaire enough time to get back to round up her brothers and start for Edinburgh.

"All good vampyres should have an opportunity ta see such a sight." Blaire dusted her hands together, extinguishing the last of her flames. She was quite proud of this little trick. Her weather-controlling coven sister Rhiannon had worked with her on it for months, teaching her exactly the right speed at which to blow the flame and exactly which way to twist her hand to start the swirling effect.

"You neglected one thing, Miss Lindsay," Sarah called from within the whirling inferno.

"And what might that be?" she called back. *Had* she

missed something? She didn't think so. Sarah could not possibly escape until her fire burned itself out. And she had no intention of letting the flames die down anytime soon.

"You forgot vampyres can heal," Sarah answered as she stepped through the sizzling blaze. Her skirts burned with a white flame while the fiery tongues lapped at the sleeves of her gown. Though she moved with purpose, her grimace told Blaire she felt pain from the flames, and that was somewhat satisfying. It would have been better, however, if the fire had kept the woman prisoner. There was nothing to do now but escape and hope Sarah's injuries kept her from the pursuit.

Blaire turned to run, but Sarah, still covered in flames, was on her immediately. Blaire's fire wouldn't hurt her; it was an extension of her, after all. The flames extinguished as soon as Sarah touched her, as soon as her arms wrapped around Blaire and pinned her hands behind her back. As soon as Sarah's teeth hovered over Blaine's neck.

Foolish! She'd been trapped by her own arrogance. Her coven sisters had always said that might happen one day.

"I may not have the desire to pleasure you, but I find the idea of killing you to be irresistible." The smell of Sarah's singed flesh burned Blaire's nose.

Blaire kicked. And tried to bite. And flung her head toward the vampyre's nose in hope of crushing it. But Sarah dodged all of her blows. Blast her, she was strong. There was not one bit of softness in her grasp. Why hadn't James mentioned how strong those of his kind could truly be?

Sarah twisted Blaire's arm behind her back, pushing it painfully up until Blaire thought it would break in two. Finally, she let out a whimper. Damn her human sense of feeling.

Sarah pushed her hair from her shoulder and gazed at her neck and lowered her head.

Suddenly, Blaire felt a blow to her side, a hard hit that bowled both her and Sarah over. She tumbled, head over heels as the vampyre rolled away from her. Blaire jumped to her feet and started a fireball glowing within her hand.

James!

His black hair shone in the light of her fire, his eyes searching her body. He held out one hand to her. "Come here, Blaire."

Without even thinking, she placed her free hand in his. His cold grip closed around her fingers as he drew her to his side. But was that where she belonged? Could he truly be trusted? Her emotions were too jumbled to know for sure.

"You've just made a grave mistake, Sarah." The steely tone of James' voice made Blaire's hair stand on end. She'd never heard anyone so angry.

Sarah shrugged unrepentantly, a ghost of a grin on her lips. "I like her fire."

Apparently, that was the wrong thing to say. James leapt toward Sarah so quickly that his movement was a blur, and then they were gone into the darkest recesses of the forest. All the air in Blaire's lungs rushed out. One moment she was between two vampyres and the next she was all alone in the silent woods. She couldn't even hear them anywhere.

"James!" she called, but there was no answer, nothing other than the icy breeze that rattled the bare branches of the nearby trees. "James!"

She stood still, trying to regain her bearings. She wasn't even certain which way they had gone. How could she even help him if she didn't know which direction to go? Then the answer hit her.

Blodswell!

James said the two of them were connected. That they could sense each other.

Blaire clutched a handful of her skirts and bolted for the castle. The icy, early morning air stung her lungs as she pushed herself through the woods faster than she'd ever gone. But there was no time to waste.

Just as she entered the clearing, Blaire spotted the Earl of Blodswell, and she nearly sagged from relief. Less than a second later, the vampyre was before her, keeping her from falling to the ground.

"James," she gasped, trying to catch her breath. "A-and Miss Reese."

The knight nodded as though he understood. "It's all right, Miss Lindsay." He gently directed her toward the castle entrance. "I know where to find him. Go back inside." And in a flash he was gone.

Blaire blinked into the darkness after him. It was as though Blodswell had never been there. The speed with which these creatures moved was incredible. How could one ever keep up with them?

She took a steadying breath and told herself that everything would be all right. Blodswell hadn't looked concerned. Instead, he'd appeared confident. That realization made her relax just a bit. Though she wanted to finish her protection spell, she needed to make certain James was all right first. Following others' commands was never something she'd readily done, but in this instance, Blodswell was probably right. She should go back inside the castle until her vampyre returned.

As she hastened toward Briarcraig, Blaire noticed a glimmer of light on the horizon. Sunrise.

Her breath stuck in her throat and she clutched her mother's ring through her heavy wool gown. She should have given it to James last night when she had the chance. It might not be his ring, but it also *could* be. And if it was, he would need it now more than ever. If he didn't survive the morning, she'd never forgive herself.

A warm, golden glow glistened off the loch, and Blaire's heart sank at the sight.

Eighteen

JAMES HELD SARAH'S COAT IN HIS GRASP AND GLARED AT his one-time lover. He'd never been as afraid as when he'd seen her nearly pierce Blaire's neck with her teeth, nearly destroy the woman who had somehow come to mean so much to him. All sense of reason and decency had drained from his soul in that moment. He still didn't feel like himself, and the longer he stared at Sarah Reese, the angrier he became. "You will leave Miss Lindsay out of this," he sneered. "This has nothing to do with her."

And it didn't. His feud with Sarah had been waged long before Blaire was born, long before her mother or grandmother had been born either, for that matter.

"Oh, I beg to differ, Jamie," she taunted him, a wicked glint twinkled in her eyes. "You forget how long I've known you. I saw the way you looked at her."

Which was neither here nor there. Blaire had nothing to do with Sarah. "How I *look* at her is none of your concern."

She leaned closer to him until her lips brushed the

side of his jaw. "Oh, it's very much my concern. You made promises to me."

James snorted. "I did no such thing." It wasn't the first time they'd had this argument.

"You most certainly did." Her voice rose with indignation. "You promised me the life I'd always wanted, a family."

"We *were* a family. You, Matthew, and me. It just wasn't enough for you."

She snorted and then wriggled from his hold. "That wasn't a family. It was an *arrangement*." She spit the word as though it was a curse. "You never said vows to me. Never promised to forsake all others." She kicked at a clump of dirt, but beneath it all, James knew she was seething inside. "That much is obvious," she finally confessed. "Yet you'd do it so easily with that *human*? That Lindsay woman?"

In a way he'd never expected to care for anyone. In a way he hadn't known he was capable of. But revealing any of that to Sarah would be the gravest mistake. "As usual, you don't know what you're talking about. I owe Miss Lindsay a debt. That is all."

"A debt?"

That was true enough. He'd still be trapped in that dank cellar if Blaire hadn't freed him. "I was in a spot of trouble, and she helped me. So, she and her family are under my protection."

Sarah scoffed. "You must think me a fool to believe such nonsense."

James shrugged. "Believe what you will. You've always made up your own mind."

Just then a searing pain hit James' arm. He glanced

down and realized morning light had filtered through the trees to land on him. Quickly, he moved to a darker area in the woods, but he couldn't stay here long.

A look of confusion lit Sarah's eyes, and then they grew wide with glee. "Have you misplaced your ring, Jamie?"

He said nothing but gritted his teeth, searching the area for the darkest place he could find. How long could he remain in the open? How bright would the sun grow? And was there any safe place to hide?

"What a foolish thing to have lost." Sarah's laugh taunted him. "You should have a wife to remember such things for you. It's such a shame you never offered the position to me." She sighed wistfully. "Well, we live and learn."

The sun grew steadily brighter, and James was forced to close his eyes to block out the light. On his hands and knees, he scrambled close to a line of heavy bushes, hoping it would help shield him from the rising sun.

Sarah knelt beside him and whispered, "Do enjoy the sunrise. It looks to be a glorious day." Then she was gone, leaving him to suffer alone.

Scorching pain washed over his body, and James hunched himself into a ball. A loud ringing echoed in his ears until he could hear nothing at all.

Finally, after what seemed a lifetime, a cool shadow of darkness encompassed him. He was able to make out a sigh and then Matthew's soothing voice, "Oh, James, whatever *would* you do without me?"

"Please tell me you didn't leave the Lindsays

unprotected," James snapped as he pulled his arm in closer to his body to fully take advantage of Matthew's shadow.

"Sarah has not returned to the castle. I would know it if she had. Besides, I believe you have more pressing matters to worry about at the moment," Matthew reminded him. "Such as how to survive the sunrise."

There was that. "If I move quickly, I could possibly make it back to Briarcraig. Perhaps," James said, mulling it over in his mind. He'd be burned to a cinder and in more pain than anyone should ever have to experience, but he'd do it if that meant getting back to Blaire. He didn't like leaving her unprotected, no matter where Matthew thought Sarah had gone.

"Perhaps if you had a heavy cloak and a parasol," Matthew added as he scratched his chin. "Somehow I don't see Miss Lindsay as someone who owns a parasol, however."

"I know, isn't it grand?" James said, a smile finally crossing his lips.

"Oh, young love," Matthew muttered. "Nearly sickening in its intensity."

"Jealous." James couldn't help but grin.

Matthew laughed. "Oh, jealous indeed." He stripped off his long greatcoat and draped it over a nearby tree, blocking out the sun. Then he tossed his jacket to James. "Keep yourself covered until I return."

"I told you I'm not suicidal," James grumbled.

The comment earned him a grin from his maker. "Indeed? You went after Sarah right before sunrise. You could have fooled me."

And given the same situation, he would have done so again. Blaire would be lifeless otherwise. "Can you castigate me later? It's too bloody bright for comfort, if you don't mind."

After a quick nod of his head, Matthew vanished. And though it felt like forever, it had to be less than five minutes later when the earl returned with a large, wool counterpane. "This should do."

After Matthew had made certain the material covered James completely, the two of them made their way back through the woods to Briarcraig. Careful to keep his eyes closed, James allowed his maker to guide him along the path and kept to the shadows as much as possible.

James ached to see Blaire. He couldn't wait to rush to her. To hold her. To ensure himself in a very basic way that she was well.

"Almost there," Matthew said as their boots moved from the soft earth to rocky gravel.

But James didn't need to be told that. He could feel her presence nearby. In the next moment, he was nearly bowled over, tackled to the ground by Blaire as her lavender scent washed over him.

She rained kisses all over his face. "Oh, I'm so glad ye're safe. I was so worried. And then the sun came up."

"Which I'm just managing to keep from scorching poor James alive," Matthew said somewhere above them. "Can we move this reunion into the castle, Miss Lindsay?"

"Oh!" Blaire leapt to her feet. "I'm so sorry, I dinna think…"

James immediately missed the glorious weight of her, pressing him into the ground.

"I'm sure," Matthew's voice held more than a hint of amusement, "that Kettering didn't mind your exuberance, my dear."

James managed to keep from growling at his maker when the earl helped him back to his feet. Not that he really had reason to be angry with the man. In fact, he owed him his life. But at the moment, he'd rather Matthew not save him from Blaire. Anytime she wanted to throw herself into his arms, he was more than willing to have her there.

"You can grumble at me later," Matthew whispered. Damn the man for being able to read him so well.

Blaire tugged James' hand into her own and dragged him the short way into the castle through the garden entrance. Once inside Briarcraig, James threw off the wool counterpane and drew Blaire into his arms. He wanted to run his hands all over her and make certain she was completely unharmed after her encounter with Sarah. Which reminded him…

"Have you lost your bloody mind?"

She reared back to get a good look at him.

"I wasna thinkin' about the sun. I am sorry."

He shook his head and was glad Blodswell had managed to disappear somewhere. "I'm not talking about the sun, Blaire. You knew Sarah and Trevelyan were lurking about. Why the devil did you go off alone this morning? Don't you know what could have happened to you?"

She rose herself up to her full height. "I'm no' some helpless waif, James."

No, she was worse. A helpless waif at least knew she was helpless. "And yet Sarah still had you by the neck. One second later, Blaire, just one more second, and you'd have been lost to me. Lost to your family. Your coven."

She had the good sense to gulp, and for a moment, James felt a bit like a cad for laying into her. But it was for her own good. She might be part of a powerful coven; but right here, right now, she was a lone witch—one who couldn't handle vampyres like Sarah or Trevelyan on her own. The quicker she understood that, the better it would be for everyone.

"I was just castin' a protection spell." Her pretty brow furrowed. "Ye said after ye had me that I would be safe. And…"

"*Safer*," he stressed the last syllable. "You can't go about taking chances, Blaire. Not with the two of them around."

"Well, clearly I dinna think I was takin' a chance, James." She folded her arms across her middle. "I was just tryin' ta protect my family."

James shook his head. Had he been a living, breathing creature, she'd have taken ten years off his life. "I told you that Blodswell and I would protect you all. Do you have so little faith in me?"

❧

Blaire stared at the vampyre. After the things Sarah Reese had told her, did she still have faith in James? It was possible the woman was lying. But how did she know word for word what James had said to Blaire, unless he'd used the same ruse time and time again?

"I'm no' used ta puttin' my faith in anyone other than the members of my coven or my brothers."

He looked as though she'd struck him. After a moment he seemed to find his voice. "I apologize. I thought we were closer than that. I thought we had a connection."

"And how many women have ye had a *connection* with?" she blurted out before she could stop herself.

James' eyes darkened to the color of a moonless night. "I beg your pardon?"

Perfect. What was she to say now? She'd been so happy he was safe. Overjoyed with relief. Why did he have to ruin it by berating her as soon as he laid eyes on her? She shrugged her answer and tried to maneuver her way around the hulking Englishman, but he easily caught her arm.

"Answer me, Blaire."

She met his eyes and straightened her spine. She wasn't certain if she could trust him. But she was not a coward. "Miss Reese told me, James."

"Told you what, exactly?"

Was he going to make her say the dratted words? She sighed. Very well. "She told me how ye've been usin' the 'the only way ta keep ye safe is for me ta claim ye as my own' ruse for decades or longer."

A muscle in his jaw ticked.

Well, that wasn't a good sign of innocence, was it? Blaire swallowed a bit of nerves and continued. "And she knew exactly where ye took from me. She described it in detail." Heat crept up her cheeks.

"So that's it, is it?" He released her hand. "Sarah Reese nearly killed you this morning, and yet you'd take her word over mine?"

Blaire's belly twisted at his words. Why did he have to say it like that?

"I risked my very life to save you from her, and you believe *her* over *me*?"

"Then how did she know?" Blaire pressed.

"Have you considered that what I told you was the truth? That the best way to keep you safe *was* for me to claim you as my own? And if that's true, if I'm *not* the liar you seem to think I am, that Sarah would know the truth of that, too? That Sarah would know that was the best way for me to protect you? She is a vampyre after all. She knows the same things I do."

Blaire's eyes dropped to the floor. She hadn't considered that at all. She'd been so shocked when the woman had repeated nearly word for word what James had said that she hadn't considered another explanation.

"I'm nearly two hundred and fifty years old, Blaire."

Her eyes slowly rose to meet his. Until now she didn't really know the first thing about him. Two hundred and fifty years old? Good heavens, the things he must have seen.

"You can't expect innocence from a man who has lived that long. Have I bedded other women? Yes. Have I taken blood from them? Yes. That's what I am. It's how I've survived. Unlike others of my kind, I don't want a woman to wear my mark on her neck or some other exposed bit of skin for all to see. If given the choice, I prefer a woman's leg to preserve her reputation, and Sarah knows that about me as well. I won't mark a woman for the world to see unless she's mine." He caught her gaze. "And I have never done so. Nor have I felt an overwhelming desire to do so. Until you."

She felt like the biggest fool. "Oh." Her voice came out very small, and it was all Blaire could do not to look away.

"Oh, indeed." He turned and stalked away from her down the small corridor, disappearing around a corner.

Blaire watched after him, unable to speak. Even if she had the ability, she wasn't certain what she could possibly say. She'd nearly gotten him killed and then questioned his honor. If he never spoke to her again, she couldn't blame him.

&

A knock sounded at James' door. He didn't even lift his head from the pillow. He glared at the handle, looking for the tiniest movement, yet he said nothing. He wasn't in the mood for friendly conversation.

"How long are you going to sulk?" Matthew's voice came through the door.

"You can go straight to the fiery depths of hell."

A laugh was his friend's response. "I see your charm is still intact." Then the man had the gall to open James' door anyway. "The role of brooding nobleman doesn't suit you."

"Then you'll have to come back when I'm feeling more jovial."

Of course, Matthew paid him no heed and stepped over the threshold. "Poor Miss Lindsay has been just as out of sorts as you are." He closed the door softly.

James growled low in his throat. If his maker didn't turn on his heel and march right back outside…

"Luckily, that little scamp of a lad was able to drag her from her doldrums."

"Bloody wonderful for her."

Matthew smirked, which was beyond annoying. "So she made a mistake," the earl began. "Who hasn't in their life?"

"Even after Sarah tried to *kill* her, Blaire believed her word over mine."

"Something I'm certain she regrets. And you, my dear friend, risked your own life to save your pretty witch this very morning."

Which was exactly his point. "And yet she *still* believed Sarah."

Matthew shrugged as though that detail meant nothing. "And you're letting Sarah win at her game."

"I'm doing nothing of the sort."

"You keep forgetting I know how you feel about Miss Lindsay."

Something James would rather forget at the moment. Blast Matthew for dredging it all back up. "I don't believe I actually invited you into my chambers."

The Earl of Blodswell laughed. "No, you wished me to the devil, a bit less delicately." He sat on the edge of James' bed. "Tell me you're not really going to let some error in judgment stand in the way of your happiness."

"She has no faith in me, Matt."

"Sarah manipulated her."

"I thought we had a bond, something…magical."

Matthew sighed. "Your eyes were closed when we returned this morning, James. So you didn't see the relief and joy that radiated from Miss Lindsay when she spotted you. It was the most beautiful sight I've ever seen. Even after listening to Sarah's poisonous tongue, even believing the worst about you, she *still* couldn't keep herself from running into your arms."

He hadn't thought about it in those terms. Still, he wasn't ready to concede. "So you're saying she's daft?"

Matthew cuffed him on the head. "No, I'm saying *you* are if you give up on Blaire Lindsay."

He'd always hated it when Matthew was right. And James knew from the depth of his soul that his friend was right this time as well. "Where is she?"

"Participating in the strangest bit of play with her brothers."

If his curiosity hadn't already been piqued, that vague statement would have done it. James pushed up on his elbows and frowned at his oldest friend in the world. "All right. You win."

Matthew winked at him. "Oh, no, my boy. In *this,* I think you are the winner."

James followed Matthew down to the castle's main floor and directly to the great hall. Once he got there, he couldn't quite believe the sight that awaited him. The newly refurbished hall was sparkling clean, the drapes replaced and new rugs lined the floors. It looked exactly like what one might find in any Highland castle, except for one thing. In the middle of the room, Captain Lindsay and Blaire were tangled together, a mass of arms and legs, wrestling for position. Matthew winced from beside him when the captain took an elbow to his midsection and bent double.

"Ye doona fight fair, Blaire," the captain groaned.

"No one said I have ta fight fair," she laughed as she released him from her grasp. Blaire stood up quickly as though she sensed James' presence. "James!" The sound seemed torn from her. "I-I mean, Lord Kettering," she corrected. Her cheeks colored prettily when she realized all the men's eyes were on her.

James couldn't drag his gaze away from her. The wounds of the morning were still fresh in his memory, but seeing the emotion in her eyes made it impossible for him to remain angry at her. Who knew he was such a fool?

Captain Lindsay stood and then dropped into a crouch, circling her as he waited for her to ready herself for his next approach. "Stop making eyes at the baron, Blaire, and prepare ta be flattened."

"Ye wish," Blaire scoffed, but she took up her fighting stance.

"Do they do this often?" Matthew asked quietly. His eyebrows were raised in awe, and James could tell Blaire had Matthew's admiration. She wasn't the average lady, his witch, not in the least. He couldn't be happier about that fact.

"Apparently they do this *very* often," Alec MacQuarrie chimed in from his seat on the settee. He shook his head and grinned, and then rubbed his hands together. "Brannock suggested I even take a turn next."

"Ye'll never best me, Alec," Blaire taunted with a grunt as she twisted free from Captain Lindsay's grasp, her moves quick and efficient. But a little piece of James' heart clenched at the familiarity between the two. MacQuarrie could find his own damn witch.

"Does he ever win?" Matthew gestured to the captain as he went to stand behind Brannock's chair.

"Only when she lets him." The lad giggled loudly.

She was a formidable lass, but a worthy opponent might make her stronger and better. James smiled to himself as he imagined the training they could engage in together.

"She doesna *let* me do anythin'," the captain grunted, quite obviously paying attention to his surroundings. A smart man he was.

"Keep tellin' yerself that, Aiden," his witch taunted. James tried to bite back a grin, while Matthew laughed aloud at her audacity. "From what I heard, ye ate an entire platter of Heather Fyfe's treacle biscuits. They've made ye more sluggish than normal."

That spurred the captain forward. He made his move, grabbing one of her legs quickly and pulling hard enough that she landed on her back with a whoosh of air escaping her lips. James stepped toward her, his need to protect her so great that it was nearly inexhaustible.

But Matthew brought him back to his senses. "Great bit of *sport*, isn't it, James?"

Aiden Lindsay grinned down at his sister. "Did ye let me do that?" he taunted from his position above her. He had her fairly well pinned to the floor. And she was none too happy about it. Something told James she could make him move but withheld her power to save his pride. Captain Lindsay called out, "Bran, come and tickle her while I have her down."

James leaned casually in the doorway. This must be something they did a lot, because Brannock jumped into the fray with enthusiasm. James couldn't fight the laugh that escaped his throat at their antics, or at Blaire's pleading for them to stop. She was ticklish. He'd have to remember that.

"Enough!" Blaire finally cried out over her own laughter. "Let me up."

The captain stood and held his hand out to her, which she took without hesitation.

When she rose, she brushed at her skirts and pulled the loose combs from her hair, which were now refusing to do their jobs. Her sable tresses spilled over her shoulders.

"Beautiful," James breathed.

"Pardon?" Captain Lindsay turned in his direction, his breathing still labored. Blaire looked no worse for the battle. She wasn't even breathing hard.

"A *dutiful* brother, I said." James shrugged. It took all his strength to pull his gaze from Blaire.

"Is it my turn?" Alec MacQuarrie said from the settee.

The devil it was. That man would put his hands on Blaire over James' dead body, though that probably wasn't the best turn of phrase. James took a step toward him.

"Actually, Mr. MacQuarrie," Matthew said as he stepped into James' path, "Miss Lindsay looks a bit winded right now, and I was hoping we might discuss your studies on the Third Crusade at greater length." Always the heroic knight, saving people from themselves or from James' temper.

"You mean Sir Matthew Halkett?" the Scot asked, his brow rising with interest.

"The first Earl of Blodswell, yes." Matthew gestured

toward the open doorway. "You mentioned him when we first met. And I've heard the family legends, of course, but I'd love to hear your take on the tale.

And see how accurately his heroics were portrayed in this day and age. Incorrigible narcissist. James suppressed a smile at his maker. It was best not to encourage the man, even though he was helping James at the moment.

"A knight?" Brannock Lindsay gushed. "Oh, can I hear, too, Mr. MacQuarrie?"

Alec MacQuarrie glanced around the room and shrugged. "I don't see why not."

"Oh, then let's retire to the library," Matthew suggested. "Always the best place to hear old legends, don't you agree?"

"I do love a good library," MacQuarrie agreed.

"Oh, then you'll love Briarcraig's," Matthew gushed. "There's a complete treasure trove of old tomes in there. I don't think they've been touched for ages."

The captain grumbled something under his breath about blasted libraries, but James couldn't make out the exact words.

"Let's take a look, shall we?" MacQuarrie suggested "My curiosity has been piqued."

Matthew directed Brannock and Captain Lindsay over the threshold and clapped his hand companionably on Alec MacQuarrie's back as they strode from the room. "I truly can't wait to hear your version, Mr. MacQuarrie."

An amused grin played on Blaire's pretty lips. "He likes ta hear tales about himself?"

"It's a weakness." James smiled back.

She stepped toward him, reaching out her slender arm. "I am so sorry about this mornin'."

James held up his hand to stop her. "I'm the one who's sorry." He moved a lock of hair from her forehead to look down at her. "I'm sorry about everything that happened with Sarah, but please believe that I've never lied to you."

She bit her lip, and he hoped beyond reason she believed him. How could he prove his honor?

"I have told you more truths, Blaire, than I have ever told anyone," he admitted. But it was true. He had.

Something James didn't understand danced across Blaire's face, and her grey eyes twinkled. "I believe ye."

Though he didn't need to breathe, James sighed with relief. "You do?"

She nodded. "Did ye want ta try yer luck with me?"

James thought he already had. And was the luckiest man alive. "Try my luck?"

"In the ring, so ta speak," she clarified. "Like with Aiden."

A challenge? God, he loved her fire.

"You shouldn't allow them to win. They'll never appreciate all your strength if you do."

"How did ye ken I let him win?"

"You have more talent for fighting in your little finger than he does in his whole body." It was a rare compliment, one he'd never paid to a lady. But something told him she liked it more than fancy earbobs or men who tried to steal kisses. She beamed under his praise like a beacon on a stormy night.

Still grinning, she shrugged. "They enjoy it. And they ken how ticklish I am. It's fun for them."

He'd taken note of that fact as well. "Ticklish, indeed?" he asked. That was one thing he'd have to find out for himself. "I *did* see a hole in your defense, however."

"Ye did no'!" she gasped, as outraged as a *normal* chit would be if he said her gown was a ghastly color.

"When he went to grab your leg, you could have pushed his head down and taken an advantage."

"Care ta show me?" she taunted. He adored the glint in her eye. And was so happy she believed in him that at the moment, he'd do anything she wanted.

"You can't win against me, Blaire," he said quietly. "It's not possible. I'm too strong, and I was trained by the very *humble* Sir Matthew Halkett, knight of legend and lore."

"Aye, I ken. But show me what ye were talkin' about." She grinned at him. "Unless ye're afraid, of course." She spun away from him, her skirts swirling around her ankles.

James tossed his jacket across the room where it landed on the settee. "Just remember you asked for this."

She laughed in response.

He could listen to the sound all day, but he'd rather get his hands on her, and she had given him the perfect excuse to do so. "Get ready, Blaire," he warned quickly.

Suddenly serious, she dropped into the same crouch she'd taken with the captain. Then he showed her the move and how she could defend herself.

"No' bad," she admitted. "One more time?" She made a come-hither motion with her hands. "This time, ye come at me."

James dropped to a sparring stance and circled her, his hands ready to grab her quickly as soon as the opportunity presented itself. Finally, she blinked a second too long and he lunged for her. A moment later, he had her rolled beneath him, the backs of her hands pressed to the floor.

"You'll have to try it with your brothers," he suggested. "You can't win with me. You should have listened when I told you the first time." He chuckled at the way she pressed her lips together.

"A wee bit cocky, are ye?" she asked. She didn't even struggle beneath him. She simply lay there and blinked her pretty grey eyes at him, her long lashes sweeping her cheeks like delicate fans. James instantly hardened.

"More than a wee bit cocky, Blaire," he assured her. Much more.

Blaire rocked her hips beneath him, which made him groan aloud. "Get off me," she commanded quietly. But there was no conviction in her voice.

"If I thought that was what you really wanted, I would be happy to oblige, Blaire. But I don't think it is," he whispered back to her, just before he let his lips graze her own, which were parted in surprise.

Never a man to pass up an opportunity, James immediately deepened the kiss, coaxing her with his tongue to respond. And respond she did. She warmed up hotter than fire on a cold winter night. What she lacked in experience, she made up for in enthusiasm.

The lass was fire and he would surely be burned, as would she, if he allowed their little game to continue. But he couldn't, for some reason, pull away from her.

Blaire shifted marginally beneath him, giving him enough room to slide one knee between her thighs, which immediately parted for him.

James kissed his way down her jaw line and then hovered over the side of her neck, watching her pulse beat frantically beneath the fragile skin of her neck. His lips touched her throat gently. He could kiss her softly there without taking from her, without sinking his teeth into her neck, couldn't he?

Unfortunately, it wasn't meant for him to find out. Blaire shifted beneath him, and he immediately caught her move. The little vixen was moving to knee him in the groin. "Oh, no, you don't want to do that," he whispered beside her ear. But he appreciated her spirit. Even then, she was plotting to escape his hold.

Before he could even think to dodge her blow, Blaire struck out with the heel of her hand and slammed it into his nose.

"Bloody hell," he grunted as he moved himself from atop her body. James wiggled his nose with his fingers to see how much damage she'd done when she shoved him over onto his back and landed on top of him.

"Doesna feel very good ta be on the bottom, does it, James?" she asked. In truth, the lass had flipped him with such force a normal man would have been knocked unconscious. He was happy in that moment not to be a normal man.

Moving as fast as he could, James dragged her entire body on top of him, untangled her skirts from around her legs and pulled her to where she lay astride his hips with one knee on the floor on each side of him, his hands holding the backs of her thighs.

"On the contrary, I like having you on top of me." He arched his hips and pressed against the center of her, letting her feel how hard he was. "I *ache* for you," he growled. The curtain that was her hair hung around them, blocking out the rest of the world. He lifted one hand and cupped the side of her face in his hand. "I want to be inside you," he softly admitted.

The lass didn't back away. In fact, she trembled above him. She wanted him, too.

"I want to taste every inch of you," he continued as he tugged the laces of her bodice. When he'd nearly freed the flesh that quivered with her every breath, she abruptly froze on top of him, catching his hand in hers and holding tightly.

"Someone is comin'," she whispered, as she lifted herself from on top of him and righted her clothing.

"That is my fondest wish," he sighed as he laid his head back against the floor in defeat.

A quizzical look sparked in her eyes, and James realized she didn't have any notion of what he was talking about. Could she be any more charming?

He moved to help her fix the neckline of her gown. The cord she wore around her neck was stretched tightly. He slid one finger beneath it and tugged. "What *is* this thing you wear around your neck?"

He pulled, and, from its safe haven between her breasts, he tugged free his *ring*. His very own ring. The witch had it all along. And hadn't even told him.

"Damn it all to hell, Blaire," he growled, before he yanked it from her neck with a hard tug.

She sputtered and reached for the cord. "I was goin' ta ask ye—"

But whatever she meant to say died on her lips the moment Captain Lindsay called from the corridor, "What are ye doin' in *here*? MacQuarrie is tellin' some stories of heroics ye willna want ta miss."

Nineteen

BLAIRE COULD ONLY STARE AT JAMES. HIS BLACK EYES darkened with fury as he pulled the ring from her cord and shoved her heirloom onto his finger.

"Miss Lindsay was just on her way," James growled, his scathing look barely touching her.

Why did he have to find her mother's blasted ring? She had every intention of showing it to him, asking if it was the one he sought. Clearly it was, or he *thought* it was. And after the morning spent in abject misery, Blaire had no intention of spending the rest of the day the same way.

She glanced at Aiden and smiled tightly. "Will ye remember the details and tell me later? I'm havin' a conversation with Lord Kettering."

Aiden's eyes shot to James and then back to Blaire, suspicion clouding his expression.

Blaire frowned at the dolt. "Do ye remember the talk we had, Aiden, on the way ta Strathcarron? The talk about Lord Kettering?"

She ignored the grumble from James' side of the room and watched realization dawn on her brother's face. Blaire raised her brow meaningfully. How many hints did Aiden need?

"That conversation?"

"Aye," she ground out. "Now can ye give us a few moments alone?"

"Uh." Aiden backed up. "Of course. Take yer time." Then he turned on his heel and quickly disappeared.

"What was that about?" James growled.

Warmth crept up Blaire's cheeks. She was not about to tell James about that silly conversation with Aiden. She shook her head. "Nothin', I just needed ta get rid of him."

The two-hundred-and-fifty-year-old vampyre scoffed. "Do you think I'm that inept? That you can bat those pretty grey eyes at me and I'll forget that you kept my ring from me? That you and," he gestured dismissively toward the doorway, "Captain Lindsay have been having mysterious conversations about me?"

Pretty grey eyes? Blaire would like to bask in the compliment, but he was still glaring at her. "It wasna like that."

"Oh, wasn't it? You and Captain Lindsay haven't been discussing what to do with the vampyre under your roof? You haven't been discussing how to finish the job your mother started by locking me in this godforsaken place to begin with?" He paced the floor, not even bothering to look at her. "You haven't been discussing what a fool you've made of me? You haven't been—"

"No!" she yelled. "That's no' it at all."

James stopped in his tracks and narrowed his eyes menacingly. "Then what is it?"

She had never felt so mortified in her life. "I told him I thought I could brin' ye up ta scratch." It came out as a whisper, and she couldn't look him in the eyes.

In a flash he stood before her. "What did you say?"

Was he going to make her repeat it? Not in this lifetime. Blaire shook her head. "He wanted ta throw ye out, and I had ta find a way ta stop him. It was the only thing I could think of."

With the crook of his finger, James tipped her chin back until she met his eyes. "Are you saying your brother would grant his blessing to a *vampyre*?"

Could she be more mortified? "Aiden doesna ken ye're a vampyre. And *if* he believed me, I'm sure he couldna care less."

A strange look crossed James' face, and Blaire had no idea how to interpret his expression. "You think it wouldn't matter to your brother if you…married a vampyre? Does he care so little for your safety?"

"That's no' it." Blaire shook free of his grasp and stepped away from James. He was too close, and the questions he was asking were too humiliating.

"Then tell me," he urged from behind her.

Blaire simply shook her head.

"Answer me, Blaire."

She didn't have to answer his questions. She started for the door, but before she reached it, he was standing before her. Blaire glared at him. "Ye're in my way."

"You're not going anywhere until you answer me."

How dare he behave like a brute? "I doona owe ye anythin', Kettering. Now, get out of my way."

He shook his head, and his dark eyes softened. "Tell me that dolt doesn't think you can't find a proper husband."

Pity. That was the look she read in his expression, and it infuriated her. No matter he was right in his estimation. She wouldn't be pitied by anyone. "Get out of my way, Kettering, or I'll knock ye on yer obnoxious vampyre arse."

He tossed back his head and laughed.

What he had to laugh about completely escaped Blaire, and she brushed past the arrogant Sassenach, ready to escape to the safety of her bedchamber.

But he snatched her waist in his hands and tugged her to him. "In all my years, you are the most delightful creature I've ever encountered."

That couldn't possibly be true.

"You must have droves of men lining up to court you. I've wanted to tear MacQuarrie's head off ever since he arrived just for looking in your direction."

Baron Kettering had most definitely lost whatever sense he'd previously possessed. "There's no need ta mock me. I've kent Alec MacQuarrie my whole life, and he's only ever *looked* at Caitrin. So ye can save yer pity."

The man smirked in response. "Pity? Do you think I pity you?"

She shrugged.

"If I pity anyone, Blaire, it's me. I should be furious with you, and part of me still is, but the rest of me…" He scratched his jaw. "Well, the rest of me wants things that are impossible. I wish I breathed the same air as you. I wish I could ask Captain Lindsay for his blessing to court you. I wish…"

Did he really want those things? "What do ye wish?" she couldn't help but ask. *Please tell me what's in your heart.*

"I wish," James winced, "that I understood what is happening to me. No matter that I should throttle you for lying to me and keeping *my* ring from me, all I want is to console you and kiss you and taste every inch of you and never let you leave my sight."

All the air whooshed out of Blaire. She didn't know what to say. "Oh."

A self-deprecating smile lit his face. "Are you pitying me?"

"Do ye really mean all those things?" She took a slight step backward.

He inclined his head once. "Fool that I am."

Blaire glanced down at the ring that now graced his finger. "Is it really yers?"

"Are you saying you didn't know?"

She shook her head. "Mama said it was passed from one generation ta the next. That I should never remove it. That it could someday save my life."

"Save your life by keeping me dormant," James muttered, but she heard it just the same.

"I beg yer pardon?"

James frowned. "They said something that night."

"The coven?"

"Yes. I asked them why they'd surrounded me, and the blond one said something about my future victims."

"Future victims?" What had Fiona Macleod seen all those years ago? Had she seen this? The future connection between herself and James? It certainly wouldn't be the first time Fiona had tried to keep an outsider from entering their circle.

"But I would never hurt you, Blaire."

And she didn't doubt the sincerity of the vampyre before her. Perhaps he wasn't the only fool in the room. "I ken."

"The same cannot be said of Sarah Reese and Padrig Trevelyan. Instead of bickering amongst ourselves, we should be mapping out our battle plan."

Battle plan! For the first time that day, Blaire felt useful. "What a wonderful idea. Tell me, James, how does one kill a vampyre?"

∾

If anyone had ever told James he'd even consider teaching a pretty little witch how to kill one of his own kind, he'd have sent for a padded coach to take the idiot straight to Bedlam. How things had changed. He was doing more than considering it now. The knowledge could very possibly save Blaire's life. In fact, he'd wager his immortal soul, if he had one, that she'd need this knowledge in the very near future.

"There are a few ways, actually," he said slowly, watching the rapt attention on her face as she narrowed her eyes and regarded him with all seriousness.

Her delicate brows lifted playfully when he hesitated. "Do ye plan ta share them with me? Or do ye simply want me ta guess?" Her cheeky grin nearly undid him. He wanted to take her in his arms and find out all the places where she was most ticklish, instead of teaching her the art of war against his own kind.

"If you will be quiet for a moment, I'd be happy to

tell you," he said as he drew her down on the settee beside him. "There are several things you need to know about vampyres." He took her hand and placed it flat upon his chest. The warmth of her seeped through his shirt. He forced himself to concentrate. "We do not have hearts."

"I doona believe that, James," she sighed at him, her fingers curling in to stroke his chest lightly. He felt that touch all the way to his toes. "Ye have a heart. I'm certain of it."

"If I did, I would give it to you," he blurted.

Blaire's cheeks pinkened. But she smiled. God, she had the most beautiful smile.

James cleared his throat. "I-I mean, we *do* have hearts, but they no longer beat, Blaire. Now stop distracting me."

"I havena done a thing," she protested, blinking her grey eyes at him coquettishly.

He swiped a hand across his mouth in an attempt to fight back his incisors, which threatened to descend at her very nearness. "That's about as likely as your brother giving me leave to court you properly," he chuckled. "You're a minx, and you know it."

"Do ye plan ta insult me all night? Or teach me how ta kill a vampyre? On with it, already," she prompted.

James smirked at her eagerness. How many women would be enthralled to learn the art of war against the undead? None he'd ever met. No, Blaire Lindsay was one of a kind. He could stay sitting there all evening, simply to bask in her presence. But that wouldn't help her learn how to defend herself. "We do not have beating hearts," he repeated, to bring his mind back to the task at hand. "So, you cannot kill us by stopping our hearts. Mine stopped beating a very, very long time ago."

She nodded as though she understood.

"We can also heal ourselves, unless the wound is grave."

Blaire scrunched up her pert little nose. "What do ye mean by that? Would I have ta chop off an appendage to have any effect at all on yer person?"

James squirmed in his chair. He didn't like the very idea of his *appendages* being handled in such a manner. There were much better ideas for what she could do with them.

"James?" she asked, interrupting his thoughts. The lass could take his attention unlike anyone ever had.

"The head," he finally said. "You'd have to chop off our *head*."

The color leached from her face as she whispered, "Bloody hell."

"No, a vampyre won't bleed much," he teased.

"That is no' humorous." She elbowed him in the stomach.

He grunted and bent forward to rub the offended area.

"Anythin' else?" She leaned closer to him on the settee, her grey eyes sparkling with interest.

If James kept staring at her, he'd never complete this lesson. "Uh, yes."

"I'm waitin', James."

What was he supposed to be telling her?

"What else will kill a vampyre?"

James rose from his spot and tried to shake himself from the enchanting spell she was weaving around him. "A wooden stake to the heart." Then he frowned. He was supposed to be teaching her how to protect herself, not how to get herself killed. "But stakes are dangerous, because most vampyres could take one from you and then use it to kill you before you'd even realize the danger."

"They could take it from *me*?" She grinned, laying her delicate little hand on her chest.

She still didn't realize who and what they were dealing with. "I took you down a moment ago," he reminded her. "I fear they could do the same."

Her grin widened and she rose to her feet, closing the distance between them. "Obviously, ye and I are rememberin' the events of the past few moments differently."

"I remember having you on top of me," he chuckled, knowing he shouldn't encourage her but was helpless to do otherwise. "But my memory of the rest of the encounter now evades me for some reason."

Blaire brushed hair from his forehead with the tips of her fingers, her mouth so close to him that he could smell the sweet scent of her breath. Her brows pushed together with worry. "When was the last time ye fed, James? Ye look a bit pale."

He shrugged. "When I was with you." A fiery blush crept up her cheeks, making him want to toss his head back and laugh at her nervousness. Such an innocent. She could eagerly learn the art of destroying those of his kind, but a simple reminder of what they'd done together had her flustered and speechless. He caught her gaze and held it, and then he slowly leaned forward. "When I pierced your flesh and drank you in," he whispered beside her ear.

She shivered delicately. She remembered their shared passion just as fondly as he, he'd wager. A cuff to his shoulder was her response, just before she tucked her head into his chest to hide her face.

He tipped her face up with a crooked finger under her chin. "Suddenly shy?" he teased.

"Mortified," she said quietly as she laid her cheek against his chest and snuggled closer, her arms wrapping around his waist. He could keep her here forever and a day.

"Yet you want to do it again?" he asked softly, waiting for her reaction. She stiffened slightly in his arms but then nodded against his chest and exhaled loudly.

She leaned back to look into his face. "How often do ye need ta feed? We've never discussed the details."

"It depends," he admitted.

"On?"

"On what pursuits we're engaged in. If we're not taxed, we don't use up what we've taken in quite as quickly. I have been fairly lazy of late. Though the sun exposure didn't help."

"That's why ye're pale?" she asked, her silver eyes clouded with worry, suddenly.

"Yes." He'd go and find an animal if he had to, though he'd love to sink his teeth into the delectable Blaire Lindsay again. He'd already had her to protect her, to remove the lure that was her innocence in Sarah and Trevelyan's eyes. But a second time? He wasn't certain she'd be amenable to being his dinner again, even if he brought her bliss during the course of the event. He felt like the worst sort of cad for even thinking of it.

She shoved her hair from her shoulder and tipped her neck to the side. "Ye can take from me. Take whatever ye need."

He touched his lips softly to the area. A tremor ran through her body. "I'd like nothing more. But not here. And you're not required to offer yourself up for my meals, you know. There are other sources."

"Other women?" she asked as she drew back from him.

Other women? That's what she was worried about? What a strange creature she was. So strong, yet still subject to the most basic of emotions like jealousy. He kissed the tip of her nose. "I would not go to another lass, Blaire."

"Ye wouldna?"

He shook his head.

She folded her arms across her chest as though she didn't quite believe him. Honestly, he didn't quite believe it himself. But ever since she woke him, he had no desire to meet other women, let alone enjoy their life's blood.

"Before I met you," he explained, "I probably would have enchanted some willing lass who wouldn't remember the act the next day. But not now. Not now that I've met you." He tugged her back to him, suddenly feeling the loss of her. "And tasted you," he added lastly. The blush crept back up her cheeks. "You're all I can think about."

"If I wasn't here, what would ye do?"

He'd probably starve. "Sheep. Cattle. There are a lot of choices."

"And those are as good as me?"

He chuckled. "Nothing tastes as sweet as you do, Blaire." And nothing ever had.

"Then ye'll need ta come ta me later," she said quietly.

A clatter arose in the hallway as Matthew called out, "I say, Kettering, are you still there with Miss Lindsay?" Thank God for Matthew's warning.

"I'll come to you later tonight, if it's what you want," he whispered quickly to Blaire.

"Please," she replied, then sprang away from him.

"I was extolling your celestial knowledge to young Master Brannock." Matthew entered the great hall with MacQuarrie and Blaire's brothers trailing behind him. "He'd very much like for you to point out Orion's two hunting dogs, James."

That didn't seem like the best idea with two rogue vampyres on the loose. James stepped to the window and peered out. Darkness had just fallen. "It appears a bit cloudy." He shot Matthew a look.

"They're not nearby," Matthew said so quietly that only James could hear it. "I'd sense Sarah if they were."

"Nonsense!" Alec MacQuarrie announced as he peered out a different window. "All looks clear to me."

Though they were looking for different things, weren't they?

James glanced again at his maker, looking for reassurance and Matthew nodded. "Miss Lindsay doesn't seem the sort who will want to spend her days hiding, James." The earl's voice only reached his ears.

The man did have a point. He couldn't let Sarah and Trevelyan dictate his every move for the rest of eternity. James smiled at Brannock Lindsay. "Orion's hunting dogs? Did you know they are forever chasing a rabbit across the night sky?"

The boy's eyes lit up. "I dinna ken he had any dogs ta be honest, my lord."

"Oh, indeed." James took a step toward the lad. "I'll be happy to point them out. But it is cold out there. So you'll need your warmest coat."

Before he even finished his sentence, Brannock bolted from the room and James could imagine the boy was searching madly for his coat and scarf. Blaire crossed the floor to James' side, a frown marring her pretty brow. He couldn't blame her after the scare she had this morning.

"But—" she began.

"They're not close." James took her hand in his and caressed small circles across her soft skin. "Blodswell would feel them—well, he'd feel Sarah. Besides, I'll be with him."

Aiden Lindsay cleared his throat, and James dropped Blaire's hand. How had he forgotten they had an audience? Well, that was simple, wasn't it? Blaire made him forget all rational thought.

"Astronomical scholar, are ye?" the captain asked as he dropped onto the settee.

Well, James had seen more night skies than most living people. "Scholar might be a bit grandiose. I just have an appreciation for the heavens and stars within it."

"I, for one, am looking forward to the lesson." MacQuarrie leaned casually against the window frame. "There's something about a starry night that has always brought peace to my soul."

Aiden Lindsay laughed. "Then perhaps I'll give it a go myself. Show me somethin' that will impress a Highland lass, will ye?"

"Whatever you wish, Captain." James brought his attention back to Blaire, and he couldn't help but grin at her. "And what about you, Miss Lindsay? Will you allow me to impress *you* with my knowledge of the stars and other heavenly bodies?"

She rolled her eyes, but a smile lingered on her lips. "I have no desire ta see Orion's dogs chase a rabbit across the sky, my lord." Then she lowered her voice so only he could hear. "Besides, if ye're all away, it'll give me a bit of time ta myself. And I have an appointment this evenin' I'm most anxious for."

James' mouth went dry. How was he supposed to point out constellations to her brothers and MacQuarrie while thoughts of her preparing for their *appointment* danced in his head? "Are you sure?"

Her grey eyes sparkled. "Ye'll keep one eye on the stars and another on my brothers and Mr. MacQuarrie?"

"I only have two eyes," he teased. "Is it all right if Blodswell shares the chore?"

Blaire laughed. "Just as long as everyone returns unharmed."

James offered her a half bow. "You have my word, madam."

"Then do have a wonderful time. Be sure ta tell me all about it later." Then she sauntered from the great hall, leaving James to stare after her delectable, departing form.

"Unharmed," Aiden Lindsay grumbled. "What sort of trouble does she think we'll stumble inta, anyway?"

"That you'll tumble head first into the icy loch?" MacQuarrie suggested with a barely concealed grin.

The captain snorted. "Oh, aye, somehow I was able ta march across the continent and back, but I'm incapable of walkin' a path on my own property without fallin' ta my death."

James shook his head. With any luck, the two gentlemen would never know the dangers that lurked just beyond Lindsay's walls. The idea of leaving Blaire unprotected niggled at the back of his mind, but he shook it away. At the first inkling of Sarah in the vicinity, he'd be back inside the castle within the blink of an eye. Blaire wasn't in any real danger. He'd never leave her if she was.

In almost no time, Brannock Lindsay returned to the group, all bundled up from head to toe. Clearly, Blaire had seen to his warmth. "Are we ready?" He bounced on his toes.

"Just as soon as the rest of us gather our own coats." James returned.

Soon, they all exited through the side garden door into the chilly Highland air.

Captain Lindsay clapped James on the back and said, "Lead the way, Kettering. Find the best place ta see these huntin' dogs."

James nodded. "Of course." He looked back over his shoulder at the castle. A lone candle flickered to life in Blaire's chamber window. He would count the moments until he could go to her.

Twenty

ALL THINGS CONSIDERED, BRANNOCK LINDSAY WAS A most delightful child, and just being around him made James wish for things he couldn't have. Neither a wife nor a family was in his immediate future. How he wished they were, though. He'd give his immortality and his very life for five minutes with his own family. To feel life growing within Blaire. To hold their child, a product of their union, in his arms.

"Woolgathering, James?" Matthew asked quietly from where he sat beside him on a large boulder. The captain, MacQuarrie, and Brannock gazed avidly at the sky. The latter had nearly exhausted James' knowledge in the realm of constellations.

"Not woolgathering, really," James said. "Just wishing for things I can't have."

"I've heard it said one can wish upon a falling star," Matthew began.

Yes, he'd heard the same thing. What a bunch of rubbish. "With my misfortune, the star would fall upon my head before I could get out the wish," James grunted.

"What's the cause of this sudden melancholy? Shall I assume it has to do with Miss Lindsay?"

"What else?" James picked up a stone and tossed it into the loch, where it landed with a plop.

"I think we've already established that Miss Lindsay is in love with you." Matt certainly had a way with words. It might be true. But he had nothing to offer her in return, aside from pleasure. She'd never be fulfilled with a man like him, one who didn't age and couldn't give her the family she so rightfully deserved. "You should allow *her* to decide what she can and cannot bear, instead of making the decision for her. She might surprise you."

Matthew suddenly tensed beside him.

"What is it?" James asked as he jumped to his feet. Sarah Reese and Padrig Trevelyan stepped into the clearing. "So, much for sensing them," James tossed at Matthew sarcastically and with more than a little anger. His eyes sought Sarah's hand. She'd removed the ring, her only tether to them. Why the devil hadn't he considered such a thing?

Dear God, was Blaire safe? James eyes flashed across the pair. No blood that he could see, and not a whiff of it hung on the air. Had they sought her out, there would be some evidence of it.

"Good evening," Sarah said quietly. Trevelyan said nothing but nodded his head.

"Evenin'," Captain Lindsay returned. "I doona believe I've had the pleasure."

At the same moment, Brannock stepped closer to his older brother, grasping Aiden's coat with his mittened hand. Captain Lindsay may not have had the honor, but James doubted poor Brannock would ever forget Sarah's incisors.

The temptress vampyre nodded in Lindsay's direction. "Oh, we're old acquaintances of Kettering and Blodswell."

Captain Lindsay shook his head. "For a man who ended up in my castle as part of some party prank, you certainly have quite a following in the area."

James ignored the man. Keeping everyone safe far outweighed whatever thoughts were running through Lindsay's mind. "Why are you here?" James glared at the woman who'd left him for dead that very morning.

A slow smile tipped the corners of Sarah's lips. "What kind of greeting is that, Jamie?" she purred at him. He wanted to wipe that sorry excuse for a smile from her lips. There was no charm behind it. Only malice and hatred.

"The only kind you're going to get," he replied as he advanced toward her. If he could get his hands on her, he could have her incapacitated before she could blink twice, he was that angry. But, a moment too late, he realized Trevelyan flanked MacQuarrie, the captain, and Brannock.

"Stop," the wicked vampyre called out, "or you will regret it."

"There's only one thing I regret. And that's allowing you to live this long."

Everything fell quiet except for the gentle lapping of the loch a few feet away. The captain must have finally sensed the threat the newcomers brought with them, as he pulled Brannock tighter to his side and wrapped his arm around the boy's shoulders. Even MacQuarrie stood taller.

"What's this about?" the captain asked warily.

Sarah smiled her silky little smile and said, "Oh, nothing much. James is simply wondering how he can save all of you."

"Beg your pardon?" Aiden Lindsay took a step closer to the pair.

"Actually, I was wondering how loud the snap will be when I break your neck," James said slowly, watching her face.

"Aiden, I'm afraid," Brannock whimpered from behind his brother. Of course, he was. But only by alerting the captain to the danger could he instill the proper amount of fear in the man. Enough to make him react. Quickly.

"Why don't you take Brannock back to the house, Captain?" James suggested.

"How about we all stay here instead?" Sarah returned sweetly.

What happened next was a blur of activity. Trevelyan moved to grab the boy, but James was faster. He tugged Brannock onto his back and yanked the captain to him. He saw Matthew reach for Sarah just as she grabbed Mr. MacQuarrie. But James didn't dare wait to see what would happen. The only way to save the Lindsay brothers was to whisk them back to the castle and pray Matthew could handle the pair while he was gone. He pulled Captain Lindsay into his embrace and ran for Briarcraig.

Fast as a flash, he burst through the main front door and deposited both Brannock and Aiden onto the stone floor. Blaire stood in the corridor before them. Her mouth fell open at the sight. A teacup fell from her grasp and shattered on the floor as a fireball flamed to life in her hand.

Something dangerous flashed in Blaire's eyes as realization apparently dawned on her. "Ye said they were no' nearby. Ye said it was safe."

"I know what I said." And he'd failed her. But Matthew was awaiting his help. "I have to get MacQuarrie." James turned back toward the door.

"Go, then!" Her fireball flamed even brighter.

"Do *not* follow me. If you leave your brothers unprotected, Trevelyan and Sarah will kill them."

"Go!" she cried again. But she reached into her boot and pulled out her knife, tossing it in the air toward him, where it landed in the wooden doorjamb right beside his head. He tugged it from the wall and flew through the door as fast as he could toward the loch.

Blaire stared at the empty space where James had stood. Fury coursed through her veins. How dare Sarah Reese and Mr. Trevelyan attack her family? She had the urge to chase after James, to end this once and for all. But Brannock's whimpering kept her rooted to the floor.

Her little brother scrambled over to her and clutched her skirts as though the material could shield him from all that was evil and scary in the world. She bent down to soothe him, stroking a hand across his hair. The hat she'd secured there earlier was long since gone.

"It'll be all right, Bran."

Aiden loomed above them. Storm clouds formed in his furious grey eyes. "Just what is goin' on around here, Blaire Garia Lindsay?"

"I doona think now is the time—" she began, once again stroking her palm across Brannock's head.

"Oh, no!" Aiden scoffed. "Now is most definitely the time. I'd like ta ken how Kettering can run faster than the wind. I'd like ta ken how he has more acquaintances in the Highlands than either of us, no' that I'd like ta ken either of those people, mind ye. And I'd like ta ken all of it right bloody now!"

Blaire gulped. "I ken as much as ye do, Aiden."

"I never knew ye ta lie ta me before now, Blaire."

What could she say? He *might* believe her, but that was neither here nor there now. James was gone. Alec hadn't returned. And her world was completely off-kilter. Blaire shrugged, hoping he'd leave her be. At least for the time being.

He sighed dramatically. "Very well." He stalked down the corridor. "I doona want ta see ye, Blaire, no' until ye can be honest with me." Then he disappeared around a corner.

Blaire looked down into Brannock's stricken eyes. "It was that woman, Blaire. The mean one with the pointy teeth."

"Ye're safe with me, Bran." And she prayed it was the truth.

❧

What James found when he arrived at the side of the loch wasn't what he'd hoped to find at all. Sarah lay prone on the ground, her body twisted at a grotesque angle, her severed head a few feet from her body. Her feet and fingers still twitched in the throes of second-death.

Alec MacQuarrie lay closer to the loch, gasping for air while Matthew hovered over him. Trevelyan was nowhere to be seen.

"Oh, God," James groaned as he leaned over MacQuarrie. He took the man's hand in his when he reached for it. MacQuarrie's blood seeped from the wound at his neck much quicker than it should have.

"Help him," James urged his maker.

"He has to make the choice," Matthew said. "You know I'll not turn him unless he wants it." Matthew sounded tortured, as though the words were ripped from his soul.

MacQuarrie's blood continued to spill.

"Do you want to live?" James barked at the dying man.

A feeble nod was the only answer.

James met Matthew's gaze. "I'll take care of him," Matthew said. "Go back to the others."

"You're certain? You will do it, won't you? Please don't change your mind." He probably sounded like a green lad pleading with his maker this way, but something inside him told him that Blaire would never forgive him if her friend died. It would be on his head. He'd promised to keep them all safe, and he'd failed miserably.

"Have you ever known me not to keep my word? I'll do it."

That was a small consolation considering all that had happened in the last little while. James nodded tightly.

"I'll have to take him to Callista."

It had been decades since James had laid eyes on the vampyre thaumaturge. "Still in London?" he asked Matthew.

"She is indeed."

Which meant that protecting the Lindsays from Padrig Trevelyan landed squarely on James' shoulders alone. "Godspeed, then." Matthew would have his own troubles trying to get MacQuarrie to Callista's door.

James fled back to the castle. Blaire met him at the door, where she must have been wearing a path in the rug with her pacing. Not to mention the sparks she was dropping in fear.

Her voice quivered. "W-whose blood is that?" she asked as she pointed to his clothing. "Is it Alec's?"

He *was* covered in MacQuarrie's blood, and he needed to remove it from his person as fast as possible. He wasn't strong enough to smell it. To wear it on his skin. He ran up the stairs to his bedchamber where he filled the washbasin with water.

James scrubbed frantically at the blood that covered his hands. The coppery smell of it assaulted his senses, pushing him toward a place where he didn't want to go. Blaire would be on him any moment. He was certain of it. She'd seen the blood on his clothes.

His nearness to MacQuarrie's life force caused the blood within *her* veins to call to him, almost as though he could taste the frantic pulse of her worry.

James shrugged out of his jacket and shirt, forcing himself not to breathe. He didn't need to exhale and inhale; he simply did it because it made him appear to be more human. The scent of MacQuarrie's blood was heavy within him, teasing him as nothing else had, aside from Blaire.

Blaire. He heard her quick little footsteps as he tugged a clean shirt over his head and tucked it into his trousers.

The door to his room flew open with a bang as Blaire strode through the opening. "How dare ye rush past me like that!"

"Not now, love." With the scent of MacQuarrie's blood still hanging in the air, James needed all of his strength to keep his incisors from descending.

She glared at him. "Doona think ta dissuade me, James Maitland. Where did the blood come from? Where's Alec?" Blaire demanded, her breaths heaving from her body like bellows that stoke a fire. A fireball hovered over her open palm.

"He's with Blodswell," James said slowly.

The fireball dropped to the floor, the flames not quite snuffed out by the fall. James stepped forward and stomped it down. "You needn't burn the castle to the ground, Blaire," he grunted.

Blaire gasped as one hand landed on her chest. "Alec's dead, is he no'?"

In a manner of speaking, though James opted not to voice that thought.

Her gaze moved over him and to the bed, where he'd discarded his blood-stained clothing. Damnation. He should have shoved it under the bed. Of course, she saw it. She was Blaire, after all.

James ducked as a fireball flew straight for his head. "Blaire," he warned.

"Doona *Blaire* me," she clipped out. "Ye havena answered me. Is Alec dead?"

"No more so than I am," he hedged.

Her eyes narrowed as she appraised him. "And what does *that* mean? So help me God, James. If ye doona tell me what happened…" Her voice cracked on the last, and she seemed unable to finish her thought.

James' heart would have broken if he still had one. Watching sorrow and panic engulf her was painful to his soul. He opened his arms to her, wanting nothing more than to offer whatever comfort she could take from him.

Blaire shook her finger at him. "No," she whimpered.

James didn't wait for her to come to him. He advanced on her and paid no heed to her struggle when she attempted to shake free of his hold.

"Let me hold you," he commanded softly as she stopped fighting him and relaxed in his arms. "MacQuarrie is…*safe*." If only she'd leave it at that for now.

"Safe? Where is he, James? What happened ta him?"

More than he wished to explain. "He's with Blodswell for the time being. He'll make sure your friend gets all the help he needs."

"He's no' dead?" She tipped her head back to look at him.

"He was nearly dead when I went back for him. Sarah and Trevelyan had done their best."

"Ye are no' answerin' my questions!" she shouted at him.

"Trust me, you don't want to know, Blaire," he replied calmly. He wanted to rail at her, too. He'd just saved her brothers. He'd done it for her. Yet he still felt tremendous guilt at having had to leave MacQuarrie behind.

The astounded look on her face was almost his undoing. If he told her MacQuarrie would be turned into one of his kind, she'd never forgive him. If he didn't tell her, she'd never forgive him for that, either.

He could almost feel Blaire's heart breaking within his arms. Her friend's health lay on her shoulders. But he'd not allow her to carry that burden. It was his. He alone would shoulder it.

"Swear it, James." She looked up at him, tugging fiercely at the fine lawn of his shirt. "Promise me he'll be all right and I'll believe ye."

"I promise," he said. He only prayed he was right and that MacQuarrie had survived one way or the other. But James knew that, no matter what, the Scot would no longer be the man she'd once known. "But for now, lass, we have other worries."

Blaire shook her head. "Other worries?"

"We have your brothers to deal with, and Trevelyan is still out there somewhere."

"And the woman?"

"No longer a concern," he grunted.

"Ye mean…?"

James nodded. "Sarah is gone, and she can't hurt anyone else."

⁓

But the man was still a worry. And if Blaire read James' expression, Trevelyan was the more dangerous of the pair. Staying at Briarcraig was no longer an option.

Blaire stepped toward her window to peer out at

the night sky. "I have ta take my family away from here, James. I have ta. I have ta take them back ta Edinburgh. My coven can keep them safe. The five of us will be together there, and we will keep them safe. Cait's already home, and Elspeth should be by now." She was rambling. She was certain of it. But she didn't know how to deal with these vampyres. She didn't know how to help Alec, whatever was wrong with him. She didn't know what else to do.

Her coven sisters could make her feel more centered. More alert. More secure. Less off-kilter.

James gently spun her around to face him. "Blaire, I told you. He'll follow. Here, I can keep you safe."

But he hadn't done that tonight, had he? She was safe and her brothers, but poor Alec… She shook her head. "I *have* ta go home, James," she whispered as she rubbed a hand down the side of his face.

He sighed, and his dark eyes bore into hers. "All right. Tomorrow, Blaire. Tomorrow, we'll go. Together."

But that was a truly awful idea. "Nay, James. Ye canna come with us." Her jaw quivered, despite her resolve.

"I'll not let you go alone, unprotected."

If only she had faith in his ability to keep them all safe, but voicing such thoughts would only result in him puffing out his chest with male pride and bravado. "Aiden willna allow it," she said instead. "He is quite furious that I wouldna answer his questions about what happened this evenin'."

"Is that all?" James' dark eyes twinkled just a bit.

"He may no' be magical, but he does have control over my future. I doona think antagonizin' him is the best way ta go about anythin'."

"I'll make him forget the whole thing," he vowed.

Blaire couldn't help but scoff. "I think ye may have overestimated yer powers of persuasion."

"I can enchant him, make him forget everything he saw."

Were his powers truly that strong? Not that she could change her mind. Whatever feud raged between James and Mr. Trevelyan had nothing to do with her brothers, and she couldn't risk their safety. If anything ever happened to Brannock or Aiden, she'd never forgive herself. "That doesna solve the problem, James. My brothers are in danger because of ye. Do ye no' see that? Ye canna go with us ta Edinburgh."

His dark eyes flashed with...anger? Hurt? She couldn't tell which. "I'll not let you go alone. The answer is no, Blaire."

Arrogant Sassenach vampyre. "Ye doona get ta make decisions for me, James. Ye're no' my father. Ye're no' my husband." She turned her back on him and crossed the room to escape him. If she had to look at his wounded expression for one more moment, she'd give in. And she couldn't afford to do that.

"I could be," he whispered. "If you'd have me. Your husband, that is."

"Ye truly want ta marry me?" Blaire gasped as she raised a hand to cover her madly beating heart. Never in her wildest dreams had she ever expected to receive a proposal from any man. But from James... She wished beyond reason she could accept it.

"I do," was all he said. He advanced toward her slowly, his steps nearly predatory. She wanted nothing more than to run to him, throw herself into his arms, and rain kisses across his face. "I want to spend the rest of my life with you throwing fireballs at my head."

This, truly, was not the best time for this conversation. Brannock and Aiden were in danger. She'd only barely gotten Brannock into bed with the aid of a potent sleeping draught, and Aiden still wasn't speaking to her. Then there was Alec. And she had no idea what had happened to him. "I need time ta think," Blaire said as she spun away from him, pressing her fingertips against her temples.

His hands landed on her shoulders, and he squeezed gently. "Take all the time you need as long as you'll have me."

She turned to face him. "Ye want ta marry me. Are ye sayin' ye love me, James?" She'd give anything to hear him say those words.

The emotion that had been evident until that moment left his face. He looked at her stoically. "I care about you, Blaire, but I don't believe creatures such as myself are capable of love."

She couldn't help the sigh of sadness that escaped her.

James' brow furrowed. "Are you disappointed, Blaire? I thought you were more practical than to believe in love."

Practical? Is that how he saw her? "I am," she stammered. "And, no, I'm no' disappointed." She had no reason to be, did she? After all, she never thought she'd find a man who could love her. Still, since he owned her heart, it did hurt a bit. "I doona need for ye ta love me." Then she quit his chamber as quickly as she'd entered it. She had to leave before he saw the tears on her cheeks. She could hear him calling from behind her, followed by a quick curse when he saw Aiden approaching. Heaven forbid her brother catch her escaping the baron's room.

Aiden's eyes narrowed on her. "Has Kettering returned?"

At least he was speaking to her. Blaire shook her head. "I was just lookin' for him."

Aiden grunted and started to pass her, but this nonsense had gone on long enough. Besides, she needed him to listen to reason, even if she didn't confide all to him. "Aiden, I need ta speak ta ye."

He folded his arms across his chest. "Indeed? And are ye goin' ta tell me the truth this time?"

As little as was necessary. She nodded her head. "Aye." Then Blaire hooked her arm with Aiden's and leaned her head toward him, keeping in mind James' sensitive hearing. "Can we talk in yer chambers?" she whispered. Besides, the location would give them a head start on packing his things at the same time.

Aiden looked over his shoulder as though he thought someone was watching them, and Blaire kept from glancing in that direction herself. Most likely he was right, and she didn't think she could take seeing James Maitland at the moment. As soon as they entered Aiden's chamber, the whole story fell from Blaire's lips. She hadn't intended to tell him all of it, but once she started talking, there was no stopping. Well, she didn't mention James *taking* from her. Vampyre or no vampyre, James would have found Aiden storming into his room and making foolish male demands to assuage his pride and Blaire's honor. And that wouldn't help their current situation at all.

Aiden sat slumped in a high-backed chair beside his bed, his mouth agape, as it had been the past ten minutes. "Vampyres?" he finally muttered.

Blaire managed to nod. "So ye see why we have ta leave at first light. Alec said Cait was home and Elspeth should already be back. With the coven complete, we can protect everyone."

"Alec," he muttered softly, apparently just now remembering their friend in the aftermath of the bizarre tale she'd shared with him.

Blaire's heart ached at the thought of the noble Alec MacQuarrie, wondering what had become of him and hoping her faith in James was not misplaced. "He's badly injured. That's all I ken. James—er—Kettering said Lord Blodswell was seein' ta him. Legend has it no man is more noble than Blodswell. All we can do is hope he can save Alec."

"Trustin' that a dyin' and bleedin' man is safe in the hands of a vampyre seems foolish, Blaire." Aiden sat forward in his seat and rubbed his brow, as though the whole evening had left him with a headache.

When he said it that way, Blaire had to agree. "There's nothin' we can do, Aiden. Nothin' I can do," she clarified. "If Elspeth was here, perhaps; but I'm sadly ill-suited for healin' anyone."

"So we're puttin' our faith with Blodswell."

"We doona have much of a choice." Blaire dropped to the edge of Aiden's bed, across from him so she could look him in the eye. "Will ye make sure we can leave at dawn?"

Wordlessly, he nodded.

"I love him." Her voice cracked.

"I'm afraid no potions can help ye with that, Blaire," Aiden said softly. "But I'm sure ye ken what's best. Will Kettering let ye leave so easily?" He tipped his head at her and watched her quietly.

"He's sleepin'. For the moment at least. That's why it's imperative that we leave immediately."

His eyebrows rose in question. "And what will keep the vampyre from hearin' us? It's no' easy ta pack an entire household and sneak out like thieves in the night."

"I can put a magical damper on the noise. He'll sleep right through it. At least long enough for us ta be well on the way ta Edinburgh before he wakes."

"I doubt this will make him very happy."

She was certain it wouldn't. But that couldn't be avoided. She turned to walk toward her chamber, the weight of the world sitting on her shoulders.

She kissed Aiden's cheek and then slipped quietly from his chamber so he wouldn't see the tears that threatened to spill down her cheeks. She hastened to her room, writing the spell to damper the noise out in her mind.

She shed her clothes, slipped into her nightrail, donned a wrapper, and padded down the hallway in her stocking feet. James would be hers. For this one night, at least.

Twenty-One

WHEN BLAIRE SLIPPED INTO HIS ROOM, JAMES FELT certain he'd finally died and gone to heaven. He'd been pacing his chamber for an hour, waiting for the household to quiet so he could go to her. He needed her. He needed to hold her. To comfort her. To love her. But the sounds of the household packing and dragging trunks down the corridors had prevented him from going to her.

She softly closed the door behind her, the soft lavender scent of her reaching him from all the way across the room. She didn't slow as she walked toward him but shrugged out of her wrapper and let it drop to the floor. He froze.

Her black-as-night hair hung like a curtain down her back. Her silver eyes flashed with something he wanted to understand. Desire? Fear? Love? She sat down on the edge of his bed and tilted her head at him.

"I was going to come to you," he said feebly. He must sound like the worst sort of fool. But at the very thought of her in his room, of her in his life, he had no idea what to do. All he wanted to do was clutch her to himself and make love to her. He wanted to ensure that she was safe. To check every inch of her body. She hadn't even been involved in the altercation. Yet he fretted over her like a…man in love.

But that couldn't be. He wanted her. He trusted her. He needed her. But love? He wasn't capable of that. Not without a heart.

"Now ye doona have ta come ta me. I've come ta ye." She held her hands out wide, as though offering herself up to him.

"Did you give more thought to my proposal?"

"I'm still thinkin' about it," she said with a slow smile.

"What do you want, Blaire?" he asked, suddenly unsure of what she was doing there. Unsure of what *he* was doing there. He wanted her with an all-consuming desire. Her heartbeat hummed to him, driving him to her side.

James tugged her gently to her feet as he began to divest her of her nightrail. He tugged it quickly over her head, leaving her in nothing but her stockings and garters. She reached for him, her hands shaking only a little as she began to pull his shirt from his trousers.

"We need to talk, Blaire," he murmured against her naked shoulder.

"We will," she assured him. "We'll talk about everythin'." He heard the unspoken "later" at the end of that. He pressed his lips to her collarbone and nibbled her gently.

She gasped as his hands slid around to her naked bottom and he lifted her breast to his mouth and tongued her nipple. He tugged his upper lip down with his lower when his fangs extended. This was not the time to scare the lass.

Blaire shoved him back none too gently. "What do I have ta do ta get ye naked, vampyre?" she asked with a grin.

Blaire sat down on the edge of the bed, obviously unashamed of her nakedness in the candlelight, and slowly rolled her stockings down her slender thighs, all the way down her calves. James feared he would spend himself in the bedclothes again before he could even get his hands on her. It had been twenty years since he'd taken a woman. But more than that, it had been several lifetimes that he'd waited for Blaire. He ached to feel her pleasure swamp him as it had before, only this time he planned to be inside her, to convince her to stay with him, to be his wife.

Her gaze didn't waver when he divested himself of his trousers and everything else, and stood before her proud and naked.

❧

Blaire stood up on trembling legs and took a step forward to press her body against his, standing on tiptoe to touch his lips to hers. She'd seen the movement when he'd tugged his lip down to cover his fangs. But she loved them. Just as she loved him. "Let me in," she whispered as she slipped her tongue between his lips and gently licked across his distended incisor. He groaned and grabbed her even tighter, drawing her naked body to him as fiercely as she'd hoped.

Blaire knew James wasn't a man of reserved passion,

just as she was coming to learn about herself. She wanted him to be as breathless and as out of control as she was.

She couldn't hold back a squeal as he scooped her up in his arms and carried her to the bed. She scooted back to where she rested on the pillows and held her arms open to him. But instead of falling into her arms as she'd anticipated, he took her hands in his and pressed them into the mattress.

"Don't think you will be in control, here, Blaire," he taunted as he bent his head to take her nipple into his mouth, where he drew it heavily between his lips.

"I want ta touch ye." She was nearly appalled by the panting sound of her own voice.

"If you touch me, I won't be able to control myself." His words came out in a low growl.

"Who said ye have ta be in control?"

"I don't want to hurt you," he explained as he lifted his head and looked into her eyes. His fangs were no longer hidden, but the gentleness of his gaze belied the ferocity of them.

He softly kissed his way down her jaw, licking and nibbling gently as he crossed her shoulder and then down her breasts.

"Doona make me wait, James," she begged, the need within her growing to a crescendo.

James settled himself between her thighs as his hand moved down to rub through her heat. He dipped one finger into the silky essence of her desire and then brought it up to rub her center, circling it slowly until she was a writhing mass of unfulfilled desire beneath him.

"Please," she begged. "Please, James."

His hardness pressed at her softness as he stared down into her eyes, his own black gaze warmer than she'd ever seen it. "What do you want, Blaire?"

"You," she pleaded, hating the weakness in her own voice while loving that he'd provoked her enough to make her want him so badly. Only James. Always James.

"You'll marry me, Blaire? You'll marry me as soon as possible?"

She froze in his arms.

"Blaire?"

His blasted honor. He wouldn't take her because his honor wouldn't let him. She closed her eyes tightly.

"Blaire?" he asked, his voice growing more concerned.

"Aye," she cried as he probed at her center. "Aye," she whispered as she cupped his face with her hands and looked into his eyes. "I love ye."

He took her in one piercing thrust that filled her completely—body, heart, and soul. He stilled within her when she felt the small pain of being owned by him. His voice was shaky when he asked, "Are you all right, Blaire? I didn't mean to hurt you."

"Ye could no' hurt me if ye tried, James." She pulled his head down to hers and touched her lips to his hungrily, hoping to remove the fear that rested there. Yes, he feared something. Perhaps it was her. Perhaps it was their destiny. Perhaps it was the feelings she created within him. If his feelings were comparable at all to what she felt having him seated within her, she could understand his fierceness.

She adjusted her hips marginally, causing a groan to erupt from his lips. He began to move within her slowly, withdrawing from her, only to plunge back in, heavy and hard.

"More," she encouraged him, arching beneath him.

He called her name as he surged within her, his voice hot, his arms strong as he held her.

When he finally flung her over that precipice of pleasure, he didn't follow her. He stilled within her and breathed heavily against her ear. "That's it, Blaire. I want all of you," he growled.

She quaked around his length, the pleasure spiraling as she fluttered around him. "James!" she cried, fearing the pleasure would cleave her in two. When she finally stilled, she found that she was still whole beneath him. He clenched his teeth above her, not moving.

"James?" She reached for the side of his face.

"Several lifetimes I've waited for you, Blaire." He pulled from her depths, still hot and hard, the silky wetness that was evidence of her pleasure sliding against her leg.

He flipped her over and stuffed a pillow beneath her hips.

"I never thought I'd find someone like you," he growled as he filled her again. His hand slid beneath her belly to tangle in her curls as he rocked within her, touching places she hadn't known existed. His bare chest rubbed against her back with every thrust, each one pushing her higher and higher. "Can't hold back, Blaire," he grunted, his lips pressed to her shoulder.

Blaire reached behind her and pushed her hair from her neck, baring the beat of her pulse to his gaze. She arched her back, pressing her neck closer to his mouth.

"Don't hold back," she coaxed him. "Take all of me, James. Please."

He licked across her shoulder and then nibbled it gently.

"Do it, James," she commanded. "Mark me. Make me yers."

Finally, just as his fingers and his thrusts within her were about to send her back over that cliff into completion, his fangs pierced the tender skin of her neck.

His pleasure poured into her as he fed upon hers. He erupted within her at the same time as he took from her, his mouth sealed over her skin as he drank her in and gave back to her all that he had to give.

He slowed within her and tugged the pillow from beneath her hips, his body covering hers completely as he pressed her into the mattress. She felt a sense of unexplainable loss when he pulled his fangs from her throat and gently licked across the wounds to close them.

He rolled onto his back and drew her on top of him, allowing her to drape herself over him. She craved the closeness. She craved his love. For she already knew that he had all of hers and always would. She snuggled into his arms and let him hold her closely. She feigned sleep, enjoying this taste of a love unlike anything she'd ever known, since she'd never be able to experience it again.

When his even breaths told her he slept, she lifted the arm that held her so tenderly and slipped out of bed. She dropped her nightrail over her head and turned back to him. "I am sorry, James," she said quietly, though he probably couldn't even hear her.

"I do love ye. I love ye more than my life. But I have ta protect my family."

She would leave for Edinburgh as soon as possible. They'd be long gone before the sun rose. He'd hate her for it when he woke. But she had to take her family out of harm's way and back to the safety of her coven.

Blaire watched as James slept heavily. He looked so peaceful, and she hoped to always keep that memory in her mind. She glanced once at the ring on his finger. Then decided to leave it in his care. The ring was his, after all.

She tossed her clothes back on and slipped quietly into the corridor. While Aiden and Brannock still rested, she had one more task to accomplish before they left. Years ago, her mother and the others had prevented James from *leaving* Briarcraig, but she would never do such an awful thing to him again. He should be able to move freely about, not caged like an unruly beast. But now to keep him safe, she needed to prevent anyone else from *entering* the castle, especially while he slept.

She was certain Trevelyan would hunt James until the end of time, and of that Blaire had no control, but she could ensure the dangerous vampyre would never step foot inside the castle. She could ensure Briarcraig would always be a safe haven for James.

Blaire walked from room to room, from one end of the castle to the next, repeating a spell that would prevent the malevolent vampyre from crossing Briarcraig's threshold. Once each room had been doused with magic, she stopped before the main entrance. She pointed her finger at the large, imposing oak door. With a fiery fingertip, she etched the *Còig*'s emblem, a five-pointed star, into the wood.

"There." She dusted her hands across her skirts. Trevelyan could never step over the threshold.

Then she climbed the stairs to her room to finish packing her things. She tossed her clothes into a trunk, packed the vials and cauldron she'd used the nights ago, and even tossed the five witch figurines Brannock had found into her bag. They were hers, after all. Why shouldn't she take them? A scrap of foolscap in her trunk taunted her. She owed James an explanation, and she prayed he wouldn't hate her once he had it.

Twenty-Two

JAMES WOKE JUST AS THE SUN BROKE THE HORIZON. He groaned loudly and pressed the heels of his hands to his eyes, grinding them fiercely. Something tickled his chin. James raised his head to look around, but the movement just made the room spin a bit. Sitting on his chest and staring back at him as though he was mad was Brannock Lindsay's feral cat. "Well, good morning." He scratched the beast between its ears. "Hiding from young Master Brannock again, are you?"

He looked slowly around the room, but Blaire was nowhere in sight.

The cat meowed.

"He can be a bit overzealous," James agreed, "but he's taken a liking to you. And you *are* all skin and bones. I'd wager if you stayed close to the lad, he'd fatten you up in no time."

James nudged the cat from his chest, and then he struggled to sit up. The counterpane fell to reveal his naked chest. What the devil had happened to him? Then the events of the night before flooded back in his memory, hitting him like a storm-carried wave.

Blaire had accepted his proposal and allowed him to make love to her. To mark her as his own. To bite her flesh and leave his mark for the *world* to see. So then where was she?

A crinkling sound caught his attention, and he looked over at Bruce the cat to find the feline gnawing on a piece of foolscap. *A note?* He snatched it from the bed, and his eyes flew over the words.

> *My dearest James,*
>
> *As I write this, I am certain you will be furious with me when you wake, and for that I am sorry. I hope you can forgive me and try to understand. I had never planned to marry. I had never dreamed I would find a man I could love, a man I wanted to spend the rest of my life with. Please know that your proposal meant more to me than you can ever imagine. It tempted me like nothing else ever has. I wish with all my heart that I could have accepted it, but we were not to be.*
>
> *I told you I was too practical to believe in love. I lied to you. I know love exists because I have seen it with my very eyes. I just never thought it would find me. It is silly I suppose, if you consider my circumstances, to refuse your offer, but I really do not have a choice. I made a promise to myself, you see, a very long time ago. My father never loved my mother, and I swore as a small lass that I would never live her life. It was too painful to watch. I cannot imagine living it. As much as I love you, I will not condemn myself to a loveless marriage. I have seen that play out, and I have no desire to see it again.*

The more pressing matter is Mr. Trevelyan. I do not blame you for whatever mishap found my dear friend, Mr. MacQuarrie. I truly believe that whatever transpired was out of your control and that you feel terribly. However, I cannot risk the chance of a similar mishap befalling one of my brothers. I feel I can better protect my family within the circle of my coven. By the time you read this, I should already be on my way home. I am not certain of the nature of the feud between you and Mr. Trevelyan, but I ask you not to bring it to my doorstep. If you truly care about me, as you have professed, then you will keep this battle far from me and my family.

I know that I will never forget you. The time we spent together was the most amazing of my life, and I would not trade it for anything in the world. I have placed a protection spell on Briarcraig to ensure that Trevelyan cannot enter the castle. You are free to come and go as you please. Briarcraig can be your refuge from that terrible creature, if you so desire.

I hope you have many wonderful years before you and that you will remember me fondly.

> *Yours Always,*
> *Blaire*

Pain flared within James' chest, pain so harsh it made him double over.

She'd left him.

The pain was unlike anything James had ever felt. He'd been injured more times than he could count. In fact, he'd been shot when he died the first time. And that hadn't compared to this blinding, searing pain.

He clutched at the counterpane to steady himself. Then he had the sudden urge to take in a breath of air. He inhaled, and air filled his once-dormant lungs as a beat started within his chest. The rhythm of his own pulse reached his ears.

"What the devil?" he muttered. How was that possible?

Bruce the cat meowed beside him.

James was worried enough for both of them. He swung his legs over the side of the bed and came to his feet. Blood pumped into his limbs, tingling like mad, moved by his beating heart. He crossed to the mirror and blew a breath across it. It fogged. "Do you see that?" he asked the cat.

Bruce rubbed his head against James' ankle, purring loudly.

James stared at his reflection. This didn't make any sense. He clearly remembered the night he had *died* along the road to London. Stopped by highwaymen, he'd been shot, fell to the ground, and watched his life's blood seep into the earth. Then Matthew had appeared out of the mist, finished off his attackers, and offered James salvation. He would never forget the moment his heart had *stopped* beating. The feeling was like nothing he'd ever felt before or since. He'd lived two hundred and twenty-five years without feeling blood coursing through his veins, his heart beating strongly in his chest.

In all his years with Matthew, James had never once heard of such a thing. Not a rumor. Not a legend. Nothing. It didn't seem fathomable. But he had no doubt that his heart was now beating just as strongly as it had when he was a living, breathing man more than two centuries earlier.

Only one thing made any sense, if any sense was to be had. He'd always been in possession of his heart. It had just lain dormant for two hundred and twenty-five years until Blaire Lindsay entered his life. He'd thought he had no heart to offer her, no love to go along with it; but apparently he was wildly mistaken. He had a heart after all, and though she might be in Edinburgh, it pounded in his chest, calling out for Blaire Lindsay.

James snatched her letter from the bed and reread it. Foolish girl. How could she take off like that? How could she put herself in danger? Hadn't he told her that Padrig Trevelyan would come after her, if for no other reason than to torture James by doing so?

Panic gripped him. Now that his heart was beating, had he lost all chance to save her? Had his powers vanished with the re-emergence of his heart? One way to find out. He dashed from one end of the room to the other. His dash was more of a sprint. He'd lost his speed. Bloody hell, how could he instantly reach Blaire without his ability to move quickly? And strength. Was he still strong? James glanced around the room. What could he test himself with?

His eyes landed on the four-poster bed, and he dashed to the foot of it. He bent at the waist and tried to lift the edge with his little finger. All he got in return was an aching digit. He picked it up with his hand. Thank God. He doubted he could move boulders anymore. But he was still a strong man. Was he a *man*? Truly? He dropped the bed back to the ground and ignored the cat's growl at the unexpected clatter. Strength and speed. He'd lost them both, or most of them at least. But he could do this. He could get to her, although by normal means and not through vampyre trickery, and pray the entire journey that Trevelyan hadn't gotten to her first.

He looked back at the cat, which had plopped down beside the wardrobe and meowed. If *that* scrawny creature was still living, he couldn't have been out too terribly long. Still, it could have been long enough for Trevelyan to have found Blaire. "Well," he said to the cat, "no time to waste, is there?" After all, a pretty witch who loved him was somewhere on the road to Edinburgh.

The cat yawned.

James couldn't help but laugh. "You can rest on the way. I have a feeling a lad in Edinburgh is missing you dreadfully." He scooped the cat up in his arms and headed for Matthew's abandoned chambers. There must be a valise or something in which he could keep the little creature until they reached their destination. Besides, the poor thing would be terrified unless he couldn't see where they were going. And James had no desire to show up on Blaire's doorstep covered in claw marks from head to toe. He may bleed, after all, now that he had a life source of his own moving through his veins.

James tugged the bellpull in the corner of the room. After the previous evening's events, bathing and starting the day refreshed would be nice, but there wasn't time. Not if he meant to catch up to his witch.

A scratch came at his door. James glanced toward the sound. "Come."

A nervous Highland maid pushed the door open wide. "Ye rang, sir?"

James nodded. "Lord Blodswell's coach is in the stables, is it not?"

"Aye, my lord."

Perfect. Matthew should already be in London; hopefully MacQuarrie had made the journey without expiring. "See that it's readied, lass. I have need of it."

"Of course, my lord."

※◦

The two day journey to Edinburgh had been a nightmare, to say the least. Blaire's sleep had been laden with nightmares, the kind that would typically make someone bound from their bed and jump into wakefulness. Yet she couldn't escape the depression-filled haze that brought her lower than she'd ever been. When she was awake, her nerves were so on edge that Blaire nearly jumped out of her skin at each bump in the road, certain James had awoken despite the dampening spell and was dead set on revenge for her trickery.

As night fell, her nerves only rattled more. Was Trevelyan chasing them? Had he finally caught up to them? And if so, would she have the power to hold him off without her coven sisters surrounding her? It was all foolishness, she well knew. Trevelyan's feud was with James, not her. Trevelyan had no reason to follow her to Edinburgh.

The carriage driver they'd borrowed from the Fergusons had been none too happy when Aiden had roused him from the warm bed of a village widow in the dead of night. The man's outlook hadn't changed during the entire drive. Adding to their misery,

Brannock had sulked ever since they left Briarcraig.
Not because he would miss the dreary place, but
because he'd been unable to locate Bruce the cat
before their departure.

Fortunately, Aiden had taken pity on her. He'd
only lamented the loss of Heather Fyfe half a dozen
times on the journey, but he had draped his arm
around her shoulders, squeezed her hands when she
fidgeted, and promised her everything would turn
out all right. She so wished her brother had Cait's
power of clairvoyance, that he could say such things
with absolute certainty. But she wouldn't truly feel
at peace until she was reunited with Caitrin, Elspeth,
Rhiannon, and Sorcha, until she could feel the power
of them surge together and protect those they loved.

As daylight faded, Blaire could finally make out
Edinburgh in the distance. She released a sigh of relief.
Just a little while longer, and they could return to their
own lives. Her heart contracted at the thought. Aiden
and Brannock would be safe, but she would never stop
missing James and wishing for a life that couldn't be
hers. Was *this* what Fiona had seen all those years ago?
That James would break her heart and leave her only
a shell of the witch she'd once been? Is *that* why the
coven tried to protect her from him?

"Almost there," Aiden said quietly beside her.

Blaire nodded. "As soon as we get things settled, I
need ta see the others."

Her older brother nodded. "Aye, I figured as much.
Give Caitrin my felicitations."

"Alec." The name rushed from Blaire. What would
she tell Cait about Alec?

Aiden squeezed her arm. "One thing at a time, lass. And with any luck, MacQuarrie will be whole and hale before ye have ta tell her anythin'."

But that wasn't true. She'd have to tell Cait the truth. She'd have to tell all of them the truth. She could never keep something of this magnitude from her coven. There was no sense going into that with Aiden, however, so she nodded her head.

"What about Alec? I–I mean Mr. MacQuarrie? Did somethin' happen ta him?" Brannock piped up after having said very little for the longest while.

With Brannock, however, Blaire wasn't ready to divulge the truth. In fact, she might never be ready. The poor lad was still having nightmares about Sarah Reese's pointy teeth. The last thing Blaire would do was add to his fears. "Nothin'. He just dinna want ta come back with us, is all."

"No' with Miss Macleod's marriage," Aiden supplied helpfully. "I suppose I should say Lady Brimsworth, though."

The fabrication seemed to placate Brannock, who turned his attention back outside as Edinburgh grew larger in the window. Blaire and Aiden exchanged a look, quietly agreeing to keep all talk of vampyres and other terrible creatures away from Brannock as long as possible.

"Doona wait for us ta get settled, Blaire. I'll have the driver take ye ta the Fergusons' first. No need ta unload and unpack. We strong Lindsay men can handle that."

Blaire leaned forward and kissed Aiden's cheek. He really was a very dear brother.

❦

Blaire bounded up the steps of Sorcha Ferguson's stately Georgian home and rapped loudly on the door. A moment later, the elderly butler with wild grey hair stood before her. "Miss Lindsay," he greeted her, "I dinna realize ye were home."

Home. In the strangest sense, it felt like home was Briarcraig Castle, beside James Maitland. She shook the melancholy thought from her mind and forced a smile to her face as she stepped over the threshold. "I've actually just returned. Please tell me Miss Ferguson is home,"

The words were barely out of her mouth, and the door closed behind her, before a high-pitched squeal assaulted her ears. Then Sorcha, with all her natural grace, appeared from nowhere and launched herself into Blaire's arms.

"Oh, we've missed ye so much. I canna wait ta hear about Aiden's castle. Is it as horrid as ye feared? Oh, and ye willna believe what's happened ta Cait." Sorcha slid her fingers against her thumb slowly and smiled as a rosebud opened within her palm.

Blaire shook her head and took it from the younger witch. "Married some English lord, I hear."

Sorcha's smile vanished. "Augh! I hoped I'd get ta tell ye," she complained. "I wished ye could've been here, Blaire. Lord Brimsworth is just as dashin' as Benjamin Westfield."

Blaire couldn't help but smile at her coven sister. Sorcha was always the most exuberant of the bunch. "Ye can tell me all the details. MacQuarrie was sparse on those."

Sorcha linked her arm with Blaire's and tugged her toward a cheerful yellow parlor. "Poor Mr. MacQuarrie. I dinna see him before he left. Was he very heartbroken?"

His heart was the least of his worries now, but Blaire couldn't bring herself to tell the tale more than once. She shook her head.

"Wallace was beside himself," Sorcha giggled. "I think he actually threatened Lord Brimsworth."

Blaire couldn't care less what Sorcha's overgrown half-brother had done. "Listen, Sorch, somethin' has happened. Somethin' terrible. We need ta gather everyone together. We're goin' ta need all our powers combined."

Sorcha dropped Blaire's arm, and fear washed across her features. "That's no' possible."

"Is Elspeth no' back?" Blaire's head pounded as she sank into an overstuffed chintz chair. "How much longer will it be, do ye think?"

"It's no' Elspeth." Sorcha frowned. "She and Benjamin returned yesterday, but Caitrin is gone."

"Gone!" Blaire bellowed. "But she just returned."

"Well, she had some vision of Lord Brimsworth's father, and she and the earl started for Kent with no time ta spare. It could be months before she's back in Edinburgh. What's happened? Why do we need all of us?"

Blaire's heart sank. Without all five of them, what would they do? Without Cait in their numbers, it was foolhardy to rouse everyone tonight. They'd have the same trouble worrying them tomorrow. "More than I can go inta tonight. Send a note ta the others for me, will ye?"

"Of course."

"Can we meet in yer orangery tomorrow for luncheon?"

Sorcha's soft brown eyes twinkled. "Oh, what a wonderful idea. I can show ye my new orchids."

Orchids were the last thing on Blaire's mind.

Twenty-Three

BLAIRE PACED SORCHA'S ORANGERY FROM ONE END OF the windowed room to the other. She was being foolish, she knew. She was early; the others weren't even late. But she couldn't help herself. All morning long she'd felt as though someone was watching her, and it made the hair at the back of her neck stand on end.

"*Havers!*" Lady Elspeth Westfield's voice stopped Blaire mid-pace.

Blaire turned on her heel and rushed toward her friend. It seemed like a lifetime since she'd seen her last, though in truth it had only been a few months. Blaire threw her arms around the healing witch's neck and held her tightly, though she was careful of Elspeth's protruding belly. Even so, she felt the bairn kick her.

Elspeth laughed and brushed her wild, red hair from her face. "She is very particular about her space." She lovingly smoothed a hand across her stomach. But her green eyes, ever knowing, remained focused on Blaire. "Ye've been cryin'."

That was something warrior witches just didn't do.

Blaire shrugged and walked toward one of Sorcha's rosebushes. "Somethin' in my eye, I'm sure."

Behind her, Elspeth scoffed. "Ye can try ta spin that yarn with someone who hasna kent ye yer whole life." She walked up behind Blaire and placed a delicate hand on her shoulder. "Cait was terrified somethin' had happened ta ye. Was she right?"

Blaire sagged forward. With Aiden and the others, she could pretend, but Elspeth could always see right through her. "My life's a mess. And I doona ken what ta do about any of it." She swiped at a traitorous tear.

"Tell me, Blaire. I'll do whatever I can ta help ye."

She turned to face her friend. "Did ye ken our mothers, all of them, trapped a man and kept him locked up in a castle in the Highlands?

Elspeth's mouth dropped open. "I beg yer pardon."

Blaire shook her head. "But he's no' really a man. A man couldna have survived such a thing."

"Then what is he?" Marriage to a Lycan had made Elspeth more accepting of the fantastical than some others might be.

"Would ye believe a vampyre?"

A strange look settled on Elspeth's face, and she frowned as though trying to remember something. "A vampyre?" Then she looked Blaire straight in the eyes. "I think I remember some talk about a vampyre, but I was so young at the time. Nothin' is comin' ta me."

Blaire nodded. "If ye remember somethin' about *this* vampyre, ye would've only been two or so."

Elspeth's green eyes widened. "Two? Do ye mean the man—the vampyre—was locked away for twenty years?"

Blaire sighed. "James remembered they said somethin' about his future victims, but I canna imagine him ever hurtin' anyone." Other than herself, that was. And he couldn't really be blamed for not loving her, could he?

"James?" Elspeth pounced right on that slip of the tongue. "The vampyre is called James?"

No use going back at this point. "James Maitland, Baron Kettering."

Her friend smiled. "And would this James be the reason yer life is a mess?"

Blaire eyes dropped to the floor. "Only I would be foolish enough ta lose my heart ta a man who doesna have one ta give me in return."

Elspeth gently touched her cheek. "Oh, Blaire sweetheart, it canna be that dire. Men are foolish creatures no matter if they're human or somethin' else. Ye can trust me on that. I love Benjamin with all my heart, but I'm no' blind ta his faults. They say things differently than we hear them and vice versa. It's a miracle we're even able ta carry on conversations with men."

Blaire smiled at her friend's kindness. Elspeth never could stand to see anyone in pain, whether it be physically or otherwise. But there was no smoothing over James' words to her. He cared for her, but he could never love her. He had said so himself. There wasn't a lot of room for misunderstanding with such a statement.

"Oh!" Sorcha's melodic voice came from the doorway. "Ye're both here already. Have ye seen Rhi?"

"No' yet," Elspeth replied and then braced herself for one of Sorcha's hugs. "No' so tight—the bairn…"

Sorcha released her instantly. "I'm sorry, El. I forgot myself." Then she directed them to a table, nearly overflowing with vines and a silver tea service. "Sit, sit. Last night Blaire said somethin' terrible had happened, and I couldna sleep all night worryin' about it."

Blaire looked toward the empty doorway. "Doona ye think we should wait for Rhi?"

Sorcha shook her head, and her perfect brown curls swayed back and forth. "If she wants ta hear things first, she should try bein' on time." She gracefully slid into one of the slat-backed chairs and tipped her chin up, daring either of the others to defy her. This was Sorcha's court after all. "Tea?" She gestured to the pot before her.

Blaire shook her head. Tea would not solve her problems, but she took a seat at the table anyway.

"Now what is this terrible thin' that happened? Can we do somethin' about it?"

Blaire sighed. "I'd hoped the five of us could do somethin' together, but with Cait gone, I doona ken that we can. But I thought ye should all ken what transpired, just the same."

Elspeth slid into an empty seat around the table, her eyes searching Blaire's. "Do go on."

So she told them. She told them about their mothers trapping James decades earlier. She told them about her mother's ring and how it really belonged to James. She told them about Sarah Reese and how she'd overpowered Blaire. She told them about Padrig Trevelyan and how the man's gaze terrified her. She told them about James returning to the castle, his clothes bloodied from Alec's injuries, though she still didn't have any details about that situation. And she told them about her escape with Aiden and Brannock from Briarcraig and the feeling of foreboding that had followed her ever since.

"I still canna believe our mothers did such a thing!" Sorcha sat back in her seat as though she was affronted. "And no' ta tell us!"

Elspeth shook her head. "I feel like the answer is just in the recesses of my mind, but I just canna remember it." She turned her gaze to Sorcha. "Do ye think Wallace might remember somethin'?" Sorcha's brother was closer to thirty than twenty.

"I doona ken, but I can ask him."

Not that Blaire held out a lot of hope. Even if Wallace Ferguson knew why their mothers had done such an awful thing, that wouldn't really solve her current predicament, would it?

Sorcha leaned forward in her seat, her soft brown eyes focused on Blaire. "There's one thin' I doona understand from yer tale."

"And that is?"

"Well, I canna believe the baron just let ye leave Briarcraig."

Of course, she hadn't told them every detail, nor did she plan to. "I had a bit of luck on my side." She'd worn him down by letting him make blissful love to her and then escaped while he slept. Blaire avoided their most interested gazes. "What do ye suppose is keepin' Rhiannon?" She wasn't the most punctual of witches, but even this was strange. One would think that after receiving a summons, she would have arrived by *now*.

Just then, the door to the orangery blew open, seemingly almost of its own volition. Rhiannon, followed by a huge gust of wind that lifted Blaire's hair, bustled through the door. The air nearly crackled with her impatience.

"Oh, my, she does have herself in a bit of a maelstrom," Sorcha mumbled.

"It would appear so," Elspeth whispered back dramatically.

Rhiannon wasted no time as she tugged her gloves from her fingers. "Somethin' is no' right," she said quickly as she shook her head with wonder. "I doona ken what it is, but somethin' is off."

"Off?" Blaire questioned. "What do ye mean?"

"I have no idea," Rhiannon said. "But I can feel it on the wind."

"What do ye feel?" Elspeth asked as she sat forward and rested her chin on the heel of her overturned hand. Rhiannon had always been able to feel trouble brewing. It was unexplainable, but her powers were ripe for any emotional disturbances that didn't plague the others quite as harshly.

Rhiannon closed her eyes and blew the door open with a heavy breath through pursed lips. Air from outside rushed into the orangery. Rhiannon shivered. "I've been tryin' ta figure it out all mornin'. It's a blamed nuisance, this gift of mine. Doesna tell me a blasted thing, aside from the fact that *somethin'* is wrong."

"It followed me home," Blaire confessed. "I'm so sorry. But I couldna think of any other way." She blinked back a tear. Battle-born witches did *not* cry.

A drop of water fell onto the top of Blaire's head.

Fantastic. If she cried, of course Rhiannon would sympathize, and then they'd all be a blasted mess.

"Someone tell her a humorous story, will ye?" Blaire said, her voice choked with emotion. "Or we'll all drown in here, and I find it very difficult to run in wet skirts."

The small rain cloud evaporated. "And ta think I missed ye," Rhiannon grumbled.

"Aye, I missed ye, as well," Blaire admitted. She'd missed them all so much. But not the same way she now missed James.

The story spilled from Blaire's lips a third time. When Blaire got to the part about Sarah Reese and her desire for Brannock, a lightning bolt flickered within the room, a brief flash of bold color.

"Doona hurt my plants!" Sorcha yelled at Rhiannon.

"My apologies," Rhiannon mumbled. Then she took a deep breath. "*That's* what I'm feelin'. He's here. This man who's huntin' ye. He's in Edinburgh."

"How do ye ken?" That was a ridiculous question. Yet Blaire found it escaping her lips anyway.

"I just do," Rhiannon shrugged. "There's a disturbance in the air. His hatred fuels his quest for ye. And I can feel how much he dislikes that ye're livin'."

Blaire jumped to her feet. "I'll have ta leave. I'll have ta take my family and go somewhere safe."

Elspeth shook her head slowly. "And leave the people of Edinburgh ta face his wrath? With only three of us ta fight him? And no' a battle-born witch among us, once ye're gone? Ye lost yer mind when ye lost yer heart. When ye lost it all." Elspeth's glance moved to Blaire's neck. Blaire felt a flush move up her cheeks. Certainly, she couldn't know...

"Do ye need a blast of cool air?" Rhiannon asked quickly as she noticed the heat that suffused Blaire's face.

"That willna be necessary," Blaire murmured. She took a deep breath. "We need a strategy. I think the best thing ta do is trap the vampyre and dispose of him."

"Dispose of him how?" Sorcha asked. Of course, the youngest witch would feel queasy at the thought of killing. But it didn't bother Blaire one bit.

"We have ta find him first," Elspeth reminded everyone.

"No' we," Rhiannon said quickly. "Ye happen ta have a bairn in yer belly, and we willna put her in danger."

A male voice broke in from the door of the orangery. "Danger?" Lord Benjamin Westfield asked, his usual wolfish grin missing from his handsome face at the very thought of Elspeth and their bairn being in danger. "Who's in danger?" he barked.

"No one," Elspeth soothed as she rose to her feet and crossed to her husband. One of his arms snaked around her waist and drew her to his side as the other hand landed on her belly. They were really so happy that it was nauseating. Yet Blaire still wished she could have what they shared. With James.

Elspeth's husband peered down into her eyes. "Don't lie to me."

"I'll no' tell this tale again," Blaire snapped as she stood up as well. "If yer husband wants ta be nosy, El, he can ask ye all the questions he likes. I have huntin' ta do."

Elspeth called out to her retreating form, "Doona walk away, Blaire. I need ta ask ye about somethin'." Her gaze once again settled on Blaire's neck.

"I doona need yer healin'," Blaire said quickly. After all, there was no way to heal from the loss of James.

"It's no' *my* healin' ye need," Elspeth said softly. "I'm aware of that. I just want ta be certain ye're all right."

"We'll talk later then." Blaire started toward the exit.

"Where are ye goin'?" Sorcha wanted to know. "May I come, too?"

Blaire nodded quickly, and Sorcha and Rhiannon fell into step behind her. No doubt, Elspeth would join them as soon as she had spilled the whole story to that beast of hers. Or perhaps not. There wasn't another man on Earth who was more overprotective than Benjamin Westfield. And that could be a blessing in disguise. Elspeth would pull every detail Blaire had kept tucked closely to her chest and spill them all across the floor. She wasn't in a hurry to divulge such secrets to anyone, not even caring, generous Elspeth.

As soon as James arrived in Edinburgh, Arthur's Seat called to him like a beacon. He wasn't certain how to go about finding his witch in the city, but she hunted like a man, shot like a man, and fought like a man. The main peak of the hills in the southern corner of the city seemed like a place she would have spent time. Looking there was most certainly a waste of time, but he didn't know where else to start.

He plopped Bruce the cat back into the traveling valise, and the pair of them left Matthew's coachman at the base of the hills, promising to return soon.

Fresh Scottish air seeped into James' lungs as he

climbed the Seat, an experience that still amazed him after centuries of not breathing. Finally, he stood at the top of Arthur's Seat and looked down at picturesque Edinburgh below. The sun warmed his hair, and the wind danced across his neck. His heart beat a quick rhythm inside his chest, slightly overtaxed by the climb up the largest hill. But it was a glorious feeling to hear his blood pumping within his veins.

A plaintive wail reached out to him from the valise at his side. His little feline companion was not a contented traveler. More than once along the journey, the cat had screamed loudly enough that James was looked upon with curiosity. He'd be very happy when he could return the cat to Brannock Lindsay. No doubt the ugly creature would be happy to be free of rocking coaches, as well, James was certain.

Freedom. It was something James had never expected to feel. He'd always assumed, from the moment of his first death, that he'd forever be tied to the need for a life source not of his own making, that he would never lead a *normal* life. It was simply unfathomable that his heart now beat. That he was human. That he was free to love as he chose. To age. To have a family. And he owed it all to Blaire.

He couldn't wait to see her, to hold her in his arms. To chastise her for running out on him. Although now he was certain her leaving was what had caused his heart to beat once more. After all, one must have a heart for it to be broken. And it wasn't until she was gone that he realized how very much he loved her, indeed.

An inhuman growl emanated from the valise, and it shook in his hand. James chuckled. "Sorry, Bruce. I know it's a bit cramped. But Matthew will kill me all over again if I let you shred his coach's interior. Besides, it won't be long before we find your master, and then you can run to your heart's content or burrow in settees or eat fishy snacks or whatever it is you're dying to do."

Just then, a sound caught his attention. Female voices coming in his direction from a trail below. And one of them was not just any female voice. James' heart soared. For once, luck had found him.

"Blaire!" he called and darted down that particular path. He must be the most fortunate man on Earth. He'd thought it would take hours to locate her in a city the size of Edinburgh. Perhaps even days. How amazingly fortuitous that she should stumble across his path. Of course, in the last little while, he'd become a complete believer in fate.

A moment later, he spotted her, traipsing up the hill wrapped in a tattered coat, the Lindsay plaid draped across her shoulders. Blaire's mouth fell open when her eyes landed on him, and the two young women flanking her on either side gasped.

"Ja—Lord Kettering," Blaire finally found her voice, though she still didn't move an inch toward him. "What are ye doin' here?"

"*That's* Lord Kettering?" the delicate brunette beside her mumbled before James could respond. "I canna believe ye left *him*. Are ye mad?"

"Shush, Sorcha," the other woman hissed.

Blaire glanced over her shoulder at the tiny brunette and frowned. "Can ye behave?"

Sorcha, at least James assumed that was her name, shrugged. A little smile tilted up her lips on one side, and her warm brown eyes twinkled when they fell on him. "Did they lock ye up, my lord, ta keep ye from breakin' hearts?"

She certainly was a saucy little thing. James almost laughed, but he kept his eyes on Blaire and lifted his brow. "You told them who I am? What happened to me?" Not that he was surprised. How many times had she told him she trusted her coven above all else, including him?

Blaire gulped under his gaze. "They had a right ta ken. Their mothers were involved as well."

James looked at the three Scottish lasses before him. Memories of the revenge he'd once wanted to take on their mothers for trapping him in that crumbling castle and keeping him locked away from the rest of the world flashed in his mind. All of it meant nothing now. If that coven long ago hadn't captured him, he might never have crossed Blaire's path. He might never have fallen for her. He might never have become human again. No, not revenge. He owed that coven and their daughters his life and so much more. "It is a pleasure to meet you, ladies." And he truly meant it.

The brunette sighed, and a dreamy expression settled on her face.

Blaire narrowed her eyes on James. "I asked ye no' ta come here."

"You did," he agreed, and then he closed the distance between them, dropped the valise at his feet, and grasped her hand in his. "But you also agreed to be my wife, and in my way of thinking, there's nowhere else I should be other than by your side."

Blaire's lip trembled, and James had the urge to kiss her right then and there with her friends looking on—and damn the consequences. "I told ye I couldna marry ye."

The brunette gasped behind them, as though the idea was an affront to her personally.

Blaire glanced over her shoulder and met the willowy witch's eye. "Rhi, can ye do somethin' with her?"

The woman draped her arm around the brunette's shoulder and began to drag her from the scene. "But she dinna tell us that part of the story, Rhi," the little one grumbled as they disappeared around a bend. "And I'm thinkin' that was the most important part!"

"I'd have to agree with your exuberant little friend." James couldn't help but smile at the comments the littlest witch threw over her shoulder.

"She's a pest."

"I should be furious with you for leaving me the way you did."

Blaire shook her head. "There was no other way. Yer as stubborn—"

"—As you are, my love. And you're right, I would never have let you leave."

"I had ta protect my brothers, James. I doona expect ye ta understand."

He sighed. "You are your own worst enemy, Blaire. Do you know that?"

She frowned and folded her arms across her chest. "I most certainly am no'."

"Oh, you are." He nodded his head to emphasize his point. "You ran off without thinking the situation through."

"I thought it through!" She insisted and jabbed him in the chest with a pointy finger.

He couldn't help but chuckle, even though the situation was far from humorous. He was just so happy to have found her. Relieved. So ecstatic he could float to the heavens. Still they had a little business to see to first. "Did you indeed? Do you recall me telling you that Trevelyan would hurt you just to get his revenge on me?"

"Only because he *thought* you cared for me."

"I *do* care for you."

"Out of sight, out of mind."

That was on the edge of enough. Did she have so little faith in his feelings? "Give me your hand."

"I beg your pardon."

"Give. Me. Your. Hand," he clipped out.

She thrust her hand behind her back. "What do ye want with it?"

"Blaire," James sighed as he pulled her hand from behind her, peeled the glove from her wrist, and then freed each slender finger. "Beautiful," he muttered, squeezing her hand before sliding it inside his overcoat, jacket, and waistcoat. He held it against the fine lawn of his shirt and pressed it against his chest. "There. Do you feel that?"

She glared at him as though he was the most inept man in existence. "What exactly am I supposed to be—" She gasped and ripped her hand from his grasp, as though she'd touched a hot stove.

James grinned. She'd felt it. He knew she had. "Out of sight, out of mind, huh?"

"Is that yer…heart?" The words seemed wrenched from her soul.

"It took you leaving to make it beat again, Blaire. One must have a heart for it to break. Evidently, mine was there all along, just waiting for you."

                          ⤝⤞

Blaire choked on a sob. She'd been trying so hard for so long *not* to cry, and yet she couldn't help the flood of tears that now streamed down her cheeks.

"Oh, my love," James crooned and dabbed her cheeks with a handkerchief. "I've never seen you so upset."

But none of it made any sense at all. "I doona understand."

"I'm not sure I understand any better than you do. I woke up alone," he glanced at the valise at his feet, "or nearly. Then I read your note, which crushed my heart by the way, and raced here as fast as I could. I'm slightly impaired without my speed and strength, so I had to travel by carriage. You haven't seen Trevelyan, have you?"

Blaire's mind was still reeling with all that he was saying. "What does that mean? How is it that yer heart is beatin'?"

James took a step away from her and tugged the crested ring from his finger.

Her heart leapt to her throat. "No!" Was he mad? He'd be burned alive. He was…laughing at her. She couldn't believe it. He *was* laughing at her.

James tossed the ring high in the air and then caught

it. "I don't need it any longer, love. My heart now beats. I'm as human as the next man." He grinned. "Well, I'm a little faster than the next man. And stronger. But that's probably just my body's response to being so strong for so long. It adapted." He shrugged. "Some traits haven't left me all together."

It was so much to take in. Blaire could only blink at him. "How?"

"Not, 'how.' *Who*." He stressed the last word. "You, Blaire. You did this to me. And I can never thank you enough."

Thank her? She shook her head. She'd never wanted his thanks. It was her mother's fault he'd been locked away all those years ago. Her fault his life had been stolen from him.

"What is it?" He grasped her elbow and tugged her toward him. "Don't tell me now that I'm human you don't love me anymore."

A gurgled laugh escaped her throat, which was mildly embarrassing. "I-I doona ken ta say."

"Say you'll have me, Blaire."

A horrible grumbling growl came from the valise at their feet, and Blaire took a startled step backward. "What the devil is that?"

James smirked. "You left Briarcraig in such a hurry that poor Bruce got left behind."

Blaire's eyes fell once more to the bag. "Ye brought that miserable creature with ye? I'd thought we were well rid of it."

"Oh, come now," James took her hand in his. "He's not that bad. And I know how much Brannock adores the thing."

James would be her brother's hero from now until the end of time. "Was that yer plan? Butter Brannock up and have him plead yer case?"

He laughed, and the rich sound encompassed Blaire's heart. He seemed so different now. Much more at ease. More lighthearted. Blaire blinked up at him. It wasn't just her imagination. He *was* different. "Your eyes," she whispered.

The smile fell from his face. "What about them?"

She shook her head, not truly believing it herself. "They're blue."

"They are?" He appeared as amazed by that fact as she was.

Blaire took a step away from him. She needed time to think, time to clear her head. "I canna do this right now."

"Do what?"

She gestured wildly between the two of them. "This. Us."

"Blaire." He reached for her, but she stepped further away.

"Just a little time, James."

He frowned at her. "Trevelyan is out there, Blaire."

She glanced up at the sky and the sun beaming down on them. "Perhaps, but I'll be safe enough until sundown."

"Very well." He sighed. "But don't take too long."

Twenty-Four

James' heart clenched as Blaire escaped down a side path. Time. She needed time. For what? He thought she loved him, though now he wasn't sure if she ever said those words. Was she regretting what they'd been to each other at Briarcraig? Did she no longer want him now that he was more than a heartless vampyre?

He heaved a sigh.

It would be God's cruel punishment to give him his heart back after nearly two hundred and twenty-five years only to have the woman he loved toss it back at him when he offered it to her.

"Ye can stop now, Rhi." An irritated whisper reached his ears. "She's gone."

James turned toward the sound to see Blaire's bubbly, brunette coven sister poking her head out from behind a tree. "Were you listening the entire time?" he asked.

She didn't even have the good grace to look ashamed. Instead she huffed indignantly. "Nay," she grumbled as she walked slowly up the path toward him. "Rhiannon whipped the air around me so loudly I couldna hear a thing."

As if on cue, the willowy witch followed her friend from behind the shrubbery and sighed. "Had the roles been reversed, ye wouldna want anyone listenin' ta yer conversation."

The brunette rolled her eyes. "Ha! *I* wouldna hold out on any of ye in the first place."

Though James' heart still ached, the youngest witch did make him smile. It would be impossible to dislike the lass.

"Anyway," she said, finally reaching him, "we were no' properly introduced. I'm Sorcha Ferguson, and that's," she gestured with her head, "Rhiannon Sinclair."

James inclined his head in greeting. "James Maitland, Baron Kettering."

"I ken." Sorcha Ferguson beamed at him. "And I'm so happy ta make yer acquaintance."

"Are you?" If Blaire's friends were honestly happy to meet him, perhaps all wasn't lost. She must have said good things about him, at the very least.

"Oh, aye!" Sorcha nodded enthusiastically. "I've never met a vampyre before."

Was that all it was? Did all of these witches prefer the undead to live, breathing men? Would Sorcha turn tail and flee him, too, if she knew that truth, that he was now just a man? "I'm really not that special."

But she shook her head as though that was nonsense. "Vampyres are new for me. I've learned all about Lycans from Lord Benjamin, but—"

"Sorcha!" the other witch hissed just as a quick breeze blasted across the youngest one's brown hair.

With an exasperated sigh, Sorcha turned to her sister witch and smoothed her hair back in place.

"That was uncalled for, Rhi. Do ye ken how long Maggie worked on my curls today?"

"Some secrets are no' ours ta divulge," Rhiannon Sinclair countered.

Sorcha snorted. "Now yer concerned about Lord Benjamin? When he first came here, I was the only one nice ta him."

"Well, I doona think he'd appreciate ye tellin' some strange vampyre ye doona even ken all of his secrets."

Sorcha turned her gaze back to James. "But yer no' some strange vampyre, are ye? Did ye really ask Blaire ta marry ye?"

He nodded once.

"See?" Sorcha tossed back over her shoulder. "He's as good as family."

James took his first relieved breath in quite a while. Sorcha Ferguson might be more chatty than was wise, but she was the closest thing to an ally he had in these parts. He glanced down at the growling valise at his feet. "Would you mind directing my driver to the Lindsay household? I have something that desperately needs to be returned to young Master Brannock."

⤜⤐

The sun was just starting to set as Blaire stepped through the front door of Lindsay House. She crossed the threshold into the parlor and groaned aloud. There, sitting in her threadbare straight-backed chair, James Maitland appeared to be the center of attention. Crowded around him was…everyone else.

In the settee beside Elspeth, Sorcha prattled endlessly about something inane. Lord Benjamin leaned casually against the window frame, nursing a glass of whisky. Brannock sat on the floor in the corner playing with that dratted cat and a ball of string. And Rhiannon paced anxiously at the far end of the room, leaving a slight breeze in her wake.

Truly, she shouldn't have been surprised at any of this. Sorcha must have gone back in search of James atop Arthur's Seat as soon as she'd realized Blaire was gone. But what else was she to do? She'd just been so surprised to see him that her confused emotions bubbled over; she had needed a little time to catch her breath, to sort out her thoughts. After all, it wasn't every day that someone met a vampyre and allowed him to take her blood, then her innocence, then her heart, perhaps not in that order. She'd nearly resigned herself to missing him the rest of her life, convinced herself it was better to live alone than with him but without his love. And then…then he turned up out of nowhere and said he was *human*. A little time to clear her head was not too much to ask.

James caught sight of her in the doorway and quickly came to his feet with a smile.

A gentle burst of wind brushed her cheek. Yes, Rhiannon. She was fine. No need to worry. Yet the weather-controlling witch couldn't help but be led by her emotions. It was part of who she was. Evidently, it was part of who Blaire was, too. Emotions. She snorted indelicately. Who'd have ever thought she had any?

Sorcha turned to look in her direction when she heard that unladylike snuffle from her nose. "Oh, there ye are," she gushed as she leaned forward, placed her tea on the table, and then jumped to her feet. She slid one slender hand into the crook of James' arm, and he smiled down at her. "Look who we found on his way down from the Seat."

"Ye *found* Lord Kettering?" Blaire asked, well aware the meddlesome wood sprite would never allow an unattached man to go about aimlessly. Particularly not one as handsome as James Maitland.

"Aye, he was lookin' for yer house." Sorcha beamed. "But we rescued him."

"I'm certain he appreciated yer assistance," Blaire said drolly. Although she'd walked about for more than two hours trying to slow the roiling thoughts within her mind, she now found that she was just as discombobulated as she had been when she'd first spied James that afternoon. And his powder-blue eyes.

"I was quite grateful," James said as he walked toward Blaire. Sorcha dropped his arm when she sensed his direction, a satisfied smirk on her face.

"Why are ye here?" Blaire asked directly.

James' back straightened a bit. "Returning Brannock's pet and to talk with the captain, of course."

"Where is Aiden?" She glanced around the room. If James had confessed all they'd been to each other to her brother, Aiden would be here awaiting her return, ready to thrash her. Strange that he was the only one absent in this unlikely gathering.

"He went ta see Mr. MacDonald," Brannock reminded her without looking up from the scraggily cat.

To discuss his new fortune and get the man's opinion on sound investments. How could she forget? "Well, ye'd best leave before he returns."

James narrowed his light blue eyes on her. She didn't think she'd ever get used to the color. "I'm not leaving, Blaire. Trevelyan is out there some-where. Besides, Captain Lindsay and I need to come to an understanding."

Arrogant as ever. Unlike his eye color, that certainly hadn't changed. "Well, then I hope ye enjoy yer discussion with Aiden whenever he returns," she said with a slow nod. "For now, I'm goin' up ta bed."

"Blaire!" Sorcha gasped. Rhiannon's wind grazed her cheek once more. Opposite ends of the spectrum, those witches were. If she wasn't so confused, it might be hysterical.

"Sleep well, love," James said quietly, his voice rumbling across her skin like a caress. She suppressed a shiver. Yet she forced herself not to look back in his direction. "I'll still be here in the morning," he added just before she passed out of sight.

"Ye doona plan ta leave?" she asked. She sounded like a dolt, she knew. But it was torturous having him around yet not being able to touch him, to love him.

"Not with Trevelyan out there."

"Perhaps ye've forgotten I can take care of myself."

A seductive smile graced his lips. "Then perhaps I'll need *you* to protect *me* from his wrath."

Blaire rolled her eyes. He could charm stars right out of the night sky. No wonder Sorcha looked so mesmerized.

"Besides," he continued, gazing directly at her, his intent unmistakable, "I do need to have that word with your brother." He meant to offer for her hand. She was certain of it. What would she do if Aiden said yes? She'd most likely jump for joy. Then she'd hate herself afterward.

She turned back toward the staircase and didn't stop until she reached her room; then she stomped across the room and flung herself onto the bed. She wanted to curl into a ball and die. No, she wanted to curl at James' side and tell him she loved him. But what she *most* wanted was to hear him tell her the same thing.

She suffered in silence for only a few moments before a quick rap on her door drew her from her misery. Before she could even call out a response, the door opened a crack and Elspeth slipped inside. She crossed the room without a word, took a chair by Blaire's head, and held out her hand. Wordlessly, Blaire clutched it with her own. They sat in silence for a moment as Blaire tried to reign in her emotions.

Finally, Elspeth let out a little giggle. "I canna believe Brannock is downstairs cuddlin' with that hideous, hairless, earless excuse for a feline."

"That would be Bruce," Blaire mumbled into her pillow. "Brannock found him at Briarcraig, and I thought we were well rid of the beast until James brought him back ta us."

"He reminds me of a patchwork quilt. A very old one."

"He *is* very old. About two hundred and fifty years."

Elspeth covered her heart with her free hand and gasped. "*Havers!* Now I ken ye lost yer mind when ye lost yer heart. I've never heard of a cat that old! Has he been enchanted?"

Blaire mumbled into the pillow again. "No' the

cat, El. The man. Kettering is two hundred and fifty years old."

"Oh, my," Elspeth breathed. "Maybe that's why he looks handsome. He has had a very long time ta get himself in shape."

Blaire sat up and swung her legs over the bed to face her friend. "Nay, I think that's part of who he is. Or was. Vampyres tend to be quite perfect, physically."

Elspeth's eyebrow shot up. "Seen enough of them ta ken?"

"More than I'd like. They're quite beastly in their own right."

"Beasts really are no' a bad lot," Elspeth reminded her as she leaned back and tucked her legs into the chair to get comfortable. "I love mine dearly, even when he shakes mud all over me under the light of the moon." Her face took on a dreamy quality. "Of course, then he gets to clean me off," she giggled.

Heat suffused Blaire's face. "There are some things that should no' be discussed so openly, El," she grumbled.

"Typically, I would keep my marital bliss out of your life, particularly the romantic parts of it. But I have a feelin' that ye've had a taste of it already." Her gaze danced across the two small pin pricks at the base of Blaire's neck. "Or *he* had a taste. I'm no' certain which description is more accurate."

"Ye've no idea what ye're talkin' about," Blaire sighed. Though she wished she did. She needed to tell someone.

"I never could tell ye before, seein' as how ye were unmarried and Ben was a Lycan and all, but I do ken what ye're feelin'." She bared her shoulder and showed Blaire the two crescent-moon-shaped mouth prints, one upper and one lower, that made the mouth print of a man. "Lycans claim their mates."

Blaire had heard about "claiming," but she hadn't known what it meant until this very moment. "He *bit* ye?" she nearly screeched as she appraised the mark.

"Oh, he most certainly did. And it was wonderful." Elspeth tilted her head at Blaire and regarded her quizzically. "How was yers?"

"Fabulous," Blaire moaned as she dropped her face into her hands. Then she looked up with a small smile she couldn't hide, no matter the situation. "Breathtakin'. Invigoratin'. It was like…" She couldn't even come up with the words.

"Like becomin' one? In more ways than just the physical?"

"That's it exactly." Blaire nodded.

"Ye must love him, or ye wouldna have given him yer innocence."

Blaire nodded again, slowly, contemplating what Elspeth had just declared. She did love him. "But he doesna love me back."

"What makes ye think that?"

"I asked him," Blaire said with a small snort.

"And he said he doesna love ye? I doona believe it." She shook her head vehemently. "No' with the way he looks at ye. No' with the way he raced ta get ta ye. He may no' be a Lycan, but he *claimed* ye, Blaire."

"He has bitten hundreds of women throughout the years. Probably thousands. He's been alive for two hundred and fifty years, doona forget. I'm nothin' special."

Elspeth blew harshly, a very unladylike sound. "Oh, open yer eyes. Ye're the reason why the man chased ye all the way here from Briarcraig Castle," she said sarcastically. "It wasna ta return that blasted cat, Blaire. It was for ye."

"Ye doona even ken the whole story."

"Oh, certainly, I do. Our Sorcha can get blood from a turnip when she sets her mind to it. She got the whole story from yer vampyre." She motioned toward Blaire's neck again. "Of course, he dinna talk about takin' yer innocence. But he told her about how his heart started ta beat when ye left him."

"Why would he do such a thing? Ta *Sorcha*?" she cried. "Why blab it all ta *Sorcha,* for heaven's sake?"

"He was probably hopin' for an ally or two. Because he certainly doesna have one in Benjamin, and I doubt he will with yer brother."

"Benjamin doesna approve?" Blaire's mouth fell open.

Elspeth shrugged. "He's a bit over protective of all of ye. Considers ye ta be his little sisters. I thought he was goin' ta take Brimsworth's head off when he found out about Cait."

Blaire giggled, not able to imagine such an occurrence. For a Lycan, Benjamin Westfield was generally affable and liked everyone. He sort of reminded her of a lapdog.

"He's worried about this Trevelyan fellow, Blaire. What is the nature of this feud between Kettering and the other vampyre?"

Blaire had no idea. It wasn't something they'd ever discussed. Before she could say as much, a loud crash and a *thunk* that nearly shook the walls of the home drew both the witches' attention.

"*Havers!*" Elspeth jumped to her feet.

"What the devil was that?" Blaire bolted for the door. If that cat was destroying her house…

∽

James had not felt such a blinding pain in two hundred and fifty years. He'd taken plenty of punches during that time, but vampyres healed themselves. Evidently, however, he'd lost that ability along with his speed and some of his strength. It was quite evident by the fact that his eye was throbbing like the devil. He looked up from the floor at the more-than-furious Aiden Lindsay, who was being held back but only marginally by the hulking Benjamin Westfield. Even if Sorcha hadn't confided all about the Lycan, James would have known him instantly for what he was. The wolfish gleam in his eye gave the man away.

"You better get up, Kettering, before I have to let him go," Westfield said drolly. "You need a fighting chance. Now you have one. Quit nursing that eye and find your feet, man." In that instant, the Lycan looked almost sorry for him.

James rolled to his feet. The pain had been a surprise. He could still take the captain in a fair fight, at least he thought he could; but putting the man to shame was the last thing he wanted, especially since what he *really* wanted was Aiden Lindsay's blessing.

Westfield released the captain just as Blaire rounded the corner. "What was that noise?" she cried. Then she stopped suddenly to take in the blood that dripped from the corner of James' eye. "What happened ta ye?" She reached to touch at his injury.

He winced and jerked his head away. "Well, right now, I have a witch probing at a very tender battle wound."

"That wasna a battle, blood-sucker," the captain snarled at him from over Westfield's shoulder. "I'll show ye a battle," he said as he pushed against the Lycan's hold again. "Blaire, doona touch him. Ye have no idea where he has been."

Oh, she had a pretty good idea where he'd been. James was certain she remembered when he'd been inside her. The very thought made his body react. This was *not* the time.

"He's no' a wild animal, Aiden," his witch scolded. "And ye shouldna call him names."

"Must we discuss wild animals?" Westfield asked, as though he was affronted.

"Good Lord," Blaire murmured. "Who would have thought ye would have such delicate feelings?"

"Keep it up, Miss Lindsay, and I'll let him go," Westfield replied, as he nodded toward Aiden, who still was trying to tear free of his hold.

"Benjamin," the red-headed witch scolded. But a smile lingered on her lips.

"Go ahead and let him go," Blaire said. "I can take him."

"That is no' humorous," the captain grunted.

"Yet so true," Blaire taunted.

James had to appreciate the man's fierce protective instinct toward his sister. If he had a daughter or a sister, he would feel the same way, he was certain.

"Why are ye still here?" Blaire asked him as she rubbed her forehead.

"I told you I'm not leaving you."

The captain growled at the announcement, and Blaire frowned at his reaction. "If ye tell him about us…" she warned quietly so that only he could hear. But Westfield's ears perked up at those words. He'd heard. Dear God, now he'd have an angry Lycan *and* an irate brother to deal with.

But the seriousness of the moment was broken when James' stomach rumbled loudly.

Blaire's eyebrows shot up quickly. Elspeth Westfield giggled, as did the littlest witch. "My apologies," James grunted. "I still haven't grown accustomed to this hunger thing."

"If ye plan ta make a meal of my sister, I'll kill ye right here!" the captain bellowed, once again fighting against Westfield's hold.

He'd love to make a meal of her but not one that involved piercing her flesh with his incisors, not anymore. "Actually, the very thought of blood turns my stomach." He mulled it over. Although it had been his life source for so long, the idea of consuming the liquid now made him feel a bit uneasy. "I might enjoy some *real* food, however."

The captain looked about as perplexed as James felt.

Twenty-Five

FROM THE THRESHOLD, BLAIRE WATCHED JAMES IN surprise as he inhaled a pot of partan bree, several helpings of stovied tatties, half a dozen oatcakes, and an entire roasted grouse. Never in her life had she ever seen anyone eat so much food. Apparently, no one else had, either, as they all stood at various places around the dining room, gaping at the one-time vampyre while he finished off a feast that could have fed a family of six.

"*Havers!*" Elspeth muttered beneath her breath.

The sentiment was echoed by all present.

"I thought," Aiden whispered in Blaire's ear, "ye said he was a vampyre."

"He is—I mean—he was," she replied.

"What do ye mean *was*?"

Blaire tore her eyes from James long enough to look at her older brother at her side. "I doona ken how ta explain it, Aiden."

He narrowed his grey eyes on her. "Start at the beginnin'."

James' chair legs scraped the floor as he pushed

away from the table. "It started…I, um, *changed*, after your sister left me."

Blaire gulped and then turned her gaze on James. "I doona think that's what he meant, Lord Kettering." Vampyre or no vampyre, she would kill him if he breathed one word of their time together to Aiden.

"What do ye mean by *when Blaire left ye?*" Aiden's voice rang out loud and clear.

"Well," Elspeth nearly sang from her corner, "this bairn is makin' me rather tired. Rhi, Sorcha, Benjamin, why doona ye wait with me in the parlor for a while? I'd like ta get off my feet."

After a mass exodus from the dining room, Blaire found herself completely alone. Well, not completely. James and Aiden still stared daggers at each other from opposite sides of the room.

"All right. I want answers," Aiden grumbled.

James heaved a sigh. "Before the three of you fled Briarcraig, your sister accepted my proposal of marriage."

"Is that true?" her brother barked.

Blaire shrugged. "Aye, but—"

"Then after *celebrating*, I, uh, woke up alone in my bed to find you'd all abandoned me to the castle."

Blaire felt Aiden's eyes narrow on her, but she couldn't meet his gaze. He'd know the truth for sure if she looked at him.

"And that's when I knew I'd changed," James continued. "My heart beats once more, Captain. I'm no longer what I was, and it's all due to your sister's love."

"My sister's *love?*" Aiden echoed.

James nodded. "Without a doubt, sir."

Blaire couldn't find her voice to say a word. She could only watch the two men eye one another as the fight slowly drained from Aiden. "Ye really should have asked for my blessin' before ye proposed ta my sister."

James agreed with an incline of his head. "You are, of course, correct, Captain. But I'm asking you for it now."

"Aiden, wait!" Blaire begged. "I doona ken what I want."

Her brother scrubbed a hand along his jaw. "I ken ye love the man, Blaire. Ye told me so yerself. And he says it was yer...*love* that transformed him. I'd say ye ken well enough what ye want, and ye made that decision at Briarcraig Castle."

And she did love James, so much it hurt. But she wasn't sure that was enough. In fact, she knew it wasn't. Without James' love in return, she'd wither away and die. "But I canna do it. I'm no' the marryin' sort. I—"

"If yer the *lovin'* sort, then yer the marryin' sort, Blaire. I doona want ta hear another word about it. Tomorrow I'll talk ta Mr. Crawford about havin' the banns read."

Which meant she had three weeks to talk James out of this madness. Three weeks to convince Aiden that spending her years as a spinster was preferable to spending her years unloved. Three weeks was, in all honesty, not a lot of time.

"Now, if ye'll excuse me, we have guests in the parlor." With that, Aiden strode from the room without a look back.

Blaire folded her arms across her chest and glared at the arrogant Sassenach across the room from her. "Well, I hope yer happy."

His brow rose in surprise. "That you'll be mine forever? I couldn't be more thrilled."

"Yer a fool, James Maitland."

"Am I?" A deep laugh erupted from him.

She snorted. "Ye've been given a chance at livin' a normal life. A natural life, and ye want ta marry *me*? Have ye lost yer mind?"

"I lost my heart to you."

How dare he say such a thing! Blaire pointed a finger at him. "If ye mock me, I swear I will engulf ye in a ball of flames. And if yer black eye is any indication of yer weakened state, ye willna survive the experience."

James frowned at her. "What the devil is wrong with you, Blaire? Do you not love me anymore?"

If only she could lie well. But there was no point to it. "Aye." She sighed, wishing it wasn't the truth. "I love ye enough, James, that I want ye ta enjoy the chance ye've been given ta start over."

"This life is only worth living if you're by my side, love."

Her heart nearly melted, which wouldn't serve her purposes at all. She was supposed to be talking him out of this foolishness, not allowing him to talk her into it. A change of tactics was most assuredly needed. "Tell me somethin'. If ye were no' so certain Mr. Trevelyan was out there somewhere, would ye have followed me ta Edinburgh? Is it simply yer noble nature that willna allow ye ta leave me in danger?"

"I would have come for you, Trevelyan or no Trevelyan."

Well, that didn't work. Blaire flopped down at the dining-room table. "Why is it he hates ye so, James? What is the history between ye?"

"We have different philosophies of life." He settled at the table across from her and leaned back in his chair. "And over the centuries, you meet up with the same people over and over again. Our paths crossed many times, and none of the encounters were particularly pleasant."

"So all of this is because the two of ye have different philosophies? That's it?"

He raked a hand through his hair as though the conversation had taken an uncomfortable turn.

"I canna marry a man who willna be honest with me, James. So—"

"Are you going to be this difficult once we're married?"

She couldn't help the grin that spread across her face. "If ye insist on this farce, Kettering, I will make yer life a miserable existence. Ye really should reconsider and run off before Aiden can speak ta the vicar tomorrow."

At that he laughed. He had the audacity to toss his head back and laugh. "You'll have to do a lot better than that, Blaire Lindsay. I've waited a quarter of a millennia for you, and nothing will make me give you up."

Blast him for being on to her. She narrowed her eyes on him. "I believe ye are evadin' my question, James. I want ta ken about this feud between ye and Trevelyan."

"And if I tell you, will you stop being so difficult and marry me?"

She scoffed. "Ye *wish* it was that simple."

He shook his head. "No, love, I don't. I love you just the way you are, and if you ever made it easy on me, I'd think you were ill."

All the air in Blaire's lungs whooshed from her body. Did he just say he loved her?

"Are you all right?" He bolted from his seat and was standing over her in the blink of an eye.

Blaire tipped her head back to look at him. "Ye are still fast." What a completely inept thing to say. Of all the questions she wanted to ask. All the things she wanted to say, and "ye are still fast" was what came out of her mouth?

A seductive smile turned up the corners of his lips. "I know how to be slow and take my time when necessary, lass."

She felt a flush creep up her neck, and she was certain her face was as red as Elspeth's fiery hair.

His breath brushed across the shell of her ear as he bent to whisper quietly to her, "You do remember what it was like being in my bed, don't you, Blaire?" His lips touched her cheek gently.

Blaire was incapable of speech. She was nearly incapable of taking a breath. How in the world could she ever speak? She gulped instead.

James chuckled lightly and then stood up tall. "I'll be back in the morning, Blaire."

"Ye're leavin'?" She jumped to her feet and spun to face him. "But ye said ye were stayin' here."

He shrugged, nearly feigning nonchalance. But she knew him too well. "I have some errands. And I doubt your brother would want me traipsing back in at some ungodly hour. But don't worry. I'll be close by."

He was definitely up to something. "What kind of errands can ye have this time of the night in Edinburgh?" Let him try to lie to her. That would be fantastic.

"The kind that involve catching rogue vampyres." She opened her mouth to speak, but he shushed her. *He shushed her? How dare he?* James continued, "It does not involve meddlesome witches, however. So, I expect you to stay here and protect your brothers, just in case Trevelyan gets past me."

Oh, he thought he would fool her with the *protect your brothers* idea. She crossed her arms over her chest. "Oh, ye doona honestly believe I'll fall for that, do ye?"

He walked close, until he stood one step before her, one hand cupping her cheek lightly. "I expect you to stay here."

She said in a sing-song voice, "Ye never could enchant me, James Maitland. And ye certainly canna now. No' since ye're very nearly human, or whatever ye are."

His eyes narrowed at her. "I wasn't trying to enchant you. I'm telling you what I expect." His voice was firm and…annoying as the devil. "I need you to trust that I can take care of you."

"Ye?"

He took a step back from her, obviously irritated. "Yes, me. I'm going to be your husband after all."

Perhaps or perhaps not. That hadn't truly been settled, but it was beside the point at the moment. "And have ye forgotten that ye're human, James? Ye can *die*, ye fool!"

He tilted his head at her. "And that would bother you, Blaire?"

She stuttered out, "O-o-of course, it would." She'd never get over such an occurrence.

"Why?" He crossed his arms over his chest.

There was no point in denying it. He knew it anyway. "Because I love ye, ye arrogant Englishman," she ground out after a moment of indecision.

"I love you, too," he said softly, his lips turned up in a small grin, before he quit the room.

James stepped out into the chilly night and searched the darkness for signs of Trevelyan. He *was* there. James was certain of it. He was in Edinburgh, and he was bent on revenge. James had nearly told Blaire what Trevelyan was about, and that it was all James' fault, but he'd rather not have to explain such things. If he could track down his old foe and dispense with the villain, they could put all of this behind them and start fresh.

His boots crunched along the cobblestone path as he walked away from Lindsay House. But he spun quickly when he heard a noise rattle the bushes by his side. "Who's there?" he asked.

"You can relax, Kettering. It's just me." Benjamin Westfield stepped out into the moonlight, his dark hair hanging over his brow. He brushed it back with an impatient hand. "I wanted to have a word with you."

James wanted to roll his eyes, but he forced himself to stand still for Westfield's set-down. He tried to keep the sarcasm from his voice when he said, "I'm well aware that I'll have to deal with Captain Lindsay simply because I am in love with his sister. Do I have to take on the entire Lycan race, as well?"

"Lycan race?" Westfield chuckled. "I think the proper term is *human* race, Kettering. With some eccentricities."

"That's one way to put it."

"Eccentricities aside, you and I have something in common. And because of that commonality, I want to give you some advice." Westfield waited patiently for his response.

"You're a werewolf—," James began, but the other man cut him off.

"Lycan, actually. Werewolf's a derogatory term." Westfield nodded once, indicating that he should continue. "But go ahead."

"Wait." James couldn't let that one pass him by. "It's a derogatory term? An insult? Truly?"

"It's a bit like Aiden Lindsay calling you a blood-sucker. I'm sure you didn't appreciate the reference."

"If the shoe fits." James shrugged. He'd always been able to slip in and out of polite society. Yet, if he truly thought about it, the blood-sucker reference was a bit offensive. "But I see your point," he finally grunted out.

"Back to the human race," Westfield said, a knowing smile tipping the corners of his lips. "I love my wife."

James appraised the moon's height in the sky. "Westfield, I hate to seem impatient, but I have somewhere to be."

"Exactly why I need to talk with you." Westfield blew in frustration. "You mean you have someone to hunt."

"My appointments are none of your concern," James snapped, finally losing his patience.

Westfield scoffed. Loudly. "I beg to differ on that point. Now would you be quiet long enough for me to tell you how to win with these witches?"

"I didn't get the impression that you approved of me, Westfield. Why would you give me any advice?"

The man shrugged. "Well, I've been where you are. Specifically, on the outside of this coven, and from what I understand," he tapped his own ear, "excellent hearing, by the way—if you and Blaire both survive the upcoming fight, Captain Lindsay will see you leg-shackled to his fiery sister. So you're about to enter our circle. That makes you as good as family, regardless of what I think about how you've gone about all of this."

James didn't care one whit what Benjamin Westfield thought about how he'd gone about all of this. The regal Lycan didn't know the first thing about his life. "How generous of you. I'll just be on my way."

"So you don't want to know how to get on with this coven? How to get what you want? These lovely witches are a formidable force. I am married to one, and I'm expecting one of my own in just a few months."

"God bless you," James muttered. Though an image of Blaire cradling their child, a little raven-haired girl who could throw fireballs, flashed in his mind. He'd give anything to see that sight for real.

"Thank you. I'll need it. These women are connected, tightly knit in every way. They do everything together, and they draw on the strength of one another," Westfield started to explain.

"Now Blaire has me, and she can draw on my strength." He turned to walk away.

"Fairly naïve for a man who has been alive for as long as you have. Or addled. I'm still trying to decide which." A small growl left the man's throat.

James was surprised when his incisors didn't descend in self-defense as that had been his natural reaction for so long. He rubbed at his upper lip in consternation. Westfield's eyebrows rose just a bit in the darkness. Annoying thing, having people know about his change and his discomfort with it. He felt certain he could hold his own in a fair fight. But not with piercing teeth and a menacing bite.

"Very well, have your say." James acquiesced. Let the man get whatever it was off his chest, and then James could get on with what he needed to do.

"If you want to find the vampyre, stay with the witches. Stay with Blaire."

"Absolutely not." Blaire was already in danger because of him, so leading Trevelyan to her was out of the question. "I can go and hunt the man on my own. I do know him fairly well. I can locate him, kill him, and be done with it."

"You're not listening to me at all."

"You sound like Blaire." James snorted. He'd never met a Lycan before, but he'd always heard they were a fierce race. This specimen was fairly lacking. "Are you a Lycan in women's skirts?"

"Be glad I have two older brothers, Kettering." Westfield did growl that time. "Or I'd knock you flat on your human ass."

"You could try," James tossed back.

"And I'd win. If Aiden Lindsay can send you crashing to the floor, I can most assuredly knock the smug expression from your face and then some."

He'd been taken by surprise, that was all. Fairly ungentlemanly of Westfield to bring it up. "Would you care to give it a try?"

"I have better things to do than show you up, Kettering. Namely, keeping my wife and the others safe." Then Westfield lowered his voice and spoke to James as though he was a small child. "These witches don't have to find trouble. It finds them. This vampyre friend of yours will find them as well. If you're gone, traipsing off on your own mission to find the blood-sucker, I can promise you one or more of those delightful witches will do the same."

Blaire. She'd done that very thing at Briarcraig Castle.

"Then it's too late," Westfield continued. "Their circle is only at four right now. They don't have the benefit of all five of them together. Alone, none of them stand a chance."

But Blaire wouldn't be so foolish again. Not after her encounter with Sarah. James started to say as much, but the Lycan held up his hand and growled again.

"I love my wife dearly. And I know she'll find a way to participate in this fight no matter what. So only by being here *with* her, with them all together, can I assure her safety. And that of her coven sisters." His hand clapped onto James' shoulder. "I could use your help. If you're of a mind to give up your solo hunt and become part of the family."

James' heart leapt at the offer. Become part of the family. Become part of something bigger than himself. Westfield truly was welcoming him into the circle of the coven. Offering to aid him with this problem instead of making James face it alone or admonishing him for bringing this trouble into their midst. It was humbling.

"From the tale you told Sorcha earlier, I have no doubt Trevelyan will come and find them. He knows that by getting to Blaire, he could kill you. Or at least torture you with the knowledge that he harmed her for the rest of your days. When he arrives, be here. Be ready. I know I will be."

And with that, Westfield turned and walked back toward Lindsay House.

James had two choices. He could go off on his own and find Trevelyan in his weakened state. Or he could take Benjamin Westfield's advice and wait for Trevelyan to find Blaire. The latter scared the life out of him, but perhaps the Lycan was right.

With a sigh, James turned back and followed Westfield's lead.

Twenty-Six

BLAIRE COULDN'T BELIEVE JAMES MAITLAND WAS such an incredible dolt. How dare he go off on his own with that arrogant swagger of his? She had no doubt that once upon a time he could have taken on Trevelyan all by himself, but now he sported a black eye because of her very *human* brother. Had James been a vampyre for so long that he couldn't imagine not being one any longer? Was he so accustomed to living, no matter what, that he couldn't envision not doing so now?

I expect you to stay here. His words echoed in her mind, and she scowled in response. He should know better than to dictate to her. If they were to be married, she certainly wouldn't put up with such nonsense.

But if they were to be married, then her one-time vampyre would have to still be breathing.

Arrogant swagger or not, he needed her help, even if he didn't realize it. But she'd faced a vampyre alone once, and *her* arrogance had nearly gotten her killed. She needed someone she could trust. Elspeth would be the best choice as she could heal any injuries Blaire might receive at Trevelyan's hand, but Benjamin would never let his wife out of his sight, especially not in her delicate condition. Irritating, lovesick, over-protective mutt. So, she'd leave the healing witch to watch over Aiden and Brannock in her absence. That decision brought her some comfort.

Rhiannon. Blaire nodded her head at the next best choice. Actually, Rhi was a fairly good option. Her wind and lightning could come in quite handy in this upcoming battle.

Her mind made up, Blaire started for the parlor but found all three of her coven sisters waiting for her in the corridor.

"I'm comin', too," Sorcha insisted before Blaire even said a word.

"Will ye keep yer voice down?" Elspeth hissed. "How many times have I told ye that Ben canna hear ye if ye whisper?"

Sorcha shrugged, but she did lower her voice. "So where are we goin'?"

Blaire shook her head. "Ye're stayin' here. Rhiannon will come with me."

Rhiannon nodded her acceptance, while Sorcha thrust out her bottom lip. "I can help, too, Blaire. And from everythin' Lord Kettering said about this Trevelyan fellow, I doona want him around anymore than ye do."

"Withered orchids will no' help, Sorcha. Stay here with El and make sure Aiden and Brannock are safe."

Sorcha folded her arms across her chest. "Lord Benjamin can help *here*!" Apparently, in her temper, the youngest witch forgot all about whispering. "And I'm a witch just like ye are! Just because I doona have fireballs in my fingertips doesna mean I canna help!"

Blaire grasped Sorcha's arm and dragged her toward the back entrance. It was either take her along or have Benjamin Westfield poking his snout where it wasn't wanted. "Will ye hush?" she ordered while Rhiannon quietly followed in their wake.

They rushed out the door, and almost instantly the chilly air nearly froze them to their bones. If Sorcha hadn't been so bloody loud, they could have put on their coats and been mildly prepared for this outing.

"It's freezin'!" Sorcha complained.

"Well, that's no one's fault but yer own," Blaire countered as she made her way through the darkened mews. Out of nowhere, a warm breeze encompassed them all and Blaire was once again thankful for the shy, considerate Rhiannon.

"Where *are* we headed?" Rhiannon asked. Her soft voice stopped Blaire in her tracks.

She turned to face her sister witches who were following her in this endeavor. Rhiannon and Sorcha had some idea of what they were facing, but Blaire owed them more than that. "Above all else, Trevelyan is a man and he thinks like a man. Where does Benjamin go when he's put out with El?"

"I doona ken where he goes, but he usually has a glass of whisky," Sorcha supplied.

"Aye. Or a whole bottle," Blaire agreed. "And Aiden heads off ta a pub every chance he gets. If Trevelyan is huntin' for food, he'd go where other men converge, especially at night."

"Do ye ken how many pubs are in Edinburgh?" Sorcha frowned. "Is that the best ye've got?"

"He canna be out durin' the daylight, so he'd also need an inn or someplace ta lay his head."

"So we're lookin' for an inn with a good-sized taproom," Rhiannon stated. "Ta give him more choices in his meal. Is that it, Blaire?"

She nodded. "Each time I've seen him, he was dressed well, as though money was no' a problem. I was thinkin' ta start at the Thistle and Thorn." It was, after all, the nicest inn in the area and one even Benjamin had stayed at a time or two in the past.

"Sounds like a good place ta start," Rhiannon agreed.

Blaire looked from one witch to the other. There was still so much they didn't know about vampyres, and she didn't have a lot of time to teach them. "Let's take a hack and I'll explain more on the way."

James stepped over the threshold of Lindsay House a bit buoyed by his decision to follow Benjamin Westfield's advice. Keeping Blaire safe with others who had the same motivation was a bit of a relief. Before now, he never would have considered teaming up with a coven of witches, or a Lycan, for that matter, to accomplish any goal. Being part of this circle would take a little getting used to. They were like a great big family, and he'd never had that, not even in his first life. As a boy, he'd had his father, and as a vampyre, he'd always had Matthew, but that was different from a whole group of people who loved and looked after each other the way these witches and their families did.

And very soon he would be a part of it all. No, according to Westfield, he was a part of them now, simply because he loved Blaire. Amazing, the blind, nonjudgmental acceptance of this group.

He made his way back to the dining room, ready to tell Blaire he'd changed his mind and they'd deal with this threat together. But she was gone. She must have joined the others in the parlor. James frowned. He'd wanted to tell her this privately. To steal a kiss or two in the process, but that was not to be.

Oh, well, he was part of this big family now. Might as well tell them all. James sighed and quickly made his way to join the others in the parlor.

Fewer people were present than when he'd left. Aiden Lindsay nursed a whisky in the far corner, and Brannock giggled while he scratched Bruce's chin. But what made James' heart clench was the hushed spat between Benjamin and Elspeth Westfield on the settee. There was no sign of the other three witches anywhere in sight. And if the vein bulging near Westfield's left eye was any indication, something was not right in Lindsay House.

"Where is Blaire?" he asked the room at large as Westfield's earlier warning echoed in his ears. Surely she wouldn't have done something so foolish.

The Lycan heaved a sigh and rose from his spot beside his wife. "I wish I knew, Kettering. I came back here to find the three of them gone." He glanced back at the red-haired witch at his side.

She knew. James could feel it in his bones. "Where are they, Lady Elspeth?"

From the corner, Captain Lindsay lifted his glass in

salute. "Blaire can take care of herself, Kettering. As her soon-ta-be husband, ye should reconcile yerself ta that fact."

Bloody idiot. Blaire could take care of herself in most situations, but not against a dangerous vampyre hell-bent on revenge. "Where is she?" he ground out, leveling his gaze at the only witch left.

"I suggest you watch your tone with my wife," Westfield growled.

James turned his glare on the Lycan. "Then you make her tell me."

Westfield shook his head. "She doesn't know. They didn't say before they left."

James' heart plummeted. How the devil was he going to find her?

"You said you knew Trevelyan," Westfield interrupted his thoughts. "So where do you suggest we start?"

"Blaire wanted ye ta stay with me, Ben," his wife pleaded. "Just in case."

Just in case the vampyre came here. So Brannock would have more than a drunken brother and an expectant witch to protect him. And had Sarah still been alive, that might not have been a bad plan. But Trevelyan had no desire to take his revenge on James through anyone other than Blaire. He blamed James for the loss of his own wife. He blamed James for making him live an eternity without the woman he loved. And now that Trevelyan knew James cared for Blaire, she'd be the only one upon whom he would exact his revenge.

"Trevelyan doesn't care about the others," James

breathed out. Dear God, how would he ever find her? He felt so dizzy that the room nearly spun.

"What do you mean?" Westfield narrowed his eyes.

"All he cares about is Blaire." Damn it, he didn't know Edinburgh at all. Where would he even go to find Trevelyan?

"But he attacked all of ye at Briarcraig," Elspeth found her feet. "And Blaire wasna even with ye at the time."

"That would have been Sarah's idea," he explained, looking toward the door. "How long have they been gone?"

"Sarah's idea?" Elspeth pressed. "The woman who died?"

"She had pointy teeth," Brannock piped up, holding his scraggly cat close to his chest. "She was scary."

"Believe me. *Trevelyan only cares about Blaire.*"

"I can find them." Benjamin Westfield started for the door. "I can follow their scent."

What a wonderful trait to possess.

"Brannock and Captain Lindsay are safe?" Elspeth followed her husband.

"I'd wager my life on it." James was quick on Westfield's tail, following him down a corridor toward a back entrance.

"Well, then I'm comin', too." Elspeth slid her arms into a long coat that billowed about her ankles.

"Ellie, go back," her husband directed over his shoulder.

"Doona order me about, Benjamin. If Blaire needs me ta heal her, I willna spend my time sittin' in the Lindsays' parlor twiddlin' my thumbs."

"Headstrong witch," her husband grumbled.

"'Til the bitter end," she confirmed.

If James' heart wasn't aching at the thought of losing Blaire, he might have smiled at the exchange. His own witch was headstrong. If he would be battling Blaire's will for a lifetime, there was no reason Westfield should get off easy.

⤶❦⤷

"So doona look him in the eyes?" Sorcha asked as they climbed from the hack. "That makes him sound a bit like Medusa."

"If ye make eye contact," Blaire explained once more, "he can enchant ye. Take over yer will."

"Oh, what a wonderful power ta possess," Sorcha gushed. "Ye dinna say—is he handsome?"

Blaire's mouth fell open as Rhiannon smothered a smile and handed the driver a few coins for his trouble.

"Honestly, Sorcha Ferguson, ye are the most fanciful witch alive," Blaire complained as the driver led his dray horse back toward the main road. And Sorcha truly *was* the most romantically inclined witch ever born. She definitely needed her own love affair in time.

Blaire had spent the entire trip detailing how dangerous Padrig Trevelyan was. He could enchant them. He was faster than a blur. He could pierce their flesh with his teeth faster than they could blink. He was as strong as a Lycan, perhaps even stronger. Blaire wasn't certain, since she'd never actually seen a battle between the two breeds, and yet all Sorcha worried about was whether or not the man was handsome.

"I doona think I'm fanciful at all. El and Cait both have Lycans, and now *ye* have a vampyre. Why should I no' wish for a handsome husband who's strong and has wonderful powers?"

Rhiannon tried to hold back a giggle, but it came out as a snort.

This was why they shouldn't have brought the littlest witch along on this excursion. Blaire folded her arms across her chest and glared at Sorcha. "I think ye're mad. We've come out here ta find a dangerous creature and finish him off, and ye're husband-huntin'."

Sorcha rolled her eyes. "I only asked if he was handsome. Ye doona have ta be so surly, Blaire."

Surly. She'd like to *surly* Sorcha right back in a hack and send her home across town. "Can ye be quiet? I canna think with yer prattlin'."

Rhiannon gestured toward the dark taproom door, and a gentle breeze rattled the hinged Thistle and Thorn sign outside the entrance to the inn. "Are ye goin' ta walk in there ta see if ye spot him?"

Well, it certainly couldn't be one of the other two. They'd never laid eyes on the vampyre before. "Aye." She retrieved a dagger from her calf and handed it to Rhiannon. "I canna imagine he'd cause a scene with the room full of patrons in there. He'll follow me back outside. Ye'll have ta use yer wind ta keep him from advancin' too quickly."

"Willna ye need this?" Rhiannon bounced the dagger in her hand as though she were testing its weight.

Blaire shook her head. "I have another. But if he gets past me, remember—go for his main append-ages. James said that would slow him down. If we can slow him enough, I can take off his head and be done with it."

"And what if ye canna?" Sorcha's mouth dropped open as though she was just now realizing what a dangerous situation they were about to put themselves in.

"Then ye'll have ta bat those pretty brown eyes at him and hope he's flattered by yer interest."

Sorcha's eyes narrowed at her. "Just be careful, will ye?"

Blaire nodded and then went straight to the taproom entrance. She could hear the laughter of men deep in their cups, and one even singing an old Gaelic love song somewhere deep inside the inn. She took a deep breath, pushed the door open, and then stepped inside. She was immediately assaulted by the smell of ale and too many bodies.

One would think the men of Edinburgh would notice a tall woman without a coat in the middle of February standing in their midst, but not one of them looked up from their tankards. Blaire scanned the room looking for her quarry, to no avail. She didn't see Trevelyan's dark head anywhere in the bunch.

However, she did spot Sorcha's brother, Wallace Ferguson, at the far side of the room, slurring his words as he asked the barmaid for another drink. For half a second she considered turning Sorcha over into her oafish brother's keeping, but dealing with Wallace Ferguson would only slow her down in the end.

She sighed at her own foolishness. Had she truly expected to locate Trevelyan so quickly? As Sorcha had said, there were numerous pubs throughout Edinburgh. Finding him at her first stop was highly unlikely. She wished they hadn't excused that hack driver so quickly. They'd do better at the next stop.

Well, there was no need to stand here all night. Blaire turned back around to escape the din and odor of the Thistle and Thorn taproom. She walked back out into the bitter cold, and the sight that met her eyes was the most terrifying she'd ever seen.

Standing in the moonlight, Padrig Trevelyan held Rhiannon's hands behind her back. He met Blaire's gaze, and a wicked smile turned up the corners of his lips. "Ah, Miss Lindsay, we meet again. I understand you've been looking for me. Pity your friends didn't heed your warnings."

Twenty-Seven

EVERY BIT OF KNOWLEDGE BLAIRE HAD ABOUT vampyres flooded her mind. Don't look him in the eyes, she reminded herself. She kept her gaze focused on Padrig Trevelyan's hairline and forced herself to ignore the tranquil sound of his voice. "Release her this instant!"

"As the lady commands." Trevelyan smoothly stepped away from Rhiannon with his hands turned upward as though he was no threat at all.

But Rhiannon didn't move an inch toward safety. No rainstorm thundered above their heads; no winds whipped violently to defend them against the vampyre. Blaire glanced at her weather-controlling coven sister, and her heart plummeted when she noticed the empty expression on Rhiannon's face.

"Ye enchanted her," she accused.

"Well, we all use the powers we're given, don't we?"

Blaire's eyes darted around the coaching yard. Where the devil was Sorcha?

"Looking for your other little friend? She didn't even get the chance to…what was it you said, 'bat her pretty brown eyes at me and hope I was flattered by her attention'?"

He'd heard everything she'd said. Blaire nearly groaned aloud. How long had he been there? Had he followed them to the Thistle and Thorn? "What have ye done with her?"

Trevelyan shrugged. "She is safe." His silky voice washed over Blaire, but she still refused to look in his eyes, even as he stepped closer to her. "And she'll remain safe, as long as you do what you're told."

Blaire shook her head and backed away from him toward the door of the Thistle and Thorn. "Sorcha!" she called out. The moonlight glinted off something on Trevelyan's hand, and Blaire recognized James' ring, or one very like it.

Trevelyan laughed. "She cannot hear you right now, Miss Lindsay. And I have no desire to hurt her, so rest easy."

Rest easy. The vampyre had put Rhiannon in a trance and absconded with Sorcha, and he wanted her to rest easy? Ha! If she could get further in the darkness and lure him closer, she'd thrust her dagger into his neck. "I just want my friend."

Trevelyan smiled as he advanced on her. "And I just want Kettering. So why don't we make a trade?"

Again Blaire shook her head, moving further into the shadows of the inn. Where had that ring come from? It wasn't James'. When she'd seen him last, the old heirloom had been on his hand; and if Trevelyan had encountered James to take his ring, he wouldn't be playing this game with her now. No, it must be the one that had belonged to Sarah Reese. "Whatever is between ye and Kettering has nothin' ta do with my friends or my family."

"Ah, but it has everything to do with you, my dear, with what you represent. And I've been waiting for this chance for over two centuries."

"And what chance might that be?" she asked. If she could engage him in casual conversation, she might be able to distract him and gain the upper hand.

"The chance to return the *favor*," he sneered the word, "Kettering did me all those years ago."

"I doona ken what ye mean."

Trevelyan snorted. "Of course not. Do you think he would admit to anything that would tarnish his good name? His unimpeachable honor?"

Bloody hell! What *had* James done?

"No." Trevelyan shook his head, answering his own question. "But he's responsible for it all the same. And now I finally get the opportunity to thank him properly for making me suffer this miserable existence."

Near the line of trees, Blaire noticed a patch of white and recognized Sorcha's dress. The youngest witch, lay lifeless on the cold ground just a few feet away. Blaire couldn't hold back the gasp that escaped her. What had Trevelyan done to the little wood nymph?

He glanced over his shoulder, and a wistful smile settled on his lips. "A sweet girl."

A fireball flared to life in Blaire's hand, and a lump formed in her throat. "How dare ye hurt her?"

His glare darkened on Blaire. "I told you she was safe."

"She doesna look *safe*," she growled in response.

At that Trevelyan tipped his head back and laughed,

for which Blaire was exceedingly grateful as it gave her the opportunity to retrieve the dagger from her sleeve without the vampyre realizing it. "For one who consorts with those of my kind, Miss Lindsay, you really are ill-prepared."

"Because I doona care for creatures who harm the innocent? She could *never* have hurt ye. She doesna have it in her." Blaire tucked her hand against her skirt, using the fabric to shield the dagger from his view.

Trevelyan shook his head as though she was the silliest lass in the world. "Your friend is merely sleeping. I didn't touch one hair on her pretty little head. I've come here for you, Miss Lindsay, and no one else will do, not right now anyway."

"Because of Kettering?"

"Because of Kettering," he agreed. "You have no idea how long I've waited for the good baron to fall, just as he has for you. Turnabout is fair play, and if I have to live the rest of this godforsaken life without my Anwen, then Kettering should suffer the same fate." There was pain beneath his words. Blaire could almost hear his agony.

"Anwen?" What *had* James done to cause such turmoil?

"My wife," he said softly and then gestured his head toward Sorcha's lifeless form. "Your friend resembles her. Porcelain skin. Innocent, trusting eyes. Her whole joyful life in front of her."

Padrig Trevelyan's expression softened, as though he was lost in the past. Blaire extinguished the ball of fire in her palm. If the man could be reasoned with, it would make everything so much easier. No one had to be hurt or killed.

Wind whipped delicately at Blaire's skirts. Apparently, delving into the past forced him to release his hold on her sister witches. Rhiannon's gentle caress was a signal of that. Blaire wanted to rejoice. "She sounds lovely."

Anguish settled on his face. "She was until Kettering killed her."

Blaire couldn't imagine James ever doing any such thing, vampyre or not. He'd had no reason to kill women even when he'd partaken of their blood.

A voice boomed from behind her. "You know as well as I, Trevelyan, that *fate* took her, not me." Blaire didn't need to look over her shoulder. She would know that voice anywhere.

James had arrived. She wasn't sure if she should celebrate or cry.

Then James stepped into the clearing, with Benjamin following in his wake. Trevelyan's eyes found the two men as well. "I know that's the story you've told for nearly two centuries. I also know it for the lie it is."

From the corner of her eye, Blaire could see the flame of Elspeth's red hair at the edge of the nearby line of trees. Why wasn't Elspeth watching over Brannock and Aiden? What if Trevelyan had gone after her brothers instead? Then a chill seeped into her bones. But he wouldn't have, would he? Trevelyan hadn't even hurt Rhiannon or Sorcha when he'd had the chance. He'd openly announced that he'd come for her and only her.

"Ye really do mean ta kill me?" Blaire refocused on the dangerous vampyre just outside her grasp.

Elspeth quietly dropped to her knees beside Sorcha, which brought Blaire a bit of comfort. If any harm had come to the littlest witch, Elspeth wouldn't rest until Sorcha was back to her irritating, bubbly self.

Trevelyan didn't seem to notice anything but Blaire, however, as his black eyes stared into her soul. "Think of it as saving you from a life of heartache, Miss Lindsay. Do you really want to grow old and die, while he stays virile and young? Or worse, do you want to become one of us to *remain* with him? That existence is far from pleasant. You can take my word on that."

"Blaire," James bellowed, "back away from him. Now!"

But she couldn't back away. This fight was hers. He'd come after her with the intent of killing her. Backing away was out of the question.

"Blaire!" James called again.

"Stay where ye are, James," she ordered. All she needed was for Trevelyan to attack James instead. He *was* human now, after all. He could die at her feet and leave her with nothing more than the pain Padrig Trevelyan had endured all these years. "We're only talkin'."

Trevelyan laughed. "Do you think you can charm me, Miss Lindsay, into changing my course? I can promise you I'm immune to ladies' charms."

The blasted vampyre wasn't helping the situation at all. She glared at him. "I doona mean ta charm ye, Mr. Trevelyan. But ye sought me out, dinna ye? That makes this between *us*, and we are only talkin'."

He smirked. "Well, then I hate to spoil your fun, Miss Lindsay, whatever amount of it you have left. What *shall* we talk about?"

She glanced at his hand and the ring upon his pinkie. "I thought ye were goin' ta tell me about Anwen."

The vampyre's smirk vanished and he sighed wearily, though Blaire knew he had no need to breathe at all. "She was full of energy. Cheerful. I couldn't deny her anything." Even after all the years spent without Anwen, Trevelyan's love for her was evident in his voice. "We should have had the rest of our lives together. Children. Grandchildren. But in the end, we'd been married only a few months before she died."

Why did he insist on blaming James? "How did she die?" From the corner of Blaire's eye, she saw ivy grow at Sorcha's feet and then start to spread toward where she stood with Trevelyan. She only hoped the vampyre didn't notice it, too.

"The Great Plague," Trevelyan replied, "not that we knew that at the time. We'd traveled to London to help care for Anwen's uncle who'd fallen ill. By the time we arrived, the old man was dead as well as half of London. And in no time, Anwen and I were struggling to hold on to life ourselves."

James could hardly be blamed for the Plague, though Blaire kept that thought to herself. Sorcha's ivy had almost reached them, and there was no reason to antagonize the man until a trap was set.

"Blaire!" James once again called out to her, pain lacing his voice.

She wished she could soothe him, but she mostly wished he'd keep his blasted mouth closed so Trevelyan wouldn't focus on him. "It's his story, James. Pray allow him ta tell it."

"And then *he* showed up." The vampyre nearly spat the last in James' direction. "Promising salvation from the pain."

"I only asked if you wanted my help," James bit out.

Trevelyan nodded, keeping his eyes leveled on Blaire. "And I did. But I wanted him to save us *both*. Living without Anwen has been a torture I wouldn't wish on anyone but him." He snorted. "And there he was, decade after decade. Wooing some pretty girl here or there, anything he had to do to get a drop of her blood. He never cared for any of them. Not until you. I've waited several lifetimes to get my revenge. I even followed that bloody Sarah Reese like a puppy so I could stay apprised of his actions. She always knew his whereabouts. She always knew where he was. Until the one day he disappeared, vanished, for twenty years."

Blaire spotted Benjamin Westfield moving a little to their left and Rhiannon positioning herself to the right, both of them helping to close the circle around Trevelyan. But he was so lost in his own torment that he either didn't notice or was unconcerned because of his proximity to Blaire.

James started to approach them, which made Blaire's heart lurch. Why couldn't the blasted man stay where he was safe? "I couldn't save Anwen. I tried, but it was too late as I've told you countless times. And none of this has a thing to do with Miss Lindsay. So if it's me you want…"

Foolish, foolish, mortal man. Blaire wanted to

scream at James. Why did he insist on putting himself in danger?

Trevelyan's mouth fell open as he finally let his eyes stray to James. "Is that a *bruise* over your eye?"

Blaire could see the man try to make sense of the situation. After all, a vampyre shouldn't sport a blackened eye. And though she doubted the villain understood the circumstances completely, because she still didn't understand them herself, James did appear more vulnerable in his current condition.

Apparently that was enough to make Trevelyan change his target.

Everything happened so quickly that there was barely time to breathe. A bolt of lightning arced in the sky, landing in front of James as though to protect him. Sorcha's vine grabbed hold of Trevelyan's boot, rooting him in place, but it wouldn't be strong enough to hold a creature of his strength for long. The vampyre's incisors descended, and he lunged for James.

Blaire's heart clenched. She stepped into the vampyre's path, her dagger outstretched. In Trevelyan's haste, he impaled himself on her weapon. He staggered backward, surprise on his face, but Blaire knew the wound wouldn't be enough. He still had his head. He still had his appendages. All he needed to do was remove the dagger and heal himself, and then he'd advance his attack once again.

She needed a more powerful weapon, one designed to attack vampyres.

"Sorcha! I need a wooden stake." The little sprite could always talk nature into doing her bidding, even in the dead of winter.

Trevelyan's eyes widened, and he turned an accusatory glare on James. "You told her how to defeat your own kind?"

"Should he have left me defenseless?" Blaire asked as a gust of wind placed a sharpened stake at her feet. She snatched it up. "Ye doona have ta do this, Mr. Trevelyan. Ye can turn around, go on yer way, and leave us be."

Trevelyan yanked the dagger from his chest and tossed it on the ground. "I never could have defeated him on my own before. He was older, stronger." And he wasn't about to give up. He didn't say those words, but Blaire could hear them in his voice.

So be it. She was battle born.

Trevelyan backed away, his eyes darting around the woods, the inn, the coaching yard, as though devising a battle plan in his mind. James was well guarded, with Benjamin flanking one side and Rhiannon on the other. Thunder rumbled overhead as a warning.

Then faster than a blur, Trevelyan moved across the yard. He reached out and caught Rhiannon, drawing her to him. "Quite a temper you have," he said to her. He grabbed her hair in a vicious grip that had the weather witch gasping in pain. He licked his lips before he said, "I've never tasted a witch before."

"Let her go!" Blaire demanded.

Trevelyan's dark eyes touched every one of them as he swept them all into his next comment. "I will kill every one of you if you stand between me and my goal of finally causing him the pain he has caused for me. I'll start with this one. I suggest you all head back to the safety of your homes."

James stepped closer to the vampyre. "No need to

hide behind the girl's skirts, Trevelyan. I'm right here, and I'm not hiding."

A wicked glint lit the vampyre's eye. He pushed Rhiannon from his path and started toward James. "Why *is* your eye black?"

James shrugged. "Because I'm human once more. My heart beats for Blaire Lindsay."

The answer shocked Trevelyan to his core, if his expression was any indication. He'd realized James was weaker, but he couldn't fathom that James was *human*. It gave Blaire enough time to rush forward with her stake, but James captured her arm and pulled her to him.

"Human?" The vampyre shook his head. "It's not possible."

"But it is. Let go of your bitterness, Padrig. Let go of your hate. Salvation *is* still possible if you embrace it. Perhaps some chit can make you whole again."

"There is no salvation without Anwen," Trevelyan whispered. "No one but her, and she's long since gone."

"I'm sure," Blaire tried to rationalize, "she wouldna want ta see ye like this, hell-bent on revenge in her name."

Something flashed in Trevelyan's eyes, something Blaire couldn't interpret. Before she could try to figure it out, he snatched the wooden stake from her grasp and thrust it into his own chest.

Sorcha gasped loudly, and the sentiment was echoed by all those present. A look of peace settled on Trevelyan's face as he fell to the ground. The others all rushed forward, creating a circle around the vampyre who lay dead at their feet.

"Good God!" Benjamin Westfield muttered.

Elspeth smoothed a hand over Rhiannon's mussed hair. "Are ye all right? Did he hurt ye?"

Rhiannon shook her head and wiped a tear from her cheek. "Frightened me was all."

"That is the saddest thing I've ever heard." Sorcha sniffed. "He knew it wasna possible. He knew his heart would only ever beat for one woman and there was no chance without her."

"I hate to be the bearer of bad news," Benjamin said, "but the body." He gestured to the ground.

A ball of fire sparked to life in Blaire's hand. There was no other way. "Anwen, I hope ye're still waitin' for him." She tossed the ball to the ground.

Flames licked at the vampyre's clothes.

"The ring," James said and reached toward the flames.

"Doona," Blaire said, stopping him. "Let it burn with him."

But little Sorcha sent a vine up through the flames, wrapped it around his finger, and tugged the ring gently from his pinkie. As she drew it back to her, the flames once again wrapped around Trevelyan, and Sorcha and Rhiannon had to turn away to keep from seeing the sight. Yet Blaire watched. She couldn't look away. She couldn't help but pray that he found his salvation in death. She couldn't help but hope that Anwen's love was waiting to envelop him on the other side of life.

James' arms wrapped around her from behind. "Don't look," he said quietly before he pressed his lips against her temple. If she could draw him into her, she would.

"He deserves ta have someone witness his fate. Ta mourn him. That person will be me," Blaire said.

"And me," James declared.

"And us," Elspeth said from within Benjamin's arms.

"Well, I willna watch," Sorcha whimpered from her place beside Rhiannon, where the witch had moved away from the smoldering fire. If Rhiannon wasn't careful, she'd put the flames out with the rain cloud that brewed overhead because of her sadness. "I canna watch, but I canna help but mourn for the poor soul."

Within moments, nothing was left of Trevelyan, no evidence that he'd ever existed.

Sorcha held out Trevelyan's ring for James. "Ye wanted this?"

He nodded and pocketed the ring that was identical to his own; and Blaire had a sinking feeling that he had left something unsaid.

"Sorcha!" came a slurred bellow from the taproom door. "Is that ye, lass? What are ye doin' out here?"

Wallace Ferguson.

Blaire nearly groaned aloud. It was fortunate Sorcha's ogre-sized brother hadn't departed the Thistle and Thorn a few moments earlier, or he would most assuredly have asked about the fire that was now gone, even in his inebriated state.

Sorcha bolted across the yard into her brother's arms. He held her while she sobbed uncontrollably.

"What is it, lass?" Wallace's eyes darted around the clearing at the others present, and a sober look settled on his face. "Is she all right?"

Sorcha pulled back from her brother and nodded

her head. "I'm sorry for cryin' all over ye. I ken how ye hate it."

Wallace shook his head. "Nay, Sorch, I'm just worried about ye." He suddenly seemed much less foxed than he had moments ago. Then again, Wallace was usually only gentle with Sorcha. If anything had the power to sober the man up, it was his little sister's distress.

A fresh deluge of tears spilled down Sorcha's cheeks. "It was just so sad. The poor vampyre never stopped lovin' his wife, and ye could see the torture in his eyes."

"Sorcha!" Blaire barked. What in the world was wrong with her, saying something like that to Wallace?

The large Scot again glanced around at the others present. "What's this about a vampyre?"

Blaire glared at Sorcha. Now what would they say? Why couldn't she have kept her bloody mouth shut? She was the one who'd begged to come along on this excursion.

"Actually, Wallace," Elspeth began as she closed the space between her and the mammoth in Scotsman's clothing. "I was goin' ta ask ye myself but in a less public place." She heaved a sigh. "I seem ta remember somethin' about our mothers and a vampyre when I was very young, but I canna remember exactly what it was. I was hopin' ye'd remember more than I do."

Wallace frowned, his bushy brows met in the middle of his head. "Aye, I remember it, El. We should probably all head over ta Ferguson House." He glanced around the innyard. "We doona want ta send the rest of Edinburgh inta a panic, do we?"

Twenty-Eight

THERE HAD BEEN VERY LITTLE DISCUSSION AS EVERYONE made their way back to the Ferguson's elegant home, which was a far cry from the shabby Lindsay abode. James noted the somber butler, stylish wall coverings, and one immaculate room after another as he and the others trailed Wallace to a good-sized parlor.

"Sit, sit," the oversized Scot directed the room at large. "I need ta find what I'm lookin' for. It might take a while." Then he hastily quit the room.

Most of the others heeded Wallace's advice, but James couldn't sit. What exactly did Ferguson know? What could he possibly be retrieving?

Blaire touched James' sleeve and brought him back to the present. "What is it ye're no' tellin' me?"

"Good God, woman!" He gaped at her. "What can you possibly think I'm hiding from you?" Hadn't he bared his soul, told her everything from the very beginning?

She was completely undeterred by his tone. Confident warrior witch. "Why did ye want Sarah Reese's ring? For sentimental reasons?"

He would have liked to have laughed at the ludicrous question, but damn her for finding the one thing he hadn't told her. Well, he *had* told her, but not in so many words; and he was loathe to do so now at any rate. "I have a feeling someone will have need of it, that's all."

Blaire frowned at the floor, and he could tell she was trying to figure out what he'd left unsaid. Then her eyes slowly rose to meet his, and he knew she could see through him. "Alec."

She was perceptive.

James nodded once. "Blodswell will teach him, the same way he did me."

Blaire's hand flew to her heart. "Dear God."

"I'm sorry," James pressed, "I had hoped he could be saved, but there was no other way."

"He hasna been saved, James. He's been doomed."

It wasn't that bad. James had lived the life himself for two-and-a-quarter centuries. "Blodswell will see that he's taken care of."

"Ye doona understand." Blaire swiped at a tear. "Alec lost the one woman he's ever loved. He'll be no better than Trevelyan."

James shook his head. "Don't even think that way. He *asked* Blodswell to save him. He wanted to live."

But Blaire didn't look convinced.

Then James noticed Benjamin Westfield staring in his direction, a frown marring the Lycan's face. "What's that about?" He motioned with his head toward the settee were Westfield sat with his wife.

Blaire glanced at the man and exchanged a look of remorse with him. "Alec was his dearest friend. They attended Harrow together as boys. He's as worried as I am."

Well, damn the man and his Lycan hearing. Some conversations should be private. James raked a hand through his hair, just as Wallace Ferguson rejoined them.

The large Scot held a golden filigreed box in his hand, and he offered it to Sorcha before sitting in an overstuffed leather chair. "That was yer mother's."

"Where did it come from?" Sorcha exclaimed.

"Can we talk about that later, Sorch?" He furrowed his brow, and the man was clearly hiding something. "I thought ye wanted ta ken about the vampyre."

"I, for one, want to hear all about it." James took a step forward. He had a fairly good idea the vampyre in question had been himself, and while he would never have found Blaire without the previous coven locking him away forever, he would still like to know their reasons for doing so.

Wallace looked from Elspeth to Rhiannon to Sorcha. "Ye ken how Fiona Macleod was."

"Unfortunately," Elspeth muttered.

"Well, she and Bonnie rarely saw eye ta eye. They fought more than any of the others."

Blaire nodded in agreement. "Fought like cats and dogs."

"Is that important?" James couldn't help but ask. What did the dynamics of the coven have to do with this situation? Five witches had captured him, and they were all in agreement.

"Aye." Wallace Ferguson looked at him as though he was an imbecile. "Because it wasna always that way, no' in the beginnin'. I remember when my father married Bonnie. In those days, she and Fiona were the closest of friends."

"I doona even remember that," Elspeth Westfield whispered.

"So what happened?" Sorcha sat forward in her seat, clutching the filigreed box tighter.

"That's a long story." Wallace scratched his head. "And I'm no' sure how much of it is important."

"The vampyre," James reminded the Scot, folding his arms across his chest.

"Of course the vampyre." Wallace sighed. "Well, Fiona had Alpina Lindsay up in arms about a vampyre who was goin' ta kill her unborn bairn."

All eyes turned to James. He tossed up his hands. "I never harmed anyone."

Wallace shook his head. "Ye're him, huh? I suppose I should've figured that."

"For the love of God, Wallace," Blaire complained. "Will ye tell the bloody story?"

The overgrown Scot frowned, and he sat back in his chair with a huff. "I dinna mean the vampyre would hurt the bairn. Fiona said he would come inta the midst of the *Còig* when the battle-born witch was in possession of all her powers and that he'd kill her then."

For the love of God! Again all eyes focused on James, and he shook his head. "That's not true."

"No, it's no'," Wallace agreed good-naturedly. "But the others dinna ken that. They blindly followed Fiona's lead. They were determined ta keep the monster from ever harmin' the bairn that would be Blaire. They were impassioned about it, like nothin' I'd ever seen from them up ta that point or since."

Which was what the woman had meant when she'd mentioned James' future victims. "But I thought this seer of yours was always correct."

Elspeth snorted. "Fiona Macleod was more concerned with preserving the purity of the coven than with honesty."

"I beg your pardon?" James frowned at the redhead. "What do you mean by that?"

"It's a long story as well, and ye'll have ta hear it another day. Just suffice it ta say, this wouldna be the first time Fiona was less than honest about a vision." Then she turned her attention back to Wallace. "Bonnie found out Fiona lied?"

Wallace nodded. "Aye. Bonnie was mortified. They had a huge argument, and their friendship never recovered." Wallace's eyes sparkled. "Did ye find the cask?"

"What cask?" James asked, his gaze roving around the group.

"The trunk full of money." The overgrown Scot refocused on Blaire, "It was supposed to be left at Briarcraig for ye. Bonnie was convinced ye would need it one day, and that she'd no' let yer father squander it before then. When ye were ready ta find the vampyre locked in the cellar, ye would also find the cask. "

"How do ye ken all of this?" Rhiannon finally spoke up. James had nearly forgotten the weather-controlling witch was still there.

A blush stained Wallace Ferguson's face, and he shrugged.

"Wallace!" Sorcha pressed.

Finally, the Scot lifted his gaze to stare at his sister.

"Bonnie was so sweet, so pretty. I used ta think she was an angel that Father somehow convinced ta live with us."

"Ye eavesdropped?" Sorcha gasped.

"No' all the time!" her brother insisted. Then he gestured to the golden box in Sorcha's hands. "She used ta tell me that when somethin' was botherin' me, I should write it down, get it off my chest. She told me that's what she did when she was troubled."

Blaire stepped forward. "Are ye sayin' Bonnie wrote all this down?"

"She kept her journal in that box."

"Where did ye get the box?" Sorcha demanded.

"In her hidden room."

From the breath of air Sorcha sucked in, James would wager this was the first time the lass knew her mother even had a secret room.

❧

James stepped across the threshold of Lindsay House and was quite surprised to find Captain Lindsay doing a wonderful impression of a large boulder whose only task was to hold the chair in place in which he reclined. It was a damned good thing that was his only job, because even that appeared to be a bit of a challenge for him, as much as he was struggling for focus in his severely inebriated state.

"Oh, good Lord," Westfield muttered as he took in the scene.

Captain Lindsay swayed as he stood up slowly and reached for his decanter of whisky. "I dinna expect ta see ye back here tonight, gentlemen," he said slowly, as though wrapping his mind around the words was difficult. Aiden glanced behind them. "Where is Blaire? Doona tell me ye lost her." He pointed one wobbly finger at James. "Because if ye tell me that, I'll have no choice but ta kick yer arse." He glanced down at his boot, as though it should be moving at that point, and flexed his foot. Then he shook his head, collapsed back in his seat, and sighed.

James spoke up, "Blaire is at the Fergusons'. The youngest witch had need of them, and they asked to be left alone for a bit." They had demanded it, actually. And Blaire had even threatened his manhood in order to make him leave. But there was no need to apprise Captain Lindsay of all the details. "Where is Master Brannock?" The man had been left in charge of the lad. And there were no servants about to care for the boy.

"I sent the lad ta bed quite some time ago," Lindsay said with a wave of his hand. Even that appeared to go astray, however. "Come and join me in a drink, Westfield." His eyes narrowed at James. "Can ye drink whisky, Kettering? Or is my sister the only refreshment ye can tolerate?"

James scrubbed a hand down his face, and stalled by taking the time to slowly remove his coat. "I told you. I have no need for blood anymore." He couldn't throttle the foxed brother of the lass he intended to marry, could he? Well, he *could*, but that would be bad form. Very bad form.

"Don't worry," Westfield said quietly. "He's harmless when he drinks."

James raised his eyebrows at the Lycan.

"He doesn't do it often. Their father was a bit of a drunkard, so he tends to avoid it most of the time. He must be fairly out of sorts to get this bad, particularly on this night."

James took the glass the captain held out. He hadn't had spirits in a very, very long time. He could barely remember what they tasted like. He looked directly at Captain Lindsay. "I can't change what I once was. The only thing I can control right now is my future. And my future is with Blaire. Even if you can't accept my past, your sister can. And I'll have her as long as she wants me. I'd love to do it with your blessing."

Westfield coughed into his hand. "What he means, Aiden, is that he doesn't plan to have your sister for dinner, but he does plan to have her for his wife."

"With your blessing, of course," James added. The blessing really didn't matter. But it sounded sincere and might appease the man.

"Nice finish," Westfield murmured to James.

James inclined his head at the Lycan. He liked him more and more as the night went on. He raised the whisky to his lips and let the smoky flavor of it wash over his tongue. It had been a very, very long time since he'd enjoyed such an indulgence.

"Careful there. Or you'll be deeper in your cups than Aiden, my friend," Westfield warned as he tossed back a glass himself and reached for the bottle.

"I never had a problem holding my drink before. You, on the other hand..." He made a motion to Westfield's second cup.

"Westfields have a higher tolerance for spirits." The Lycan shrugged. He noted that the man didn't say *Lycan*. So, the captain didn't know what he was. Interesting. There were *some* secrets within this circle after all.

Captain Lindsay chuckled. "Or could it be that ye drink them like water so yer body is used ta them?"

"That, too," Westfield admitted with a wolfish grin.

"So, what happened tonight? Why do I have the feelin' there's a story ta be told. Probably one I willna like." The captain adjusted his body marginally in the chair. But even that appeared to be too much for him.

Westfield glanced up at James and muttered, "Proceed at your own risk."

James took the time to toss back his glass of whisky, grimace, pour another, and think about the situation. "Honestly, Captain, we met up with a rogue vampyre with a debt to settle. Unfortunately, it was my debt, but Blaire got dragged into the middle of it."

"But Blaire and the others are all right?" the captain asked. He looked marginally more sober. But only marginally. And the look was gone so quickly that James could have sworn he'd missed it. James wasn't in the mood at all to recount the events of the night, but the captain was, evidently. A fighting man himself, Lindsay devoured the details of the battle as quickly as James and Benjamin Westfield consumed the man's whisky. James found himself pouring his heart out to the man, something he never would have done ordinarily. Soon the captain knew all there was to know about James' feelings for Blaire. The Lycan did as well, but James suspected he was well caught by his own witch so it didn't bother him over much.

Before long, James raised his hand to point

something out to the captain and found out his own motions weren't as well coordinated as they once had been. He tugged his watch fob from his pocket and flipped open the lid. It was getting awfully late. "I wonder where Blaire is. I thought she'd be home by now. Maybe it wasn't safe to let them travel alone."

"No worries," Westfield said as he crossed one foot over his knee. "Sorcha will have them sent them home in her carriage." He shrugged.

A soft snick sounded at the front door.

"There they are now, I'd imagine," Westfield said as he rose to his feet. Even the Lycan was so deeply in his cups that he weaved as though the floor moved beneath him. James knew any effort on his part to stand would be for naught. So, he remained sitting quietly and hoped Blaire wouldn't notice how foxed he was. He had a feeling he'd never live this one down if she did.

James smiled at the love of his life and the fiery-haired witch who belonged to his new friend as they came through the door.

"We were about to send a search party out to find you," Westfield said slowly.

Both the witches stopped in the doorway. The red-haired one crossed her arms over her chest as her toe began to tap against the floor. "What have ye been doin' while we were out?" she asked, eyeing her husband. "Though I have a fairly good idea."

Westfield merely shrugged unapologetically.

Blaire folded her arms across her chest, her gaze boring into James. "Talking," he replied, although it felt like he had a mouth full of cotton. "I was getting to know your brother, here."

Blaire crossed the room and picked up the empty whisky decanter. "Gettin' ta ken him?" she asked. "Is that what ye call it?"

The captain sat forward and brushed his hair back from his brow. Bloody hell, the man had gone from being a bumbling idiot one moment to sober as a vicar the next. "Actually, Blaire, I just had a nice discussion with yer betrothed. The man canna hold his liquor worth a damn."

"Are ye foxed, James?" Blaire asked as she placed a hand upon his shoulder.

James tried to fight the insane smile that he knew spread across his face. He failed. Terribly. "Quite foxed, love," he grunted.

Westfield chimed in. "It appears as though the good captain was on a fact-finding mission and he duped us both." Thank God, Westfield wasn't sober as well. Otherwise, James would have been so angry he wouldn't have been able to control himself. But the Lycan appeared to be nothing more than a pawn in Lindsay's game.

"Aiden, I canna believe ye got him like this," Blaire complained.

The man smirked. "Well, what was I supposed ta do? Ye were keepin' things from me, Blaire. And I dinna like it. I *still* doona like it. But at least now I ken what's goin' on with my own sister." He bent quickly and kissed her cheek. "I'm goin' ta bed. Big day tomorrow."

Blaire thought it over for a moment. "Wait," she called to his retreating back. He stopped and turned slowly toward her. "What happens tomorrow?"

"Tomorrow ye marry Kettering. The man canna hold his spirits worth a damn. If ye ever want ta ken what's goin' on in his head, just ply him with whisky. It worked for me." He gave Blaire a telling glance that made her blush. "We'll no' be waitin' for the banns, no' after the tale I heard tonight. So ye'll marry tomorrow, and Kettering can pay the fine for the irregular marriage. He's fairly plump in the pockets, or so I hear."

James grunted loudly. But it came out more as a belch. "Apologies," he murmured. "Still not quite used to this human body." Mortifying it was.

Westfield chuckled loudly. The man found everything to be humorous when he was foxed, evidently.

"What did ye tell him?" Blaire demanded, her hands on her hips. He wanted to replace them with his own. He reached for her, but he grabbed at air as she stepped away from him. "Bloody hell, Blaire. Would you be still?" he grumbled. That earned another laugh from Westfield. Blast the man.

"Plan yer day around a weddin' tomorrow, Blaire. The good baron will take ye as his wife. We'll see it completed before the sun sets on another day." Captain Lindsay turned and whistled a little tune as he disappeared down the corridor.

"But ye *said* we'd call the banns!" Blaire cried. "I was supposed ta have three weeks."

"Tomorrow, Blaire!" Aiden yelled back. She could tell from his tone that he wouldn't take no for an answer.

"Speaking of weddings," James called after the Captain. "I bumped into a certain Miss Fyfe as I was fleeing Strathcarron. The lass seemed quite distraught at your sudden departure."

Aiden Lindsay actually blushed. "I, uh, have plans ta return ta Briarcraig at my earliest convenience. Well, as soon as I see my sister well and truly united in matrimony ta ye, Kettering."

"I'm certain the lass will be glad to hear of your return."

Westfield's witch crossed the room and tugged him to his feet. "Let's go home, ye fierce beast," she teased as he leaned into her.

"Bloody good time it was, Kettering," the Lycan murmured at him. But he followed his wife to the waiting coach without looking back. If James wasn't mistaken, he was watching the sway of her bottom as she walked in front of him. Smart man.

"Thinking of arses," James muttered as he reached out as quickly as he could and grabbed a handful of Blaire's skirts. "Bring yours over here." He tugged her down into his lap and locked his arms around her waist.

"Who was thinkin' of arses?" his witch asked.

"All good men think of arses, Blaire. Don't you know that?" He grinned what he knew was a foolish grin at her.

"I do now." She rolled her eyes. Then she sighed deeply and tucked herself into his arms. "Married tomorrow?" she asked. "How could ye let Aiden fool ye like that?"

"He seemed so sincere," James admitted.

"He might no' be a battle-born witch, but he was raised by one and he's fairly wily. Ye should have kent he was up ta somethin'." She punched James lightly in the shoulder. He still held the watch open in his lap. "Why do ye have this out?" she asked.

He'd show her the inscription inside his watch fob after they were married, and not a moment before. He tucked it into his pocket before she could become curious. "You were out awfully late. Did you get everything settled with Sorcha?" The lass had been quite distraught when he'd left them.

"That might take some time," Blaire hedged.

"The secret room?" he pressed.

"Aye, it exists." She bent and touched her lips to his.

"And why I was locked up? It's in the journals?"

She was awfully distracting when she wanted to be.

"Ye were imprisoned in the bowels of Briarcraig because ye're my destiny, ye fool." She kissed him again, ever so softly, and he wrapped his arms around her.

But then a bellow sounded from the corridor. "Go ta bed, Blaire!" Aiden yelled.

James sighed and rested his forehead against hers. "Tomorrow, you will be mine."

"And ye will be mine," she reminded him.

"Bed, Blaire!" the bellow sounded again.

"Bloody hell, I'm goin'!" she cried as she kissed James quickly and scurried from his lap. He watched her cute little arse until she turned the corridor. Tomorrow, indeed.

Twenty-Nine

WHAT WAS TAKING SO BLOODY LONG? BLAIRE WOULD have been pacing the aisle of the church if Rhiannon and Sorcha hadn't forced her into a pew and then sat on either side of her to keep her still. Their presence, their support, did nothing to quell the anxiety stirring deeply within her. Blaire's eyes strayed back to the door at the end of the chapel that led to Mr. Crawford's office.

"What can they possibly be talkin' about?" she grumbled under her breath.

A warm hand settled on her shoulder, and Blaire glanced up at Benjamin Westfield standing behind her. "Do you really want an answer to that?"

He could hear them! Thank heavens. She silently vowed to refrain from any more dog jokes at his expense for at least a fortnight. "Aye," she whispered.

Rhiannon and Sorcha leaned in closer, and Elspeth crossed from the far side of the church to stand beside her husband. None of her sister witches wanted to miss one word, either.

"Well," Benjamin began and tucked his wife's arm

in the crook of his arm, "the good vicar is not happy with the number of irregular marriages he's performed this last year. He says it won't look good for him with his superiors."

"He doesna mean ta refuse?" Blaire gasped, now resigned to her fate of becoming Baroness Kettering. And now that she'd accepted it, she wanted to get on with it. After all, she'd never been the most patient witch to begin with, but now... Well, now she couldn't wait to say before God and her friends how much she loved James Maitland and wanted with all her heart to be his wife. "There are other ways. We can make our declarations if Crawford willna perform the ceremony."

Benjamin chuckled. "Anxious, are you?"

"Ben," his wife chided.

He sighed as though all his fun had just been taken away. "No, Blaire, he will not refuse. But he's giving Aiden and Kettering the devil of a time about it. He doesn't understand why you can't just wait for the banns to be read."

"Well, what did they say?" Blaire gulped.

Benjamin winked at her. "Kettering gave a rather impassioned plea. Said that when you've waited your whole life for the right woman to come along, waiting three more weeks to make her your wife is a special kind of torture."

Blaire's heart skipped a beat. What a beautiful thing to say. "Did he really?"

At that moment, the office door opened. Aiden and the vicar, Mr. Crawford, entered the chapel, but she paid them no attention as she could see

James' large frame behind them. He stood in the threshold, the picture of confidence and arrogance. She wouldn't have him any other way. His light blue eyes twinkled as he followed the other two men into the chapel.

"Well." Mr. Crawford cleared his throat. "I suppose all is in order. Miss Lindsay, if ye'll please join us." He gestured to the altar at the front of the room.

She was on her feet in the space of a single beat of her heart, more than ready to embrace her future.

Then the vicar's eyes narrowed on her friends still sitting on the pew. "But while I have the rest of yer attention, let me make myself very clear. I doona ken what has gone on in my parish recently, but I've had quite enough of it. Miss Sinclair, Miss Ferguson, if either of ye come ta me wantin' an irregular marriage, I'll turn ye right back around and I willna listen ta another word. Do ye hear me?"

"And then you can either make your declarations or have the always popular anvil wedding at the border," Benjamin Westfield joked.

Mr. Crawford's face turned as red as an over-ripe tomato. "Lord Benjamin!" the vicar sputtered. "As ye were the one who started this unfortunate trend, I will ask ye ta hold yer tongue in my church!"

"Sorry, sir." Benjamin replied, though he didn't sound sorry in the least.

"Well, then…" Mr. Crawford opened his Bible. "Let's move forward, shall we? Miss Lindsay, Lord Kettering."

Then they were standing before the vicar, and James took Blaire's hands in his. The rest was a blur. She didn't hear a word Mr. Crawford said and didn't realize she even needed to say, "I do," until she saw the panic in James' eyes.

"Blaire," he urged.

How could she have missed her cue? "Aye, of course. I do." And she did, more than she ever could have imagined.

James' expression relaxed, and he squeezed her hand.

"Do ye have a ring, my lord?" the vicar asked.

"I've had it all my life." James reached inside his jacket pocket and retrieved his ring, the one her mother had stolen from him all those years ago. A lump formed in Blaire's throat. "Are ye sure?"

"Without it, I would never have found you, my love." Then he slid the ring on her finger. It was so big and heavy that it nearly slipped back off. James folded her hand in his to keep his heirloom in place. "We'll get it fitted."

All Blaire could manage was a nod.

"Lord Kettering, ye may now kiss yer bride."

Still holding his hand over hers, James tugged Blaire closer to him, very slowly lowered his head, and brushed his warm lips across hers.

❧

In all the days James had lived, none had ever seemed as long or tiring as his wedding day. After the marriage ceremony, he and Blaire had been rushed off to a wedding breakfast at Benjamin Westfield's opulent estate outside the city, along with everyone else in Edinburgh, it seemed. James had never seen so many Scots. They'd filled nearly every corner of the manor, and they hadn't seemed inclined to leave. Ever.

It was late that evening before he was finally able to retire to the room Westfield had graciously offered for their wedding night. Now if only his bride would join him.

He collapsed into a high-backed chair that was more stylish than comfortable, but he didn't move from it. He'd wait until he had a reason to get up. He'd wait for Blaire.

How long would it take for her to extricate herself from her sister witches? James flipped open his watch fob. He'd meant to check the time, but the lamplight caught his inscription, and his eyes retraced the words he'd read for more than two centuries.

We know what we are, but not what we may be.

He smiled to himself, realizing that the sentiment meant so much more now than it ever had before. He had never imagined that he could be something different than he was. He had never imagined that a pretty girl who could hold fireballs in the palm of her hand could change him, make him more than he had ever dreamed possible.

"Woolgatherin'?" His wife's voice from the threshold interrupted his thoughts.

James shook his head and leaned back in the chair. It was becoming more comfortable by the minute. "Just waiting for you, my love."

A dazzling smile lit her lips as she shut the door behind her before crossing the room and dropping onto his lap. James chuckled. He could get quite used to this.

"It was so nice of Benjamin ta offer us a place of our own for the night."

"Nice," James agreed. Then he kissed the tip of her nose. "I'll be forever in his debt."

"Lindsay House isna that bad." She frowned at him.

"Oh, I beg to differ, my darling witch. Lindsay House has your two brothers in residence. One of them can shoot better than I, he once told me. So, when I make love to my wife this evening, I'd rather not have the good captain within hearing or shooting distance."

"If he was goin' ta shoot ye, he would have done it last night when ye confessed all yer sins ta him."

She might have a point. Still, he'd rather not take any chances just yet. His heart was beating once more, and he wasn't in any hurry for it to stop again.

"Lookin' at your watch again?" Blaire asked. "Ye do seem a mite obsessed with it."

"I'm only obsessed with you."

She rolled her eyes in a way he found most endearing. "Can I see it?"

"Are you going to steal it again?"

She smacked his chest lightly. "I never stole yer watch."

James snorted.

"All right, I did steal it. I used it for a spell when I was tryin' ta figure out what ye were."

"And now you know what I am?"

"My husband, for now and always."

"For now and always." He brushed his lips against hers. Then he sat back against the seat and handed her his watch.

She clicked it open and read the inscription. "We

know what we are, but no' what we might be." Blaire looked over at him. "Shakespeare."

He shook his head. "Why are you always trying to attribute sayings to William Shakespeare?"

Blaire blew a strand of hair from her eye as though he was the most troublesome creature known to man. "I ken the line, James Maitland. It's from *Hamlet*."

"It is," he agreed. "But Shakespeare didn't come up with it."

"What do ye mean?"

"Blodswell tried to pound the sentiment into my head. He finally took my watch, which was a gift from the Queen, by the way, and had the phrase engraved inside. He said if I looked at it long enough, it might someday seep in."

A look of pure joy settled on her face. "And Mr. Shakespeare?"

"Asked for the time one night in a pub. I flicked open the watch to show him, and the blackguard ended up stealing my line—or Matthew's line, really. Can you believe it?"

Blaire giggled. "I find, my love, that when ye're involved, I should believe almost anythin'."

About the Author

Lydia Dare is a pseudonym for the writing team of Tammy Falkner and Jodie Pearson. Both are active members of the Heart of Carolina Romance Writers and have sat on the organization's board of directors. Their writing process involves passing a manuscript back and forth, with each one writing 1,500 words after editing the other's previous installment. Jodie specializes in writing the history and Tammy in writing the paranormal. They live near Raleigh, North Carolina.

Cooper House, London - April 1817

Sisters were a blasted nuisance. And it made no matter whether the sisterhood came by blood or by coven. Rhiannon Sinclair had often wanted to dispense with them all and be afforded a chance to live a normal life. Yet she found herself chasing her younger sister from Edinburgh to London, just so she could ensure her safety.

Rhiannon paced the entryway of her aunt's home on Hertford Street, smarting more than a bit at not having been invited to wait inside in a parlor. Instead, the Coopers' butler had looked down his craggy, beaklike nose as she explained who she was and why she'd come. Then he'd left her standing in the entryway while he walked much too slowly down the corridor. If the disdainful servant wasn't careful, she'd zap him with a bolt of lightning and show him the error of his ways. Perhaps he'd move a bit faster if she did. Before she could summon even one thought of a storm, he vanished around a corner.

After what felt like a lifetime, the butler returned and nodded briefly at her. "You may follow me, Miss Sinclair." What had taken the man so long? Had he gone to hide the silver before showing her in? That was as likely as not. There was no wonder what her aunt had said about her.

With a beleaguered sigh, the servant led her to a tidy blue parlor where her aunt and new uncle waited. Having been married less than a year, Rhi didn't know Mr. Cooper well at all. But her Aunt Greer was another matter entirely. In fact, the aunt in question was her mother's younger sister, and unfortunately she knew her quite well.

"Rhiannon," Aunt Greer gushed. "It's so nice to see you." As fraudulent as ever. The woman even tried to hide the brogue she'd been born with. And her tone was so sickly-sweet it made Rhiannon want to cast up her accounts. Because, truth be told, her aunt resented her more than a little. She'd resented her enough to take her younger sister to London in the dead of night, and had left her at home with nothing more than an absent-minded father and a house-full of servants for company. "What brings you to Town, dear?"

As though she didn't know. What brought her to Town? How could the woman even say that with a straight face? Rhiannon took a deep breath as thunder rolled outdoors. "I came ta check on Ginny. Could ya send someone ta fetch her? I'd like ta speak with her."

Aunt Greer sucked her teeth lightly. It was a habit that had always annoyed Rhiannon to no end. "Unfortunately, she has already retired for the evening." She raised her eyebrows at Rhiannon. "Perhaps another time?"

It was rather late. But Rhi didn't mind waking Ginny, if need be. "Certainly, she's still awake. If I could just see her for a moment." She pointed down the corridor. "Which way ta her chambers?"

"Not now, Rhiannon."

Thunder rumbled outdoors again.

"As I said, Ginessa is already abed. So, let me walk you out, dear," her aunt said as she grabbed Rhiannon's elbow in her gnarly little grasp and shoved her toward the doorway. Of course, Rhiannon could make the woman release her. She could do it in a way her aunt would never forget with a nicely aimed zap. But it would probably be best not to burn those bridges in case she had to cross them later. Her aunt's voice dropped to frantic whisper. "My husband is not aware of your particular affliction, Rhiannon. And I'd prefer to keep it that way. Keep your powers in check when he—or anyone else, for that matter—is present. Your mother never managed it. But you are still young enough to learn."

Rhi tried to keep the scorn from her voice when she replied, "I'm sorry ye were no' born magical, Aunt Greer. There's no' much I can do about that. But, really, ye should have accepted the situation by now."

"I will never, ever accept that my sister was born an anomaly. And you and your little coven of witches will never have my approval. In fact, from this point forward, I plan to limit your access to Ginessa so you don't inhibit your sister's chances of a successful launch in society. Her name will not be associated with scandal. Do you hear me?" She hissed the last.

"A successful launch in society?" Rhi's mouth fell open. Truly it was the last thing she expected. Ginny was barely seventeen and a rather naïve seventeen at that.

"Don't look at me like that, Rhiannon Sinclair."

"But Ginny's so young." And London would swallow her whole.

"Well, you're not her guardian, are you? Besides, your father welcomed my invitation."

Papa probably hadn't lifted his head long enough from whatever tome consumed him to even hear a word Aunt Greer had said. He couldn't possibly think this was a good idea, not if he'd actually thought about it. Her aunt had never offered a thing where either she or Ginny was concerned. Not until now. Rhi must be missing something but whatever it was escaped her completely.

"How did you come to be here?" Aunt Greer's frown deepened. "You didn't travel south with that coven in tow, did you? I won't have you hurt Ginessa's chance at finding a proper husband."

"Proper husband? What is that supposed ta mean? Are ye plannin' ta marry her off ta some blasted Sassenach?" Rhiannon hissed.

"Better than what she'd find in Scotland."

Rhi sucked in a lungful of air. "Why can she no' marry a man from Scotland? Ginny is Scottish, after all."

"Because in Scotland, Ginessa can't escape the taint of your creation, Rhiannon." Her aunt sighed deeply as though dealing with her was the worst sort of trial. "And I'll expect you and whoever you brought with you to return to Edinburgh as soon as possible. I'm certain your fondest wish is for your sister to find happiness."

Of course, she wanted Ginny to find happiness. But there was no reason to remove her to London in order to do so. Rhiannon was the older of the two. And she had never been launched upon society. Her aunt would never do such a thing. Not with all the resentment she held in her heart for the members of the *Còig*, members of the coven of witches she'd so badly wanted to belong to when she was younger. Unfortunately, only the oldest daughter in each family was born magical. And her aunt had never recovered from the slight of being second born.

"The taint of my creation is the least of yer worries," Rhiannon warned.

Her aunt's shoulders went back and she lifted her nose a little higher in the air.

"Know this, Aunt," she said, as she pointed a finger in the woman's face. "I willna allow ye ta run rough-shod over her life just ta spite me. Or ta spite the fact that ye were born average."

Rhiannon could almost see the storm-cloud forming in the air and her aunt could as well, if her smirk was any indication. Unfortunately, Rhi's powers were often ruled by her emotions and, while most people could blink back the tears that welled behind one's lashes, the tell-tale patter of raindrops in a room full of people could give her aunt much more insight into her feelings than she wanted her to have.

Rhiannon turned on her heel and fled. The butler looked supremely satisfied as he quickly opened the door. She was surprised not to feel the press of his boot against her backside as she neared the threshold. He yelped lightly as Rhiannon passed him. Teach the English dog to mess with Rhiannon Sinclair. She'd hit him with the force of power that one might feel after dragging their feet on the carpet, for which he should be immeasurably thankful as she could have done much worse.

Rhiannon slipped out into the dark night. She was quite used to skulking about under the moonlight. And with her powers, had little fear that anyone would accost her and do harm. So, she took a short walk to Hyde Park, where she could take a seat on a bench alone and plan what she would do next.

She hadn't expected her aunt to ask her to stay with her. In fact, she'd already sent her belongings on to Thorpe House in Berkeley Square, the home of her coven-sister, Caitrin, now the Marchioness of Eynsford, and her wolfish husband Dashiel. She supposed, she probably should have mentioned as much to Cait, but her friend would forgive her popping in unannounced as it had been months since they'd seen each other.

Cait would welcome her into her home, unlike Aunt Greer.

In all honesty, she hadn't expected Aunt Greer to welcome her, but couldn't her aunt at least have allowed her to see Ginny, to be sure she was all right? Rhi sighed. Apparently not. Aunt Greer had treated her as she always had. Not as a revered member of the *Còig*. Not as someone with superior strength and cunning. Not as someone capable of being loved. She treated her as something vile. Something that should be squashed from the face of the earth.

A lone tear trickled down Rhiannon's cheek as a raindrop landed atop her head. Fantastic. She'd be drenched within moments if she didn't pull herself together. Yet the longer she sat there, the more distraught she felt, and the angrier she became.

Rhi jumped to her feet. The wind swirled around her, raising her hair and the trailing end of her traveling dress in its haste to circle her. She glanced about the park. Thank goodness she was alone. She could have the devil's own temper-tantrum and there wasn't a soul to watch. Lightning flashed and thunder boomed overhead. Rhiannon raised her hands in the air and called the wind and the rain, stirring it to the point where she was drenched within seconds.

She felt only slightly better. So, she stomped her feet and the air crackled with her anger. Better. Much better.

Despite the chit lounging across his lap, Matthew Halkett, the Earl of Blodswell, had more than a meal on his mind. He needed to find his new charge and be sure all was well with the newly reborn Scot. Alec MacQuarrie had turned out to be more work than he'd ever expected. When he'd first met the gentleman in the lowlands, the Scot had seemed a gregarious sort; and when they'd become reacquainted later in the Highlands, Matthew had no idea the man had since suffered a broken heart. If he had, it may have altered his decision to turn him into one of his kind. Now the damage was done, and Matthew had to deal with the consequences, even if it meant following the younger man from room to room as he learned to use his new baby teeth.

Matthew lifted the wench from his lap, wiped his mouth with the back of his hand and thanked the woman with a soft smile. She curtsied quickly and said, "It was my honor, sir."

Of course, he'd brought her great pleasure before he'd pulled his incisors from the nape of her neck. That was very much the reason why so many women lingered around Brysi, the gentlemen's club for those of his kind. They craved the emotion and satisfaction a vampyre could bring. And almost all of them were in it for the pleasure, if not for the coin. He rarely even had to enchant them to make a meal of them. Or to draw one beneath him. Or to do both at once.

"Have you seen Mr. MacQuarrie about?" he asked casually as she adjusted her clothing.

"He's above stairs with Charlotte, I believe. I saw him go up there just before you arrived."

He pressed a coin into her palm. "How many of you has he enjoyed tonight?" he asked casually, dreading the answer.

She giggled. "Quite a few. The man is insatiable." She shivered delicately. Obviously, she'd been with him recently, if her reaction was any indication.

Matthew sighed. "I'd best go and find him." He started for the stairs. If he waited for MacQuarrie to be free of the Cyprians who lined these halls, Matthew would have to wait decades. Thankfully, Brysi was a safe place for the newborn to test his mettle. Matthew glanced in doorways and down corridors until he finally heard the guttural sound of the man's voice when he moaned.

"Don't," a woman cried.

Oh, good lord. MacQuarrie could find trouble unlike any other. Matthew didn't even knock. He thrust the door open and stepped inside. He paused when the paramour cried out again.

"Don't... stop!" she begged.

So that was a cry of pleasure and not of distress. Bloody wonderful. Matthew wanted to snort.

MacQuarrie didn't even bother to look up. He had a blond straddling his lap, where he lifted and lowered her slowly, her bodice down around her waist, her dress up around her hips. Damn it to hell. Matthew hated walking in on scenes like this.

Yet something about it made him pause. A thin trail of blood dripped down the woman's back from where the infernal Scot had failed to seal his lips across her skin properly before he sank his teeth into her.

"Please," she begged, her voice raspy and strained. She glanced over her shoulder and was fully aware that Matthew was in the room. "Please finish it," she cried. She didn't make a move to cover herself. Or to remove herself from MacQuarrie's swollen member.

"Make the seal and finish the chit," Matthew grumbled. He'd told Alec the same bloody thing over and over. She was waiting for the seal, for the transfer of emotions between them, for MacQuarrie to share his desire with her, and take her pleasure in return.

Alec looked up and spoke around the woman's flesh. "I don't want to. I don't want to feel it. This is enough for me." He mumbled against her skin, but Matthew heard every word.

"It's not enough for her."

MacQuarrie shot him a look that told him to go to the devil.

What was a mentor for if not to teach? "Finish it," Mathew commanded.

"Bloody hell," the man said as he leaned forward and sealed his mouth over the bite with fervor. The chit cried out in ecstasy and Matthew turned his head to avoid seeing MacQuarrie shudder beneath her.

What was he thinking? The blasted Scot was in no condition to leave Brysi, at least not at the moment. Matthew sighed again. Damn if he wasn't doing that a lot lately. And he didn't even need to breathe. "I'll be back in a few hours, but I expect you to stay here. And to stay out of trouble," he warned as he turned and left.

Alec MacQuarrie's laughter followed him all the way down the corridor. Keeping that man out of trouble was like trying to return a whore to chastity.

He slipped from the club out into the night and walked and walked until the scenery of Covent Garden disappeared behind him. He needed to clear his head and decide what to do about his charge. It had been much easier when he'd tutored Kettering in this life a few hundred years ago. Was he getting too old to deal with the foolishness of youth? Or was this generation of man particularly trying?

Before he knew it, he walked all the way to Mayfair

and yet still had no idea of how to continue. Out of nowhere, a crushing wind nearly knocked him from his feet. He braced himself. What the devil? He'd never seen a storm come on so quickly, and he'd seen more than most.

That was when the rain started in earnest. Only moments before, the stars had been twinkling in the sky. Yet now, thunder crashed and lightning flashed. Hail clattered on the cobbled path where he walked. He covered his head with his arm and ducked beneath a tree.

That was when he saw her. Standing directly in the middle of the fray was the loveliest sight he'd ever seen in his life. Her black hair was slicked back with water but it trailed all the way down to her waist. Her gown was pasted to her body, sodden with water. She laughed loudly and sardonically as a bolt of lightning flashed at her feet.

The chit was likely daft. Did she not know any better than to come in out of the rain? Likely, she would be killed by the ferocity of this sudden storm if he didn't intercede. Matthew dashed across the park to where she stood. She clapped her hands in time with the crashes of thunder that made even him jump. And looked ridiculously pleased by it all. She didn't even see him as he bolted toward her. Had she escaped from Bedlam?

He yelled over the wind and thunder. "Miss? Are you all right?"

She spun to face him. "Oh!" Her eyes flashed with the same ferocity as the storm. Yet the wind calmed and the thunder stopped crashing when her hands dropped to her sides. Then the beauty brushed the sodden mass of her hair from her forehead. "Who are ye?" she asked.

The lovely Scottish lilt nearly startled him as much as the timber of her voice. She sounded like she'd recently been crying, but with the rain that continued to fall, he couldn't tell if her cheeks were wet from more than just rain. He found himself with the absurd desire to reach out and brush her cheeks dry with the pads of his thumbs.

"Doona tell me ye're some knight in shinin' armor come ta save a lass from the storm?" She laughed loudly, the tinkling sound of it making him want to smile with her.

"Well, actually..." he started. He was a knight of old. Or he once was. Before his first death, but that was well more than six hundred years ago. Matthew shook his head. "... I was just concerned to see a lady about to be overcome by such a vicious storm. I thought I'd rescue you."

The storm clouds lifted. The rain stopped. She glanced down at her drenched gown, which now hugged her body like a second skin, and crossed her arms in front of her chest. And that was when he realized it. She wasn't caught by the storm. She was the storm. Saint George's teeth! She was a force to be reckoned with. She was one of them.

THE
TAMING
OF THE
WOLF

BY LYDIA DARE

REGENCY ENGLAND HAS GONE TO THE WOLVES!

Lord Dashiel Thorpe has fought the wolf within him his entire life. But when the moonlight proves too powerful, Dash is helpless, and a chance encounter with Caitrin Macleod binds the two together irrevocably. Though Caitrin is a witch with remarkable abilities, she is overwhelmed and runs back to the safety of her native Scotland. But Dashiel is determined to follow her—she's the only woman who can free him from a fate worse than death. Caitrin will ultimately have to decide whether she's running from danger, or true love...

Praise for Lydia Dare

"The authors flawlessly blend the historical and paranormal genres, providing a hint of the lycan lifestyle with a touching romance... lots of feral fun." —ROMANCE NOVEL NEWS

978-1-4022-4437-7 • $6.99 U.S./$8.99 CAN/£4.99 UK

A CERTAIN WOLFISH CHARM

BY LYDIA DARE

REGENCY ENGLAND HAS GONE TO THE WOLVES!

The rules of Society can be beastly...

...especially when you're a werewolf and it's that irritating time of the month. Simon Westfield, the Duke of Blackmoor, is rich, powerful, and sinfully handsome, and has spent his entire life creating scandal and mayhem. It doesn't help his wolfish temper at all that Miss Lily Rutledge seems to be as untamable as he is. When Lily's beloved nephew's behavior becomes inexplicably wild, she turns to Simon for help. But they both may have bitten off more than they can chew when each begins to discover the other's darkest secrets...

"*A Certain Wolfish Charm* has bite!"

—SABRINA JEFFRIES, *NEW YORK TIMES* BESTSELLING AUTHOR OF *WED HIM BEFORE YOU BED HIM*

978-1-4022-3694-5 • $6.99 U.S./$8.99 CAN/£3.99 UK

TALL, DARK AND WOLFISH

BY LYDIA DARE

REGENCY ENGLAND HAS GONE TO THE WOLVES!

He's lost unless she can heal him

Lord Benjamin Westfield is a powerful werewolf—until one full moon when he doesn't change. His life now shattered, he rushes to Scotland in search of the healer who can restore his inner beast: young, beautiful witch Elspeth Campbell, who will help anyone who calls upon her healing arts. But when Lord Benjamin shows up, everything she thought she knew is put to the test…

Praise for *A Certain Wolfish Charm:*

"Tough, resourceful, charming women battle roguish, secretive, aristocratic men under the watchful eye of society in Dare's delightful Victorian paranormal romance debut."

—*PUBLISHERS WEEKLY* (STARRED REVIEW)

978-1-4022-3695-2 • $6.99 U.S./$8.99 CAN/£3.99 UK

THE WOLF
NEXT
DOOR

BY LYDIA DARE

REGENCY ENGLAND HAS
GONE TO THE WOLVES!

Can she forgive the unforgivable?

Ever since her planned elopement with Lord William Westfield turned to disaster, Prisca Hawthorne has done everything she can to push him away. If only her heart didn't break every time he leaves her. Lord William throws himself into drinking, gambling, and debauchery and pretends not to care about Prisca at all. But when he returns to find a rival werewolf vying for her hand, he'll stop at nothing to claim the woman who should have been his all along, and the moon-crossed lovers are forced into a battle of wills that could be fatal.

"With its sexy hero, engaging heroine, and sizzling sexual tension, you won't want to put it down even when the moon is full."

—SABRINA JEFFRIES, *NEW YORK TIMES* BESTSELLING AUTHOR OF *WED HIM BEFORE YOU BED HIM*

978-1-4022-3696-9 • $6.99 U.S./$8.99 CAN/£3.99 UK

THE
FIRE LORD'S
LOVER

BY KATHRYNE KENNEDY

IF HIS POWERS ARE DISCOVERED, HIS FATHER WILL DESTROY HIM...

In a magical land ruled by ruthless Elven lords, the Fire Lord's son Dominic Raikes plays a deadly game to conceal his growing might from his malevolent father—until his arranged bride awakens in him passions he thought he had buried forever...

UNLESS HIS FIANCÉE KILLS HIM FIRST...

Lady Cassandra has been raised in outward purity and innocence, while secretly being trained as an assassin. Her mission is to bring down the Elven Lord and his champion son. But when she gets to court she discovers that nothing is what it seems, least of all the man she married...

"As darkly imaginative as Tolkien, as richly romantic as Heyer, Kennedy carves a new genre in romantic fiction."
—Erin Quinn, author of *Haunting Warrior*

"Deliciously dark and enticing." —Angie Fox, *New York Times* bestselling author of *A Tale of Two Demon Slayers*

978-1-4022-3652-5 • $7.99 U.S./$9.99 CAN/£4.99 UK

Hundreds OF YEARS TO REFORM A RAKE

BY LAURIE BROWN

HIS TOUCH PULLED HER IRRESISTIBLY ACROSS THE MISTS OF TIME

Deverell Thornton, the ninth Earl of Waite, needs Josie Drummond to come back to his time and foil the plot that would destroy him. Josie is a modern career woman, thrust back in time to the sparkling Regency period, where she must contend with the complex manners and mores of the day, unmask a dangerous charlatan, and in the end, choose between the ghost who captivated her or the man himself. But can she give her heart to a notorious rake?

"A smart, amusing, and fun time travel/Regency tale." — *All About Romance*

"Extremely well written…A great read from start to finish." —*Revisiting the Moon's Library*

"Blends Regency, contemporary and paranormal romance to a charming and very entertaining effect." —*Book Loons*

978-1-4022-1013-6 • $6.99 U.S./$8.99 CAN

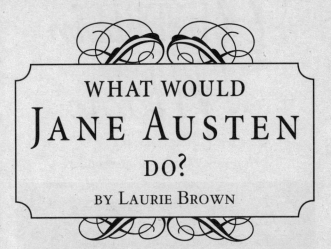

WHAT WOULD
JANE AUSTEN
DO?

BY LAURIE BROWN

Eleanor goes back in time to save a man's life, but could it be she's got the wrong villain?

Lord Shermont, renowned rake, feels an inexplicable bond to the mysterious woman with radical ideas who seems to know so much…but could she be a Napoleonic spy?

Thankfully, Jane Austen's sage advice prevents a fatal mistake…

At a country house party, Eleanor makes the acquaintance of Jane Austen, whose sharp wit can untangle the most complicated problem. With an international intrigue going on before her eyes, Eleanor must figure out which of two dueling gentlemen is the spy, and which is the man of her dreams.

978-1-4022-1831-6 • $6.99 U.S. / $7.99 CAN

Uncertain Magic

BY LAURA KINSALE
New York Times bestselling author

"Laura Kinsale creates magic."
—Lisa Kleypas, *New York Times* bestselling
author of *Seduce me at Sunrise*

A MAN DAMNED BY SUSPICION AND INNUENDO

Dreadful rumors swirl around the impoverished Irish lord
known as "The Devil Earl." But Faelan Savigar hides a
dark secret, for even he doesn't know what dark deeds he
may be capable of. Roderica Delamore, cursed by the gift
of "sight," fears no man will ever want a wife who can
read his every thought and emotion, until she encounters
Faelan. Roddy becomes determined to save Faelan from his
terrifying and mysterious ailment, but will their love end up
saving him… or destroying her?

"Laura Kinsale has managed to break
all the rules…and come away shining."
—*San Diego Union-Tribune*

"Magic and beauty flow from Laura
Kinsale's pen." —*Romantic Times*

978-1-4022-3702-7 • $9.99 U.S./$11.99 CAN